D0039968

READ.
IF YOU
DARE

CT

N

DEMCO

READ
IF YOU
DARE

TWELVE TWISTED TALES
FROM THE EDITORS
OF READ MAGAZINE

The Millbrook Press
Brookfield, Connecticut

Published by The Millbrook Press, Inc.
2 Old New Milford Road
Brookfield, Connecticut 06804

Copyright © 1997 by Weekly Reader Corporation
Printed in the United States of America
All rights reserved
Lib. ed. 6 5 4 3 2 1
Pbk. ed. 6 5 4 3 2 1

Library of Congress Cataloging-in-Publication Data
Read if you dare : twelve twisted tales from the editors of Read Magazine.
p. cm.
Summary: A collection of stories by such authors as Nathaniel Hawthorne,
Ambrose Bierce, and Stephen King, exploring the notions of fate, destiny, and
coincidence.
ISBN 0-7613-0046-5 (lib. bdg.). — ISBN 0-7613-0343-X (pbk.)
1. Fate and fatalism—Juvenile fiction. 2. Children's stories, American.
[1. Fate and fatalism—Fiction. 2. Short stories.] I. Read magazine.
PZ5.T88   1997
[Fic]—dc20 96-44221   CIP   AC

Book design by Tania Garcia

ACKNOWLEDGMENTS

"Battleground" by Stephen King. Reprinted with permission. © Stephen King. All rights reserved.

"Deadline" by Richard Matheson. Reprinted by permission of Don Congdon Associates, Inc. © 1960 by Richard Matheson.

"Night Burial" by Ken Siebert. Reprinted by permission of the author.

"Reverse Insomnia" by Jonathon Blake. Reprinted by permission of the author.

"The Right Kind of House" by Henry Slesar. Reprinted by permission of the author.

"The Ruum" by Arthur Borges. Reprinted by permission of the author and the author's agents, Scott Meredith Literary Agency, L.P., 845 Third Avenue, New York, NY 10022.

"Skater" by Catherine Gourley was inspired by the poem "The Skater of Ghost Lake" by William Rose Benét.

"Snow Cancellations" by Donald R. Burleson. Reprinted by permission of the author.

Read is a literature magazine published for students in middle and senior high school by the Weekly Reader Corporation. Published biweekly during the school year, the magazine features the best of contemporary young adult fiction and nonfiction with classical literature adaptations and historical theme issues. The Best of *Read* series celebrates the magazine's fiftieth anniversary.

INTRODUCTION

The ancient Greeks believed that Night and Air united and gave birth to the three Fates. Robed in white, the three sisters determine the destiny of all humans. Clotho is the spinner of life. For each man and woman, she spins a fine linen thread on her spindle. Lachesis is the measurer of life. She determines the worth of the linen thread, deciding if it will be woven into goodness or evil. Atropos, the shearer of life, is the smallest and most terrible of the sisters. She determines how long each mortal's life will be, then with her sharp shears snips the linen thread.

Some mortals greatly feared the Fates. Others scoffed at the sway the Fates supposedly held over mortals. Still others believed that the Fates could be tempted and the linen threads of life twisted, if only just a little.

In celebration of fifty years of publishing, the editors of *Read* are proud to bring you this collection of tales, each a twist of fate. We have blended contemporary young adult short stories with literary classics. What the stories—both classic and contemporary—have in common is this: Each has appeared in the pages of *Read* over the years and each tells a tale of a person who faces an unexpected turn of events. But is the unexpected simply a coincidence or is it destiny? Are the mortals in these tales innocent victims of circumstance? Or have they tempted the Fates and brought the dreaded twist upon themselves?

Read on ... if you dare.

CONTENTS

CONTENTS

PART II — LACHESIS, WEAVER OF GOOD AND EVIL

CONTENTS

PART III — ATROPOS, TRIMMER OF THREADS

READ.
IF YOU
DARE

PART I
CLOTHO,
SPINNER OF LIVES

SKATER

by Catherine Gourley

She said his name as if she had known him forever,
as if they were already good friends.

The air is December-cold on Ghost Lake, but Jeremy
Randall's cheeks are hot and flushed. He grunts as
he elbows the other skaters away from the puck. Their
shouts echo across the frozen lake. The puck spins free of
the tangle of hockey sticks and bladed feet, skidding out
beyond the dock. The boys chase the rubber disk, a blur
now in the growing darkness of late afternoon. The score
is tied, and the game is in sudden-death overtime.
Whoever makes the next goal wins.

Jeremy reaches the puck first. Shaving ice, he pivots,
then skates the puck back toward shore. In an instant, he
slaps the puck. It whizzes past the goalie's legs.

"Yes!" Jeremy shouts. He holds his arms high in victory
as Don and Hugh leave the ice. His jacket, like theirs, is

tossed on the lakeshore, but Jeremy skates out again beyond the dock. His movements are effortless, the blades like wings on his feet.

A sudden wind bends the tops of the fir trees fringing the far shore. Like the echo of a crying bird, the wind whips across the frozen lake, but Jeremy doesn't hear its moan or feel its sting. Orange and violet streaks darken the sky minute by minute, but Jeremy doesn't notice that either. Instead, he hears again the whack of his hockey stick and sees the puck skid into the goal. At that moment, Jeremy is his own hero, and he shouts into the wind, "I could skate forever!" He imagines himself in Chicago in a brightly lit arena, wearing a Blackhawk uniform and circling the ice to earsplitting cheers from thousands of fans. "Jer! Jer! Jer!" Chicago Stadium vibrates with the noise.

"Jer!" Don cups his hands around his mouth and calls again, "Jer!"

Jeremy looks over his shoulder. On shore, Don and Hugh seem far, far away. Jeremy digs in and starts back.

That's when he sees her.

She is kneeling in the snow in a small clearing, not far from the public beach where Don and Hugh are waiting. She rises and steps onto the ice. She is dressed in white; otherwise, Jeremy might not have seen her in the almost darkness.

Jeremy turns and skates backward so he can watch

her. He skates slowly now, but she is too far away for him to see her face.

"Jer! C'mon. We're going!"

Jeremy turns again and skates to shore. "Did you see that girl?" He sits on the frozen ground and quickly unlaces a skate.

"What girl?"

Jeremy looks across the lake, but the white figure is gone, hidden perhaps behind the trees on the point. Only the dark shadow of a bird sweeps across the ice now. "There was a girl," Jeremy says, pulling off the other skate. "Out there. Just coming onto the ice."

"No one comes to Ghost Lake after dark," says Hugh.

"Especially not a girl," says Tom. "Alone."

The two boys start along the path through the trees to the park road. The last threads of orange and violet light melt into the ebony ice and trees. From where he stands, Jeremy cannot see even the end of the dock now.

"But I saw her." He speaks out loud. "Didn't I?"

Later, at home in his room, Jeremy lies on his bed and stares at the poster of Mario Lemieux on the wall. He studies the grim determination in the hockey player's face. He can almost feel the adrenaline pumping through Mario's veins as he battles for control of the puck.

"Jer?"

Jeremy's mother opens the door, breaking the dream.

She has just come home from work. "How was school today?" she asks.

Jeremy shrugs. "School's school."

She steps inside the room, decorated with professional hockey memorabilia. At first, she was happy about her son's interest in the sport. It got his mind off the divorce, and a year ago, when she and Jeremy moved back to Pennsylvania from Chicago, hockey was an easy way for Jeremy to make new friends. Now she worries that hockey is the only thing her son thinks about.

"Did you spend some time with your grandfather this afternoon?" she asks.

"Poppy was asleep when I got home." Then, unable to avoid his mother's penetrating stare, Jeremy admits, "I kind of got home late."

She crosses her arms in front of her. "Playing hockey, right?"

Jeremy grins. "I really smoked them. I made a slapshot the length of the whole dock!"

"Weren't you going to do something for me and Poppy today?"

Jeremy looks at her with innocent eyes. "What?"

"You know Poppy can't climb a ladder anymore."

"Oh yeah. The Christmas lights."

His mother turns for the door. "Do it now, Jer."

Years ago, his mother had told him about the winter solstice and how burning candles in the windows was an ancient custom urging the sun to burn brightly on the shortest day of the year—December 21. Jeremy gets up, but he sighs deeply to let his mother know that he's too old now for trees and tinsel, colored lights and superstitions.

Jeremy pokes through the boxes in Poppy's attic, looking for the decorations. He has lived with his grandfather only since January, and so things in the house are still new for him. He finds the box of Christmas lights and digs deeper to find the extra bulbs. As his hand pushes through a tangle of wires, he sees an old card and picks it out of the box.

It is a Christmas postcard, yellow with age. Bits of silver glitter stick to the snow scene. Suddenly, Jeremy recognizes the place as Ghost Lake. In the picture, fir trees line the shore. Even the old dock is there. Printed in red-ribboned letters across the winter sky are the words *Season's Greetings!*

He is about to toss the card back into the box when he notices the girl. In the picture, she is kneeling in the snow in the clearing, lacing up her skates. He flips the card over. It is addressed to George Mellon, Jeremy's grandfather. The written message—*I can't wait to see you again. Love, Cecily*—makes Jeremy slightly uncomfortable, as if he is peeking through a keyhole at Poppy's life. The date on the card is December 14, 1922. Something inside Jeremy Randall quickens, like wings batting against his chest. Today is December 14 — seventy-five years later!

He stares at the picture again. The girl is wearing a long coat trimmed in white fur. "It's her!" Jeremy says out loud.

"Who?" His mother is coming up the attic steps with two mugs of hot chocolate.

Quickly, though he is not sure why, Jeremy slips the postcard into his hip pocket. He turns and lifts the rope of Christmas lights to show his mother. "I got them, spare bulbs and all."

"Good," she says. She settles down in the nest of boxes on the floor. She spies an angel tree topper with yellow fiberglass hair. "Oh, look at this!" she cries happily. "These ornaments have been in my family for years," she says, talking more to herself now than to Jeremy.

After a few minutes, he quietly leaves his mother alone with her memories.

Late the next day, Jeremy stands in the shadows of the steep firs at Ghost Lake. He is not surprised when the girl appears again in the clearing. As before, she kneels to lace up her skates. He watches as the wind ripples the white fur collar on her coat. She steps onto the ice, glides in a wide circle, and then, step-over-step, gains speed. She twists, leaping gracefully into the air, and lands on one skate, gliding backward.

On the next jump, she lands off-balance and falls, hard. Jeremy rushes out of the shadows and, flat-soled, runs across the ice to help her. "Are you all right?" he asks.

Her cheeks are flushed—from the cold or from the exercise, Jeremy isn't sure which. Thin streams of late afternoon sun fall through the trees and glitter like tinsel in her dark hair. She's beautiful, Jeremy thinks, amazed.

"Were you spying on me?" she asks angrily.

"No! No, I was just...." He turns and points at the trees. "I was just walking and...." He faces her again. "Yeah, I guess I was spying on you."

"You're Jeremy," she says. When he looks surprised, she laughs. "I've been spying on you, too. You play hockey after school. You're good."

Jeremy grins, embarrassed but pleased, too. "You're Cecily," he says, remembering Poppy's Christmas postcard.

If she is surprised that he also knows her name, she doesn't show it. "I'm visiting my grandfather. His name is John Culver. He's an artist. Do you know him?"

Jeremy shakes his head. "I'm kind of new around here."

A sudden rush of wings startles them, but it is only an owl circling low over the ice. "You shouldn't skate here alone at night," Jeremy says protectively.

"Oh, I'm not alone," she laughs, her voice like a bird's.

"Why do you think they call it Ghost Lake, Jer?"

She says his name like she has known him forever, like they are already good friends. "Wait here," he tells her. "My skates are on shore. I'll go with you."

The next morning at breakfast, Jeremy asks his mother if she knows John Culver. She looks up from the newspaper. "John Culver? Who told you about John Culver?"

"He's some kind of painter, right?"

"He was. John Culver has been dead for years."

Again, Jeremy feels the wings of a nervous bird fluttering inside his ribs. "He's dead? But he can't be!"

"But he is. He was an old man when I was a kid growing up here. We used to call him 'the hermit.' He lived over by the lake. Poppy warned me not to go there, but I always did." Jeremy's mother looks curiously at her son. "Why?"

Jeremy pulls the postcard from his pocket. "I found this in the attic."

"Pretty," she says. "And look! It was painted by him, see?" She points a fingernail at John Culver's name printed in the corner. She turns the card over. "Whoever sent this to Poppy sent it seventy years ago when Poppy was—"

"Fifteen," Jeremy says. "My age." He'd figured that out the night he found the card. "Grandma's name wasn't Cecily, was it?"

"No," says Jeremy's mother, amused at having discovered a secret love of Poppy's. "It definitely wasn't!"

"Then ... who *was* Cecily?"

"I've no idea, but your grandfather was a handsome man once," she says. "Just like you. And he loved to skate, just like you do."

His mother crosses to the refrigerator and uses a decorative magnet to tack the card on the door. "It's our first card of the season. Kind of like getting a holiday hello from the past, isn't it?" She smiles at the picture. "I like it."

Jeremy says nothing. His mother would never believe him if he told her that he had been skating with that same girl from the postcard last night on Ghost Lake.

"Why didn't you tell me your grandfather was dead?" Jeremy asks Cecily late that afternoon at the lake.

Her voice is sad. "Because I don't think of him as being dead. I prefer to remember him the way he was when he was alive. What's wrong with that?"

Jeremy regrets now bringing it up. It doesn't matter about John Culver. He takes her hand and they skate together.

The moon, already risen, is pale in the sky. But as night deepens, the moon glows into life like a candle in a window celebrating the solstice. It casts the bird-like shadows of Jeremy Randall and Cecily Culver on the ice. Cold crackles in the trees. Jeremy feels Cecily's fingers tighten around his hand. "You aren't scared, are you?" he asks.

"No," she answers. "Just a little cold."

"Who put this here?" Surprised, Poppy turns and looks at Jeremy.

"Mom thought you'd like to see it. I found it in the attic."

Jeremy stares at his grandfather, a thin man now with white hair. His eyes are a watercolor blue, like Jeremy's own. Jeremy remembers what his mother said about Poppy being handsome and strong once and loving to skate. As Poppy stares at the picture on the postcard, his annoyance melts away.

"Who is she, Poppy?"

"An old friend," he answers quietly.

"Did you love her?"

Poppy smiles sadly. "I thought I did. But her father wouldn't let anybody near her. No one was good enough for Cecily Culver."

Then Poppy looks up, willing the memory away. He is about to toss the card into the garbage, but Jeremy stops him. "Don't!" Poppy looks at him, surprised. "She's back," Jeremy says. "I mean, her granddaughter is back. She's staying at the lake."

Poppy's eyes go wide. "What?"

"Her name is Cecily, too."

"No, Cecily Culver couldn't have had a granddaughter."

"Why not?"

"Because...." Poppy hesitates. Jeremy stares at him, waiting. "Because I was with her on the ice when it happened."

"When what happened, Poppy?" Jeremy says, exasperated.

"The ice cracked. I tried to save her, but she slipped out of my hands. I ran for help, but it was too late."

An eerie feeling shivers through Jeremy. "You mean, she died?"

"Her father blamed me. He never forgave me." Poppy looks at the card in his hands, then at Jeremy. In one quick movement, he rips the card in half.

"What are you doing?" Jeremy cries.

Poppy tosses the two pieces of the card into the garbage. "Don't go there again, Jer," warns Poppy. "Stay away from that place." His grandfather walks from the room.

At first, Jeremy is too stunned to move. But a few minutes later, he goes to the wastebasket and retrieves the two pieces of the card. Alone in his room, he tapes the pieces together again.

Jeremy doesn't listen to Poppy. He goes back to Ghost Lake at dusk and waits for Cecily. For four days, they meet secretly on the shore. Arms laced together, they skate, and skate, and skate. Sometimes she sings.

Sometimes she tells him stories. "Do you know about Alcyone and King Ceyx?"

"No," he says, not embarrassed.

"They lived in ancient Greece and they were in love," Cecily says. "Like us."

Jeremy stops skating and stares at her with nervous surprise. "What did you say?"

Cecily giggles and skates away. He chases her and catches her around the waist. "What did you say?" he teases. "Tell me what you said."

"He drowned," she says at last, seriously.

"Who?"

"King Ceyx. And Alcyone was so sad that she threw herself into the sea and drowned, too."

Abruptly, Jeremy turns away from her. "I don't like that story."

Now it is Cecily who follows him across the ice. "But it's not over. Zeus felt so sorry for them that on the night of the winter solstice, he turned them into birds—kingfishers—and they lived forever."

"It's late. I gotta go." Jeremy turns for shore.

Still, Cecily follows him. "But the story has a happy ending, Jer."

He turns then and says sharply, "Don't talk about drowning, OK? You don't know what happened out here a long time ago. Poppy told me—"

"Poppy? Your grandfather?"

Jeremy stares at her, so pretty, so perfect like a picture. Still, he is not sure who Cecily really is and why she would lie to him about being John Culver's granddaughter.

She steps forward to touch his cold, unmittened hand. "Don't be mad at me," she says.

"I'm not mad. I'm just…" Suddenly, he feels a little frightened of her. He moves away from her touch.

"I'm leaving," she says then.

"What?"

"We're going home. Tomorrow will be our last night together, Jer."

They step off the ice and begin to remove their skates. Jeremy's hands are numb. He fumbles with the laces. He hadn't thought that one day Cecily might not be here. His head spins. He wants to tell her he is sorry for shouting at her. He wants to ask her if she really meant it when she said she loved him. But no words come out.

"Meet me here tomorrow," Cecily says, standing. Her skates are tied over her shoulder.

"Cecily, wait!" Jeremy is still fumbling with his own shoes, but she disappears into the shadows of the firs.

It is late afternoon. The hockey game is not even close. Jeremy misses an easy shot, and Hugh shouts at him.

When the game is over, they leave him behind, shaking their heads. "What's gotten into him lately?" Tom asks. Hugh shrugs.

It is the night of the winter solstice, and darkness comes early to Ghost Lake. The dim moon rises above the trees. Alone now, Jeremy skates out beyond the dock. His eyes search for the gleam of moonlight on her winged feet. He listens hard for the skurring sound of her skates, but hears only a crisp, thin sound—like a violin. It drifts on a bluish mist from the lake's far shore.

"Only a bird," he says out loud.

He leans forward into the wind as he skates, one long stride after another. "What if she doesn't come?" he thinks. No girl has ever told Jeremy Randall that she loved him, and he doesn't want to lose her the way Poppy lost his Cecily years ago.

Then he sees her. She moves from tree to tree, then kneels in the snow and laces her skates.

They join arms, and they skate. All day in front of his bedroom mirror, he has practiced what he wants to tell her. But now that she is laced to his side, he can't remember a word. He says without looking at her, "I don't want you to go."

"You don't?" Her breath is a frosty feather close to his cheek.

"Can't you stay a little longer?"

"Maybe you could come with me," she says.

He shakes his head. "How can I?"

Suddenly, over her shoulder, he sees a large shadow. It flits and swoops, startling him.

"What is it?" she asks, not letting him go.

"Nothing." Then he teases her. "Maybe a ghost. Why do you think they call it Ghost Lake?"

But Cecily doesn't laugh.

The shadow swoops again, nudging them farther away from shore.

"Jeremy?"

"It's just a bird," he says. "An owl probably."

"Or," she whispers, "a kingfisher."

He changes direction, pointing north of the dock. But the shadow follows, gliding between them and the shore.

Then he hears it. The skurring of steel following closely behind him. He skates faster, bringing Cecily with him. But the skurring comes faster, too.

"Jeremy!" Her voice is frightened now that they are far, far from the dock. Into the blue mist Jeremy skates to escape the phantom.

Then, suddenly, the ice seems to light up beneath them in jagged bolts, shooting forward and sideways. The ice crackles and pops. A split second later, a roar fills their ears.

Then all is quiet again. Only the shadows of two night birds sweep low over the frozen lake to the far shore.

"Jer?"

His mother knocks on his bedroom door. It is after nine o'clock, and it is not like Jeremy to be so late getting home. She pushes the door open, feels for the light switch on the wall, and flips it on.

The room is as it was this morning when she left for work. She picks up a sweatshirt tossed on the bed and folds it. As she opens the bureau drawer to put it away, she spies Poppy's postcard. It has been ripped and taped together again. The girl is still there and the boy too, skating on Ghost Lake.

Something is different about the picture, but Jeremy's mother can't quite place it. She shrugs and turns away, leaving the light on for Jeremy when he comes home.

NIGHT BURIAL

by Ken Siebert

Terry wanted to explore the unknown. Sure, it was risky, but someone with guts and brains—and planning—could pull it off.

Terry heaved the last shovelful of dirt aside, then jumped into the three-foot hole he and Sara had just dug. "Do you think it should be deeper?" he asked, looking up at her.

"It's deep enough," she said and dropped her shovel. In the moonlight that filtered through the pine trees, he thought he saw her shiver.

"You're right," he said. "Deep enough." He scrambled out of the hole again. "Ready for the box now?" he asked.

"I don't know about this," Sara said suddenly. "Now that we've dug the hole and I can actually see how long and deep it is...."

"I know," he said grinning. "It makes it real."

"Terry, I'm scared."

"So am I, a little. But that's the whole point. If there's no risk, why do it?"

"Why *are* you doing this?"

"Why does somebody go over Niagara Falls in a barrel? Why did Harry Houdini let himself be handcuffed, nailed inside a crate, and lowered into a river?"

"What you're doing is different."

He grinned. "I know."

"Let's just forget it and go home. OK, Terry?"

"No way. I started this, and I'm going to finish it. Just think of it as, well, an experiment."

A chill wind swirled through the branches of the pines. Sara hugged herself. "And what if the experiment fails?"

"Look. I've explained it all to you before. Houdini didn't jump into a tank of water with his arms and legs locked in chains and then just hope he could get them unlocked in time. He practiced. He built up his endurance. He thought of every possibility ahead of time. That's why he was so brilliant."

"And you're sure you thought of everything?"

"Of course I have. I wouldn't be doing this if I wasn't ready. I'm not stupid." He looked at his watch. The red numbers glowed 9:25. "Let's get the box. I want everything in place by ten o'clock, just the way we planned."

Reluctantly, Sara followed him across the graveyard to

where she had parked her father's truck outside the gate. Belden Park was a small, old burial ground. A high wrought-iron fence enclosed the two dozen graves. Time and weather had bleached the faces of the stone markers. The names of the dead could be read on only a few stones. No one used the cemetery for burials anymore. That was why Terry had chosen this place. It was part of his plan. No one ever came to Belden Park, so no one would interfere with his experiment.

The idea had come to him during the summer, when he'd read a biography of Harry Houdini. Houdini, considered the world's greatest magician, had been more than just a trickster who created illusions. He had been a powerful athlete who had conditioned his body to do amazing things—he could dislocate his shoulders in order to slip out of a straitjacket. Houdini had made himself a master artist. There wasn't any magic about his stunts. Terry wanted to be like him.

The challenge was to test his resolve. His feat would be the ultimate contest between willpower and emotion. That was the most important point. Even someone as great as Houdini, who had a hundred different stunts, must have been scared when he had himself tied into a straitjacket and lowered headfirst from the eaves of a New York City skyscraper. To escape, he had to defeat his emotions. If he panicked, he was a dead man.

It was simple, really—if he could remain calm and under control while buried alive for eight hours, he could handle anything. Strong people didn't take the easy road. They were always testing themselves, building their inner power. Eight hours wasn't all that long if you were mentally tough.

In a sense, the experience would be a controlled nightmare. He would tape-record his reactions. When it was all over, he would play the tapes in the comfort of his bedroom and coolly analyze the experience.

For weeks, he had planned every detail, right down to the heavy rubber tubing that would be his lifeline. He needed Sara's help, of course. Even Houdini had had an assistant. No one was more reliable than Sara. She would dig him up on schedule—8:00 A.M. sharp.

Even if there was some unforeseen delay, there would be enough water if he rationed it. And there would always be plenty of air coming through the tube.

At the cemetery gate, Terry checked everything a final time—blankets, a full canteen, the rubber tubing, a pillow, a cassette recorder and a tape, and a homemade, six-foot pine box. First, they carried the box and a lantern to the grave. Terry noticed with some interest that he would be lying close to Rufus James, 1850–1899, according to the tombstone. Of all the graves nearby, that one alone seemed to have been tended recently.

"Shouldn't you have some sandwiches or something?" Sara asked after they carried the rest of the gear to the newly dug grave.

"No," Terry said, "it's not exactly a picnic." He smiled at Sara, but she just looked away.

A cloud bank moved in and switched off the moon. Suddenly the night was very dark. As Sara watched Terry light a lantern, a new thought occurred to her.

"What if I stay here, right in the truck, just to make sure you're all right?"

"I'm going to be fine. I'll probably sleep most of the night away."

"Still, I'd feel a lot better if you'd let me stay and watch."

"Watch for what? This cemetery is a forgotten place. No one comes here. I've checked it out for two weeks."

"Right. All part of your perfect plan," she said.

"Sara, you don't get it. I want total isolation. It's a very important part of the experiment. Knowing you were here would wreck everything. A crowd might as well hang around and dig me up every five minutes to see how I'm doing."

Sara sighed. "Do you think the air tube is wide enough?"

"Quit worrying, will you? We tried it above ground, and it worked fine. Why should it be any different with a foot of dirt over it?"

"I can't believe we're really doing this," Sara said as Terry spread the blankets in the pine box. "We need a couple of those Houdini straitjackets."

"You think it's crazy, and I think it's an exploration."

"Of what?"

"Of me. Of who I am. I'm not like anyone else. I'm different."

That much Sara agreed with. Terry wasn't like other people. Maybe that was why she found him so attractive. Being with him was like taking a journey and not knowing what would be around the next bend.

He climbed down into the box. There was just enough room for him to stretch. "OK, now hand me the rest of the stuff."

Sara handed him the canteen of water, the pillow, the portable tape player. Then she helped him push the stiff rubber tube snugly into the hole in the lid. It was a perfect fit. No dirt could come in around it.

"That's it, I guess, Terry said. "I'll see you at eight o'clock."

Sara leaned over him. "It's not too late to change your mind," she said.

"I can't do this without you, Sara. Don't let me down. I'm counting on you."

She nodded grimly, then tried to smile. "See you in the morning."

Terry grinned. "You'd better—or I'll never speak to you again."

"That's not funny!"

Lying there, looking at the moonless sky, Terry felt a kinship with anyone who had ever explored anything first—the first person to submerge in a submarine, the first person to crawl into a space capsule. Now it was his turn to explore the unknown.

Sara carefully placed the lid on top of the box and hammered a nail into each corner, leaving part of the nail-head sticking up for easy removal. Terry had said four would be enough. The air hose stuck out about a foot above ground level. As she shoveled dirt over the box, Sara was careful that no dirt got into the tube opening.

When she had finished, she knelt and spoke into the tube. "Are you OK?" She put her ear to the tube, listening. When there was no answer, she started to panic. "Terry," she yelled, "say something!"

The answer came at once. "Sweet dreams, Sara."

Sara knelt, shaking, near the fresh mound of dirt. Clouds had completely blotted the sky now, and the moon was hidden. She looked at the tombstones bathed in pale lantern light. For the first time, she began to feel a sense of violating sacred ground.

She waited a few minutes longer, listening in case Terry had changed his mind after all. But the cemetery was silent. Not even the wind was blowing now. She turned off the lantern and started toward the truck.

She sat in the cab and stared at the cemetery. The darkness had swallowed the tombstones. From where she sat, it was impossible to see that anything had been disturbed. Once more she considered spending the night in the truck. Terry would never know she was there. But it was Saturday night, and her parents expected her home by 11:00. Besides, Terry had turned down the idea, and that was that. No way could she betray his trust.

She turned on the motor and, after a final glance at the cemetery, drove toward town.

Terry lay in the black confinement, sweating from every pore. Mistake number one—not figuring on the heat. There was enough air to breathe but not enough to evaporate the perspiration. He kept brushing the sleeve of his sweater across his forehead and eyes.

He tried fanning himself. As long as he kept it up, things were a little better. When he stopped, he was right back where he started. He pressed the button on his watch, and the little red numerals sprang at him in the blackness. 12:10. Only an hour gone? Incredible.

He spoke into the recorder: "Twelve-ten, and all is not well."

He was startled by his voice, so hollow and alien. "The heat is miserable. I've got to squirm out of these clothes as much as possible. The air smells pretty bad by now. I can breathe well enough, but I'm melting. More later."

A sudden sharp cramp in his right calf made him rise up quickly and crack his forehead on the lid of the box. It hurt some, but the pain in his calf was the main concern. He tried to massage the aching muscle but couldn't reach it. After a time, the pain slowly began to ebb away.

Sweat ran in rivulets, stinging his eyes and puddling up in his ears. Mistake number two—wrong clothing. Outside, frost crystals might be forming on the blades of grass. Outside, he might have needed the sweater, the blankets.

Twisting back and forth, he tried to get out of his sweater and T-shirt. In his struggle, he used the air too quickly, and he started to black out. Giving up, he lay motionless until he slowly regained his senses. His head began to throb where he had hit it, and his drenched clothes hung to his body like leeches.

Sara couldn't sleep. She had been foolish to think she could put Terry out of her mind. She could still see him, lying in that awful box, looking up at her and the moon. A dozen what-ifs ran through her mind. What if he didn't have enough air after all? What if the truck broke down as she was driving to the cemetery? What if her parents thought up some dumb chore she had to do before she left the house in the morning?

The clock on her bed table read 2:30. *Impossible!* she cried silently. She got out of bed and looked out her window. Dawn was still endless hours away.

What if he had panicked and was shouting for her?

If she took the truck now, her parents would surely hear her. She had to wait until at least 6:00. She sat on the edge of her bed, then lay back, staring at the blank ceiling of her room.

Terry looked at his watch again through watery eyes. The tiny numerals danced and wavered like a red mirage—2:45. A little more than five hours. He mustn't struggle. Getting enough air had become a serious problem.

Or was it a problem? Maybe the heat and the sweating and the suffocating lack of air were only in his imagination. Still, it seemed as if the box had somehow shrunk. Mistake number three—he hadn't realized he was claustrophobic.

He reached for the canteen and took a long drink, then cursed himself for spilling some of the precious water over his chin and neck. Still, the water gave him some relief. How stupid to misjudge the amount of heat his body would generate inside a closed box. He tried to think of Houdini, how his mind had controlled his emotions while he calmly had gone about his escape. Then something occurred to him. Houdini had died in a freak accident—someone had punched him in the stomach and burst his appendix.

What if Sara doesn't come? What if some freak accident happens to her? He pushed the button on his recorder, but the red numerals on his watch were somersaulting again. "I don't know what time it is. I must not move."

He wasn't sure why he shouldn't move. Something about air. His mind was confused. The point of the whole experiment was escaping him. Only one thought filled him.

"Sara?" he called hoarsely into the recorder. "I'm counting on you."

Edith James drove to Belden Park in her old Ford with her poodle, Misty, and a large potted mum to put on the grave of her grandfather Rufus. She had risen before dawn, as always, and by the time she reached the old graveyard at 6:00 A.M., the first light of day was filtering through the pine trees. She loved this part of the day best of all, and she wanted to get things done early so she could get back to study her Bible lesson for the class before church.

When she was four, her father had died in World War I and had been buried somewhere in France. She'd never really known him, but she had a vague memory of him throwing her laughing into the air on her third birthday. She could not bring flowers to her father, but she could bring them to her grandfather—and in that way honor the man whose memory she would always cherish.

She drove her car to the end of the dirt road and parked near the gate. "All right, Misty," she said as she opened the door, "go have yourself a good run." Misty leaped outward and immediately began sniffing a small bush. His mistress primped for a second in the rearview mirror, patting her gray hair carefully into place. Then she took the plant and followed the dog into the cemetery.

She went straight to the grave, the one she visited every two months to keep it neat and tidy. She placed the plant with its pretty orange blossoms in front of Rufus's stone and was just beginning to say a prayer when she thought she heard a faint voice.

Turning her head, she saw the freshly dug grave. Misty was sniffing curiously, pawing a bit of the bare dirt. No one had been buried in the cemetery for years, Edith knew. She shook her head sadly. "Must be some pauper's grave," she spoke aloud. "Someone with no money buried here secretly during the night."

Again, she thought she heard a voice. She decided it must have been Misty whining in excitement or just her tired old ears playing tricks on her again. Then she saw the tube coming from the ground near the head of the grave. "What a pathetic little flower holder," she sighed. "And so empty. Well, whoever you are, you won't be forgotten today."

Terry had drifted in and out of frightening dreams all through the night. His throat was raw, as if he had been yelling, but he remembered nothing about it. He fumbled for his canteen and managed to get it to his mouth. Only a few drops trickled onto his lips. Sara. There was something about Sara he should remember. He wondered whether he had been dreaming of her. His chest ached dully. Why was it so difficult to breathe? *Hang on,* he whispered to himself, but he wasn't sure why he should hang on or to what.

Edith James snapped half a dozen mums from the plant she had brought for her grandfather and stuck the stems snugly into the rubber flower holder. "There," she said, standing up to admire their feathery orange heads. "That certainly brightens things up!" Satisfied, she called Misty and returned to her car.

A mile or two down the road, she was quite surprised to pass a pickup truck heading the other way. A girl was driving, driving fast. A pretty young thing, but her face looked anxious as the truck flashed by. What on earth, Edith James wondered, would bring one of today's teenagers racing out here at this hour of the morning? Well, that wasn't her worry. She had plenty of time to take Misty home and then head off for Bible study.

Edith smiled gently. How nice, she thought, to have already done her good deed for the day.

SNOW CANCELLATIONS

by Donald R. Burleson

It was something all kids prayed for. But this time...

Snow wrapped around the house like the shroud of a mummy. From his bedroom window, Jamie could just make out the vague outline of the bird feeder on the edge of the deck. Beyond the backyard, the pines and spruces were snow-covered ghosts waving in the wind, nodding to each other, whispering.

It was going to be a big storm. Jamie liked that. Sort of. There was something exciting about a snowstorm burying everything. But it was also a little eerie.

Jamie heard his mother in the kitchen as she prepared breakfast. He knew better than to get in her way while she was getting herself ready for work. His father worked the early shift at the mill and had left an hour earlier. Jamie had heard him, too, outside, scraping the shovel blade on the surface of the driveway. It must have begun snowing during the night. And the air visible through the frosted window was still a frenzy of flakes, falling thick and fast.

The bedroom door opened. "Jamie? Are you awake? You should get dressed for school."

Jamie turned away from the window. "But it's snowing."

"They haven't cancelled school yet," she said and left. Jamie slipped on his jeans and went into the kitchen. The radio on the shelf over the dishwasher was turned up so his mother could hear it as she moved about the house.

"...*before it's over, folks, we expect fifteen to eighteen inches accumulation in some locations. If you have to go out, friends, give yourself a lot of extra time to get where you're going. And please drive with care. Hey, we like you and we want you to get there safe and sound. I'm Rick Phillips from Storm Center Radio, 1360 on your dial. The cancellations are coming in, and we'll have a complete rundown following these messages, so stay tuned.*"

Jamie, still half-asleep, ate his toast and watched the swirling fingers of snow tapping against the kitchen window. Maybe they were going to cancel school! He'd heard it happened up here in the north all the time. In Arizona, where his family had lived till this past year, school had never been cancelled for snow. Ever. The only time he'd ever seen snow was on that trip to Colorado when he was six.

"Maybe they'll close up at Sanborn's," Jamie called to

his mother, "and you won't have to go to work."

She shook her head ruefully as she came back into the kitchen. "Sanborn's wouldn't close if it was the end of the world."

On the radio, the commercials ended and the cancellation announcements began. Jamie set his spoon down and listened.

"*...Bedford Senior Center is open but no transportation. Hooksett, no school, all schools....*

Come on! Jamie thought, finishing his cereal. *Come on! Who cares about all that stuff? What about Merrimack?*

"*...Derry, no school. Salem, no school. Dingdong Bell Nursery School in Goffstown closed today. This just in,*"— Jamie had a feeling and held his breath— "*Merrimack, no school....*"

"Mom?"

"I heard it, Jamie."

"All right!" he cried. "No school." Suddenly, he felt very much awake. He went now to the living room window. Fresh snow had already covered the driveway where his father had shoveled. It was beautiful stuff, but somehow also darkly suggestive, as if saying: *See, you people think you're so smart, but I can shut you down anytime I feel like it, and I feel like it right now.* A snowplow turned onto his street and rumbled past, pushing a sliding hill of snow with its wide-mouth blade.

"I guess you'll have to be here by yourself," his mother said. She had her coat on and her boots.

He shrugged. "No problem."

"I guess you can watch TV or play tapes. For lunch, make yourself a peanut butter and jelly sandwich. I'll call you at lunchtime, but you know my number at work if you need me."

"OK, Mom. Bye."

Still, she hesitated. "I hate to leave you alone. Maybe I can work through my lunch hour and get home early. OK?"

"It's no big deal," he said again.

He watched as she trudged out across the drive and brushed snow off her car. She climbed in and slowly backed out. The car's taillights winked red through the wind-driven flakes and then were gone around the corner.

Now he was alone. Alone in the house, alone with the snow brushing against every window.

Outside, the wind swirled and howled and slashed the snow like a torn curtain. Jamie heard the floorboards creak, and he turned. Funny, he thought, how an empty house could make sounds.

Well. He stacked his breakfast dishes in the sink, then went to his bedroom. He fumbled through the mess of socks and underwear in his dresser and uncovered his emergency supply of candy bars. Taking three, he went to his parents' bedroom.

He crawled onto the bed and arranged the sheets snugly around his legs like a bird's nest. He had decided on this room rather than his own because this room had a phone. He was going to call Kevin Riley.

He unwrapped a candy bar and took a bite and leaned across to the phone beside the bed. After tapping out Kevin's number, he straightened back out in his nest with the phone in hand. A boy's voice answered on the other end.

"'Lo?"

"Hey, Kevin, your mother sniffs gym socks."

"Cheez. Jamie, you're weird."

"Yeah, and you're a total geek."

"Hey, what are you eating?"

"Dog boogers." At this they both collapsed into laughter. Then Kevin said, "Great about school bein' closed, huh? What're you doin'?"

"Sittin' here talkin' to you on the phone. Whadda ya think I'm doin'?"

"Your folks home?"

"No," Jamie said. "Yours?"

"Naw, they both had to go to work. Wicked neat bein' home by yourself, huh?"

"Sure. Yeah, I guess so."

Kevin guffawed. "Whadda ya mean, you guess so? You scared bein' alone, Jamie?"

"No, no, I'm not scared. What's there to be scared of?" He really wasn't scared. Not exactly.

"Hey," said Kevin. "I'll tell you what's to be scared of. You're from Arizona, right? You don't know. Cars skid off the road and plough into snowbanks. People walking in a blizzard get lost all the time. They get snow-blind, and then their toes and fingers fall off from frostbite."

"Their fingers and toes fall off?" Jamie repeated incredulously.

"See you *are* scared. Go find your mommy, Jamie."

"Hey," Jamie had just realized that the radio was still going in the kitchen. "Hey, hold on. I'm gonna go get the radio and bring it in here so I can listen in bed."

"You in bed, Jamie? What a wimp."

Jamie went for the radio. When he had it plugged in and playing on his mother's bureau, he resettled himself in the middle of the bed and picked up the phone. "I want to check out the cancellations."

"How come? You already know they cancelled school. What else matters?"

Jamie watched the snow falling ever harder and faster beyond the windowpanes. "I thought if it got bad enough, they might close the mill early and—"

"And our dads would come home, right? I told you you were scared."

"Stick it in your ear, Kevin."

"What station you listenin' to?" Kevin asked. Jamie could hear him tuning a radio across the dial, a jumble of stations fading in and out.

"Got it," Kevin said, and Jamie could hear the radio sound over the phone slide into agreement with his own radio.

"*. . . and storm-related information continues to come in. It's a big one out there, folks, so stay with us and we'll keep you up to date as this whole region gets buried.*"

"Hey, Jamie, this is neat. The whole town's covered up with snow."

Jamie had been to Kevin's apartment building across town several times and knew that you could see just about the whole town from Kevin's fourteenth-floor living room window.

"Kevin?"

"Huh?"

"Can you see Sanborn's from there?"

"Sanborn's? Yeah, of course I can see Sanborn's. It's got snow all over the roof. What's the matter, puddin'-face, oo miss oo mommy?"

"Suck toe jam, Kevin."

"Munch navel fuzz, Jamie."

They were both quiet for a while; the radios murmured the same commercials, the same chatter.

"...*cancelled, and also the meeting of the Franco-American Friendship Club for this evening has been cancelled.*"

"Hey, Kevin?"

"What?"

"Listen, you don't have to hang on the line if you got things you want to do."

A moment of silence. Then: "Naw, I don't have nothin' I want to do. I'll stay on."

Jamie said, "Sort of nice having someone to talk to, right?"

"Yeah, I guess it is, kind of. Even if I have to talk to some chickenskin like you."

They became thoughtful again, neither speaking for a good while. Outside, the snow seemed heavier, more insistent than ever. It brushed against the frosty panes with jittery fingers of white, worrying at the glass.

Then Jamie said, "We never had this stuff in Arizona. Something about it is kind of eerie, huh?" Jamie steeled himself for Kevin's smart-mouth reply.

But Kevin was slow in replying, and surprisingly he said, "Yeah, kind of."

What do you know, Jamie thought, *he feels it too.* "Kevin, can you see the mill?"

"Yeah, just barely. It's a long way off. I can just see it. Looks all wrapped up like a...a mummy."

"A mummy! That's weird. That's just what I was thinking this morning when I got out of bed and looked out the—"

"*...I'm Rick Phillips for Radio 1360, your information center for this storm.*"

Something in the tone of the announcer's voice had stopped Jamie. The voice sounded, well...different.

"Kevin?"

"Mmm?"

"That guy on the radio—did you think he sounded kind of strange?"

"I guess I wasn't paying much attention to him. I was looking at the snow. It kind of hypnotizes you, you know?"

Somehow Kevin seemed different now, more serious. Jamie had never known Kevin to be serious about anything. The music that had been playing on the radio stopped, and the voice was back.

"*Time now is 8:25, and that snow just keeps coming down. And do we have some new cancellations for you!*"

The wind outside moaned and shifted the snow in crazy patterns. That voice *was* different, and Jamie didn't like the way it sounded. It was—what? A little like some kind of cartoon-character villain, sort of half-mocking like. Sort of...unreal.

"Hey, you're right," he heard Kevin say. "That voice sounds—"

"Shh, listen."

"Here's the big one, friends. Listen carefully." He pronounced carefully the way Bela Lugosi might say it in a Dracula movie, drawing out the *a-a-r* sound with a special menace. *"Here it is. Merrimack Valley Mill is cancelled."* The radio went immediately to music again, some goofy love song.

For a long while, neither boy spoke. Finally, Kevin broke the silence. "Jamie?"

"I'm here."

"Jamie, I'm lookin' out the window, and somethin' looks funny."

"What do you mean, something looks funny?"

Kevin waited a long time before answering. "This isn't right. I can see Pennacock Park."

"So? You can see practically everything in the city from your apartment."

"Yeah, but not the park. I never could see it before."

"Aw, c'mon, Kevin, it's as big as a football field. Bigger. You must have seen it."

"No, no, I'm tellin' you Jamie, I never could see it before. The mill was always in the way. Oh, no!"

Jamie heard Kevin draw in a shocked-sounding breath. "What?" Jamie asked.

"I can see the park because the mill isn't there."

Jamie laughed, but the laugh came out a little hollow. "Give me a break, Kevin. Of course the mill is there. You're talking goofy, dufus."

Kevin sounded angry. "Look, Jamie, I oughta know where that mill is from my own window, and I'm tellin' you it disappeared. That's why I can see the park, because the mill ain't hidin' it anymore."

Outside Jamie's window, the wind whooped up into a howl and threw snow against the pane. "Kevin, what are you saying? My dad works there."

"I know," Kevin said quietly. "So does mine."

"...at 8:39, this is Radio 1360, your Voice of the Storm." The voice had that mocking, Dracula tone again, more so than before. "And in case you thought we were through with cancellations, consider this one, my friends. This just in — Sanborn's in Merrimack. Sanborn's has been cancelled."

Immediately there was more music.

"Kevin?"

"I'm here."

"Kevin, my mom works at Sanborn's."

"I know."

"Kevin, can you see Sanborn's?"

After a moment, Kevin replied, "I can't tell, there's so much snow."

"Kevin, look, I'm going to hang up for a minute. I'll call you back."

"Promise?"

"Promise." Jamie clicked down the receiver. Then, after a pause, he punched out the familiar digits of Sanborn's, digits he had used so many times before to call his mother when he had a question or a problem. As he looked up from the phone, his eye caught the photo on his mother's bureau—his mom, his dad, and himself smiling in the sun on summer vacation two years ago. Somehow he felt oddly moved by the photo and other familiar objects placed on the bureau.

He listened for the phone to ring at Sanborn's, straining to hear that soft burring sound. He heard only a blank hissing on the line and the murmuring of the wind outside, where, he could see, the snow was falling harder than ever. Finally he gave up and dialed Kevin back. Kevin answered before the first ring was finished, "Jamie?"

"Yeah, it's me. Look, I tried to call my mom, but there's no answer at Sanborn's. It doesn't even ring. So maybe the telephone lines are down. That sometimes happens in a snowstorm, right? I mean, you ought to know. You've lived through other snowstorms before, right?" Jamie realized he was speaking rapidly, nervously, but he couldn't help it.

"*... We hope you're staying tuned, because we're having more snow cancellations. Exotron Technologies has been can-*

celled. *Compton Industries has been cancelled. Pennacock Mall has been cancelled."*

"Jamie!" Jamie had never heard Kevin's voice sound the way it did now.

"Your mom works at Pennacock Mall, doesn't she?"

"Jamie—there's something awful wrong. The downtown, out my window. There's, like, parts of it gone. I mean, really gone. Like holes in it."

"OK, maybe it's a mirage. Sometimes in the desert, you know, the heat waves coming up from the ground and all make things blurry and wavy and you think you see things...."

"Shh. Jamie, listen. The radio!"

"...and still more Storm Center Radio updates for you. Ready for this one?" The voice sounded thick, gloating, dreadful. *"Reeds Ferry Apartments, in Merrimack, cancelled."* Music. Some woman was singing, "Let it snow, let it snow, let it snow."

A brittle finger of ice wormed its way up Jamie's spine. Kevin lived in the Reeds Ferry Apartments complex. Jamie swallowed hard to get his voice back.

"Kevin?"

Nothing.

"Kevin? This isn't funny, anymore. You're just trying to scare me." Jamie laughed nervously. "So, OK, you win. You scared me. Now stop it!"

Nothing.

"Kevin!!!"

Nothing on the line at all but a dead, dry hissing, like the sound that might come out of the grinning and remorseless mouth of a reptile.

"Kevin, please be there. *Please!*"

Silence. Silence on the phone, and the radio crooning softly along, unconcerned.

Jamie hung up the phone and sat looking at the snow, which had grown into a nightmare of whiteness pressing at the window, blotting out everything, tumbling and turning and writhing in the madness of the wind.

He looked at the photo of himself and his parents smiling in the Arizona sun. Quickly, he jumped from the bed and ran to grab the frame. He glanced out of the window. Everything was wrapped in white. He could see nothing, not the woods beyond the backyard, not the bird feeder outside the window, not the driveway—nothing. Jamie dashed back to the mattress. Pulling the sheets closer around him and pressing the photo to his cheek, he waited for the music to end.

THE RUUM

by Arthur Porges

*The animals were paralyzed, preserved as
living specimens. Now the ruum intended
on preserving one more — a human.*

Then: The cruiser *Ilkor* had just passed beyond the
orbit of Pluto when a worried officer reported to the
Commander.

"I regret to inform you, sir," he said nervously, "that a
Type H-9 Ruum has been left behind on the third planet,
together with anything it may have collected."

The Commander's three eyes turned from green to
blue, but her voice remained level.

"How was the ruum set?"

"For a maximum radius of 30 miles, and 160 pounds,
plus or minus 15."

The Commander was silent for several seconds. Then
she said, "We cannot change course now. We will retrieve

the ruum on our return in a few weeks. In the meantime, confine the person responsible to quarters."

But at the end of its outward run, the cruiser met an enemy raider. When the battle was over, both ships, radioactive and loaded with dead, began a billion-year orbit around the star.

And on Earth, it was the age of the dinosaurs.

Now: When the two men had unloaded the supplies, Jim Irwin watched his partner climb into the little plane with pontoons.

"Don't forget to mail that letter to my wife," Jim shouted.

"The minute I land," Walt Leonard called back. "And you find some uranium. Make us millionaires. And don't rub noses with any grizzlies."

Jim thumbed his nose as the plane skimmed across the lake and rose into the sky. Suddenly he felt a strange chill. For three weeks he would be alone in this remote valley of the Canadian Rockies. If anything happened, he would be completely on his own until Walt returned. And if there was any uranium in the valley, he had to find it in twenty-one days.

To work then—and no gloomy thoughts. With the unhurried skills of a trained woodsman, he built a lean-to in the shelter of a rocky overhang. He piled his supplies back under the ledge, covered by a tarp and protected from animal prowlers. All but the dynamite—he hid that carefully two hundred yards away.

The first two weeks went by swiftly but with no finds. Only one good area remained, and just enough time to explore it. Early one morning Jim set off for the northeast part of the valley.

He took the Geiger counter and his rifle. The .30-06 was a nuisance, but huge grizzlies have touchy tempers and take a lot of killing. The .22 pistol he left in his holster in the lean-to.

Jim walked all morning, sometimes feeling a burst of hope as the counter began to chatter. But its sputter always died down. Apparently, he and Walt had picked the wrong valley. Jim's cheerfulness faded.

He decided to think about his lunch. The sun, as well as his stomach, said it was time. He had just prepared to fish a foaming brook, when he rounded a grassy knoll and came across a sight that made him stiffen to a halt.

The scene was like some giant outdoor butcher shop. A wide variety of animals, neatly lined up in threes, stretched almost as far as the eye could see. Those nearest him were ordinary deer, bear, cougar, and mountain sheep. But down the line were many strange beasts. One near the extreme end he recognized at once. There had been a specimen like it in the museum at home.

No doubt about it—the body was that of a stegosaur, no bigger than a pony.

Fascinated, Jim walked down the lines. Glancing at one lizard, he saw an eye flutter. Then it came to him—the animals were not dead but paralyzed and somehow preserved. *Still alive?* Perspiration prickled Jim's forehead. *A stegosaur still alive after 150 million years?*

All at once he noticed something else. The victims were roughly the same size. Nowhere was there a really large animal. No tyrannosaur. No mammoth. Each specimen was about the size of a large sheep. He was puzzling this out, when the underbrush rustled behind him.

For a second, Jim wondered if a blob of mercury had rolled into the clearing. The rounded object moved with just such a liquid motion. It whipped out and retracted a number of metal rods with lens-like structures at their tips. The object rolled steadily toward him at about five miles per hour. From its look, Jim had no doubt that it meant to add him to the heap of living-dead specimens.

He sprang back a number of spaces, unslinging his rifle. A grim smile touched his lips as he pulled the trigger. He knew what one of those 180-grain slugs could do at 2,700 feet per second.

Wham. The familiar kick against his shoulder. *E-e-e-e-!* The whining screech of a ricochet. He sucked in his breath. At a mere twenty yards, the bullet had bounced off the ruum.

Quickly, Jim blasted two more rounds. The ruum kept coming. When it was six feet away, he saw a gleaming hook flick out and a stinglike probe waiting between them. The stinger dripped green liquid.

Jim ran.

He weighed exactly 149 pounds—light, trim, and fit. He had no trouble pulling ahead. The ruum seemed unable to increase its speed. But Jim felt no relief on that score. No animal on Earth could keep a steady five-mile-per-hour pace forever.

As he ran, Jim began to shed all surplus material. He hesitated over the rifle, but military training impelled him to keep the weapon. The Geiger counter he placed gently on a flat rock while barely breaking his stride.

One thing was certain. This would be a fighting retreat. He'd use every survival trick he learned in his hazard-filled lifetime. Whatever that thing was, wherever it had come from, it would find him no easy prey.

Taking deep, measured breaths, he loped along, looking with shrewd eyes for anything that might be used to his advantage in this weird contest. Suddenly he came upon a sight that made him pause. It was a point where a huge boulder overhung the trail. He grinned as he remembered a Malay mantrap that had once saved his life.

Purposely dragging his feet, he made a clear trail directly under the boulder. Then he walked backward in his own prints and jumped up to a point behind the balanced rock.

After digging under it with his belt knife and ramming it with his shoulder, he felt it teeter. He was crouching there, panting, when the ruum rolled over the hill.

Seemingly intent on the footprints, the alien sphere rippled along directly under the boulder. As it did so, Jim gave a savage shout and, thrusting with his whole weight against the boulder, toppled it directly on the machine below. Five tons of snow fell from a height of twelve feet.

After another shout, this time of triumph, Jim scrambled down to the trail. He stared at the huge boulder, shaking his head dazedly. Then he gave the solid rock a kick in celebration of his victory. "Take that, you bloody butcher," he said out loud.

Then he leaped back, his eyes wild. The giant rock was shifting. Even as he stared, part of a gray form appeared under the nearest edge, somehow working its way loose from the tons of weight. With a choked cry, Jim turned and resumed his flight.

He ran hard a full mile down the trail. Looking back, he could just make out a dark dot moving away from the boulder. He sat down and put his head in his hands. What now?

He forced himself to relax and nibbled some dried beef, biscuits, and chocolate. A few sips of water, and he felt ready to resume the struggle.

After running fifteen minutes, he came to a sheer face of rock about thirty feet high. If he could make it to the top of that rock, the ruum would have to detour and might lose the trail.

He looked at the sun. Huge and crimson, it was almost touching the western horizon. He would have to move fast before darkness came. Using every crack and tiny ledge, he fought his way up the cliff. He had just reached the top when the ruum rolled up to the base of the wall of rock. But the machine did not detour. It hesitated for only a few seconds. Then it began to send out metallic wands. One of these, topped with lenses, waved in the air. Jim drew back too late—their unblinking gaze had spotted him peering down.

Immediately, all the wands retracted, and a slender rod began to shoot straight up toward him. As he watched, its barbed tip gripped the cliff almost under his nose.

Jim leaped to his feet. Already the rod was shortening as the ruum swallowed it, pulling itself up along the slender metal track. Seizing a length of dry branch and inserting one end under the hook, Jim began to pry.

There was a flash, and Jim felt a surge of power that shattered the end of the branch. He dropped it with a gasp of pain and backed off several yards, full of rage. Snarling, he unslung his rifle. Now he had the ruum where he wanted it.

Kneeling to steady his aim, Jim sighted at the hook and fired. The hook disappeared in an explosion of rock and dust, and there was a soggy thud at the base of the cliff. Jim shouted with relief and joy. Not only had the heavy slug blasted the metal claw loose, it had also smashed a big gap in the cliff's edge. The ruum would have a hard time using that part of the cliff again.

Jim looked down and saw a gray form at the bottom. He grinned. Every time the ruum clamped a hook over the bluff, he'd blow the hook loose. He had plenty of ammunition. Sooner or later that devilish machine would have to accept a detour.

Then he looked again. Down below, the squat machine was sending up three rods at the same time. The rods snagged the cliff's edge at intervals of about four feet.

Jim whipped the rifle to his shoulder. The first shot was a bulls-eye, knocking loose the left-hand hook. His second shot knocked off the center barb. But even as he whirled to level at number three, he saw it was hopeless.

The first hook was back in place. No matter how well he shot, one rod would always be pulling the ruum to the top.

Jim hung the rifle muzzle down from a small tree and ran into the deepening dark. All those years he had spent to toughen his body were paying off now. But so what? What could he do? Was there anything that would stop the infernal machine behind him?

The he remembered the dynamite.

Gradually he changed his course back toward his camp by the lake. Overhead, the stars brightened, pointing the way. At times he stopped to rest or to check his direction. But he could never rest long before the sound of the ruum came to his ears.

Shortly after sunrise he reached the lake and his camp. He staggered from exhaustion and his eyes closed. He struck himself feebly on the nose, popping his eyes open. There was the dynamite. The sight of those greasy sticks snapped him wide awake.

He forced himself to stay calm and to think carefully. The dynamite must be set off from a distance at the very moment the ruum passed over it. He couldn't use a fuse—the rate of burning wasn't constant enough to allow precise timing. Sweat poured down his face. He had to think of an answer, but he was so tired, so tired. His head drooped. He snapped it up—and saw the .22 where he had left it in the lean-to.

His sunken eyes flashed.

Moving with frantic haste, he piled all the percussion caps along the dynamite sticks. Then, staggering out to his trail, he carefully placed the box about twenty yards from a rocky ledge.

Jim had scarcely hunched down behind the ledge when his tireless pursuer appeared five hundred yards away. He slid into a crack where he could aim at the dynamite and still be shielded from the blast. If it was a shield...when all those sticks blew up at only twenty yards.

Suddenly he was in full awareness. A huge form had come along the edge of the lake and was sniffing at the explosive. Of all the times for a grizzly to be snooping about! It had the whole camp to explore. Why did it have to choose the dynamite? Just a touch could blow one of the percussion caps. And then....

The grizzly heard a noise and raised its massive head to stare at the strange object approaching. Jim snickered. Until he had met the ruum, the giant North American grizzly was the only thing in the world he had feared. And now the two terrors of his life were meeting head-on— and he was laughing.

About six feet from the bear the ruum paused. The grizzly reared with a ferocious growl, terrible teeth flashing white against red lips. The ruum started to roll past, still intent on its specimen. The bear closed in, roaring, and gave the ruum a hard swat with one mighty paw armed with razor-sharp claws. The blow would have ripped apart a rhinoceros. Dust flew from the machine, and it was knocked back several inches. It paused, then rippled on, ignoring the bear.

The lord of the woods wasn't settling for a draw. With incredible speed it pulled the ruum to its chest with shaggy forearms and clamped its jaws on the gray surface. Jim half rose. "Get it!" he croaked.

Then silver metal gleamed bright against the gray. There was a flash, swift and deadly. The roar of the king became a gurgle, and its one-ton bulk fell to the ground. Blood poured from its slashed throat as it died.

And the ruum rolled past the giant corpse, still intent on the man's trail. "OK, baby," Jim said under his breath, "come and get it." And very calmly he squeezed the trigger of his pistol.

Sound first. Then giant hands lifted his body from where he lay and let him go. He came down hard in a patch of nettles. But he didn't care. He noticed that the birds were silent. Then there was a fluid thump as something heavy struck the ground a few feet away. Then all was quiet.

Jim lifted his head. He saw an enormous smoking crater in the earth. He also saw, gray-white now from powdered rock, the ruum.

The machine was under a handsome pine tree. Even as Jim watched, wondering if the ringing in his ears would ever go away, the machine began to roll toward him.

He fumbled for his pistol. It was gone. It had dropped somewhere out of reach. He wanted to pray but couldn't get his brain to focus....

The ruum was a foot away now, and Jim closed his eyes. He felt cool, metallic fingers touch, grip, lift. His body was raised several inches and juggled oddly. Helpless but strangely serene, he waited for the stinger with the green liquid. He thought of the lizard with the trembling eye and wondered what it would be like to lie paralyzed but mentally aware for a million years.

Then, gently, the ruum put him back on the ground. When he opened his eyes some seconds later, the sphere was rolling away. Watching it go released a flood of emotions, and he began to sob softly. It seemed only a matter of moments before he heard the seaplane's engine and opened his eyes to see Walt Leonard peering down at him.

Later, in the plane, Walt grinned suddenly and said: "Well, no uranium, but we'll do OK. I can get a helicopter, a big one. We'll pick up some of those prehistoric specimens, and museums will pay us plenty."

Jim shook his head. "What about that robot keeping watch on its collection?"

"It can't fly, can it?"

"Who knows?' Jim responded. "I wouldn't bet on it."

"Well, maybe we can work out some rig that will let us retrieve the bodies from the air. Maybe grab the robot too."

"No way," said Jim. "I'm through messing with that thing." He paused, "All that running I did, and then the stupid thing didn't want me at all."

"Yeah," Walt said, "that was really weird. And after that marathon. I admire your guts, man." He glanced sideways at Jim Irwin's haggard face. "That run cost you plenty. I figure you lost over ten pounds."

PART II
LACHESIS, WEAVER
OF GOOD AND EVIL

A MEETING WITH DEATH

Adapted from the "Pardoner's Tale" from
The Canterbury Tales
by Geoffrey Chaucer

*They were rakes, rascals, scoundrels—all three.
But they had made a pact. Together they
would seek out death and destroy him.*

During the 1300s, a terrible pestilence swept across Asia and Europe claiming hundreds of thousands of victims. Some people called the dreadful disease the Plague. Others called it the Black Death. No one knew the cause of the dying or from where the pestilence had come. No one then understood how the Black Death could steal so silently, so swiftly from one village to the next. In fear, some people fled their homes to seek a safer place. Others remained behind to confront, perhaps even to defeat, the deadly specter. The setting *of the story that follows is a rural village in England, a village in which Death walks boldly among the people.*

Early one morning, before the church bells have rung to announce the start of day, three young men gather in a tavern. They are dressed as gentlemen, but their drunken behavior gives away their true nature. They are rakes, rascals, scoundrels—all three.

This morning they have come not to feed their empty bellies, but to quench their thirst for more wine. A skinny boy, whose mother is the tavern keeper, sets another jug of wine on their table. Suddenly from outside comes the low and mournful bong of a funeral bell. Villagers file past the tavern door, carrying a corpse on a stretcher. The first rascal wipes the wine from his lips and goes to the door to watch. "Do you see this?" Oswald calls to his companions. "A funeral starts our day."

"You, boy!" shouts Roland, the second rascal. "Go quickly and ask whose corpse this is that passes by here."

"And look to it that you report his name correctly," adds John, the third rake in the group.

"But, sirs, there is no need for that," the boy answers. "It was told to me two hours before you came in here. The dead man was an old companion of yours."

"A friend of ours? Tell us the name!"

"I don't know his name, only that I have seen him here with you. Last night he was sitting on that very bench when suddenly there came a thief who, with a spear, smote the man's heart in two." The boy demonstrates by thrusting a make-believe sword forward. "Then, just as quickly, the thief went away without a word."

"A thief?" says Oswald, turning from the door and looking at the other rakes. "Who is this vile creature?"

"The people call the thief Death."

"Death! Ha!" Roland scoffs and reaches for the jug to pour himself more wine. "The stupid boy spins tales to tease us."

Marie, the boy's mother, has been listening and now she steps forward. "The child speaks the truth. Death has slain both man and woman, child and laborer in a large village over a mile hence. I believe Death must live there."

"If I were you," the boy tells the rakes, "I'd take care or Death will do you harm too."

Roland mocks him. "Do *us* harm! Now the boy thinks he can frighten us."

"I would not laugh if I were you," warns Marie. "A thousand people, I tell you, have died!"

Roland pushes back his stool and stands, made bold by the liquid courage of the wine he has drunk. "I vow by holy bones to seek out this mad creature. I shall seek Death on the highways and byways!" He turns to his two companions and challenges them. "Listen, my friends. We three are all of one mind. Let each of us hold up his hand to the other two and each of us become the others' brother, and we will slay this traitor, this thief Death."

Oswald glances anxiously at the open tavern door. The mournful sounds of the funeral bell still echo along the street outside.

"Well? Are we brothers?" Roland presses. "Do we pledge our word of honor to live and die for each other? Together we can defeat Death!" He holds out his hand.

John hesitates, then he leaps to his feet and clasps Roland's hand. "Yes! Death shall be slain!"

The two rascals look at Oswald. "The thief who has slain so many, on my honor, will be slain before night falls." He steps to the table and places his hand on theirs. "Brothers."

The pact made, the three rakes storm from the tavern into the morning sun.

Because Marie has said that Death lives in the neighboring village, the three rakes head in that direction. They go not quite a half mile when they come upon an old woman on the road. A dirty cloth is wrapped about her head and shoulders. Her face is pale and withered; her fingers, bony and twisted with age.

"Good morrow, lords," she greets in a voice as old and brittle as bone. "May the saints protect you."

"Bad cess to you, old woman!" Roland says with a grimace. "Why are you all wrapped up except for your face?"

"Yes," says Oswald. "Why do you live so long, in such old age?"

The old woman uses a twisted branch for a cane. She leans upon it and gazes into Oswald's face. "Because even if I walked to India I could not find a man either in a city or in a village who would exchange his youth for my age. Therefore, I must keep my age for as long as I live."

"She's making up riddles, I think," laughs John.

"Move out of our way, you old crone," barks Roland. "Your old bag of a body takes up too much of the road."

"It is wrong of you to speak rudely to an old woman," she whines. "Have I injured you by word or deed?"

"*You* injure us? That's a howl!" All three rascals laugh.

"I warn you," says the crackling voice. "Do no harm to an old woman any more than you would wish others to do to you in your old age—*if* you live till then."

"Leave her be. Her mind is as old as her body, and she makes no sense."

Roland shoves her aside, and the three rakes walk on.

"Not even Death will take my life," says the old woman. "And so I walk like a restless prisoner. Lo! How I fade away, flesh and blood and skin!"

Roland turns. "Death you say? You have seen Death?"

The old woman mumbles to herself, "Oh, when shall my old bones be at rest? I am cursed to wander from village to village. I must go where I have to go."

Roland grabs the old woman's thin arm. "You spoke just now of this traitor Death, who slays all our friends in this country. Where is Death? Tell us! Or you shall pay for it!"

John peers closely at her wrinkled face. "Perhaps she is Death's spy. Finding young lives for Death to snatch away!"

With eyes dark and clouded, the old woman stares without fear into their arrogant faces. "Well, sirs, if you are so eager to find Death, then turn up this crooked path. By my faith, I left him there in that grove, under a tree, and there he will stay."

"We mean to slay him for all the young people whose lives he has stolen," Oswald says. "What do you think of that, you old crone?"

Her blistered lips crack into a thin smile. "Your boasting won't make him hide himself at all. Death is not afraid of rascals like you. Do you see that large oak? You shall find him there, waiting for you."

Roland lets go of her arm. At once, the three rakes turn and run along the crooked path.

"Is this the tree?" Roland cries. "But I see no one!"

The three rakes stand before the large oak, looking now up into its branches, looking now through the surrounding shadows for Death.

"The old crone has tricked us," says John. "I told you she spoke in riddles."

"Here! What's this?" cries Oswald. Partially hidden in the tangle of grass and thorns at the base of the oak tree is a large sack. Oswald frees it and unties the rope around its closed neck. "Why it's gold!" he gasps. "GOLD!"

"Let me see!" Roland grabs the bag from Oswald and spills some of the coins into his palm. They fall in a glittering stream to the ground. John quickly scoops the fallen coins into his own hands.

"It *is* gold!" cries John. "Two hundred pieces of gold at least!"

"We're rich!" laughs Oswald. "Rich!"

The three hoot wildly with joy. Already they have forgotten their pledge to find and slay Death.

"What shall we do? How shall we divide it?" asks John.

The three sit on the ground with the sack of gold in the center.

Roland speaks first. "Brothers, pay attention to what I have to say. Fortune has given us this treasure so that we can live our lives in mirth and jollity. As lightly as it came, so we shall spend it!"

"Who would have guessed that we should have such

good luck today!" muses Oswald. "A day that began with a funeral! Let's take it now and go."

"Not so quick!" warns Roland. "Think but a minute. If we carry this gold from this hidden place to my house—"

"*Your* house?" interrupts John.

"Or else to yours," Roland quickly adds, "Someone will see us. They will think us thieves and hang us for our treasure."

"Yes, yes," agrees John. "We cannot carry the gold to our homes in the daylight."

"We shall draw lots to see who among us will return to the village and secretly bring back food and wine," suggests Roland. "One shall go and two shall remain here to guard the treasure."

The three rascals look at one another. Once more Roland holds out his hand to make a pact. And once more first John, then Oswald, agree to the deal. Roland draws three straws from his pocket, snaps off the end of one, then holds all three in his fist. John draws first. Then Oswald picks. At the same time, each rake opens his hand. Oswald's straw is the shortest, but he does not leave at once. "We are brothers?" he asks.

"We made a pledge, didn't we?"

"And you will wait for me here?" Oswald asks, still unsure.

"Yes, yes!" says John. "We shall wait for you here. Do

you think I would let *him*," he nods to Roland, "get away with our shares of the gold?"

Oswald hurries away, back down the crooked path. No sooner is he out of sight when Roland leans closer to John. "It is a great deal of gold."

"Yes, indeed it is."

"It would be greater if divided by two instead of three," suggests Roland.

John grins. "What are you thinking?"

"That two are stronger than one."

Roland cups the coins and lets them fall, glittering from his hand into John's. John stares at the golden pool in his palm.

"Yes," says John, "two *are* stronger than one."

As Oswald hurries back to the village, he imagines gold falling like yellow sunshine from Roland's hand to the ground. Why, he wonders, should he share it? After all, he was the one who discovered the happy sack. *If I should have it all*, he thinks as he nears the village, *why I'd be the happiest man alive!*

In the village, he spies an apothecary shop, where herbs and medicines of all kinds—poisons too—are sold. He doesn't hesitate, but enters the shop at once. "I have a problem," he tells the apothecary.

"What problem is that?"

"Rats," Oswald answers at once. "Many rats. Under my house. And a polecat too. The beast has been killing my chickens."

"I have just the thing you need. No creature in all this world, if it eats or drinks of this mixture, will not lose its life at once." He hands Oswald a glass jar.

"Are you certain of this? It must work quickly, very quickly."

"Oh, yes. The rats shall die in less time than it would take you to take ten steps."

The young rake pays for his poison, then hurries to another shop and buys three skins of wine. Carefully, he pours the poison into two of the skins, then makes a small mark on the third. Smiling slyly, he raises the skins. "To your health, dear friends."

Quite pleased with himself, Oswald returns to the tavern to order some food. The tavern owner recognizes him. "Ah, it is you. Have you found Death?"

"Don't be foolish. Why should I want to find Death?" Oswald asks. "That was only a boasting game we played hours ago."

"Where are your two companions?"

"Gone. As far away from this village as they can get. They shall not return."

Marie gives the young man bread and cheese, and he

hurries away, heading back toward the grove of trees and the gold that awaits him.

John stands and points down the crooked road. "I see him. He is coming."

"Remember our plan," Roland says. "Do not betray me."

Oswald returns and sets the skins of wine in the grass. Although seeming to do so casually, he makes sure that the marked skin is the one nearest him. Roland reaches hungrily for a crust of bread. Oswald watches as John picks up the skin nearest him. He raises it to his lip, then hesitates. "What took you so long?" he asks suspiciously.

"That foolish woman in the tavern wanted to know if we had found Death." Oswald grins. "I told her it was a game we were playing, that we had better things to do. It is not our worry where Death may go."

"A game. That's right," says Roland, his mouth full of cheese. "Death may come and go as he pleases. It is no skin off our backsides, is it?" He laughs and John laughs, as well. Soon all three rakes are slapping their knees and hugging their sides.

Then suddenly, John lunges at Oswald, pinning him to the ground. "Here is another game to play, brother." In a flash, Roland pulls out his knife and plunges it into

Oswald's heart. Oswald's struggle lasts but a few moments, and then he is still.

John and Roland sit back, stunned at what they have done. The air around them seems to hold its breath. And then Roland laughs in triumph. "It is done. The gold is ours. Come, let us celebrate."

"What about—" John nods toward the body.

"What about him? It was his misfortune to draw the shortest straw. We'll bury him later. But first," Roland holds up a skin of wine, "we drink. To our fortune!"

John brings his own skin of wine to his lips. "To long and idle lives," he toasts.

Each man throws back his head and drinks.

The apothecary's words are true. The poison is violent, strong, and quick. So quick, in fact, that when the old woman steps from the shadows of the grove to retrieve her gold, the three rakes offer no resistance at all. How can they? They are as silent and unmoving as the tree trunks that surround them.

"You think you can defeat Death?" she asks the scoundrels who stare back at her with unblinking eyes. "It cannot be done. Your greed was the poison that killed you. May someone bury your flesh before it rots in the sun."

And with that, Death shuffles away.

THE BIRTHMARK

by Nathaniel Hawthorne

*The birthmark was nature's flaw. But what
nature could not perfect, science could.*

Aylmer gazed unhappily at his wife, Georgiana, across
the room. She was beautiful, except for a small
birthmark on her cheek. Aylmer was a scientist, not a doctor, and before his marriage to Georgiana, he had scarcely
noticed the mark. But for weeks now it had been troubling him. It was like a stain upon white marble. He had
begun to hate it.

"My dear," he ventured one day, "has it ever occurred
to you that the mark upon your cheek could be
removed?" he asked.

Georgiana smiled uneasily. "It is so faint, I often forget it is even there. To tell you the truth, it has been so
often called a charm that I was simple enough to imagine it might be so."

"Upon another face perhaps it might," replied her husband. "But never on yours. I find it shocking!"

Georgiana was alarmed. "Shocking?" she cried, deeply hurt; at first reddening with momentary anger, but then bursting into tears. "Then why did you take me from my mother's side? You cannot love what shocks you!"

The singular mark was deeply interwoven with the texture and substance of her face. In the usual state of her complexion—a healthy though delicate bloom—the mark wore a tint of deeper crimson, which imperfectly defined its shape amid the surrounding rosiness. When she blushed it gradually became more indistinct, and finally vanished amid the triumphant rush of blood that bathed the whole cheek with its brilliant glow. But if any shifting motion caused her to turn pale, there was the mark again. Although quite small, its shape bore a similarity to the human hand.

Aylmer stood, agitated now. The birthmark was a fatal flaw of nature. "If it were not for the mark, you would be perfect!"

Georgiana turned away, and Aylmer was left brooding. He was a scientist. He had spent his entire life in his laboratory working on perfecting what nature could not. A simple birthmark was a small thing compared to the larger experiments with which he was concerned. But he said nothing more.

Day after day, whenever she looked up, Georgiana found Aylmer staring at her, sometimes with a sour expression, other times with a look of appalled disgust. Georgiana soon learned to shudder at his gaze. A glance from him would change the roses of her cheeks into a deathlike paleness, amid which the crimson hand was brought out strongly. Soon, she too began to hate the sight of the mark.

Late one night, when the lights were growing dim so as hardly to betray the stain on the poor wife's cheek, she herself, for the first time, voluntarily took up the subject.

"Do you remember, my dear Aylmer," said she, with a feeble attempt at a smile, "having a dream last night about this odious birthmark?"

"None! None whatever!" replied Aylmer, startled that somehow his wife had read his nightmare. But then he added, in a dry, cold tone, trying not to betray his emotion, "I might have dreamed of it. Perhaps I did, for I have thought of the mark often before I fall asleep."

"You *did* dream of it!" she pressed. "And it was a terrible dream! I wonder that you can forget it. I heard you speaking in your sleep. You cried out, 'It is in her heart now; we must have it out!' Do you not remember the dream now?"

Indeed he did remember. It was very clear to him. He was in his laboratory, and he was pressing the blade of a knife into the soft skin of Georgiana's cheek. The deeper he cut, the deeper the birthmark sank. He could not get to the root of it. Aylmer had wakened in a cold sweat. Beside him, Georgiana was sleeping peacefully. The mark was still there, as grotesque to him as ever.

"Aylmer," resumed Georgiana, solemnly, "I know not what may be the cost to both of us to rid me of this fatal birthmark. Perhaps its removal may cause cureless deformity; or it may be the stain goes as deep as life itself. But let the attempt be made. You have learned science. Cannot you remove this little, little mark, which I cover with the tips of two small fingers? Is this beyond your power? To do so would give you peace and save your poor wife from madness."

Aylmer beamed. "Noblest, dearest, tenderest wife," he cried, "doubt not my power. I have already given this matter the deepest thought. I feel fully competent to remove the mark without error or danger to you. I shall make you perfect!"

Aylmer kissed his wife's cheek—her unblemished cheek. "No one will equal your beauty," he promised.

"Is that so important to you, Aylmer?" Georgiana asked, sadness in her voice.

"Your happiness is what is important to me," he answered. "And you have just admitted that you are dreadfully unhappy knowing how the mark disturbs me."

And that, of course, was quite true.

The dream he had dreamt was only foolishness. Aylmer had no intention of removing the birthmark by an operation. He had a different method, a chemical solution. For days, then weeks, he worked in his laboratory until at last he had discovered the right combination of chemicals. With the liquid mixed and ready, Aylmer drew his wife into the laboratory.

As she stepped over the threshold, Georgiana was cold and tremulous. Aylmer looked cheerfully into her pale face, with intent to reassure her, but was so startled with the intense glow of the birthmark that he shuddered violently. His wife fainted.

Quickly, he lifted her and carried her into a private room where he sometimes slept and studied. When Georgiana recovered consciousness she found herself breathing a sweet, penetrating fragrance. "Where am I? Ah, I remember," she said, faintly, and she placed her hand over her cheek to hide the terrible mark from her husband's eyes.

The scene around her looked like enchantment. Aylmer had converted the smoky, dingy, somber room into a beautiful apartment. The walls were hung with gorgeous curtains, which fell from ceiling to floor and shut out all light that might interfere with his chemical experimentations. Perfumed lamps emitted flames of various hues—blues, corals, pale greens—uniting in a soft radiance.

He told her he had been working to perfect a liquid to prolong life for years, perhaps forever. "Death is the ultimate flaw of nature, is it not? One day I shall discover an elixir of life that will bring man immortality," he said enthusiastically.

"Aylmer, are you in earnest? It is terrible to possess such power, or even to dream of possessing it."

"Do not tremble, my love," said her husband. "I would not wrong either you or myself with my experiments. I mean to improve the world."

Georgiana loved her husband, despite his aversion to the mark upon her cheek. But she felt sorry for him, as well. For a man of science who dreams of perfecting nature can never be satisfied. He is doomed to fail even if the experiment succeeds.

Aylmer bid her to follow him into the laboratory. In comparison to the boudoir, the laboratory was a gray room of brick. The furnace, hot and feverish, caught her eye. Quantities of soot clustered above it and seemed to have been burning for ages. Around the room were glass tubes, cylinders, crucibles, and other apparatus of chemical research. The room seemed naked after the elegance and sweet perfume of the boudoir. Aylmer, too, seemed more serious, more pale, as if the laboratory's gaseous odors were seeping inside his soul.

"Behold," Aylmer said, and he held up a vial of silver

liquid. On the table stood a geranium diseased with yellow blotches which had overspread all its leaves. Georgiana watched as Aylmer poured a small quantity of the liquid upon the soil in which it grew. In a little time, when the roots of the plant had taken up the moisture, the unsightly blotches began to be extinguished as new, green tips of vegetation began to sprout and uncurl. Within minutes, the geranium was lush and green, a perfect plant again. Crimson blooms crowned its head.

"Why, it is magical!" Georgiana cried.

"No, it is not magic," Aylmer said. "I am not a sorcerer with a book of spells and potions. I am a scientist. That is why you must trust me, my dear."

"Will you put this silver liquid on my face?" she asked.

"Oh, no. The mark runs too deep beneath the skin. You must drink the liquid. Unless science deceives me," he told her, "it will not fail."

"I submit," she replied, calmly. "I will quaff whatever draught you bring me; but it will be on the same principle that would induce me to take a dose of poison if offered by your hand."

"My dear wife," said Aylmer, deeply moved. "I knew not the height and depth of your nature until now. But why do you speak of poison, of dying? The liquid cannot fail. There is no danger. I have tested it. The strength of the potion is right."

"Danger? There is but one danger—that this horrible stigma shall be left upon my cheek and I shall go mad!" she cried. "Give me the goblet."

"Drink then," exclaimed Aylmer, with admiration for his wife, "and you shall be perfect."

She quaffed the liquid and returned the goblet to his hand.

"I am grateful," she said. "Now, dearest, let me sleep. My senses are closing over my spirit like the leaves around the heart of a rose at sunset."

She spoke the last words with a gentle reluctance, as if it required almost more energy than she could command to pronounce the syllables. Scarcely had they loitered through her lips when she was lost in slumber.

Aylmer sat by her side, watching her closely. Not the minutest symptom escaped him. Her cheeks flushed; her eyelids quivered. Each tiny detail he recorded in his notebook. So engrossed was he in the progress of the operation that he failed to notice that the geranium on the table had begun to droop. The bloom's crimson petals drifted silently to the table top.

With each breath in and each breath out, the outline of the crimson hand upon Georgiana's cheek became less noticeable. She stirred in her deep sleep and murmured, then sighed, and the mark faded even more. Aylmer scribbled another note. When he looked up again, he was jubilant.

"By Heaven! It is gone!" said Aylmer. "I can scarcely trace it now. Success! Success! But why is she so pale?"

He rose and drew aside the window curtain and suffered the light of natural day to fall into the room and rest upon Georgiana's cheek. Slowly she unclosed her eyes and gazed into the mirror that her husband now gave her. A faint smile flitted over her lips. But then her eyes sought Aylmer's face with a trouble and anxiety that he did not understand.

"My poor Aylmer," she murmured.

"Poor? No, I am the richest, happiest husband. Do you not see? It is a success. You are a perfect woman."

"My poor Aylmer," she repeated. "You have aimed high. Do not repent that. But you have rejected the best that earth could offer."

He knelt beside her on the couch and took her hand. Her fingers were cold. "Rejected you? Never!"

"I am dying."

Alas! It was too true. The fatal hand had grappled with the mystery of life.

The presence of the birthmark had been awful to him; its departure now was more awful still. Watch the stain of the rainbow fading out of the sky, and you will know how that mysterious symbol faded from Georgiana's face. As the last crimson tint of the birthmark faded from her cheek, the parting breath of the now perfect woman passed into the atmosphere, and her soul, lingering a moment near her husband, took its heavenward flight.

On the laboratory table, the geranium was bone dry. Its fallen leaves lay like autumn about its base of clay.

ARRESTED

by Ambrose Bierce

*A posse with a pack of bloodhounds was on
his track. His chance of escape was slender.*

Orrin Brower of Kentucky was a fugitive from justice.
A jury had found him guilty of murdering his
brother-in-law and had sentenced him to hang by the
neck until dead. But on the night before he was to die,
Brower made a daring escape. He knocked down his
jailer with an iron bar, robbed him of his keys, and, opening the outer door, walked out into the dark night.

Neither moon nor stars were visible. Brower ran for the
forest beyond town. But he was not from this part of the
state, and he was soon lost. He could not tell if he was
running away from the town or back toward it. He knew
that in either case, a posse of citizens with a pack of

bloodhounds would soon be on his track, and his chance of escape was very slender, for the jailer he had struck with the iron bar had been unarmed.

Brower had no weapon now with which to defend himself. Yet he thought that even an added hour of freedom was well worth having.

Just then, as he emerged from the thick wood onto an old road, he saw a man standing motionless in the gloom. It was too late for Brower to retreat. The fugitive felt that at the first movement back toward the wood he would be filled with buckshot. For a long moment, the two men stood as trees. Brower was nearly suffocated by the activity of his own pounding heart.

A moment later—though it seemed like an hour—the moon sailed into a patch of unclouded sky. The hunted saw that the other man was Burton Duff, the jailer that Brower had struck with the bar. The jailer was as white as death, and upon his brow was the livid mark where the iron bar had cracked open his skull.

The jailer raised an arm and pointed. Brower understood. He was a courageous criminal. That much was obvious from his escape. But even a criminal, when beaten, submits.

Turning his back to his captor, Brower walked submissively away in the direction indicated, looking neither to the right nor to the left, hardly daring to breathe. His head ached with the imagined pain of being shot in the back should he attempt again to flee from his jailer.

Eventually, they entered the town, which was all alight but deserted. Straight toward the jail the criminal walked. He laid his hand upon the knob of the heavy iron door of the main entrance, pushed it open, and entered.

A half-dozen men, armed, were in the room. They faced him, amazed. Brower turned to look over his shoulder at the man who had brought him back, but nobody was there. No one at all was behind him.

But there, on the floor in the corridor, exactly where Brower had left him, lay the dead body of Burton Duff.

THE RIGHT KIND
OF HOUSE

by Henry Slesar

Rotted beams, blistered paint, wet basement—
Sadie Grimes's house was a real fixer-upper.
Who would ever want to buy it?

The automobile that stopped in front of Aaron
Hacker's real estate office had New York license
plates. Aaron didn't need to see the license plates to know
that its owner was new to the elm-shaded town of Ivy
Corners. The car was a red convertible. There was nothing else like it in town.

The man got out of the car and headed straight for the
door.

"It seems to be a customer," said Mr. Hacker to the
young lady at the other desk. "Let's look busy."

It was a customer, all right. The man had a folded

newspaper in his right hand. He was a bit on the heavy side and wore a light gray suit. He was about fifty with dark, curly hair. The skin of his face was flushed and hot, but his narrow eyes were frosty-clear.

He opened the door and nodded at Aaron. "Are you Mr. Hacker?"

"Yes, sir," Aaron smiled. "What can I do for you?"

The man waved the newspaper. "I saw the name of your agency in the real estate section of the newspaper."

"Yep. I take an ad every week. Lots of city people are interested in a town like ours, Mr. —"

"Waterbury," the man said. He pulled a handkerchief from his pocket and mopped his face. "Hot today."

"Unusually hot," Aaron answered. "Doesn't often get so hot in our town. We're near the lake, you know. Well, won't you sit down, Mr. Waterbury?"

"Thank you." The man took the chair and sighed. "I've been driving around. Thought I'd look the town over before I came in. Very nice little place."

"Yes, we like it," said Aaron.

"Now I really don't have much time, Mr. Hacker. Suppose we get right down to business. I saw a house at the edge of town, across the way from an old deserted building."

"Was it an old yellow house with pillars?" asked Aaron.

"That's the place. Do you have that house listed?"

Aaron chuckled softly. "Yep, we got it listed." He flipped through a looseleaf book and pointed to a type-written sheet. "But you won't be interested for long."

"Why not?"

Aaron turned the book around. "Read it for yourself."

"Authentic colonial," the man read. "Eight rooms, two baths, large porches, trees and shrubbery. Near shopping and schools. $300,000."

"Still interested?"

The man stirred uncomfortably. "Why not? Something wrong with it?"

"Well." Aaron scratched his temple. "If you really like this town, Mr. Waterbury—I mean if you really want to settle here, I have any number of places that'd suit you better."

"Now, just a minute!" The man looked indignant. "I'm asking you about this colonial house. You want to sell it or not?"

"Do I?" Aaron chuckled. "Mister, I've had that property on my hands for five years. There's no house I'd rather collect a commission on. Only my luck ain't that good."

"What do you mean?"

"I mean you won't buy. That's what I mean. I keep the listing on my books just for the sake of old Sadie Grimes. Otherwise, I wouldn't waste the space. Believe me."

"I don't get you."

"Then let me explain. Mrs. Grimes put her place up for sale five years ago, when her son died. She gave me the job of selling it. I told her then that the old place ain't even worth *$50*,000!"

The man swallowed. "And she wants *$300*,000?"

"That's right. It's a real old house. I mean old. Some of the beams rotted. Basement's full of water half the time. Upper floor leans to the right about five inches. And the grounds are a mess. Not that it couldn't be fixed up, you understand. But the price has got to be right. And it isn't. I told her that right to her face."

"But why does she want so much?"

Aaron shrugged. "Sentiment, I suppose. The house has been in her family since the Revolution."

The man looked at the floor. "That's too bad," he said. He looked up at Aaron and smiled sheepishly. "And I kinda liked the place. It was—I don't know how to explain it—the right kind of house."

"I know what you mean. It's a friendly old place. A good buy at $50,000, but $300,000?" He laughed. "I think I know Sadie's reasoning, though. You see, she doesn't have much money. Her son was supporting her, doing well in the city. Then he died suddenly, and she knew it was sensible to sell. But she couldn't bring herself to part with the old place. So she set a price tag so high that nobody would buy it. That eased her conscience." Mr. Hacker shook his head softly. "It's a strange world, ain't it?"

"Yes," Waterbury said thoughtfully. Then he stood up. "Tell you what, Mr. Hacker. Suppose I drive out to see Mrs. Grimes? Suppose I talk to her about it, get her to change her price."

"You're fooling yourself, Mr. Waterbury. I've been trying for years."

"Who knows? Maybe if somebody else tried—"

Aaron Hacker shrugged his shoulders. "Who *knows,* is right. It's a strange world, Mr. Waterbury. If you're willing to go to the trouble, I'll be only too happy to lend a hand. Just let me ring Sadie. I'll tell her you're on your way."

Waterbury parked his car beside the rotted picket fence that faced Sadie Grimes's house. The lawn was a jungle of weeds and crabgrass, and the columns that rose from the front porch were covered with flaking paint. He reached for the hand knocker on the door and banged it twice.

The woman who came to the door was short and plump. Her hair was white and her face was lined. She wore a heavy wool sweater, despite the heat. "You must be Mr. Waterbury," she said.

The man smiled. "How do you do, Mrs. Grimes?"

"About as well as I can expect. I suppose you want to come in?"

"It's awfully hot out here." He chuckled.

"Hm. Well, come in then. I've put some lemonade in the icebox. Only don't expect me to bargain with you, Mr. Waterbury. I'm not that kind of person."

"Of course not," the man said, following her inside.

They entered a square parlor with heavy furniture. The only color in the room was in the faded hues of the worn rug in the center of the floor. The old woman headed straight for a rocker and sat motionless, her wrinkled hands folded sternly. "Well?" she said. "If you have anything to say, Mr. Waterbury, I suggest you say it."

The man cleared his throat. "Mrs. Grimes, I've just spoken with your real estate agent...."

"I know all that," she snapped. "Aaron's a fool. All the more for letting you come here with the notion of changing my mind. I'm too old for changing my mind, Mr. Waterbury."

"Er—well, I don't know if that was my intention, Mrs. Grimes. I thought we'd just—talk a little."

She leaned back, and the rocker squeaked. "Talk's free. Say what you like."

"Yes." He mopped his face again, and shoved the handkerchief back into his pocket. "Well, let me put it this way, Mrs. Grimes. I'm a businessman, a bachelor, never married; I live alone. I've worked for a long time, and I've made a fair amount of money. Now I'm ready to retire—

to somewhere quiet. I like Ivy Corners. I passed through here some years ago on my way to—er, Albany. I thought one day I might like to settle here."

"So?"

"So, when I drove through your town today, and saw this house, it just seemed—right for me."

"I like it too, Mr. Waterbury. That's why I'm asking a fair price for it."

Waterbury blinked. "Fair price? You'll have to admit, Mrs. Grimes, these days a house like this shouldn't cost more than—"

"That's enough!" the woman cried. "I told you, Mr. Waterbury, I don't want to sit here all day and argue with you. If you won't pay my price, then we can forget all about it."

"But, Mrs. Grimes—"

"Good day, Mr. Waterbury!" She stood up, indicating that he was expected to leave.

But he didn't. "Wait a minute, Mrs. Grimes," he said. "Just a moment. I know it's crazy, but—all right. I'll pay what you want."

She looked at him for a long moment. "Are you sure, Mr. Waterbury?"

"Positive! I've enough money. If that's the only way you'll have it, that's the way it'll be."

She smiled. "I think that lemonade'll be cold enough.

I'll bring you some—and then I'll tell you something about this house."

He was mopping his brow when she returned with the tray. He gulped at the frosty yellow beverage greedily.

"This house," she said, easing back in her rocker, "has been in my family since 1802. It was built fifteen years before that. Every member of the family, except my son, Michael, was born in the bedroom upstairs. After Michael was born, there was a flood in the basement, and we never seemed to get it dry since. I love the old place, though, you understand."

"Of course," Waterbury said.

"Michael's father died when Michael was nine. There were hard times then. I did some needlework, and my own father had left me some money, which supports me today. Not in grand style, but I manage. Michael missed his father, perhaps even more than I. He grew up to be, well, wild is the only word that comes to mind."

The man nodded in understanding.

"When he graduated from high school, Michael left Ivy Corners and went to the city. He went there against my wishes, make no mistake. But he was like so many young men—full of ambition, wild ambition. I didn't know what he did in the city. But he must have been successful—he sent me money regularly. However, I didn't see him for nine years."

"Ah," the man sighed, sadly.

"Yes, it wasn't easy for me. But it was even worse when Michael came home. Because, when he did, he was in trouble."

"Oh?"

"I didn't know how bad the trouble was. He showed up in the middle of the night, looking thinner and older than I could have believed possible."

Waterbury took another gulp of lemonade, wondering how much longer he would have to listen to the old woman talk. He suddenly felt very tired.

"He had no luggage with him," she continued. "Only a small black suitcase. When I tried to take it from him, he almost struck me. Struck me—his own mother!" She leaned forward in the rocker to stare into Waterbury's sweating face. "I put him to bed myself, as if he were a little boy again. I could hear him crying out during the night. The next day, he told me to leave the house. Just for a few hours. He wanted to do something, he said. He didn't explain what. But when I returned that evening, I noticed that the black suitcase was gone."

The man's eyes widened over the lemonade glass. "What did it mean?" he asked.

"I didn't know then. But I found out soon, too terribly soon. That night, a man came to our house. I don't even know how he got in. I first knew when I heard voices in Michael's room. I went to the door, and tried to listen, tried to find out what sort of trouble my boy was in. But I heard only shouts and threats, and then..."

She paused, and her shoulders sagged.

"A shot," she continued, "a gunshot. When I went into the room, I found the bedroom window open and the stranger gone. And Michael—he was on the floor. He was dead!"

"Dead?" Waterbury croaked. His dry throat seemed to be tightening.

"That was five years ago," she said. "Five long years. It was a while before I realized what had happened. The police told me the story. Michael and this other man had been involved in a crime, a serious crime. They had stolen close to one million dollars."

Waterbury's chair creaked as he shifted uncomfortably. He was having trouble keeping his eyes open in this dreadful heat.

"Michael had taken that money, and run off with it. He wanted to keep it all for himself. He hid it somewhere in this house—to this very day I don't know where. The other man had come looking for my son, looking to collect his share. When he found the money gone, he—he killed my boy."

She sat back in her rocker. "That's when I put this house up for sale—at $300,000. I knew that, someday, my son's killer would return to look for the money. Someday, he would want this house at any price. All I had to do was wait until I found the man willing to pay much too much for an old lady's house."

She rocked gently.

Waterbury put down the empty glass and licked his lips. He was growing dizzy, very dizzy.

Sadie Grimes smiled sweetly. "More lemonade, Mr. Waterbury?"

"Oh!" he gasped, his throat closing on itself. "This lemonade ... is so bitter."

BATTLEGROUND

by Stephen King

*By Mr. King's request, "Battleground" appears
in its entirety here and is not the abridged
version that appeared in* Read *magazine.*

"Mr. Renshaw?"

The desk clerk's voice caught him halfway to
the elevator, and Renshaw turned back impatiently, shifting his flight bag from one hand to the other. The
envelope in his coat pocket, stuffed with twenties and
fifties, crackled heavily. The job had gone well and the pay
had been excellent—even after the Organization's 15
percent finder's fee had been skimmed off the top. Now
all he wanted was a hot shower and a gin and tonic and
sleep.

"What is it?"

"Package, sir. Would you sign the slip?"

Renshaw signed and looked thoughtfully at the rec-

117

tangular package. His name and the building's address were written on the gummed label in a spiky backhand script that seemed familiar. He rocked the package on the imitation-marble surface of the desk, and something clanked faintly inside.

"Should I have that sent up, Mr. Renshaw?"

"No, I've got it." It was about eighteen inches on a side and fitted clumsily under his arm. He put it on the plush carpet that covered the elevator floor and twisted his key in the penthouse slot above the regular rack of buttons. The car rose smoothly and silently. He closed his eyes and let the job replay itself on the dark screen of his mind.

First, as always, a call from Cal Bates: "You available, Johnny?"

He was available twice a year, minimum fee $10,000. He was very good, very reliable, but what his customers really paid for was the infallible predator's talent. John Renshaw was a human hawk, constructed by both genetics and environment to do two things superbly: kill and survive.

After Bates's call, a buff-colored envelope appeared in Renshaw's box. A name, an address, a photograph. All committed to memory; then down the garbage disposal with the ashes of envelope and contents.

This time the face had been that of a sallow Miami businessman named Hans Morris, founder and owner of the Morris Toy Company. Someone had wanted Morris out of the way and had gone to the Organization. The Organization, in the person of Calvin Bates, had talked to John Renshaw. *Pow.* Mourners please omit flowers.

The door slid open, he picked up his package and stepped out. He unlocked the suite and stepped in. At this time of day, just after 3 P.M., the spacious living room was splashed with April sunshine. He paused for a moment, enjoying it, then put the package on the end table by the door and loosened his tie. He dropped the envelope on top of it and walked over to the terrace.

He pushed open the sliding glass door and stepped out. It was cold, and the wind knifed through his thin topcoat. Yet he paused a moment, looking over the city the way a general might survey a captured country. Traffic crawled beetlelike in the streets. Far away, almost buried in the golden afternoon haze, the Bay Bridge glittered like a madman's mirage. To the east, all but lost behind the downtown high rises, the crammed and dirty tenements with their stainless-steel forests of TV aerials. It was better up here. Better than in the gutters.

He went back inside, slid the door closed, and went into the bathroom for a long, hot shower.

When he sat down forty minutes later to regard his package, drink in hand, the shadows had marched halfway across the wine-colored carpet and the best of the afternoon was past.

It was a bomb.

Of course it wasn't, but one proceeded as if it were. That was why one had remained healthy and upright and taking nourishment while so many others had gone to that great unemployment office in the sky.

If it was a bomb, it was clockless. It sat utterly silent; bland and enigmatic. Plastique was more likely these days, anyway. Less temperamental than the clocksprings manufactured by Westclox and Big Ben.

Renshaw looked at the postmark. Miami, April 15. Five days ago. So the bomb was not time-set. It would have gone off in the hotel safe in that case.

Miami. Yes. And that spiky backhand writing. There had been a framed photograph on the sallow businessman's desk. The photo had been of an even sallower old crone wearing a babushka. The script slanted across the bottom had read: "Best from your number-one idea girl—Mom."

What kind of number-one idea is this, Mom? A do-it-yourself extermination kit?

He regarded the package with complete concentration, not moving, his hands folded. Extraneous questions, such as how Morris' number-one idea girl might have discovered his address, did not occur to him. They were for later, for Cal Bates. Unimportant now.

With a sudden, almost absent move, he took a small

celluloid calendar out of his wallet and inserted it deftly under the twine that crisscrossed the brown paper. He slid it under the Scotch tape that held one end flap. The flap came loose, relaxing against the twine.

He paused for a time, observing, then leaned close and sniffed. Cardboard, paper, string. Nothing more. He walked around the box, squatted easily on his haunches, and repeated the process. Twilight was invading his apartment with gray, shadowy fingers.

One of the flaps popped free of the restraining twine, showing a dull green box beneath. Metal. Hinged. He produced a pocket knife and cut the twine. It fell away, and a few helping prods with the tip of the knife revealed the box.

It was green with black markings, and stenciled on the front in white letters were the words: G.I. JOE VIET-NAM FOOTLOCKER. Below that: 20 Infantrymen, 10 Helicopters, 2 BAR Men, 2 Bazooka Men, 2 Medics, 4 Jeeps. Below that: a flag decal. Below that, in the corner: Morris Toy Company, Miami, Fla.

He reached out to touch it, then withdrew his hand. Something inside the footlocker had moved.

Renshaw stood up, not hurrying, and backed across the room toward the kitchen and the hall. He snapped on the lights.

The Vietnam Footlocker was rocking, making the

brown paper beneath it rattle. It suddenly overbalanced and fell to the carpet with a soft thud, landing on one end. The hinged top opened a crack of perhaps two inches.

Tiny foot soldiers, about an inch and a half tall, began to crawl out. Renshaw watched them, unblinking. His mind made no effort to cope with the real or unreal aspect of what he was seeing—only with the possible consequences for his survival.

The soldiers were wearing minuscule army fatigues, helmets, and field packs. Tiny carbines were slung across their shoulders. Two of them looked briefly across the room at Renshaw. Their eyes, no bigger than pencil points, glittered.

Five, ten, twelve, then all twenty. One of them was gesturing, ordering the others. They lined themselves up along the crack that the fall had produced and began to push. The crack began to widen.

Renshaw picked one of the large pillows off the couch and began to walk toward them. The commanding officer turned and gestured. The others whirled and unslung their carbines. There were tiny, almost delicate popping sounds, and Renshaw felt suddenly as if he had been stung by bees.

He threw the pillow. It struck them, knocking them sprawling, then hit the box, and knocked it wide open. Insectlike, with a faint, high whirring noise like chiggers, a cloud of miniature helicopters, painted jungle green, rose out of the box.

☠

Tiny *phut! phut!* sounds reached Renshaw's ears and he saw pinprick-sized muzzle flashes coming from the open copter doors. Needles pricked his belly, his right arm, the side of his neck. He clawed out and got one—sudden pain in his fingers; blood welling. The whirling blades had chopped them to the bone in diagonal scarlet hash marks. The others whirled out of range, circling him like horseflies. The stricken copter thumped to the rug and lay still.

Sudden excruciating pain in his foot made him cry out. One of the foot soldiers was standing on his shoe and bayoneting his ankle. The tiny face looked up, panting and grinning.

Renshaw kicked at it and the tiny body flew across the room to splatter on the wall. It did not leave blood but a viscid purple smear.

There was a tiny, coughing explosion and blinding agony ripped his thigh. One of the bazooka men had come out of the footlocker. A small curl of smoke rose lazily from his weapon. Renshaw looked down at his leg and saw a blackened, smoking hole in his pants the size of a quarter. The flesh beneath was charred.

The little bastard shot me!

He turned and ran into the hall, then into his bedroom. One of the helicopters buzzed past his cheek, blades whirring busily. The small stutter of a BAR. Then it darted away.

The gun beneath his pillow was a .44 Magnum, big enough to put a hole the size of two fists through anything it hit. Renshaw turned, holding the pistol in his hands. He realized coolly that he would be shooting at a moving target not much bigger than a flying light bulb.

Two of the copters whirred in. Sitting on the bed, Renshaw fired once. One of the helicopters exploded into nothingness. That's two, he thought. He drew a bead on the second... squeezed the trigger...

It jigged! God, it jigged!

The helicopter swooped at him in a sudden deadly arc, fore and aft overhead props whirring with blinding speed. Renshaw caught a glimpse of one of the BAR men crouched at the open bay door, firing his weapon in short, deadly bursts, and then he threw himself to the floor and rolled.

My eyes, the bastard was going for my eyes!

He came up on his back at the far wall, the gun held at chest level. But the copter was retreating. It seemed to pause for a moment, and dip in recognition of Renshaw's superior firepower. Then it was gone, back toward the living room.

Renshaw got up, wincing as his weight came down on the wounded leg. It was bleeding freely. And why not? he thought grimly. It's not everybody who gets hit point-blank with a bazooka shell and lives to tell about it.

So Mom was his number-one idea girl, was she? She was all that and a bit more.

He shook a pillowcase free of the tick and ripped it into a bandage for his leg, then took his shaving mirror from the bureau and went to the hallway door. Kneeling, he shoved it out onto the carpet at an angle and peered in.

They were bivouacking by the footlocker, damned if they weren't. Miniature soldiers ran hither and thither, setting up tents. Jeeps two inches high raced about importantly. A medic was working over the soldier Renshaw had kicked. The remaining eight copters flew in a protective swarm overhead, at coffee-table level.

Suddenly they became aware of the mirror, and three of the foot soldiers dropped to one knee and began firing. Seconds later the mirror shattered in four places. *Okay, okay, then.*

Renshaw went back to the bureau and got the heavy mahogany odds-and-ends box Linda had given him for Christmas. He hefted it once, nodded, and went to the doorway and lunged through. He wound up and fired like a pitcher throwing a fast ball. The box described a swift, true vector and smashed little men like ninepins. One of the jeeps rolled over twice. Renshaw advanced to the doorway of the living room, sighted on one of the sprawling soldiers, and gave it to him.

Several of the others had recovered. Some were kneeling and firing formally. Others had taken cover. Still others had retreated back into the footlocker.

The bee stings began to pepper his legs and torso, but none reached higher than his rib cage. Perhaps the range was too great. It didn't matter; he had no intention of being turned away. This was it.

He missed with his next shot—they were so small—but the following one sent another soldier into a broken sprawl.

The copters were buzzing toward him ferociously. Now the tiny bullets began to splat into his face, above and below his eyes. He potted the lead copter, then the second. Jagged streaks of pain silvered his vision.

The remaining six split into two retreating wings. His face was wet with blood and he swiped at it with his forearm. He was ready to start firing again when he paused. The soldiers who had retreated inside the footlocker were trundling something out. Something that looked like...

There was a blinding sizzle of yellow fire, and a sudden gust of wood and plaster exploded from the wall to his left.

...a rocket launcher!

He squeezed off one shot at it, missed, wheeled and ran for the bathroom at the far end of the corridor. He slammed the door and locked it. In the bathroom-mirror an Indian was staring back at him with dazed and haunted eyes, a battle crazed Indian with thin streamers of red paint drawn from holes no bigger than grains of pepper. A ragged flap of skin dangled from one cheek. There was a gouged furrow in his neck.

I'm losing!

He ran a shaking hand through his hair. The front door was cut off. So was the phone and the kitchen extension. They had a rocket launcher and a direct hit would tear his head off.

Damn it, that wasn't even listed on the box!

He started to draw in a long breath and let it out in a sudden grunt as a fist-sized section of the door blew in with a charred burst of wood. Tiny flames glowed briefly around the ragged edges of the hole, and he saw the brilliant flash as they launched another round. More wood blew inward, scattering burning slivers on the bathroom rug. He stamped them out and two of the copters buzzed angrily through the hole. Minuscule BAR slugs stitched his chest.

With a whining groan of rage he smashed one out of the air barehanded, sustaining a picket fence of deep slashes across his palm. In sudden desperate invention, he slung a heavy bath towel over the other. It fell, writhing, to the floor, and he stamped the life out of it. His breath was coming in hoarse whoops. Blood ran into one eye, hot and stinging, and he wiped it away.

There. There. That'll make them think.

Indeed, it did seem to be making them think. There was no movement for fifteen minutes. Renshaw sat on the edge of the tub, thinking feverishly. There had to be a way out of this blind alley. There *had* to be. If there was only a way to flank them...

He suddenly turned and looked at the small window over the tub. There was a way. Of course there was.

His eyes dropped to the can of lighter fluid on top of the medicine cabinet. He was reaching for it when the rustling noise came.

He whirled, bringing the Magnum up...but it was only a tiny scrap of paper shoved under the crack of the door. The crack, Renshaw noted grimly, was too narrow for even one of *them* to get through.

There was one tiny word written on the paper:

Surrender

Renshaw smiled grimly and put the lighter fluid in his breast pocket. There was a chewed stub of pencil beside it. He scrawled one word on the paper and shoved it back under the door. The word was:

NUTS

There was a suddenly blinding barrage of rocket shells, and Renshaw backed away. They arched through the hole in the door and detonated against the pale blue tiles above the towel rack, turning the elegant wall into a pocket lunar landscape. Renshaw threw a hand over his eyes as plaster flew in a hot rain of shrapnel. Burning holes ripped through his shirt and his back was peppered.

When the barrage stopped, Renshaw moved. He climbed on top of the tub and slid the window open. Cold stars looked in at him. It was a narrow window, and a narrow ledge beyond it. But there was no time to think of that.

He boosted himself through, and the cold air slapped his lacerated face and neck like an open hand. He was leaning over the balance point of his hands, staring straight down. Forty stories down. From this height the street looked no wider than a child's train track. The bright, winking lights of the city glittered madly below him like thrown jewels.

With the deceptive ease of a trained gymnast, Renshaw brought his knees up to rest on the lower edge of the window. If one of those wasp-sized copters flew through that hole in the door now, one shot in the ass would send him straight down, screaming all the way.

None did.

He twisted, thrust one leg out, and one reaching hand grabbed the overhead cornice and held. A moment later he was standing on the ledge outside the window.

Deliberately not thinking of the horrifying drop below his heels, not thinking of what would happen if one of the helicopters buzzed out after him, Renshaw edged toward the corner of the building.

Fifteen feet...ten...There. He paused, his chest pressed against the wall, hands splayed out on the rough surface. He could feel the lighter fluid in his breast pocket and the reassuring weight of the Magnum jammed in his waistband.

Now to get around the corner.

Gently, he eased one foot around and slid his weight onto it. Now the right angle was pressed razorlike into his chest and gut. There was a smear of bird guano in front of his eyes on the rough stone. Christ, he thought crazily. I didn't know they could fly this high.

His left foot slipped.

For a weird, timeless moment, he tottered over the brink, right arm backwatering madly for balance, and then he was clutching the two sides of the building in a lover's embrace, face pressed against the hard corner, breath shuddering in and out of his lungs.

A bit at a time, he slid the other foot around.

Thirty feet away, his own living-room terrace jutted out.

He made his way down to it, breath sliding in and out of his lungs with shallow force. Twice he was forced to stop as sharp gusts of wind tried to pick him off the ledge.

Then he was there, gripping the ornamented iron railings.

He hoisted himself over noiselessly. He had left the curtains half drawn across the sliding glass partition, and now he peered in cautiously. They were just the way he wanted them—ass to.

Four soldiers and one copter had been left to guard the footlocker. The rest would be outside the bathroom door with the rocket launcher.

Okay. In through the opening like gangbusters. Wipe out the ones by the footlocker, then out the door. Then a quick taxi to the airport. Off to Miami to find Morris' number-one idea girl. He thought he might just burn her face off with a flame thrower. That would be poetic justice.

He took off his shirt and ripped a long strip from one sleeve. He dropped the rest to flutter limply by his feet, and bit off the plastic spout on the can of lighter fluid. He stuffed one end of the rag inside, withdrew it, and stuffed the other end in so only a six-inch strip of saturated cotton hung free.

He got out his lighter, took a deep breath, and thumbed the wheel. He tipped it to the cloth and as it sprang alight he rammed open the glass partition and plunged through.

The copter reacted instantly, kamikaze-diving him as he charged across the rug, dripping tiny splatters of liquid fire. Renshaw straight-armed it, hardly noticing the jolt of pain that ran up his arm as the turning blades chopped his flesh open.

The tiny foot soldiers scattered into the footlocker.

After that, it all happened very rapidly.

Renshaw threw the lighter fluid. The can caught, mushrooming into a licking fireball. The next instant he was reversing, running for the door.

He never knew what hit him.

It was like the thud that a steel safe would make when dropped from a respectable height. Only this thud ran through the entire high-rise apartment building, thrumming in its steel frame like a tuning fork.

The penthouse door blew off its hinges and shattered against the far wall.

A couple who had been walking hand in hand below looked up in time to see a very large white flash, as though a hundred flashing guns had gone off at once.

"Somebody blew a fuse," the man said. "I guess—"

"What's that?" his girl asked.

Something was fluttering lazily down toward them; he caught it in one outstretched hand. "Jesus, some guy's shirt. All full of little holes. Bloody, too."

"I don't like it," she said nervously. "Call a cab, huh, Ralph? We'll have to talk to the cops if something happened up there, and I ain't supposed to be out with you."

"Sure, yeah."

He looked around, saw a taxi, and whistled. Its brake lights flared and they ran across to get it.

Behind them, unseen, a tiny scrap of paper floated down and landed near the remains of John Renshaw's shirt. Spiky backhand script read:

Hey, kids! Special in this Vietnam Footlocker!
(For a Limited Time Only)
1 Rocket Launcher
20 Surface-to-air-"Twister" Missiles
1 Scale-Model Thermonuclear Weapon

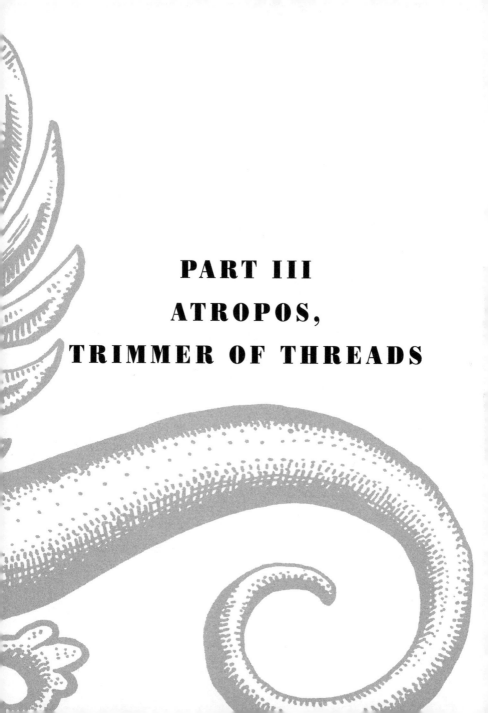

PART III
ATROPOS,
TRIMMER OF THREADS

THE BARGAIN

A retelling of the Greek myth of
Admetus and the Shadow of Death

He had until dawn to find someone to take his place.
Surely there must be one person who loved him
enough to agree to the bargain.

Admetus was young, not old. He was healthy, not ill. Solid muscles shaped his arms, back, chest, and legs. He had just assumed power as King of Pherae in ancient Greece. And he had just married the most beautiful woman. Together they would have sons who would be heroes. Yes, Admetus had many sweet reasons to live.

But during the night, the shadow of Death came for Admetus. "Your hour has struck, Admetus," the tall shadow whispered in his ear. "You must die."

Admetus woke in a cold sweat, thinking surely the

voice he had heard came from a nightmare. But the shadow still hovered over him. "Come," he beckoned. "Come now."

"No!" Admetus cried. "I am not ready! Take another whose life is less valuable than mine!"

The shadow disliked such arrogance in mortals. Nevertheless, he was willing to bargain. "If you can find one person to take your place, I will spare your life. You have until dawn."

Then the shadow dissolved.

Admetus looked at his wife asleep beside him. Life without her would not be life at all. But there were others in the palace who also adored him. He was their king. Surely they would die for him.

Admetus hurried down the cold marble floors to the room where the old nurse who had cared for him during his childhood coughed in her sleep. The woman's lips were cracked, and her eyes were yellow with sickness. Admetus woke her. "The shadow of Death has come for me. But if you take my place, I will live."

The nurse sobbed when she heard that Admetus must die. "You are so young, so strong."

"And you are so old, so ill. Dying will be a peaceful sleep for you."

"Each breath I take may be my last," the old nurse admitted. "But that is why each breath is a gift I cherish."

"You will not do it? You will not take my place?"

The old nurse hacked and wheezed. "No, life is precious, even to my old bones."

Outside the window Admetus heard the first cries of the birds. It was almost dawn. He hurried next to his parents' chambers. "You gave me life once," he pleaded with them. "You can give me life again."

"You think that because we are old we no longer enjoy the warm sun on our faces? Oh, Admetus, our son, we will miss you terribly, terribly," his parents cried.

The pink streaks of dawn were just now creeping over the horizon. Admetus returned to his bed. His wife reached for him. "Let me hold you one last time," she cried. "My sweet husband."

She slipped her arms around him. Her hands felt so cold.

"How did you know?" he asked.

"I heard the shadow come for you during the night," she answered in a voice that was thin and weak.

"I asked the old nurse. I asked my parents. No one would give me my life back."

"Why didn't you ask me, Admetus?"

"You?" He looked at his beautiful wife, the woman who would give him sons that would be heroes. In the growing light of morning, her face was ghostly pale. "No, not you."

"Did you not think I loved you enough to take your place?" she asked.

Admetus saw then the poison hemlock and the empty cup from which she had drunk. "No!" he cried, hugging her to him, but she was already cold in his arms.

The tall shadow had returned. "So, you have found someone who valued your life over her own," the shadow spoke. "You will live, Admetus." The shadow raised his arms and covered Admetus's dead wife, still cradled in his arms.

"You can't have her!" the king shouted. "Get back. She is mine."

"You agreed to the bargain," the shadow said.

The first rays of sunlight seeped through the curtained window. "No!" Admetus cried. "I take it back. Life without her is no life at all!"

But the shadow and the only woman Admetus would ever love were gone.

REVERSE INSOMNIA

by Jonathon Blake

All he could do was sleep, and sleep some more.
It didn't make any sense, especially the dreams.

Here I am again.

I've slept for two days straight this time. I'm beginning to believe that this may be unhealthy. The doctor says I have "reverse insomnia," but he also looks at me as if I were crazy.

I don't trust my doctor. *He* looks crazy. We just sit in his office and eyeball each other, wondering how crazy we both really are. Until he gives me some pills and tells me it's reverse insomnia.

I hate that idiot doctor.

His pills don't help. Did I mention that I slept for two days straight? Right through my son Andy's birthday. Right through the cake and ice cream and presents and everything.

Julie was upset with me. But I just shrugged and apologized. What could I do? I was asleep. I really think something's wrong. It's happening more and more frequently every week. A day of sleep here, two days there. It's crazy.

Thank goodness I had a lot of off-time coming to me at the office. My boss is angry with me, though. Ever since I started having this abundance of sleep, my work has slipped. Well, truthfully, it's backslid terribly.

I'm a journalist, but for some reason the words aren't coming the way they used to. The other day I thought I'd written a fantastic article on drunken driving and violence in the United States. Turns out all I'd written was a single word in the middle of a snow-white sheet.

Crash.

I couldn't make any sense of it. Neither could my boss.

I've got to get up and eat. I want Bran Flakes, but I can't recall which cabinet they're in. Everything is a little fuzzy at the edges.

There's Julie sitting on the couch in the den. Geez, I love her. That's funny. She's dressed in black. Hmm, I thought she hated that color. In the pantry. Next to the refrigerator. That's where the Bran Flakes are. How strange. I was just about to ask Julie where the cereal was, but it just popped into my head. Go figure.

Andy's sitting at the kitchen table eating Fruit Loops and chocolate kisses. I want to tell him to stop, but I'm ashamed, having missed his birthday and all.

Andy has a black balloon wrapped around his tiny right wrist. For some reason, I feel like crying.

Later, the helium must have found a way out somehow. The balloon floats, almost touching the table, looking like a shrunken head, wrinkled and distorted.

I don't want cereal anymore. In fact, I'm sure the Bran Flakes taste like cardboard now. I hate them. But not as much as I hate that doctor.

I look at Andy again. Now his forehead is touching the table. His left hand is gently resting in his bowl of Fruit Loops. Droplets of milk are clinging to his skin, making his hand and arm seem surrealistically white.

I want to reach out and draw Andy up in my arms, but I can't. I know I shouldn't touch him, but I don't know why. He seems very distant, far away. The balloon is no longer attached to his wrist. Instead, he wears a watch. I get close enough to look over his shoulder. 12:42. It says 12:42. His watch has stopped. I must remember to send his watch to the store to be fixed.

Suddenly, now I am standing beside Julie. She's still on the couch, watching television. The screen is blank, black, yet she stares at it as if it were the most important thing in the world. I want to speak to her, ask her how her day was, but I know I shouldn't. Or maybe I can't. Instead, I look at the black screen too.

Julie says she's fine, but her lips never move. I tell her I'm fine too, but the words never reach my mouth.

Julie nods her head, and suddenly the television lights up. I see a small child standing in a field of white grass. He is dressed entirely in black. So is Julie; she's there too. The boy is holding a large black balloon with green numbers printed on it.

I strain to see the boy and the numbers.

It's Andy. The balloon reads 12:42.

I blink, and Julie is gone. The TV shuts off. Andy is gone. The kitchen is empty. Have I fallen asleep again? I just don't know.

I have to find out what time it is! But my watch, like Andy's, is broken. The numbers stare at me as if I am somehow wrong, deathly wrong.

"12:42. *12:42!*"

I can't breathe! I am surrounded by clocks. Clocks upon clocks upon clocks. "12:42," they are singing to me. "12:42!" they scream. And I begin to scream along with them.

Suddenly, I am in my bed. I must have been sleeping. Or dreaming.

I climb out of bed and see that I am wearing black silk pajamas. I don't recall ever changing into these. Then again, I don't remember anything but black.

I slowly walk to Andy's room. The door is shut. I hear crying.

I knock, but no one answers my call. I knock louder. Still, no answer. I open the door. The room is bare, white. All of it—the floor, the ceiling, the walls. White.

I am in bed again, naked. My left leg itches uncomfortably and is very, very cold. Julie is lying next to me. Her lips are blue, like fingers of clay.

I swing my legs over the side of the bed and grab a robe that once was red. It has faded to gray, dark gray. If I didn't know any better, I'd say it was black.

I am staring at the doctor in his linoleum room. He tells me I am crazy and gives me some pills. He says I have reverse insomnia again. I throw the pills away, but they never hit the ground. Instead, the doctor opens his mouth and swallows them whole. His mouth becomes wider and wider until the whole room is sucked into his orifice.

The doctor swallows me.

I'm back in Andy's room, but this time it looks as it should—a bunk bed, a dresser, model airplanes I helped him make hanging from the ceiling. Andy is sitting on his bed coloring. I quietly step over the little cars on his floor, noticing that he had been playing demolition derby again. I look at the page he is so busily scribbling on. In large dark letters is the word *CRASH.*

I have to eat something. I go back to the kitchen. On

the expansive kitchen table are three white cots. I don't remember Julie buying new furniture. And why would she have put cots on the kitchen table? Are they some kind of strange decorations?

The cots are disturbing somehow. They remind me of the crazy doctor and his stupid pills. The brightness of the white cots becomes all-consuming. My head begins to throb in time to the pulsing itch of my left leg.

I deny the existence of the furniture, try to block the cots out completely. It is better that way. But they loom before me with something new attached to each of them—large white intercoms. They remind me of my trip to Radio Shack with Julie and Andy. We were looking for a toy robot for Andy's birthday. The salesman was trying to sell me an intercom system for my home. He was very bothersome, and now all I can see are bright, bright lights.

I feel like a deer. Trapped. Transfixed by headlights, unable to run.

The intercoms are looking at me, accusing me. They stand there like all-powerful gods on their metal poles attached to the cots. A black sound oozes from them. I want to stop their noise. I have to stop them! But I cannot.

I listen.

"The woman and the boy were DOA, doctor. The

man is identified as Richard Young. He is comatose and has multiple contusions on the head and upper torso. His left leg was amputated. We had to do it. There was nothing we could do to save it. His condition is critical, sir."

The doctor's voice comes through another intercom. "How did it happen?"

From the third intercom: "Drunken driver. Hit the family head-on coming out of a shopping mall parking lot.

"Estimated time of death for the woman and boy— 12:42."

The oozing black noise ceases.

A plug dangles like a limp snake from one of the white cots. It is plugged into everything and nothing.

Crying, I yank it forcefully.

Suddenly, I am asleep. Deep, deep asleep.

DEADLINE

by Richard Matheson

*The old man's story was fantastic, the confused
memory of a dying man. It could not possibly be true.*

There are two nights a year that a doctor just doesn't
make plans—Christmas Eve and New Year's Eve.
On Christmas Eve, the emergency was Bobby Dascouli's
arm burns. I was cleaning and swathing them instead of
nestling on the couch with Ruth, eyeing the twinkling
colors of our Christmas tree. On New Year's Eve, the call
from my answering service came ten minutes after I had
arrived at a party at my sister's house. Ruth smiled sadly
and shook her head. Then she kissed me on the cheek.
"Poor Bill," she said.

"Poor Bill indeed," I grumbled and set down my glass
of punch. I gently touched her much evident stomach.

"Don't go having our baby until I get back," I instructed. This was our first child, and although Ruth still had a few weeks yet before her due date, babies sometimes didn't pay attention to the calendar.

"I'll do my best to wait until after the New Year," she answered. "Be careful," she added. "The roads are snowy, and with so many people celebrating tonight.... "

"Don't worry about me. Just take care of yourself."

With wry acceptance, I said my hurried good-byes to everyone and left. I turned up the collar of my overcoat against the cold and crunched over the snowpacked sidewalk to the car.

It was after 11:00 when I reached a deserted East Main Street on the far side of town. I drove three blocks north to the address the service had given me and parked in front of what had once been an elegant apartment building when my father was in practice. Now it was a ramshackle boardinghouse. Time had rusted through the gutters and rotted out the windowsills. Inside the lobby, the plaster was cracked and falling. The place smelled of must and decay.

I rang the landlady's bell and waited. A heavy woman appeared at the door. She wore a black sweater over her wrinkled green dress, striped anklets over her heavy support stockings, saddle shoes over the anklets. She wore no makeup. The only color in her face was a chapped redness in her cheeks. Wisps of steel-gray hair hung across her temples.

She was a former patient of my father's, which is why she had asked for me. But we had never met. "You the doctor?" she asked.

I said I was.

"I'm the one who called. There's an old guy up on the fourth floor. He says he's dying."

"What room?" I asked, eager to make my visit and return to the more pleasant atmosphere of my sister Mary's house. To be honest, I was worried about Ruth. For two days, she had felt tired and achy. We had even considered not going to the New Year's Eve party at all.

"This way," the landlady said.

I followed her wheezing ascent up the stairs. We stopped in front of room 4-7, and she rapped on the thin paneling of the door, then pushed it open.

The old man was lying on an iron bed pushed against the wall. Even lying down, his body had the floppiness of a discarded doll. At his sides, frail hands lay motionless. His skin was the brown of old page edges, his face a wasted mask. On the bare pillow, his head lay still. His pale blue eyes were open, fixed on the cracked ceiling above him.

As I slipped off my coat, I saw that he was in no obvious pain. His expression was peaceful, accepting. I sat down on the bed and took his wrist. His eyes shifted as if just realizing I had come. He looked at me.

"Hello," I said and smiled.

"Hello."

The clearness of his voice startled me. However, his pulse was what I expected—a bare trickle of life, its beat barely felt beneath my pressing fingers. I set his hand back on the bed and leaned forward to place my palm against his forehead and to gaze into his eyes. He had no fever. He was not sick. He was only running down.

I patted the old man's shoulder reassuringly, then stood and gestured to the landlady. She clumped across the floor to the window.

"How long has he been in bed?" I asked her.

"Just since this afternoon," she answered. "That's what troubles me. It only began to happen this afternoon."

"What happened exactly?"

"He came down to my room and said he was going to die tonight."

I'd read about such a thing, how an old man or a woman announces that, at a certain time, they will die. And when that time comes, they do. Who knows what it is—a longing for death? A premonition? Perhaps a little of both.

"Has he any relatives?" I asked.

"None I know of," she said.

I nodded. It was not unusual for old folks to die alone. Suddenly, I was glad I had answered the call and had come.

"I don't get it," the landlady whispered.

"He is an old man. Everyone dies, eventually," I answered.

"No," she said. "When he first moved in about a month ago, he didn't look like he looks now, all wrinkled and gray. Even this afternoon he didn't look sick."

"He isn't in any pain. There really isn't anything I can do for him. It's just a matter of time."

"I see," she said.

I glanced at my watch—11:48. I thought of Ruth and that I should leave, but I hesitated. I glanced across the room at the figure in the bed. "How old is he anyway?" I asked. "Ninety? A hundred?"

"He never told me. And I never asked. I figure that's none of my business," she answered.

"I heard you," the old man said.

Both the woman and I turned, surprised.

"You want to know how old I am," the old man said. He opened his mouth to say something more, but a dry cough choked him.

A glass of water was on the bedside table, and I hurried to the old man's side, propped him up, and held the glass to his lips. When he had finished drinking, I gently laid his head back on the pillow.

"I'm one year old," he said.

I stared at his calm face. Then, I set the glass down on the table.

"You don't believe me," he said. "But it's true. I was born on December 31, 1996."

"You were?" I replied, thinking he was confused and really meant 1886.

"New Year's Eve, 1996," he repeated. Then he added, "At the stroke of midnight."

I felt a nervous shiver across my shoulders, as if for a split second my mind actually believed him.

The old man closed his eyes. "I've told a hundred people, and not one believes me. Not one understood."

I sat down on the edge of the bed once again. "Why not tell me about it," I offered. No one should die alone. As a doctor, the least I could do was provide the old man some comfort and company.

He drew in a breath slowly.

"A week after I was born, I was walking and talking. I was eating by myself. My mother and father couldn't believe their eyes."

"Well, that would be very advanced for a one-week-old," I said, humoring him.

"They took me to a doctor. I don't know what he

thought, but he didn't do anything. What could he do? I wasn't sick. I've never been sick. He sent me home with my mother and father."

"You remember this? Or is it something your parents told you long ago?" I asked.

The old man stared at the ceiling. "They were afraid of me."

"Who?"

"My mother and father."

I narrowed my eyes, studying the old man's face more closely, wondering where his story might lead. "Why were they afraid of you?"

"Because I grew old so quickly, too quickly. The doctors didn't know what to do. They called in specialists, but they didn't know what to do with me, either. I was a normal four-year-old boy, except I wasn't four years old. I was only weeks old."

The calmness and confidence of his voice suggested that the old man believed what he was saying. I felt another involuntary shiver through my body.

"They took tests. Made observations. I didn't see my parents anymore."

"You mean," I asked, trying to phrase the question gently, "your parents institutionalized you? Put you in a hospital?"

"Yes. Because, you see, I kept growing, aging. One

week I was six years old. The next week, I was eight. And then I was ten and twelve and fourteen."

The old man was delusional. His mind, like his body, had worn out, worn down. I thought it best not to encourage him to speak anymore. But he had begun his story and was determined now to finish it.

"After a while I figured it out," he said. "I understood what the doctors didn't. That's when I left the hospital. I walked out, because I knew there was nothing they could do to help me."

"What did you figure out?" I asked.

"That there have been men like me through all time. That's how the story got started," he said.

"What story?"

"About the old year and the new year. The old year is an old man with a beard and a scythe. And the new year is a little baby." The old man smiled weakly, as if remembering.

I heard a tire-screeching car in the street below, and I remembered how late it was—11:56—and Ruth's warning to be cautious about reckless drivers.

"People think it is a fable, but it isn't," the old man said. "There really are men who live for just one year. I don't know how it happens or why, but it does."

"What is your name?" I asked. It was foolish of me not to have asked it sooner.

"My name is unimportant. Who I am, what I am is." He

turned his worn face toward the wall. "I'm 1997," he said.

The landlady covered her mouth with her hand. I had quite forgotten that she was still in the room. Abruptly, as if caught in guilt, she turned and hurried out of the room. I watched her close the door behind her.

I heard a deep, heavy sigh, and I looked back at the old man. Suddenly, my heart seemed to have stopped beating. I leaned over and picked up his hand. I could feel no pulse at all. I leaned a little closer to gaze once more into his staring eyes. And then, gently, I brushed my fingers over them, closing his eyelids.

I stood looking down at him. Then, from where I don't know, a chill laced up my back. Without thought, I extended my left hand, and the sleeve of my coat slid back across my watch.

To the second.

I drove back to Mary's house, unable to get the old man's story out of my mind — or the weary acceptance in his eyes. I kept telling myself it was only a coincidence that he should have died at the stroke of midnight. Somehow, I couldn't quite convince myself.

My sister Mary opened the door. The living room was empty.

"Don't tell me the party has broken up already," I said.

"Why it's not quite one o'clock."

Mary was smiling happily. "No, not broken up," she said. "It just sort of changed location."

I also smiled. "To where?"

"The hospital."

I stared at her, my mind swept blank. Then it hit me. "You mean … Ruth?"

Mary laughed and hugged me. "You'll never guess," she giggled, "what time Ruth had the sweetest little boy … to the second!"

THE OLD REGIME

AND THE

FRENCH REVOLUTION

ALEXIS DE TOCQUEVILLE

TRANSLATED BY JOHN BONNER

DOVER PUBLICATIONS, INC.
Mineola, New York

Bibliographical Note

This Dover edition, first published in 2010, is an unabridged republication of the work originally published by Harper & Brothers, New York, in 1856 under the title *The Old Regime and the Revolution*.

Library of Congress Cataloging-in-Publication Data

Tocqueville, Alexis de, 1805–1859.
    [Ancien régime et la Révolution. English]
    The Old Regime and the French Revolution / Alexis de Tocqueville; translated by John Bonner.
       p. cm.
    "Unabridged republication of the work originally published by Harper & Brothers, New York, in 1856 under the title The Old Regime and the Revolution"—T.p. verso.
    ISBN-13: 978-0-486-47602-5
    ISBN-10: 0-486-47602-2
    1. France—History—Revolution, 1789–1799—Causes. I. Bonner, John, 1828–1899. II. Title.

DC138.T6313 2010
944.04—dc22

                          2009053583

Manufactured in the United States by Courier Corporation
47602201
www.doverpublications.com

CONTENTS.

CONTENTS.

CHAPTER III.

CHAPTER IV.

CHAPTER V.

CHAPTER VI.

CHAPTER VII.

CHAPTER VIII.

CHAPTER IX.

CHAPTER X.

CHAPTER XI.

CHAPTER XII.

CONTENTS.

PREFACE.

THE book I now publish is not a history of the Revolution. That history has been too brilliantly written for me to think of writing it afresh. This is a mere essay on the Revolution.

The French made, in 1789, the greatest effort that has ever been made by any people to sever their history into two parts, so to speak, and to tear open a gulf between their past and their future. In this design, they took the greatest care to leave every trace of their past condition behind them; they imposed all kinds of restraints upon themselves in order to be different from their ancestry; they omitted nothing which could disguise them.

I have always fancied that they were less successful in this enterprise than has been generally believed abroad, or even supposed at home. I have always suspected that they unconsciously retained most of the sentiments, habits, and ideas which the old regime had taught them, and by whose aid they achieved the Revolution; and that, without intending it, they used its ruins as materials for the construction of their new society. Hence it seemed that the proper way of studying the Revolution was to forget, for a time, the France we see before us, and to examine, in its grave, the France that is gone. That is the task which I have here endeavored to perform; it has been more arduous than I had imagined.

The early ages of the monarchy, the Middle Ages, and the period of revival have been thoroughly studied; the labors of the authors who have chosen them for their theme have acquainted us not only with the events of history, but also with the laws, the customs, the spirit of the government and of the nation in those days. No one has yet thought of examining the eighteenth century in the same close, careful manner. We fancy that we are familiar with the French society of that age because we see clearly what glittered on its surface, and possess detailed biographies of the illustrious characters, and ingenious or eloquent criticisms on the works of the great writers who flourished at the time. But of the manner in which public business was transacted, of the real working of institutions, of the true relative position of the various classes of society, of the condition and feelings of those classes which were neither heard nor seen, of the actual opinions and customs of the day, we have only confused and frequently erroneous notions.

I have undertaken to grope into the heart of this old regime. It is not far distant from us in years, but the Revolution hides it.

To succeed in the task, I have not only read the celebrated books which the eighteenth century produced; I have studied many works which are comparatively unknown, and deservedly so, but which, as their composition betrays but little art, afford perhaps a still truer index to the instincts of the age. I have endeavored to make myself acquainted with all the public documents in which the French expressed their opinions and their views at the approach of the Revolution. I have derived much information on this head from the reports of the States, and, at a later period, from those of the Provincial Assemblies. I have freely used the *cahiers* which were presented by the three orders in 1789. These *cahiers*, whose originals form a large series of folio volumes, will ever remain as the testament of the old French society, the final expression of its wishes, the authentic statement of its last will. They are a historical document that is unique.

Nor have I confined my studies to these. In countries where the supreme power is predominant, very few ideas, or desires, or grievances can exist without coming before it in some shape or other. But few interests can be created or passions aroused that are not at some time laid bare before it. Its archives reveal not merely its own proceedings, but the movement of the whole nation. Free access to the files of the Department of the Interior and the various prefectures would soon enable a foreigner to know more about France than we do ourselves. In the eighteenth century, as a perusal of this work will show, the government was already highly centralized, very powerful, prodigiously active. It was constantly at work aiding, prohibiting, permitting this or that. It had much to promise, much to give. It exercised paramount influence not only over the transaction of business, but over the prospects of families and the private life of individuals. None of its business was made public; hence people did not shrink from confiding to

it their most secret infirmities. I have devoted much
time to the study of its remains at Paris and in the
provinces.*

I have found in them, as I anticipated, the actual
life of the old regime, its ideas, its passions, its prejudices, its practices.   I have found men speaking freely
their inmost thoughts in their own language.   I have
thus obtained much information upon the old regime
which was unknown even to the men who lived under
it, for I had access to sources which were closed to
them.

As I progressed in my labors, I was surprised to
find in the France of that day many features which are
conspicuous in the France we have before us.   I met
with a host of feelings and ideas which I have always
credited to the Revolution, and many habits which it
is supposed to have engendered; I found on every side
the roots of our modern society deeply imbedded in
the old soil.   The nearer I drew to 1789, the more
distinctly I noticed the spirit which brought about the
Revolution.   The actual physiognomy of the Revolution was gradually disclosed before me.   Its temper,
its genius were apparent; it was all there.   I saw
there not only the secret of its earliest efforts, but the
promise also of its ultimate results—for the Revolu-

---

* I have made especial use of the archives of some of the greater
intendants' offices, such as those of Tours, which are very complete;
they refer to a very large district (*généralité*), placed in the centre of
France, and containing a million of souls.   My thanks are due to the
young and able keeper of the archives, M. Grandmaison.   Other intendants' offices, such as that of Ile de France, have satisfied me that
business was conducted on the same plan throughout most of the
kingdom.

tion had two distinct phases: one during which the
French seemed to want to destroy every remnant of
the past, another during which they tried to regain a
portion of what they had thrown off. Many of the
laws and political usages of the old regime which disappeared in 1789 reappeared some years afterward,
just as some rivers bury themselves in the earth and
rise to the surface at a distance, washing new shores
with the old waters.

The especial objects of the work I now present to
the public are to explain why the Revolution, which
was impending over every European country, burst
forth in France rather than elsewhere; why it issued
spontaneously from the society which it was to destroy; and how the old monarchy contrived to fall so
completely and so suddenly.

My design is to pursue the work beyond these limits. I intend, if I have time and my strength does not
fail me, to follow through the vicissitudes of their long
revolution these Frenchmen with whom I have lived on
such familiar terms under the old regime; to see them
throwing off the shape they had borrowed from this
old regime, and assuming new shapes to suit events,
yet never changing their nature, or wholly disguising
the old familiar features by changes of expression.

I shall first go over the period of 1789, when their
affections were divided between the love of freedom
and the love of equality; when they desired to establish free as well as democratic institutions, and to acknowledge and confirm rights as well as to destroy
privileges. This was an era of youth, of enthusiasm,
of pride, of generous and heartfelt passions; despite

its errors, men will remember it long, and for many a
day to come it will disturb the slumbers of those who
seek to corrupt or to enslave the French.

In the course of a hasty sketch of the Revolution, I
shall endeavor to show what errors, what faults, what
disappointments led the French to abandon their first
aim, to forget liberty, and to aspire to become the equal
servants of the master of the world; how a far stronger and more absolute government than the one the
Revolution overthrew then seized and monopolized all
political power, suppressed all the liberties which had
been so dearly bought, and set up in their stead empty
shams; deprived electors of all means of obtaining information, of the right of assemblage, and of the faculty
of exercising a choice, yet talked of popular sovereignty; said the taxes were freely voted, when mute or enslaved assemblies assented to their imposition; and,
while stripping the nation of every vestige of self-government, of constitutional guarantees, and of liberty of
thought, speech, and the press—that is to say, of the
most precious and the noblest conquests of 1789—still
dared to claim descent from that great era.

I shall stop at the period at which the work of the
Revolution appears complete, and the new society created. I shall then examine that new society. I shall
try to discover wherein it resembles and wherein it
differs from the society which preceded it; to ascertain
what we have gained and what we have lost by the
universal earthquake; and shall lastly attempt to foresee our future prospects.

A portion of this second work I have roughly sketched, but it is not yet fit for the public eye. Shall I be

permitted to finish it? Who knows? The fate of individuals is even more obscure than that of nations.

I trust I have written this work without prejudice; but I do not claim to have written dispassionately. It would be hardly decent for a Frenchman to be calm when he speaks of his country, and thinks of the times. I admit that, in studying every feature of the society of other times, I have never lost sight of that which we see before us. I have tried not only to detect the disease of which the patient died, but to discover the remedy that might have saved him. I have acted like those physicians who try to surprise the vital principle in each paralyzed organ. My object has been to draw a perfectly accurate, and, at the same time, an instructive picture. Whenever I have found among our ancestors any of those masculine virtues which we need so much and possess so little—a true spirit of independence, a taste for true greatness, faith in ourselves and in our cause—I have brought them boldly forward; and, in like manner, whenever I have discovered in the laws, or ideas, or manners of olden time, any trace of those vices which destroyed the old regime and weaken us to-day, I have taken pains to throw light on them, so that the sight of their mischievous effects in the past might prove a warning for the future.

In pursuing this object, I have not, I confess, allowed myself to be influenced by fears of wounding either individuals or classes, or shocking opinions or recollections, however respectable they may be. I have often felt regret in pursuing this course, but remorse, never. Those whom I may have offended must forgive me, in

consideration of the honesty and disinterestedness of
my aim.

I may perhaps be charged with evincing in this work
a most inopportune love for freedom, about which I am
assured that Frenchmen have ceased to care.

I can only reply to those who urge this charge that
in me the feeling is of ancient date.   More than twenty years have elapsed since I wrote, in reference to another society, almost these very words.

In the darkness of the future three truths may be
plainly discerned.   The first is, that all the men of our
day are driven, sometimes slowly, sometimes violently,
by an unknown force—which may possibly be regulated or moderated, but can not be overcome—toward
the destruction of aristocracies.   The second is, that,
among all human societies, those in which there exists
and can exist no aristocracy are precisely those in
which it will be most difficult to resist, for any length
of time, the establishment of despotism.   And the third
is, that despotisms can never be so injurious as in societies of this nature; for despotism is the form of government which is best adapted to facilitate the development of the vices to which these societies are prone,
and naturally encourages the very propensities that are
indigenous in their disposition.

When men are no longer bound together by caste,
class, corporate or family ties, they are only too prone
to give their whole thoughts to their private interest,
and to wrap themselves up in a narrow individuality
in which public virtue is stifled.   Despotism does not
combat this tendency; on the contrary, it renders it
irresistible, for it deprives citizens of all common pas-

sions, mutual necessities, need of a common understanding, opportunity for combined action: it ripens them,
so to speak, in private life.   They had a tendency to
hold themselves aloof from each other: it isolates them.
They looked coldly on each other: it freezes their souls.

In societies of this stamp, in which there are no
fixed landmarks, every man is constantly spurred on
by a desire to rise and a fear of falling.   And as money,
which is the chief mark by which men are classified
and divided one from the other, fluctuates incessantly,
passes from hand to hand, alters the rank of individuals, raises families here, lowers them there, every one
is forced to make constant and desperate efforts to acquire or retain it.   Hence the ruling passions become
a desire for wealth at all cost, a taste for business, a
love of gain, and a liking for comfort and material
pleasures.   These passions pervade all classes, not excepting those which have hitherto been strangers to
them.   If they are not checked they will soon enervate and degrade them all.   Now, it is essential to
despotism to encourage and foster them.   Debilitating
passions are its natural allies; they serve to divert attention from public affairs, and render the very name
of revolution terrible.   Despotism alone can supply
the secrecy and darkness which cupidity requires to be
at ease, and which embolden men to brave dishonor
for the sake of fraudulent gain.   These passions would
have been strong in the absence of despotism: with its
aid they are paramount.

On the other hand, liberty alone can combat the
vices which are natural to this class of societies, and
arrest their downward progress.   Nothing but liberty

can draw men forth from the isolation into which their independence naturally drives them—can compel them to associate together, in order to come to a common understanding, to debate, and to compromise together on their joint concerns.   Liberty alone can free them from money-worship, and divert them from their petty, every-day business cares, to teach them and make them feel that there is a country above and beside them. It alone awakens more energetic and higher passions than the love of ease, provides ambition with nobler aims than the acquisition of wealth, and yields the light which reveals, in clear outline, the virtues and the vices of mankind.

Democratic societies which are not free may be rich, refined, ornate, even magnificent, and powerful in proportion to the weight of their homogeneous mass ; they may develop private virtues, produce good family-men, honest merchants, respectable landowners, and even good Christians—for their country is not of this world, and it is the glory of their religion that it produces them in the most corrupt societies and under the worst governments—the Roman empire during its decline was full of such as these ; but there are things which such societies as those I speak of can never produce, and these are great citizens, and, above all, a great people. I will go farther; I do not hesitate to affirm that the common level of hearts and minds will never cease to sink so long as equality and despotism are combined.

This is what I thought and wrote twenty years ago.   I acknowledge that nothing has since happened that could lead me to think or write otherwise.   As I made known my good opinion of liberty when it was in favor, I can not be blamed for adhering to that opinion now that it is in disgrace.

I must, moreover, beg to assure my opponents that I do not differ from them as widely as they perhaps imagine. Where is the man whose soul is naturally so base that he would rather be subject to the caprices of one of his fellow-men than obey laws which he had helped to make himself, if he thought his nation sufficiently virtuous to make a good use of liberty? I do not think such a man exists. Despots acknowledge that liberty is an excellent thing; but they want it all for themselves, and maintain that the rest of the world is unworthy of it. Thus there is no difference of opinion in reference to liberty; we differ only in our appreciation of men; and thus it may be strictly said that one's love for despotism is in exact proportion to one's contempt for one's country. I must beg to be allowed to wait a little longer before I embrace that sentiment.

I may say, I think, without undue self-laudation, that this book is the fruit of great labor. I could point to more than one short chapter that has cost me over a year's work. I could have loaded my pages with foot-notes, but I have preferred inserting a few only, and placing them at the end of the volume, with a reference to the pages to which they apply. They contain examples and proofs of the facts stated in the text. I could furnish many more if this book induced any one to take the trouble of asking for them.

THE

OLD REGIME AND THE REVOLUTION.

BOOK FIRST.

CHAPTER I.

CONTRADICTORY OPINIONS FORMED UPON THE REVOLUTION WHEN
IT BROKE OUT.

PHILOSOPHERS and statesmen may learn a valuable lesson of modesty from the history of our Revolution, for there never were events greater, better prepared, longer matured, and yet so little foreseen.

With all his genius, Frederick the Great had no perception of what was at hand. He touched the Revolution, so to speak, but he did not see it. More than this, while he seemed to be acting according to his own impulse, he was, in fact, its forerunner and agent. Yet he did not recognize its approach; and when at length it appeared full in view, the new and extraordinary characteristics which distinguished it from the common run of revolutions escaped his notice.

Abroad, it excited universal curiosity. It gave birth to a vague notion that a new era was at hand. Nations entertained indistinct hopes of changes and reforms, but no one suspected what they were to be. Princes and ministers did not even feel the confused

presentiment which it stirred in the minds of their subjects.   They viewed it simply as one of those chron-
ic diseases to which every national constitution is subject, and whose only effect is to pave the way for political enterprises on the part of neighbors.   When
they spoke truly about it, it was unconsciously.   When
the principal sovereigns of Germany proclaimed at Pil-
nitz, in 1791, that all the powers of Europe were menaced by the danger which threatened royalty in France,
they said what was true, but at bottom they were far
from thinking so.   Secret dispatches of the time prove
that these expressions were only intended as clever pre-
texts to mask their real purposes, and disguise them
from the public eye.   They knew perfectly well—or
thought they knew—that the French Revolution was a
mere local and ephemeral accident, which might be
turned to account.   In this faith they formed plans,
made preparations, contracted secret alliances ; quar-
reled among themselves about the booty they saw before them; were reconciled, and again divided; were
ready, in short, for every thing except that which was
going to happen.

Englishmen, enlightened by the experience of their
own history, and trained by a long enjoyment of political liberty, saw, through a thick mist, the steady advances of a great revolution ; but they could not discern its form, or foresee the influence it was destined
to exercise over the world and over their own interests.
Arthur Young, who traveled through France just before the outbreak of the Revolution, was so far from
suspecting its real consequences that he rather feared
it might increase the power of the privileged classes.

"As for the nobility and the clergy," says he, "if this revolution enhances their preponderance, I fear it will do more harm than good."

Burke's mind was illumined by the hatred he bore to the Revolution from the first; still he doubted for a time. His first inference was, that France would be weakened, if not annihilated. "France is at this time," he said, "in a political light, to be considered as expunged out of the system of Europe. Whether she can ever appear in it again as a leading power is not easy to determine; but at present I consider France as not politically existing, and most assuredly it would take up much time to restore her to her former active existence. *Gallos quoque in bellis floruisse audivimus*—'We have heard that the Gauls too were once noted in war,' may be the remark of the present generation, as it was of an ancient one."

Men judged as loosely on the spot. On the eve of the outbreak, no one in France knew what would be the result. Among all the contemporaneous *cahiers*, I have only found two which seem to mark any apprehension of the people. Fears are expressed that royalty, or the court, as it was still called, will retain undue preponderance. The States-General are said to be too feeble, too short-lived. Alarm is felt lest they should suffer violence. The nobility is very uneasy on this head. Several *cahiers* affirm that "the Swiss troops will swear never to attack the citizens, even in case of affray or revolt." If the States-General are free, all the abuses may be corrected; the necessary reform is extensive, but easy.

Meanwhile the Revolution pursued its course. It

was not till the strange and terrible physiognomy of
the monster's head was visible; till it destroyed civil
as well as political institutions, manners, customs,
laws, and even the mother tongue; till, having dashed
in pieces the machine of government, it shook the
foundations of society, and seemed anxious to assail
even God himself; till it overflowed the frontier, and,
by dint of methods unknown before, by new systems
of tactics, by murderous maxims, and "armed opinions" (to use the language of Pitt), overthrew the landmarks of empires, broke crowns, and crushed subjects, while, strange to say, it won them over to its
side: it was not till then that a change came over
men's minds.   Then sovereigns and statesmen began
to see that what they had taken for a mere every-day
accident in history was an event so new, so contrary
to all former experience, so widespread, so monstrous
and incomprehensible, that the human mind was lost
in endeavoring to examine it.   Some supposed that
this unknown power, whose strength nothing could enhance and nothing diminish, which could not be checked, and which could not check itself, was destined to
lead human society to complete and final dissolution.
M. de Maistre, in 1797, observed that "the French
Revolution has a satanic character."   On the other
hand, others discerned the hand of God in the Revolution, and inferred a gracious design of Providence to
people France and the world with a new and better
species.   Several writers of that day seem to have
been exercised by a sort of religious terror, such as
Salvian felt at the sight of the barbarians.   Burke,
pursuing his idea, exclaims, "Deprived of the old government, deprived in a manner of all government,

France, fallen as a monarchy to common speculators, appears more likely to be an object of pity or insult, according to the disposition of the circumjacent powers, than to be the scourge and terror of them all; but out of the tomb of the murdered monarchy in France has arisen a vast, tremendous, unformed spectre, in a far more terrific guise than any which ever yet have overpowered the imagination and subdued the fortitude of man. Going straight forward to its end, unappalled by peril, unchecked by remorse, despising all common maxims and all common means, that hideous phantom has overpowered those who could not believe it was possible she could at all exist except on the principles which habit rather than nature has persuaded them are necessary to their own particular welfare and to their own ordinary modes of action."

Now, was the Revolution, in reality, as extraordinary as it seemed to its contemporaries? Was it as unexampled, as deeply subversive as they supposed? What was the real meaning, what the true character of this strange and terrible revolution? What did it actually destroy? What did it create?

It appears that the proper time has come to put these questions and to answer them. This is the most opportune moment for an inquiry and a judgment upon the vast topic they embrace. Time has cleared from our eyes the film of passion which blinded those who took part in the movement, and time has not yet impaired our capacity to appreciate the spirit which animated them. A short while hence the task will have become arduous, for successful revolutions obliterate their causes, and thus, by their own act, become inexplicable.

CHAPTER II.

THAT THE FUNDAMENTAL AND FINAL OBJECT OF THE REVOLUTION
WAS NOT, AS SOME HAVE SUPPOSED, TO DESTROY RELIGIOUS AND
TO WEAKEN POLITICAL AUTHORITY.

ONE of the first measures of the French Revolution was an attack upon the Church. Of all the passions to which that Revolution gave birth, that of irreligion was the first kindled, as it was the last extinguished. Even when the first enthusiasm of liberty had worn off, and peace had been purchased by the sacrifice of freedom, hostility to religion survived. Napoleon subdued the liberal spirit of the Revolution, but he could not conquer its anti-Christian tendencies. Even in the times in which we live, men have fancied they were redeeming their servility to the most slender officials of the state by their insolence to God, and have renounced all that was free, noble, and exalted in the doctrines of the Revolution, in the belief that they were still faithful to its spirit so long as they were infidels.

Yet nothing is easier than to satisfy one's self that the anti-religious war was a mere incident of the great Revolution; a striking, but fleeting expression of its physiognomy; a temporary result of ideas, and passions, and accidents which preceded it—any thing but its own proper fruit.

It is generally understood—and justly so—that the philosophy of the eighteenth century was one of the chief causes of the Revolution; and it is not to be denied that that philosophy was deeply irreligious; but it was twofold, and the two divisions are widely distinct.

One division or system contained all the new or revived opinions with reference to the conditions of society, and the principles of civil and political law. Such were, for example, the doctrines of the natural equality of man, and the consequent abolition of all caste, class, or professional privileges, popular sovereignty, the paramount authority of the social body, the uniformity of rules . . . . . These doctrines are not only the causes of the French Revolution; they are, so to speak, its substance; they constitute the most fundamental, the most durable, the truest portion of its work.

The other system was widely different. Its leaders attacked the Church with absolute fury. They assailed its clergy, its hierarchy, its institutions, its doctrines; to overthrow these, they tried to tear up Christianity by the roots. But this portion of the philosophy of the eighteenth century derived its origin from objects which the Revolution destroyed: it naturally disappeared with its cause, and was, so to speak, buried in its triumph. I purpose returning to this great topic herafter, and will add but one word here in order to explain myself more fully. Christianity was hated by these philosophers less as a religious doctrine than as a political institution; not because the priests assumed to regulate the concerns of the other world, but because they were landlords, seigniors, tithe-holders, administrators in this; not because the Church could not find a place in the new society which was being established, but because she then occupied the place of honor, privilege, and might in the society which was to be overthrown.

See how time has confirmed this view, and is still confirming it under our own eyes! Simultaneously with the consolidation of the political work of the Revolution, its religious work has been undone. The more thoroughly the political institutions it assailed have been destroyed; the more completely the powers, influences, and classes which were peculiarly obnoxious to it have been conquered, and have ceased in their ruin to be objects of hatred; in fine, the more the clergy have held themselves aloof from the institutions which formerly fell by their side, the higher has the power of the Church risen, and the deeper has it taken root in men's minds.

This phenomenon is not peculiar to France; every Christian Church in Europe has gained ground since the French Revolution.

Nothing can be more erroneous than to suppose that democracy is naturally hostile to religion. Neither Christianity nor even Catholicism involves any contradiction to the democratic principle; both are, in some respects, decidedly favorable to it. All experience, indeed, shows that the religious instinct has invariably taken deepest root in the popular heart. All the religions which have disappeared found a last refuge there. Strange, indeed, it would be if the tendency of institutions based on the predominance of the popular will and popular passions were necessarily and absolutely to impel the human mind toward impiety.

All that I have said of religious I may repeat with additional emphasis in regard to political authority.

When the Revolution overthrew simultaneously all the institutions and all the usages which had governed society and restrained mankind within bounds, it was, perhaps, only natural to suppose that its result would be the destruction, not of one particular frame of society, but of all social order; not of this or that government, but of all public authority. There was a degree of plausibility in assuming that it aimed essentially at anarchy; yet I will venture to say that this also was an illusion.

Less than a year after the Revolution had begun, Mirabeau wrote secretly to the king, " Compare the present state of things with the old regime, and console yourself and take hope. A part—the greater part of the acts of the national assembly are decidedly favorable to a monarchical government. Is it nothing to have got rid of Parliament, separate states, the clerical body, the privileged classes, and the nobility? Richelieu would have liked the idea of forming but one class of citizens; so level a surface assists the exercise of power. A series of absolute reigns would have done less for royal authority than this one year of Revolution." He understood the Revolution like a man who was competent to lead it.

The French Revolution did not aim merely at a change in an old government; it designed to abolish the old form of society. It was bound to assail all forms of established authority together; to destroy acknowledged influences; to efface traditions; to substitute new manners and usages for the old ones; in a word, to sweep out of men's minds all the notions which had hitherto commanded respect and obedience. Hence its singular anarchical aspect.

But a close inspection brings to light from under the ruins an immense central power, which has gathered together and grasped all the several particles of authority and influence formerly scattered among a host of secondary powers, orders, classes, professions, families, and individuals, sown broadcast, so to speak, over the whole social body. No such power had been seen in the world since the fall of the Roman empire. This new power was created by the Revolution, or, rather, it grew spontaneously out of the ruins the Revolution made. If the governments it created were fragile, they were still far stronger than any that had preceded them, and their very fragility, as will be shown hereafter, sprang from the same cause as their strength.

It was the simple, regular, grand form of this central power which Mirabeau discerned through the dust of the crumbling institutions of olden time. The masses did not see it, great as it was. Time gradually disclosed it to all; and now, princes can see nothing else. Admiration and envy of its work fill the mind, not only of the sovereigns it created, but of those who were strangers or inimical to its progress. All are busy destroying immunities, abolishing privileges throughout their dominions; mingling ranks, leveling, substituting hired officials in the room of an aristocracy, a uniform set of laws in the place of local franchises, a single strong government instead of a system of diversified authorities. Their industry in this revolutionary work is unceasing; when they meet an obstacle, they will sometimes even borrow a hint or a maxim from the Revolution. They have been noticed inciting the poor against the rich, the commoner against the noble, the peasant against his lord. The French Revolution was both their scourge and their tutor.

CHAPTER III.

THAT THE FRENCH REVOLUTION, THOUGH POLITICAL, PURSUED THE
SAME COURSE AS A RELIGIOUS REVOLUTION, AND WHY.

ALL political and civil revolutions have been confined to a single country.   The French Revolution had no country ; one of its leading effects appeared to be to efface national boundaries from the map.
It united and divided men, in spite of law, traditions,
characters, language ; converted enemies into fellow-
countrymen, and brothers into foes ; or, rather, to
speak more precisely, it created, far above particular
nationalities, an intellectual country that was common
to all, and in which every human creature could obtain
rights of citizenship.

No similar feature can be discovered in any other
political revolution recorded in history.   But it occurs
in certain religious revolutions.   Therefore those who
wish to examine the French Revolution by the light
of analogy must compare it with religious revolutions.

Schiller observes with truth, in his History of the
Thirty Years' War, that one striking effect of the Ref-
ormation was that it led to sudden alliances and warm
friendships among nations which hardly knew each
other.   Frenchmen were seen, for instance, fighting
against Frenchmen, with Englishmen in their ranks.
Men born on distant Baltic shores marched down into

the heart of Germany to protect Germans of whom they had never heard before. All the foreign wars of the time partook of the nature of civil wars; in all the civil wars foreigners bore arms. Old interests were forgotten in the clash of new ones; questions of territory gave way to questions of principle. All the old rules of politics and diplomacy were at fault, to the great surprise and grief of the politicians of the day. Precisely similar were the events which followed 1789 in Europe.

The French Revolution, though political, assumed the guise and tactics of a religious revolution. Some further points of resemblance between the two may be noticed. The former not only spread beyond the limits of France, but, like religious revolutions, spread by preaching and propagandism. A political revolution, which inspired proselytism, and whose doctrines were preached abroad with as much warmth as they were practiced at home, was certainly a new spectacle, the most strikingly original of all the novelties which were presented to the world by the French Revolution. But we must not stop here. Let us go further, and try to discover whether these parallel results did not flow from parallel causes.

Religions commonly affect mankind in the abstract, without allowance for additions or changes effected by laws, customs, or national traditions. Their chief aim is to regulate the concerns of man with God, and the reciprocal duties of men toward each other, independently of social institutions. They deal, not with men of any particular nation or any particular age, but with men as sons, fathers, servants, masters, neighbors.

Based on principles essential to human nature, they
are applicable and suited to all races of men.   Hence
it is that religious revolutions have swept over such
extensive areas, and have rarely been confined, as political revolutions have, to the territory of one people,
or even one race ; and the more abstract their character, the wider they have spread, in spite of differences
of laws, climate, and race.

The old forms of paganism, which were all more or
less interwoven with political and social systems, and
whose dogmas wore a national and sometimes a sort of
municipal aspect, rarely traveled beyond the frontiers
of a single country.   They gave rise to occasional
outbursts of intolerance and persecution, but never to
proselytism.   Hence, the first religious revolution felt
in Western Europe was caused by the establishment
of Christianity.   That faith easily overstepped the
boundaries which had checked the outgrowth of pa-
gan systems, and rapidly conquered a large portion of
the human race.   I hope I shall exhibit no disrespect
for that holy faith if I suggest that it owed its suc-
cesses, in some degree, to its unusual disentanglement
from all national peculiarities, forms of government,
social institutions, and local or temporary considerations.

The French Revolution acted, with regard to things
of this world, precisely as religious revolutions have
acted with regard to things of the other.   It dealt with
the citizen in the abstract, independent of particular
social organizations, just as religions deal with mankind in general, independent of time and place.   It inquired, not what were the particular rights of French

citizens, but what were the general rights and duties of mankind in reference to political concerns.

It was by thus divesting itself of all that was peculiar to one race or time, and by reverting to natural principles of social order and government, that it became intelligible to all, and susceptible of simultaneous imitation in a hundred different places.

By seeming to tend rather to the regeneration of the human race than to the reform of France alone, it roused passions such as the most violent political revolutions had been incapable of awakening. It inspired proselytism, and gave birth to propagandism; and hence assumed that quasi religious character which so terrified those who saw it, or, rather, became a sort of new religion, imperfect, it is true, without God, worship, or future life, but still able, like Islamism, to cover the earth with its soldiers, its apostles, and its martyrs.

It must not be supposed that all its methods were unprecedented, or all the ideas it brought forward absolutely original. On many former occasions, even in the heart of the Middle Ages, agitators had invoked the general principles on which human societies rest for the purpose of overthrowing particular customs, and had assailed the constitution of their country with arguments drawn from the natural rights of man; but all these experiments had been failures. The torch which set Europe on fire in the eighteenth century was easily extinguished in the fifteenth. Arguments of this kind can not succeed till certain changes in the condition, customs, and minds of men have prepared a way for their reception.

There are times when men differ so widely that the

bare idea of a common law for all appears unintelligible. There are others, again, when they will recognize at a glance the least approach toward such a law, and embrace it eagerly.

The great wonder is not that the French Revolution employed the methods it did, and conceived the ideas it brought forth; what is wonderful and startling is that mankind had reached a point at which these methods could be usefully employed, and these ideas readily admitted.

CHAPTER IV.

HOW THE SAME INSTITUTIONS HAD BEEN ESTABLISHED OVER NEAR-
LY ALL EUROPE, AND WERE EVERY WHERE FALLING TO PIECES.

THE tribes which overthrew the Roman empire, and eventually constituted modern nations, differed in race, origin, and language ; they were alike in barbarism only.   They found the empire in hopeless confusion, which they aggravated; and thus, when they settled, each was isolated from the others by the ruins it had made.   Civilization was almost extinct.   Social order had ceased to exist.   International communication was difficult and dangerous.   Safety dictated the division of the great European family into a thousand little states, which soon became exclusive and hostile to each other.

Yet out of this chaos uniform laws suddenly issued.

They were not borrowed from Roman legislation. They were, indeed, so much opposed to it that the old Roman law was the instrument afterward used to transform and abolish them.[a]   Their principles were original, and wholly different from any that had ever been broached before.   Composed of symmetrical parts, knit together as closely as the articles of any modern code, they constituted a body of really learned laws for the use of a semi-barbarous people.

It is not my design to inquire how such a system was formed and spread over Europe.   I merely note

the fact that, during the Middle Ages, it existed to
some extent in every country; and in many, to the
total exclusion of all other systems.

I have had occasion to study the political institutions which flourished in England, France, and Germany during the Middle Ages. As I advanced in the
work, I have been filled with amazement at the wonderful similarity of the laws established by races so
far apart and so widely different. They vary constantly and infinitely, it is true, in matters of detail,
but in the main they are identical every where. Whenever I discovered in the old legislation of Germany a
political institution, a rule, or a power, I knew that a
thorough search would bring something similar to light
in France and England; and I never failed to find it
so. Each of the three nations enabled me to understand the other two.

In all three the government was carried on in accordance with the same principles: the political assemblies were constituted from the same materials, and
armed with the same powers; society was divided into
the same classes, on the same sliding-scale; the nobles
occupied the same rank, enjoyed the same privileges,
were marked by the same natural characteristics—in
short, the men were, properly speaking, identically the
same in all.

The city constitutions resembled each other; the
rural districts were governed on one uniform plan.
There was no material difference in the condition of
the peasantry; land was held, occupied, cultivated on
the same plan, and the farmer paid the same taxes.
From the confines of Poland to the Irish Sea we can

trace the same seigniories, seigniors' court, feuds, rents, feudal services, feudal rights, corporate bodies. Sometimes the names are the same, and, what is still more remarkable, the same idea pervades all these analogous institutions. I think it is safe to say that in the fourteenth century the various social, political, administrative, judicial, economical, and literary institutions of Europe were more nearly alike than they are now, though civilization has done so much to facilitate intercourse and efface national barriers.

The task I have undertaken does not require me to relate how this old constitution of Europe gradually gave way and broke down; I merely state that in the eighteenth century it was in proximate ruin every where.[b] Decay was least conspicuous in the eastern half of the continent, and most in the west; but old age and decrepitude were prominent on all sides.

The records of the old Middle-Age institutions contain the history of their decline. It is well known that land registers (*terriers*) were kept in each seigniory, in which, century after century, were entered the boundaries of the feuds and seigniories, the rents due, the services to be rendered, the local customs. I have seen registers of the fourteenth and thirteenth centuries, which are masterpieces of method, perspicuity, and intellect. The more modern ones grow more obscure, more incomplete, more confused as they approach our own day. It would seem as though the civilization of society had involved the relapse of the political system into barbarism.

The old European constitution was better preserved in Germany than in France; but there, too, a portion

of the institutions to which it had given life were already destroyed.   One can judge of the ravages of
time, however, better from the portion which survived
than from that which had perished.

Of the municipal franchises which, in the thirteenth
and fourteenth centuries, had converted the chief cities
of Germany into rich and enlightened republics,[c] a mere
empty shadow remained.   Their enactments were un-
repealed; their magistrates bore the old titles, and appeared to perform the old duties; but the activity, the
energy, the civic patriotism, the manly and fruitful virtues of olden time had vanished.   These venerable institutions seemed to have sunk down without dis-
tortion.

All the surviving mediæval sources of authority had
suffered from the same disease; all alike were decayed and languishing.   Nor was this all: every thing
which, without actually growing out of the mediæval
system, had been connected with it and marked by its
stamp, seemed equally lifeless.   Aristocracy wore an
air of servile debility.   Even political freedom, which
had filled the Middle Ages with its works, became
sterile in the dress in which they had clothed it.   Those
provincial assemblies which had preserved their old
constitution in its integrity were rather a hindrance
than a help to civilization.   They presented a stolid,
impenetrable front to the march of intellect, and drove
the people into the arms of monarchs.   There was
nothing venerable in the age of these institutions; the
older they grew, the smaller their claims to respect;
and somehow, the more harmless they became, the more
hatred they seemed to inspire.   A German writer, whose

sympathies were all on the side of the old regime under which he lived, says, "The present state of things
is shameful for all of us, and even contemptible. It
is strange how unfavorably men look upon every thing
that is old. Novelty penetrates even the family circle, and overturns its peace. Our very housekeepers
want to get rid of their old furniture." Yet in Germany, as in France, society was then thrilling with activity, and highly prosperous; but (mark this well! it
is the finishing touch to the picture) every living, acting, producing agent was new, and not only new, but
contrary to the old.

Royalty had nothing in common with mediæval
royalty; its prerogatives were different, its rank had
changed, its spirit was new, the homage it received was
unusual. The central power encroached on every side
upon decaying local franchises. A hierarchy of public functionaries usurped the authority of the nobles.
All these new powers employed methods and took for
their guide principles which the Middle Ages either
never knew or rejected, and which, indeed, were only
suitable for a state of society they never conceived.

At first blush it would appear that the old constitution of Europe is still in force in England; but, on a
closer view, this illusion is dispelled. Forget old
names, pass over old forms, and you will find the feudal system substantially abolished there as early as the
seventeenth century: all classes freely intermingled,
an eclipsed nobility, an aristocracy open to all, wealth
installed as the supreme power, all men equal before
the law, equal taxes, a free press, public debates—phenomena which were all unknown to mediæval society.

It was the skillful infusion of this young blood into the old feudal body which preserved its life, and imbued it with fresh vitality, without divesting it of its ancient shape.　England was a modern nation in the seventeenth century, though it preserved, as it were embalmed, some relics of the Middle Ages.

This hasty glance at foreign nations was essential to a right comprehension of the following pages.　No one can understand the French Revolution without having seen and studied something more than France.

CHAPTER V.

WHAT DID THE FRENCH REVOLUTION REALLY ACHIEVE?

THE object of the preceding inquiries was to clear the way for the solution of the question I originally put: What was the real object of the Revolution? what was its peculiar character? why was it brought about? what did it achieve?

It is an error to suppose, as some have done, that the object of the Revolution was to overthrow the sovereignty of religious creeds. Despite appearances, it was essentially a social and political revolution. It did not tend to perpetuate or consolidate disorder, to "methodize anarchy" (as one of its leading opponents remarked), but rather to augment the power and the rights of public authority. It was not calculated to change the character of our civilization, as others imagined, or to arrest its progress, or even to alter, essentially, any of the fundamental laws upon which our Western societies rest. When it is disengaged from the extraneous incidents which imparted a temporary coloring to its complexion, and is examined on its own proper merits, it will be seen that its sole effect was to abolish those institutions which had held undivided sway over Europe for several centuries, and which are usually known as the feudal system; in order to substitute therefor a social and political organization marked by more uniformity and more simplicity, and resting on the basis of the equality of all ranks.

That alone required a stupendous revolution; for these old institutions were not only connected and interwoven with all the religious and political laws of Europe, but had, besides, created a host of ideas, and feelings, and habits, and customs, which had grown up around them. To destroy and cut out of the social body a part which clung to so many organs involved a frightful operation. This made the Revolution appear even greater than it was. It appeared the universal destroyer; for what it did destroy was linked, and, in some degree, incorporated with almost every thing else.

Radical as it was, the Revolution introduced fewer innovations than has been generally supposed, as I shall have occasion to show hereafter. What it really achieved was the destruction—total, or partial, for the work is still in progress—of every thing which proceeded from the old aristocratical and feudal institutions, and of every thing which clung to them or bore in any way their distinguishing mark. It respected no legacy of the past but such as had been foreign to these institutions, and could exist without them.

It was, least of all, a casual accident. True, it took the world by surprise; yet it was the mere natural result of very long labors, the sudden and violent termination of a task which had successively engaged ten generations of men. Had it never taken place, the old social edifice would none the less have fallen, though it would have given way piecemeal instead of breaking down with a crash. The Revolution effected suddenly, by a convulsive and sudden effort, without transition, precautions, or pity, what would have been gradually effected by time had it never occurred. That was its achievement.

It is surprising that this fact, which we discern so plainly to-day, should have once been hidden from the eyes of the shrewdest observers. Burke appeals to the French: "Had you but made it to be understood that, in the delusion of your amiable error, you had gone farther than your wise ancestors; that you were resolved to assume your ancient privileges while you preserved the spirit of your ancient and your recent loyalty and honor; or, if diffident of yourselves, and not clearly discerning the almost obliterated constitution of your ancestors, you had but looked to your neighbors in this land, who had kept alive the ancient principles and the models of the old common law of Europe.... "

Burke can not see that the real object of the Revolution is to abolish that very common law in Europe; he does not perceive that that, and nothing else, is the gist of the movement.

But, as society was every where prepared for this Revolution, why did it break out in France rather than abroad? Why did it present features here which were either wholly dropped or only partially reproduced in other countries? This secondary inquiry is worth resolving: it will form the subject of the following Book.

BOOK SECOND.

CHAPTER I.

A PARADOX meets us at the threshold of the inquiry. The Revolution was designed to abolish the remains of the institutions of the Middle Ages: yet it did not break out in countries where those institutions were in full vitality and practically oppressive, but, on the contrary, in a country where they were hardly felt at all; whence it would follow that their yoke was the most intolerable where it was in fact lightest.

At the close of the eighteenth century there was hardly any part of Germany in which serfdom was completely abolished.[d] [e] Generally speaking, peasants still formed part of the stock on lands, as they had done during the Middle Ages. Nearly all the soldiers in the armies of Maria Theresa and Frederick were absolute serfs.

In 1788, the general rule with regard to German peasants was that they should not leave the seigniory, and if they did that they should be brought back by force. They were subject to dominical courts, and by them punished for intemperance and idleness. They could not rise in their calling, or change it, or marry without leave from their master. A great proportion of their time was given up to his service. Seigniorial *corvées* were rigorously exacted, and absorbed, in some places, three days of the week. The peasant rebuilt and kept in repair his seignior's house, took his produce to market, served him as coachman and messenger. Many years of his youth were spent in domestic service on the manor. A serf might obtain a farm, but his rights of property always remained inchoate. He was bound to farm his land under his seignior's eye, according to his seignior's directions; he could neither alienate nor mortgage it without leave. He was sometimes bound to sell the produce of his farm, sometimes forbidden to sell; he was always bound to keep his land under cultivation. His estate did not wholly pass to his children; a portion went to the seignior.

I have not groped through antiquated laws to find these rules; they are to be found in the code drawn up by Frederick the Great, and promulgated by his successor just before the French Revolution broke out.[f]

Nothing of the kind had existed for many, many years in France. Peasants came and went, bought and sold, wrought and contracted without let or hindrance. In one or two eastern provinces, acquired by conquest, some stray relics of serfdom survived; but it had disappeared every where else; and that so long ago, that even the period of its disappearance had been forgotten. Elaborate researches of recent date establish that it had ceased to exist in Normandy as early as the thirteenth century.

But of all the changes that had taken place in the condition of the French peasantry, the most important was that which had enabled them to become freehold-

ers. As this fact is not universally understood, though
it is so important, I shall dwell upon it briefly.

It has been commonly believed that the subdivision
of farms began with and was caused by the Revolution.
All kinds of evidence establish the very reverse.

Twenty years before the outbreak, agricultural societies deplored the subdivision of farm lands. About
the same period Turgot declared that " the division of
estates was so general that a property barely sufficient
to maintain a family was often parceled out among five
or six children, who were consequently unable to support themselves by agriculture alone." A few years
later, Necker observed that the number of small rural
estates had become *immense*.

A few years before the Revolution a steward of a
seigniory informed his employer, in a secret report,
that " estates are being subdivided so equally that the
fact is growing alarming : every body wants to have a
piece of this and a piece of that, and farms are incessantly split into shreds." What more could be said
of our own time ?

I have myself taken infinite pains to reconstruct the
cadastres, so to speak, of the old regime, and I have
occasionally succeeded.   The law of 1790, imposing a
land tax, devolved upon each parish the duty of pre-
paring a schedule of the estates within its limits. Most
of these schedules have disappeared. I have, however, discovered them in some villages, and I find, on
comparing them with our modern rolls, that the number of landed proprietors was formerly one half and
sometimes two thirds of what it is now ; a surprising
fact, as the total population of France has, since that
time, increased more than twenty-five per cent.

Then, as now, a sort of mania for the acquisition of land pervaded the rural population. A judicious contemporary observer notes that "land is selling above its value, owing to the rage of the peasantry to become landowners. All the savings of the lower classes, which in other countries are lodged in private hands or invested in public securities, are used for the purchase of land in France."

None of the novelties which astonished Arthur Young on his first visit to France appeared to him so striking as the infinite subdivision of land among the peasantry, who, he estimated, held among them one half the landed property in the kingdom. " I had no idea of such a state of things," he writes more than once; nor, indeed, could he have, for no such phenomenon existed beyond the frontiers of France or their immediate neighborhood.

There had been peasant proprietors in England, but they were, even then, growing rare. In Germany, too, there had been, from time to time, in every section of the country, free farmers owning portions of the soil.[g] The oldest German customs recognized a freehold peasantry, and embraced curious regulations regarding land held by them; but the number of such landholders was always small, and their case an exceptional one.

The only portions of Germany where, at the close of the eighteenth century, the peasantry were landholders, and comparatively free, were those which bordered on the Rhine;[h] and it was in the Rhenish provinces that the French revolutionary fever developed itself first and raged most fiercely. Those portions of Ger-

many which resisted the Revolution the longest were
those where neither freeholds nor rural liberty had
made their appearance; a significant fact.

It is, then, a vulgar error to suppose that the subdivision of property in France dates from the Revolution.
It began much farther back.   It is true that the Revolution was the means of bringing into market the
Church property and many of the estates of the nobility; but it will be found, on examination of the
sales (a task which I have occasionally had patience
to perform), that the bulk of these lands passed into
the hands of persons who held land already, so that no
great increase in the number of landowners can have
taken place.   They were already, to use the ambitious
but accurate expression of M. Necker, *immensely* numerous.[i]

The Revolution did not divide, it freed land.   All
these small landowners were bound to render various
feudal services, of which they could not get rid, and
which gravely impeded a proper development of their
property.

That these services were onerous can not be questioned.   Still, the very circumstance which it would
seem ought to have lightened their burden rendered it
intolerable.   A revolution scarcely less radical than
that which had enabled them to become freeholders had
released the peasantry of France, alone out of all Europe, from the government of their rural lords.

Brief as is the interval which divides us from the old
regime, and often as we see persons who were born under it, it seems already lost in the night of time.   So
radical was the revolution which has intervened, that

it appears to have perished ages ago, and to be now buried in obscurity. Hence there are but few persons who can give a correct answer to the simple question —How were the rural districts governed before 1789? Nor, indeed, can any precise and comprehensive answer be found in books, or elsewhere than in the official records of the time.

I have often heard it remarked that, long after the nobility had ceased to participate in the government of the kingdom, the rural administration remained in their hands, and the seigniors still governed the peasantry. This too looks like a misconception.

In the eighteenth century, all parochial business was transacted by functionaries who were not seigniorial agents, and who, instead of being chosen by the seigniors, were either appointed by the intendant of the province or elected by the peasantry. It devolved upon these officers to distribute the taxes, to repair the churches, to build schools, to convene and preside over parish meetings; to administer and superintend the expenditure of the funds of the *commune;* to institute or answer, on behalf of the community, all necessary legal proceedings. The seignior had lost not only the management, but even the supervision of these petty local matters. All parish officers were subject to the government or the central power, as I shall show in the following chapter. Nor did the seignior figure any longer as the king's deputy in the parish. The execution of the laws, the assembling of the militia, the levying of the taxes, the promulgation of the king's commands, the distribution of his alms, were no longer intrusted to the seignior. They devolved upon new functionaries. The seignior was in fact nothing more than a simple individual, isolated from his fellows by the enjoyment of peculiar immunities and privileges; his rank was different—his power no greater than theirs. The intendants were careful to remind their sub-agents that "the seignior is nothing more than the first peasant in the parish."

The *cantons* exhibit the same spectacle as the parishes. Nowhere do the nobles, either collectively or separately, administer public affairs.

This was peculiar to France. Every where else, that striking feature of the old feudal system, the connection between the ownership of land and the government of its inhabitants, had been partially preserved. England was administered as well as governed by its chief landholders. In parts of Germany, such as Prussia and Austria, the sovereigns had contrived to shake off the control of the nobility in state affairs; but they still abandoned the government of the rural districts to the seigniors, and even where they assumed to control, did not venture to supersede them.

In France, the only public department in which the nobles still had a hand was the administration of justice. Leading noblemen still preserved a right of jurisdiction over certain cases (which were decided by judges in their name), and occasionally issued police regulations for the use of their seigniories; but their jurisdiction had been so curtailed, and limited, and overridden by the royal courts, that the seigniors who still enjoyed it viewed it rather as a source of income than as a source of power.

The other rights of the nobility had shared the same

fate. They had lost their political significance, but their pecuniary value had been retained and occasionally augmented.

I am alluding now only to those tangible privileges which were known as feudal rights proper, as they alone affected the people.

It is no easy matter to point out what they actually were in 1789, for their number had been immense, and their diversity prodigious. Many had disappeared altogether. Others had undergone modifications, so that the words used to describe them were not easily understood even by contemporaries; they are necessarily full of obscurities for us. Still, a careful study of the writers on feudal law in the eighteenth century, and a searching inquiry into the various local customs, permits us to range the then existing feudal rights in a few leading classes, all others being mere isolated cases.

Seigniorial *corvées* were almost wholly disused. Many of the tolls on highways were either substantially reduced or abolished, though they were still met with in a majority of the provinces. The seigniors still levied a toll upon fairs and markets. It is well known that they enjoyed an exclusive privilege of hunting. Generally speaking, none but they could keep pigeons or own dove-cotes. The farmers were every where bound to carry their grain to the seignior's mill, their grapes to his wine-press. Mutation fines—a tax paid to the seignior on every purchase or sale of lands within the seigniory—were universally in force. On all land, moreover, ground-rents (*cens et rentes foncières*) and returns in money or kind were exacted from the proprietor by the seignior, and were essentially ir-

redeemable.   One single feature is common to all these
various rules : all bear upon the soil or its produce ;
all are leveled at the farmer.

Clerical seigniors enjoyed the same advantages as
their lay brethren ; for, though there was no similitude
between the Church and the feudal system in point of
origin, destiny, or character, and though they were never actually incorporated into one, they clung together
so closely that they seemed incrusted one upon the
other.[k] [l]

Bishops, canons, *abbés* held feuds and seigniories in
virtue of their ecclesiastical rank ; convents were usually the seigniors of the village in which they stood.[m]
They owned serfs at a time when no other seignior in
France did.   They exacted *corvées*, levied toll upon
fairs and markets, owned the only oven, the only mill,
the only wine-press, the only bull in the seigniory.
Besides these rights as seigniors, the French clergy,
like the clergy elsewhere, levied tithes.

The main point, however, to which I wish to draw
attention just now, is the fact that analogous feudal
rights were in force all over Europe at that time, and
that in France they were far less burdensome than in
other parts of the Continent.   As an illustration of
the difference I may cite *corvées*, which in France
were rarely claimed and slight, in Germany universally and rigorously exacted.

More than this, the feudal rights which roused most
indignation among our ancestors, as being not only unjust, but inimical to civilization—such, for instance,
as tithes, inalienable ground-rents (*rentes foncières*),
interminable rent-charges, and mutation fines, which,

in the somewhat forcible idiom of the eighteenth century, were said to constitute the "slavery of the land,"
were all more or less in force in England. Many of
them are still in full vigor, and yet English agriculture is the most perfect and richest in the world. The
English people hardly notice their existence.

How did it happen, then, that these usages roused
in France a hatred so fierce that it survived its cause,
and seems as though it would never be extinguished?
The phenomenon is due partly to the fact that the
French peasant was a landholder, and partly to his
emancipation from the government of his seignior.
Other causes co-operated, no doubt; but, I take it,
these were the main reasons.

Had the peasantry not been landholders, they would
have paid no attention to many of the burdens laid by
the feudal system on real estate. Tithes, which are
levied on produce, interest no one but farmers. Rent-
charges are immaterial to those who do not own land.
Legal hindrances to the development of property are
no serious inconvenience to those who are hired to develop it for others. And, on the other hand, if the
French peasantry had still been governed by their
seigniors, they would have borne with the feudal rights
more patiently, for they would have viewed them in
the light of a natural consequence of the constitution
of the country.

Aristocracies, which possess not merely privileges,
but actual power, which govern and administer public
affairs, may exercise private rights of great magnitude
without attracting much attention. In the old feudal
times people looked upon the nobility as they now look

on government : they bore its impositions for the sake
of the protection it afforded.   If the nobility possessed
inconvenient privileges and exacted onerous duties, it
secured public order, administered justice, executed the
laws, succored the weak, managed public affairs.   It
was when it ceased to do these things that the burden
of its privileges began to be felt, and its very existence
became inexplicable.

Picture to yourself, I beg, the French peasant of the
eighteenth century, or, rather, the peasant you see to-
day, for he is still the same ; his condition has changed,
but not his character.   Picture him, as the documents
of the time depict him, so eager for land that he saves
all his money to buy, and buys at any price.   In order to purchase, he is bound, in the first place, to pay a
tax, not to the government, but to some neighbors of
his, who have no more authority, and no more to do
with public business than he.   Still he buys, and puts
his heart into his land with his seed.   The idea that
this little corner of the vast universe belongs to him
alone fills him with pride and independence.   But the
same neighbors pass along and compel him to work on
their land without wages.   If he tries to protect his
harvest from the game, they prevent him.   He can not
cross the river without paying them toll.   He can not
take his produce to market and sell it till he has bought
leave to do so from them ; and when, on his return
home, he wants to consume in his family the surplus
of his produce—sown by his hands and grown under
his eyes—he finds he must first send his grain to their
mill to be ground, and to their oven to be cooked.
The largest part of the income of his little estate goes

to the same parties in the shape of rents, which can not be redeemed or got rid of in any way.

Let him do what he like, he can not but meet at every step of his life these same neighbors, who interfere with his enjoyments, impede his work, consume his produce; and when he has done with these, others, dressed in black, make their appearance, and sweep off the clearest part of his harvest. Picture, if you can, the condition, the wants, the character, the passions of such a man, and estimate the store of hatred and envy he is laying up in his heart![n]

The feudal system, though stripped of its political attributes, was still the greatest of our civil institutions;[o] but its very curtailment was the source of its unpopularity. It may be said, with perfect truth, that the destruction of a part of that system rendered the remainder a hundred-fold more odious than the whole had ever appeared.

CHAPTER II.

THAT WE OWE "ADMINISTRATIVE CENTRALIZATION," NOT TO THE
REVOLUTION OR THE EMPIRE, AS SOME SAY, BUT TO THE OLD RE-
GIME.

I ONCE heard an orator, in the days when we had political assemblies, call administrative centralization
"that noble conquest of the Revolution which Europe
envies us." I am willing to admit that centralization
was a noble conquest, and that Europe envies us its
possession ; but I deny that it was a conquest of the
Revolution. It was, on the contrary, a feature of the
old regime, and, I may add, the only one which outlived the Revolution, because it was the only one that
was suited to the new condition of society created by
the Revolution. A careful perusal of this chapter will
perhaps convince the reader that I have more than
proved this.

I must, at the outset, beg to be permitted to set aside
those provinces known as *pays d'états*, which did actually, or, at least, had the appearance of partially controlling the administration of their own government.

The *pays d'états*, situated at the extremities of the
kingdom, contained barely one fourth of the total population of France ; and, with one or two exceptions,
their provincial liberties were in a dying condition. I
shall have occasion hereafter to return to them, and to
show how far the central power had rendered them
subject to the ordinary rules.*

* See Appendix.

I purpose to devote attention at present chiefly to those provinces which were styled, in administrative parlance, *pays d'élection*, though there were fewer elections there than any where else. They surrounded Paris on all sides, bordering each on the other, and constituting the fairest portion of France.

A first glance at the old government of the kingdom leaves an impression of a host of diversified rules, and authorities, and concurrent powers. France seems to be covered with administrative bodies and independent functionaries, who, having purchased their offices, can not be displaced. Their functions are often so intertwined and similar that it seems they must clash and interfere with each other.

The courts are invested with some legislative authority. They establish rules, which are binding within the limits of their jurisdiction. They occasionally join issue with the government, blame its measures loudly, and decry its agents. Single judges make the police regulations in the cities and boroughs where they live.

City charters differ widely. Their magistrates bear different titles, or derive their authority from different sources. In one place we find a mayor, in another consuls, in a third syndics. Some of these are chosen by the king; others are appointed by the old seignior, or by the prince in whose domain the city lies; others are elected by the people for a year; others, again, have purchased their office, and hold it for life.

These are all old ruined authorities. Among them, however, is found an institution either new or lately transformed, which remains to be described. In the heart of the kingdom, and close to the monarch, an administrative body of singular power has lately grown up and absorbed all minor powers. That is the Royal Council.

Though its origin is ancient, most of its functions are modern. It is every thing at once: supreme court of justice, for it can reverse the decision of all ordinary tribunals and highest administrative authority, from which all subordinate authorities derive their power. As adviser of the king, it possesses, under him, legislative powers, discusses all and proposes most of the laws, levies and distributes the taxes. It makes rules for the direction of all government agents. It decides all important affairs in person, and superintends the working of all subordinate departments. All business originates with it, or reaches it at last; yet it has no fixed, well-defined jurisdiction. Its decisions are the king's, though they seem to be the Council's. Even while it is administering justice, it is nothing more than an assembly of "givers of advice," as the Parliament said in one of its remonstrances.

This Council is not composed of nobles, but of persons of ordinary or low extraction, who have filled various offices and acquired an extensive knowledge of business. They all hold office during good behavior.

It works noiselessly, discreetly, far less pretentious than powerful. It has no brilliancy of its own. Its proximity to the king makes it a partner in every important measure, but his greater effulgence eclipses it.

As the national administration was in the hands of a single body, nearly the whole executive direction of home affairs was in like manner intrusted to a single agent, the comptroller-general.

Old almanacs furnish lists of special ministers for each province, but an examination of the business records shows that these ministers had very little important business to transact. That fell to the lot of the comptroller-general, who gradually monopolized the management of all money affairs—in other words, the whole public administration. He was alternately minister of finance, of the interior, of public works, of commerce.

On the same principle, one agent in each province sufficed. As late as the eighteenth century, some great seigniors were entitled provincial governors. They were the representatives, often by hereditary descent, of feudal royalty. They enjoyed honors still, but they were unaccompanied by power. The substantial government was in the hands of the intendant.

That functionary was not of noble extraction. He was invariably a stranger to the province, a young man with his fortune to make. He obtained his office neither by purchase, election, nor inheritance; he was selected by the government from among the inferior members of the Council of State, and held his office during good behavior. While in his province, he represented that body, and was hence styled in office dialect the absent commissioner (*commissaire départi*). His powers were scarcely less than those of the council itself, though his decisions were subject to appeal. Like the Council, he held administrative and judicial authority: he corresponded with ministers; he was, in his province, the sole instrument of the will of government.

Under him he appointed for each canton an officer called a sub-delegate (*subdélégué*), who also held office during good behavior.   The intendant was usually the first noble of his family ; the sub-delegate was always a commoner, yet the latter was the sole representative of the government in his little sphere, as the intendant was in his province.   He was subject to the intendant, himself subject to the minister.

The Marquis d'Argenson tells us in his Memoirs that one day Law said to him, " I never could have believed beforehand what I saw when I was comptroller of finances.   Let me tell you that this kingdom of France is governed by thirty intendants.   You have neither Parliament, nor estates, nor governors; nothing but thirty masters of requests, on whom, so far as the provinces are concerned, welfare or misery, plenty or want, entirely depend."

These powerful officials were, however, outwardly eclipsed by the remains of the old feudal aristocracy, thrown into the shade by its lingering splendor ; hence it was that even in their day one saw so little of them, though their hand was every where felt.   In society, the nobility took precedence of them in virtue of their rank, their wealth, and the respect always paid to what is ancient.   In the government, the nobility surrounded the king and constituted the court; noblemen led the armies and commanded the fleet ; they performed those duties, in a word, which are most noticed by contemporaries, and too often best remembered by posterity.   A seignior of high rank would have felt himself insulted by the offer of a place of intendant; the poorest gentleman of his house would have disdained to accept it. In their eyes the intendants were the types of usurped authority, new men, employed to look after burghers and peasants; at best, very poor company. For all this, these men governed France, as Law said, and as we shall soon discover.

Let us begin with the right of levying taxes, which may be said to involve all other rights.

It is well known that a portion of the taxes were farmed out to financial companies, which levied them under the directions of the Royal Council. All other taxes, such as the *taille*, capitation-tax, and twentieths, were established and levied directly by the agents of the central administration, or under their all-powerful control.

Every year the Council fixed and distributed among the provinces the amount of the *taille* and its numerous accessories. The session and decision of the Council were secret; the *taille* increased year after year, and no one was aware of it.

The *taille* was a very old tax; in former times it had been apportioned and levied by local agents, who were independent of government, and held office in virtue of their birth, or by election, or by purchase. Such were the " seignior," the " parochial collector," the " treasurers of France," the " select-men" (*èlus*). These titles were still in existence in the eighteenth century; but some of the persons who bore them had ceased wholly to have to do with the *taille*, while others were only concerned with it in a subordinate and secondary capacity. The whole real authority on the subject was in the hands of the intendant and his agents; it was he who apportioned the *taille* among the parishes, directed and overlooked the collectors, granted delays or remissions.

More modern imposts, such as the capitation-tax, were regulated by government without interference from the surviving officers of the old system. The comptroller-general, the intendant, and the Council fixed the amount of each impost, and levied it without the intervention of the taxables.

Let us pass from money to men.

Surprise has been expressed at the docility with which the French bore the burden of the conscription during and after the Revolution; but it must be borne in mind that they had long been used to it. The militia system which had preceded it was more onerous, though the contingents raised were smaller. From time to time, in the country parts, young men were drawn by lot to serve in militia regiments for a term of six years.

As the militia was a comparatively modern institution, none of the feudal authorities interfered with it; it was wholly under the control of the central government. The entire contingent, and the proportion to be borne by each province, were regulated by the Council. The intendant fixed the number of men to be furnished by each parish. His sub-delegate presided over the lottery, awarded exemptions, decided who were to remain at home and who were to march. It was his duty to hand over the latter to the military authorities. There was no appeal from him but to the intendant and the Council.

It may be added here that, except in the *pays d'états*, all public works, including those which were exclusively local, were decided upon and undertaken by the agents of the central power.

Other authorities, such as the seignior, the department of finance, the road trustees (*grands voyers*), were nominally entitled to co-operate in the direction of these works. But practically these old authorities did little or nothing, as the most cursory glance at the records shows. All highways and roads from city to city were built and kept in repair out of the general public fund. They were planned and the contracts given out by the Council. The intendant superintended the engineering work, the sub-delegate mustered the men who were bound to labor. To the old authorities was left the task of seeing to parish roads, which accordingly became impassable.

The chief agent of the central government for public works was the Department of Bridges and Roads (*ponts et chaussées*). Here a striking resemblance to our modern system becomes manifest. The establishment of Bridges and Roads had a council and a school; inspectors, who traveled each year throughout France; engineers residing on the spot, and intrusted, under the orders of the intendant, with the direction of the works. Most of the old institutions which have been adopted in modern times—and they are more numerous than is generally supposed—have lost their names while retaining their substance. This one has preserved both —a very rare instance.

Upon the central government alone devolved the duty of preserving the peace in the provinces. Mounted police (*maréchaussée*) were scattered over the kingdom in small detachments, ready to act under the orders of the intendants. It was with these troops, and, in case of need, with the aid of the regular army, that the intendant met all sudden outbreaks, arrested vagabonds, repressed mendicity, crushed the riots which the price of food constantly excited. It never happened that the government was driven to call upon its subjects for assistance, as had been common enough at one time, except in cities, where there was usually a civic guard, composed of men selected and officers appointed by the intendant.

The courts had preserved and frequently exercised the right of making police regulations ; but they were only applicable to the territory within the court's jurisdiction, and not unfrequently to a single place. They were liable to rejection by the Council, and were often so rejected, especially regulations made by inferior courts. On the other hand, the Council constantly made regulations that were applicable to the whole kingdom, as well on matters beyond the authority of the courts as on those which were within the scope of that authority. These regulations, or, as they were then called, Orders in Council (*arrêts du conseil*), were immensely numerous, especially toward the period of the Revolution. It is hardly possible to mention a branch of social economy or political organization which was not remodeled by Orders in Council during the last forty years of the old regime.

In the old feudal society, the seignior's extensive rights were counterpoised by extensive obligations. He was bound to succor the indigent on his domain. A trace of this principle is to be found in the Prussian code of 1795, where it is said, "The seignior must see to it that poor peasants receive education. He should, as far as he can, procure means of subsistence for those of his vassals who own no land. If any of them fall into poverty, he is bound to aid them."

No such law had existed in France for many years. When the seignior's rights were taken from him, he shook off his obligations. No local authority, or council, or provincial, or parochial association had taken his place. The law obliged no man to take care of the poor in the rural districts; the central government boldly assumed charge of them.

Out of the proceeds of the taxes a sum was annually set apart by the Council to be distributed by the intendant in parochial charities. The needy were instructed to apply to him. In times of distress, it was he who distributed corn or rice. Annual Orders in Council directed that benevolent work-houses should be opened at places which the Orders took care to indicate; at these, indigent peasants could always obtain work at moderate wages. It need hardly be observed that charity dispensed from such a distance must often have been blind and capricious, and always inadequate.[p][q]

Not content with aiding the peasantry in times of distress, the central government undertook to teach them the art of growing rich, by giving them good advice, and occasionally by resorting to compulsory methods. With this view it distributed from time to time, by the hands of its intendants and sub-delegates, short pamphlets on agriculture, founded agricultural

societies, promised prizes, kept up at great expense
nurseries for the distribution of seeds and plants.
Some reduction of the burdens which weighed on agriculture would probably have proved more efficacious;
but this was never contemplated for a moment.

At times the Council endeavored to force prosperity
on the people, whether they would or no. Innumerable Orders compelled mechanics to make use of certain specified machinery, and to manufacture certain
specified articles ;[r] and as the intendants were not always able to see that their regulations were enforced,
inspectors-general of industry were appointed to travel
through the provinces and relieve them of the duty.

Orders were passed prohibiting the cultivation of
this or that agricultural product in lands which the
Council considered unsuited to it. Others required
that vines planted in what the Council regarded as bad
soil should be uprooted. To such an extent had the
government exchanged the duties of sovereign for those
of guardian.

CHAPTER III.

THAT WHAT IS NOW CALLED "THE GUARDIANSHIP OF THE STATE"
(TUTELLE ADMINISTRATIVE) WAS AN INSTITUTION OF THE
OLD REGIME.

MUNICIPAL liberty outlived the feudal system in France. Long after the seigniors had ceased to administer the government of the rural districts, the cities retained the right of self-government. As late as the close of the seventeenth century, several towns continued to figure as little democratic republics, with magistrates freely elected by the people. Municipal life was here still active and public; the citizens were proud of their rights and jealous of their independence.[s]

Elections were not generally abolished till 1692; after that date municipal business was transferred to offices (*mis en offices*), that is to say, the king sold to certain citizens of each town the right of governing the others forever.

This was destroying, not the freedom of the cities alone, but their prosperity also; for, though the sale of offices has often been followed by happy results in the case of judges, whose independence is the first condition of their usefulness, it has never failed to be most disastrous in every administrative branch of government, because there responsibility, subordination, and zeal are the conditions of efficiency. The government of the old monarchy made no mistake in the matter; it took good care to steer clear of the system it imposed on the towns—it never sold posts of intendant or sub-delegate.

History may well note with scorn that this great revolution was accomplished without the least political design.[t]   Louis XI. had curtailed municipal franchises because their democratic tendency frightened him; Louis XIV. abolished, though he did not fear them, for he sold them back again to all the towns which could afford to purchase.   His object, indeed, was less to destroy their liberties than to traffic in them. When he did abolish them, it was, so to speak, a mere financial experiment, and, singular to relate, the game was kept up for eighty years.   Seven times during that period did the towns purchase the right of electing their magistrates, and seven times was it taken away as soon as they had learned to appreciate its value.   The motive of the measure was never varied or concealed.   In the preamble to the edict of 1722, the king avowed that "the necessities of our finances compel us to resort to the most effective remedy." The remedy was effective enough, but it was ruinous to those upon whom this new impost was laid.   "I am struck," says an intendant to the comptroller-general in 1764, "with the enormous aggregate of the sums that have been paid from time to time for the redemption of municipal offices.   Had these sums been laid out in works of utility in each city, the citizens would have been great gainers; as it is, the offices have only been a burden."   I am at a loss to find another feature as shameful as this in the whole range of the old regime.

It seems difficult to tell precisely how towns were

governed in the eighteenth century; for not only did
the source of municipal power change continually, in
the manner just described, but each city had preserved
some shreds of its old constitution and its peculiar local customs. No two cities in France were, perhaps,
alike in every respect, though the contrasts between
them are deceptive, and conceal a general similarity.

In 1764, the Council undertook to make a general
law for the government of cities. It obtained from its
intendants reports on the municipal organization of
each town within their province. I have discovered
a portion of these reports, and a perusal has completely satisfied me that municipal matters were managed
very similarly in all. There are superficial and apparent diversities; substantially the plan was the same
every where.

In most cases, cities were governed by two assemblies. This is true of all the large cities, and of most
of the small ones.

The first assembly was composed of municipal officers, whose number varied in different localities. This
was the executive of the *commune*, the city corporation (*corps de ville*), as it used to be called. When
the city had obtained or purchased from the king its
municipal franchise, members of this assembly were
elected for a fixed term. When the king succeeded
in selling the municipal offices (which did not always
happen, for this kind of merchandise was cheapened
by each submission of the municipal to the central authority), they had a life-interest in the posts they
bought. In neither case did the municipal officers receive a salary: in both they enjoyed privileges and

exemptions from taxes. All were equal in rank; they discharged their functions collectively. No magistrate was charged with any particular supervision, authority, or responsibility. The mayor presided over the corporation, but did not administer the government of the city.

The second assembly, known as the "general assembly," elected the corporation (wherever elections were still held), and participated in the chief affairs of the city.

In the fifteenth century, the general assembly consisted of the whole population. One of the reports mentioned above observed that this usage was "in accordance with the popular sympathies of our forefathers." Municipal officers were chosen by the whole people. The people were consulted from time to time, and to them account was rendered by outgoing officials. This custom is still occasionally met with at the close of the seventeenth century.

In the eighteenth century the people no longer constituted the general assembly. That body was almost invariably representative. But it must be carefully borne in mind that it was, in no single city, elected by the people generally, or imbued with a popular spirit. It was invariably composed of *notables*, some of whom were entitled to seats in virtue of their individual station, while others were delegates from guilds and companies, and were instructed as to their course by their constituents.

With the advance of the century, the number of notables *ex officio* increases in these assemblies, while the deputies from industrial associations fall off, or disappear entirely. But deputies from guilds are still present; that is to say, mechanics are excluded to make room for burghers. But the people are not so easily duped by sham liberties as many imagine; they cease to take an interest in public affairs, and live at home as unconcernedly as if they were foreigners. In vain do the magistrates endeavor to revive that patriotism which did such wonders in the Middle Age; no one listens to them. No one takes the least thought for the most momentous interests of the city. The polls—deceitful relic of departed liberty—are there still, and the magistrates would be glad if people would vote; but they resolutely abstain. History teems with similar sights. Very few monarchs, from Augustus to our day, have failed to keep up the outward forms of freedom while they destroyed its substance, in the hope that they might combine the moral power of public approval with the peculiar conveniences of despotism. But the experiment has usually failed, and it has soon been found impossible to maintain a deceitful semblance of that which really has no existence.

In the eighteenth century, then, municipal government in cities had universally degenerated into oligarchy. A few families controlled the public affairs in favor of private interests, without the knowledge of or any responsibility to the public. The disease pervaded every municipal organization in France. It is perceived by all the intendants, but the only remedy they can suggest is the still farther subordination of local authorities to the central government.

They were already under pretty extensive subjection. Not only did the Council modify city govern-

ments generally, from time to time,[u] but not unfrequently the intendants proposed for particular cities special
laws, which the Council passed without preliminary inquiry, and often without the knowledge of the people ;
and these laws went into effect without the formality
of registration.   " This measure," said the inhabitants
of a city at which such an Order had been leveled, "has
astonished all classes ; nothing of the kind was expected."

Cities were prohibited from establishing town-dues,
or levying taxes, or hypothecating, selling, leasing, or
administering their property, or going to law, or employing their surplus funds without an order in Council first rendered on the report of the intendant.[v]   All
public works in cities were executed according to plans
and specifications approved by an order in Council.
Contracts were adjudged by the intendant or his sub-
delegates ; the state engineer usually exercised a general superintendence over all.   Those who imagine that
all we see in France is new will not read this without
surprise.

But the Council had even a larger share of the direction of city affairs than might be inferred from these
rules.   Its power was, in fact, greater than the law allowed.

I find, in a circular addressed to intendants by the
comptroller-general about the middle of last century,
the following language: " You will pay particular attention to the proceedings of municipal assemblies.   You
will require a full report of all their proceedings and
debates, and transmit the same to me with your observations thereon."

The correspondence between the intendants and their sub-delegates shows that the government had a hand in the management of all the cities in the kingdom, great and small. It was consulted on all subjects, and gave decided opinions on all; it even regulated festivals. It was the government which gave orders for public rejoicing, fireworks, and illuminations. I find it mentioned that an intendant once fined some members of the burgher guard twenty *livres* for absenting themselves from the *Te Deum*.

Municipal officers were impressed with a suitable consciousness of their nonentity. Some of them wrote their intendant, " We pray you most humbly, monseigneur, to grant us your good will and protection. We shall try to prove ourselves worthy of it by our submission to the orders of your highness." Others, who style themselves grandly " city peers," write to say that they " have never resisted your will, monseigneur."

It was thus that the burghers were being prepared for government, and the people for liberty.

If this close subjection of the cities had but preserved their financial standing! But it did nothing of the kind. It is said that, were it not for centralization, our cities would ruin themselves. How this may be, I know not; but it is quite certain that, in the eighteenth century, centralization did not save cities from ruin. The financial history of the period is full of city troubles.[w]

Let us pass from cities to villages. We shall find new authorities, new forms, but the same dependence.

I have discovered many indications that, in the Middle Ages, the people of villages formed communities apart from the seigniors. The seigniors used them, superintended, and governed them; but they owned property exclusively, elected their rulers, and administered their government on democratic principles.

This old parochial system may be traced through all the nations which were once organized on a feudal basis, even to the dependencies to which they transported their decaying laws. It is easily discernible in England. Sixty years ago it was in full vigor in Prussia, as the code of Frederick the Great is there to prove. Some vestiges of it still lingered in France in the eighteenth century.

I remember that the first time I examined the archives of an intendant's office, in order to discover what a parish really was under the old regime, I was quite struck with the discovery, in that poor enslaved community, of several features which I had noticed in the rural districts of America, and erroneously considered as peculiarities of New World institutions. Both communities were governed by functionaries acting independently of each other, and under the direction of the community at large; in neither was there a permanent representative body, or municipal assembly proper. In both, from time to time, the people at large met to elect magistrates, and transact important business. They resembled each other, in fact, as closely as a living body resembles a corpse. Nor is this a matter of surprise, for the two systems, different as their destinies were, had the same origin.

When the rural parish of the Middle Ages was removed beyond the reach of the feudal system and left uncontrolled, it became the New England township. When it was cut loose from the seignior, but crushed in the close grasp of the state in France, it became what remains to be described.

In the eighteenth century parochial officers differed in number and title in the several provinces. Old records show that when the parishes were in full vigor, the number of these officers was greater than when the stream of parochial life became sluggish. In the eighteenth century we find but two in most parishes: the collector, and another officer usually known as the syndic. Generally speaking, these officials were elected, really or nominally, but they served far more as instruments of the state than as agents of the community. Collectors levied the *taille* under the orders of the intendant. Syndics, receiving orders from day to day from the sub-delegates, acted as their deputies in all matters bearing on public order or government; such, for instance, as militia business, state works, and the execution of general laws.

It has already been observed that the seignior had no part in these details of government. He neither superintended nor assisted the officials. His real power gone, he despised contrivances used to keep up its semblance, and his pride alone forbade him to take any share in their establishment. Though he had ceased to govern, his residence in the parish and his privileges precluded the formation of a sound parochial system in the stead of that in which he had figured. Such a personage, so isolated in his independence and his privileges, could not but weaken or militate against the authority of law.

His presence drove to the cities all persons of means and information, as I shall have occasion to show hereafter. Around him lived a herd of rough, ignorant peasants, quite incapable of administering their collective business. It was Turgot who described a parish as "a collection of huts not more passive than their tenants."

The records of the eighteenth century abound with complaints of the inefficiency, the carelessness, and the ignorance of parochial collectors and syndics. Every body deplores the fact—ministers, intendants, sub-delegates, even men of rank, but nobody thinks of looking for its true cause.

Until the Revolution the government of rural parishes in France preserved some traces of that democratic aspect which characterized it during the Middle Ages. When municipal officers were to be elected, or public affairs discussed, the village bell summoned the peasantry, poor and rich alike, to the church door. There was no regular debate followed by a vote, but all were free to express their views, and a notary, officiating in the open air, noted, in a formal report, the substance of what was said.

The contrast between these empty semblances of liberty and the real impotence which they concealed furnishes a slight indication of the ease with which the most absolute government may adopt some of the forms of a radical democracy, and aggravate oppression by placing the oppressed under the ridiculous imputation of not being aware of their real state. The democratic parish meeting was free to express its wishes, but it was as powerless to enforce them as the municipal councils of cities; nor could it utter a word till its mouth had been opened by authority. No meeting could be convened until permission had been obtained in express terms from the intendant: this granted, the villagers, who called things by their right names, met "by his good will and pleasure." No meeting, however unanimous, could impose a tax, or sell or buy, or lease, or go to law, without permission from the Royal Council. The church which a storm had unroofed, or the presbytery wall which was falling to pieces, could not be repaired without a decree of Council. This rule applied with equal force to all parishes, however distant from the capital. I have seen a petition from a parish to the council praying to be allowed to spend twenty-five *livres*.

In general, the parishioners were still entitled to elect magistrates by universal suffrage; but the intendant frequently took pains to recommend a candidate, who never failed to obtain the votes of the small electoral body. Again, he would occasionally declare of his own authority that an election just held was null and void, would appoint a collector and syndic, and temporarily disfranchise the community. Of this course I have noticed a thousand examples.

No more wretched station than that of these parochial functionaries can be conceived. They were subject to the whim of the lowest agent of the central government, the sub-delegate. He would fine or imprison them, and they could lay no claim to the usual guarantees of the subject against arbitrary oppression. An intendant wrote in 1750, "I have imprisoned a few of the principal grumblers, and made the community pay the expense of sending for the police. By these measures I have checkmated them without difficulty." Naturally enough, under these circumstances, parochial office, instead of being an honor, became a burden from which all sought to escape.

Yet still, these last traces of the old parochial system were dear to the peasant's heart. To this very day that system is the only branch of government which he thoroughly understands and cares for. Men who cheerfully see the whole nation submit to a master, rebel at the bare idea of not being consulted in the government of their village. So pregnant with weight are hollow forms!

The remarks I have made upon cities and villages apply also to almost every corporate body which had a separate existence and corporate property.

Under the old regime, as in our own day, neither city, nor borough, nor village, nor hamlet, however small, nor hospital, nor church, nor convent,ˣ nor college, could exercise a free will in its private affairs, or administer its property as it thought best. Then, as now, the administration was the guardian of the whole French people; insolence had not yet invented the name, but the thing was already in existence.

CHAPTER IV.

THAT ADMINISTRATIVE TRIBUNALS (LA JUSTICE ADMINISTRA-
TIVE) AND OFFICIAL IRRESPONSIBILITY (GARANTIE DES FONC-
TIONNAIRES) WERE INSTITUTIONS OF THE OLD REGIME.

IN no country in Europe were the courts more independent of the government than in France; nor
was there any in which more abnormal tribunals existed. The one involved a necessity for the other.
Judges whose position was beyond the king's reach,
whom he could neither dismiss, nor displace, nor promote, and over whom he had no hold either by ambition or by fear, soon proved inconvenient. That led
to the denial of their jurisdiction over cases to which
the administration was a party, and to the establishment of another class of courts, less independent, which
presented to the subject's eye a semblance of justice,
without involving, for the monarch, any risk of its
reality.

In countries like Germany, where the judges were
never as independent of the government as they were
in France at this time, no such precaution was ever
taken, and no administrative tribunals ever established.
The monarch held the common courts in such subjection that he did not need extraordinary ones.

Very few of the royal edicts and declarations, or of
the Orders in Council, issued during the last century
of the old monarchy, were unprovided with a clause
stating that all disputes that might arise, and lawsuits

that might grow out of them, must be referred to the intendants and to the Council. The ordinary form of words was, "His majesty ordains that all disputes which may arise concerning the execution of the present decree, its accessories and corollaries, shall be tried before the intendant, and decided by him, subject to appeal to the Council. We forbid our courts and tribunals to take cognizance of any such disputes."

In cases arising out of laws or old customs which made no similar provision, the Council constantly intervened by process of evocation, and took the suit out of the hands of the common judges to bring it before itself. The Council registers are full of such decrees of evocation. Frequently they gave to the practice the force of theory. A maxim, not of law, took root in the public mind to the effect that suits, in which state interests were involved, or which turned on the interpretation of a law, were not within the jurisdiction of ordinary courts, and that these latter were restricted to the decision of cases between private individuals. We have embodied this idea in a set form, but its substance belongs to the old regime.

In those days, the intendant and Council were the only court that could try cases growing out of questions of taxation. They alone were competent to decide suits concerning common carriers and passenger vehicles, public highways, canals, river navigation, and generally all matters in which the public interest was concerned.

Nothing was left undone by the intendants to extend their jurisdiction. Representations to the comptroller-general, and sharp hints to the Council, were incessant. One of the reasons assigned by a magistrate of this rank for issuing a writ of evocation is worth preserving. " Ordinary judges," says he, "are bound by rule to repress illegal acts ; but the Council can always overstep rules for a salutary purpose."

This principle often led intendants and Council to assume jurisdiction over cases whose connection with the administration was so slight as to be invisible, and even over cases which had obviously no connection with it at all. A gentleman went to law with his neighbor. Dissatisfied with the tone of the court, he begged the Council to evoke the case. The intendant, to whom it was referred, reported that, " though the interests involved were wholly of a private nature, his majesty could always, if he chose, take cognizance of all classes of suits, without rendering account of his motives to any one."

Individuals arrested for riot were usually tried on evocation before the intendant or the Provost of Police (*prévôt de la maréchaussée*). In times of scarcity, evocations of this kind were common, and the intendants appointed several "graduates" to assist them in their duties. They formed a sort of prefect's council, with criminal jurisdiction. I have seen sentences rendered by these bodies condemning culprits to the galleys and to the scaffold. At the close of the seventeenth century, criminal jurisdiction was still frequently exercised by intendants.

Modern legists assure us that we have made great progress in administrative law since the Revolution. They tell us that " before that event the powers of the judiciary and those of the administration were intermingled and confused, but that since then they have been severed, and a line drawn between them." A right appreciation of the progress here mentioned can only be formed when it is well borne in mind that if the judiciary under the old regime occasionally overstepped its natural sphere, it never filled the whole of that sphere. Both of these facts must be remembered, or a false and incomplete view will be taken of the subject. True, the courts were allowed to travel out of their sphere to make laws on certain subjects for the government of the public; but, on the other hand, they were denied cognizance of legitimate lawsuits, and thus excluded from a part of their proper domain. We have stripped the courts of the right of intruding into the administration of government, which they very improperly possessed under the old regime, but we have continued to suffer the government to intrude into the courts of law; yet it is even more dangerous for the government than for the judiciary to transcend its scope; for the interference of the latter in the administration of government only injures the public business, whereas the interference of government in the administration of justice tends to deprave the public mind, and to render men servile and revolutionary at one and the same time.

In one of the nine or ten constitutions which have been established in France within the last sixty years, and designed to last forever, an article was inserted declaring that no government official could be prosecuted before the common courts until permission had been obtained from the executive. The idea seemed so happy that, when the constitution was destroyed, the article in question was rescued from destruction, and has ever since been carefully sheltered from revolution. Officials commonly allude to the privilege secured to them by this article as one of the great triumphs of 1789, but here again they are in error. The old monarchy was quite as solicitous as more modern governments to protect its servants from responsibility to the courts, like mere citizens. Between the two eras the only substantial difference is this : before the Revolution government could not come to the rescue of its agents without having recourse to arbitrary and illegal measures ; since then it has been legally authorized to let them violate the law.

When, under the old regime, an agent of the central government was prosecuted before any of the ordinary courts, an Order in Council usually forbade the judges to proceed with the case, and referred it to commissioners named in the order. The ground for the proceeding was, according to the opinion of a councilor of that day, because the ordinary judges were sure to be biased against a government official, and thus the king's government was likely to be brought into contempt. Cases of evocation were not rare occurrences. They took place daily, and the lowest officials were as often protected by them as the highest. The most slender connection with government secured immunity from all authorities, save the Council only. A farmer liable to *corvées* prosecuted an overseer of the Bridge and Road department for having maltreated him. The Council evoked the case. The chief engineer reported confidentially to the intendant that " the overseer was no doubt much to blame, but that

was no reason why the case should be allowed to take
its course.   It is of the highest importance to the department of Bridges and Roads that the ordinary courts
should not take cognizance of complaints against the
overseers made by workmen bound to service, for if
they did, the works would soon be brought to a stand
by the lawsuits which the public dislike of these officials would excite."

On another occasion, a state contractor had taken
from a neighboring field materials which he required,
and used them.   The intendant himself wrote to the
comptroller-general, "I can not lay sufficient stress on
the injury the government would incur if contractors
were left at the mercy of the ordinary courts, for their
principles are wholly at variance with those by which
the administration is guided."

A century has elapsed since these lines were written, and yet these public officers would pass for contemporaries of our own.

CHAPTER V.

HOW CENTRALIZATION CREPT IN AMONG THE OLD AUTHORITIES, AND
SUPPLANTED WITHOUT DESTROYING THEM.

LET us briefly recapitulate the points established
in the three preceding chapters.

A single body, placed in the centre of the kingdom,
administering government throughout the country; a
single minister managing nearly all the business of the
interior; a single agent directing the details in each
province; no secondary administrative bodies, or authorities competent to act without permission: special
tribunals to hear cases in which government is concerned, and shield its agents. What is this but the
same centralization with which we are acquainted?
As compared with ours, its forms are less sharply
marked, its mode of action less regular, its existence
less tranquil; but the system is the same. Nothing
has been added, nothing taken away from the old plan;
when the surrounding edifices were pulled down, it
stood precisely as we see it.

Frequent imitations of the institutions I have just
described have since made their appearance in various
places,ʸ but they were then peculiar to France. We
shall see presently how great an influence they exercised over the French Revolution and its sequel.

But how did these modern institutions find place
among the ruins of the old feudal society?

By patient, adroit, persevering labor, rather than by

violent arbitrary effort.   At the outbreak of the Revolution, the old administrative system of France was
still standing, but a new system had been built up inside it.

There is no reason for believing that this difficult
exploit was the fruit of a deep scheme laid by the old
government.   On the contrary, it appears to have been
accomplished almost unconsciously, instinct teaching
the government and its various agents to acquire as
much control as possible.   The old officials were left
in possession of their titles and their honors, but stripped of their power.   They were led, not driven out of
their domain.   The idleness of one, the selfishness of
another, the vices of all, were skillfully turned to account.   No attempt was made to convert them, but
one and all were quietly replaced by the intendant,
whose name had never even been heard at the time
they were born.

The only obstacle in the way of the change was in
the judiciary department; but there, as elsewhere, the
government had contrived to seize the substance, leaving its rivals the outward show of power.   It did not
exclude the Parliaments from administrative business,
but it gradually absorbed their duties till there was
nothing for them to do.[z] On some few rare occasions,
as, for example, in times of scarcity, when popular ex-
citements tempted the ambition of magistrates, it allowed the Parliaments to exercise administrative authority for a brief interval, and let them make a noise
which has often found an echo in history ; but it soon
silently resumed its functions, and discreetly assumed
sole control of men and things.

A close study of the struggles of the Parliaments against the power of the king will lead to the discovery that they were invariably on political issues, and never on points of administration. Quarrels usually began on the creation of new taxes — that is to say, the belligerents contended for legislative authority, to which neither had any claim, and not for administrative power.

This becomes more apparent as we approach the revolutionary era. As the people's feelings become inflamed, the Parliament mixes more in politics; and simultaneously, the central government and its agents, with skill enhanced by experience, usurp more administrative power. The Parliament grows daily less like an administration, and more like a tribune.

Day after day, the central government conquers new fields of action into which these bodies can not follow it. Novelties arise, pregnant with cases for which no precedents can be found in parliamentary routine: society, in a fever of activity, creates new demands, which the government alone can satisfy, and each of which swells its authority; for the sphere of all other administrative bodies is defined and fixed; that of the government alone is movable, and spreads with the extension of civilization.

Impending revolution unsettles the mind of the French, and suggests a host of new ideas which the central government alone can realize: it is developed before it perishes. Like every thing else, it is brought to perfection, as is singularly proved by its archives. There is no resemblance between the comptroller-general and the intendant of 1780 and the like officials in

1740: the system has been transformed. The agents are the same, but their spirit is different. Time, while it extends and exercises the power of the government, imparts to it new skill and regularity. Its latest usurpations are marked by unusual forbearance; it rules more imperatively, but it is far less oppressive.

This great institution of the monarchy was thrown down by the first blow of the Revolution: it was raised anew in 1800. It is not true that the principles of government which were then adopted were those of 1789, as so many persons have asserted; they were those of the old monarchy, which were restored, and have remained in force ever since.

If it be asked how this portion of the old regime could be bodily transplanted into and incorporated with the new social system, I reply that centralization was not abolished by the Revolution, because it was, in fact, its preliminary and precursor; and I may add, that when a nation abolishes aristocracy, centralization follows as a matter of course. It is much harder to prevent its establishment than to hasten it. Every thing tends toward unity of power, and it requires no small contrivance to maintain divisions of authority.

It was natural, then, that the democratic Revolution, while it destroyed so many of the institutions of the old regime, should retain this one. Nor was centralization so out of place in the social order created by the Revolution that it could not easily be mistaken for one of its fruits.

CHAPTER VI.

OF OFFICIAL MANNERS AND CUSTOMS UNDER THE OLD REGIME.

IT is impossible to read the correspondence of intendants of the old regime with their superiors without being struck with the resemblance between the officials of that day and those of our own. Like institutions produced like men; across the Revolutionary gulf which divides them they appear hand in hand. As much may be said of the people governed. Never was the power of legislation to shape men's minds more powerfully illustrated.

Already in those days ministers were seized with a mania for seeing with their own eyes the details of every thing, and managing every thing at Paris. The mania increased with time and practice. Toward the close of the eighteenth century, a work-house could not be established in any corner of a distant province but the comptroller must insist on overseeing its expenditure, providing it with rules, choosing its site. If a poor-house were founded, the same minister required to know the names of all paupers relieved, their exits and their entrances. Before the middle of the century, in 1733, M. D'Argenson wrote, "Ministers are overloaded with business details. Every thing is done by them and through them, and if their information be not coextensive with their power, they are forced to let their clerks act as they please, and become the real masters of the country."

Comptrollers-general were not content with business reports ; they insisted on minute information about individuals.   Intendants expected the same from their sub-delegates, and rarely failed to repeat, word for word, in their reports, what these subordinates stated in theirs, as though they were stating matters within their own knowledge.

A very extensive machinery was requisite before the government could know every thing and manage every thing at Paris.   The amount of documents filed was enormous, and the slowness with which public business was transacted such that I have been unable to discover any case in which a village obtained permission to raise its church steeple or repair its presbytery in less than a year.   Generally speaking, two or three years elapsed before such petitions were granted.

The Council itself confessed, in a decree of 29th March, 1773, that " administrative forms cause infinite delays, and frequently give rise to very just complaints ; yet these forms are all necessary."

I was under the impression that a taste for statistics was peculiar to the government officials of our own day : this I find to be an error.   Toward the close of the old regime, printed forms were constantly sent to the intendant, who sent them on to his sub-delegates, who sent them on to the syndics, who filled the blanks. The subjects on which the comptroller thus sought information were the character of lands and of their cultivation, the kind and quantity of produce raised, the number of cattle, and the customs of the people.   Information thus obtained was fully as minute and as reliable as that which sub-prefects and mayors furnish in our own day. Sub-delegates seem, from these tabular reports, to have formed in general an unfavorable judgment upon the character of the people. They reiterate the opinion that "the peasant is naturally idle, and would not work if he could live without it." That economical doctrine appears to be very generally received among these government officials.

Nor is the official style of the two periods less strikingly similar. Official writers then, as now, affected a colorless, smooth, vague, diffuse style; each writer merged his identity in the general mediocrity of the body to which he belonged. Read a prefect, you have read an intendant.

When, toward the close of the century, the peculiarities of Diderot and Rousseau spread into the language of the day, the affected sensibility of these writers was adopted by the officials and even by state financiers. Official style, usually dry enough, then became unctuous and even tender. A sub-delegate complained to the intendant of Paris that his "feelings were so sensitive that he could not discharge the duties of his office without moments of poignant grief."

The government distributed, as it still does, certain sums in charity in each parish, on condition that the parishioners raised something on their side for the same purpose. When the sum raised by them was sufficient, the comptroller made a memorandum on the margin of the scheme of distribution, " Good—express satisfaction ;" but when it was considerable, he wrote, " Good—express satisfaction and sensibility."

Government officials, none of whom were of noble descent, already formed a class apart, with feelings, traditions, virtues, and notions of honor and dignity all their own. They constituted the aristocracy of the new society, ready to take their rank as soon as the Revolution had cleared the way.

A marked characteristic of the French government, even in those days, was the hatred it bore to every one, whether noble or not, who presumed to meddle with public affairs without its knowledge. It took fright at the organization of the least public body which ventured to exist without permission. It was disturbed by the formation of any free society. It could brook no association but such as it had arbitrarily formed, and over which it presided. Even manufacturing companies displeased it. In a word, it objected to people looking after their own concerns, and preferred general inertia to rivalry. Still, as the French could not exist without some sort of liberty, they were permitted to discuss as freely as they chose all sorts of general and abstract theories on religion, philosophy, morals, and even politics. Provided its agents were not meddled with, the government had no objection to attacks on the fundamental principles of society, and even on the existence of a God. Officials fancied these were no concerns of theirs.

Though the newspapers of those days, or, as they were usually called, the gazettes, contained more poetry than politics, they were none the less viewed with a jealous eye by the government. Careless about books, it was very strict with regard to journals, and being unable to suppress them, it undertook to make them a government monopoly. A circular, dated 1761, which I have seen, announced to all the intendants in the kingdom that the *Gazette de France* would be thereafter composed under the eye of the king (Louis XV.), "his majesty desiring to render it interesting and superior to all others. You will, therefore," continues the circular, "have the goodness to let me have a report of all events of interest within your province, especially such as bear upon natural philosophy and natural history, together with other singular and striking occurrences." To the circular was attached a prospectus of the *Gazette*, informing the public that, though it appeared oftener and contained more matter than its rival, its subscription price would be considerably less.

Armed with these documents, an intendant applied to his sub-delegates for information, but the latter replied that they had none to give. Then came a second letter from the minister, complaining bitterly of the dearth of news from the province in question, and winding up with, "His majesty commands me to say to you that it is his will that you give your serious attention to this affair, and issue the strictest orders to your subordinates." Under the pressure, the sub-delegates did their best. One reported that a salt-smuggler had been hanged, and had displayed great courage; another, that a woman in his neighborhood had been delivered of three girls at one birth; a third, that a terrible storm had taken place, but, happily, had done no mischief. A fourth declared that he had not been able, notwithstanding great exertions, to discover any news of interest, but that he took pleasure in subscribing personally to so useful a gazette, and would recommend all his neighbors to do the like. Still, these remarkable efforts seem to have produced inadequate results, for it appears from a fresh letter that "the king, who has graciously deigned to give his attention to the best means of perfecting the *Gazette*, and wishes to secure for this journal the superiority and fame which it deserves, has expressed much dissatisfaction at the manner in which his desires have been seconded."

History, it is easily perceived, is a picture-gallery containing a host of copies and very few originals.

It must be admitted, however, that the central government of France never followed the example of those southern governments which seem to have sought to be despotic only in order to blight their realms. The former was always active, and often intelligently so. Its activity was often fruitless and even mischievous, however, because it essayed to achieve feats beyond its reach, and even impossibilities.

It seldom undertook, or soon abandoned projects of useful reform which demanded perseverance and energy, but it was incessantly engaged in altering the laws. Repose was never known in its domain. New rules followed each other with such bewildering rapidity that its agents never knew which to obey of the multifarious commands they received. Municipal officers complained to the comptroller-general of the extreme instability of the minor laws. "The financial regulations alone," say they, "vary so constantly that it would require the whole time of a municipal officer, holding office for life, to acquire a knowledge of the new regulations as they appear from time to time."

When the substance of the laws was allowed to remain the same, their execution was varied. Those who have not studied the actual working of the old regime in the official records it left behind can form no idea of the contempt into which the laws fall, even in the minds of their administrators, when there are no political meetings or newspapers to check the capricious activity and set bounds to the arbitrary tendencies of government officials.

Very few Orders in Council omitted to repeal former and frequently quite recent enactments, which, though quite regular, had never been carried into effect. No edict, or royal declaration, or registered letters patent was strictly carried out in practice. The correspondence of the comptrollers-general and the intendants shows plainly that the government was constantly in the habit of tolerating exceptions to its rules. It rarely broke the law, but it daily bent it to either side, to suit particular cases or facilitate the transaction of business.

An intendant wrote to the minister, in reference to an application of a state contractor to be relieved from paying town dues, "It is certain that, according to the strict letter of the laws I have cited, no one can claim exemption from these dues, but all who are acquainted with business are aware that these sweeping provisions, like the penalties they impose, though contained in most of the edicts, declarations, and decrees establishing taxes, were not intended to be literally construed, or to exclude exceptional cases."

These words contain the whole principle of the old regime. Strict rules, loosely enforced—such was its characteristic.

To attempt to form an opinion of the age from its laws would lead to the most ridiculous errors. A royal declaration of 1757 condemned to death all writers or printers of works assailing religion or government. Booksellers in whose shops they were found, peddlers who hawked them, were liable to the same penalties. Was this the age of Saint Dominic? No, it was exactly the period of Voltaire's reign.

Complaints are heard that Frenchmen show contempt for law. Alas! when could they have learned to respect it? It may be broadly said that, among the men of the old regime, the place in the mind which should have been occupied by the idea of law was vacant. Petitioners begged that established rules might be departed from in their case as seriously and as earnestly as if they had been insisting on the honest execution of the law; nor were they ever referred to the law unless government intended to give them a rebuff. Custom, rather than volition, still inculcated submission to authority on the part of the people; but whenever they did break loose, the least excitement gave rise to violent acts, which were themselves met, not by the law, but by violence on the other side, and arbitrary stretches of power.

Though the central power had not acquired in the eighteenth century the strong and healthy constitution it has since possessed, it had, notwithstanding, so thoroughly destroyed all intermediate authorities, and left so wide a vacant space between itself and the public, that it already appeared to be the mainspring of the social machine, the sole source of national life.

Nothing proves this more thoroughly than the writings of its assailants. During the period of uneasiness which preceded the Revolution, a host of schemes for new forms of society and government were brought to light. These schemes sought various ends, but the means by which they were to be reached were invariably identical. All the schemers wanted to use the central power for the destruction of the existing system, and the substitution of their new plan in its stead: that power alone seemed to them capable of accomplishing so great a task. They all assumed that the rights and powers of the state ought to be unlimited, and that the only thing needed was to persuade it to use them aright. Mirabeau the father, whose aristocratic prejudices led him to denominate the intendants intruders, and to declare that if the government had the sole right of appointing magistrates, the courts of justice would soon be mere " bands of commissioners," relied on the central power alone for the realization of his chimerical plans.

Nor were these notions confined to books ; they pervaded men's minds, gave a color to society and social habits, and were conspicuous in every transaction of every-day life.

Nobody expected to succeed in any enterprise unless the state helped him. Farmers, who, as a class, are generally stubborn and indocile, were led to believe that the backwardness of agriculture was due to the lack of advice and aid from the government. A letter from one of them, somewhat revolutionary in tone, inquired of the intendant " why the government did not appoint inspectors to travel once a year through the provinces, and examine the state of agriculture throughout the kingdom? Such officers would teach farmers what to plant, what to do with their cattle, how to fatten, raise, and sell them, and where to send them to market. They would, of course, be paid officials. Some honorary distinction should be conferred on successful agriculturists."

Inspectors and honorary distinctions! These are the last encouragements a Suffolk farmer would have thought of expecting.

The masses were quite satisfied that the government alone could preserve the public peace. The mounted police alone commanded the respect of the rich, and inspired terror among the people. Both viewed that force rather as the incarnation of public order than as one of its chief instruments. The provincial assembly of Guienne observed that "every one has noticed how quickly the sight of a mounted policeman will subdue the most riotous mob." And every body wanted, accordingly, to have a troop of them at his door.[a] Petitions to that effect overloaded the registers of the intendants: no one seemed to suspect that the protector might be a master in disguise.

Nothing astonished the exiles who fled to England so much as the absence of any such force there. Some express surprise, others contempt at the phenomenon. A man of some merit, but who had not been taught to expect such a contrast, exclaimed, "It is positively true that an Englishman congratulates himself on being robbed, with the reflection that, at all events, there are no mounted police in his country. An Englishman is sorry to see riots, but when rioters escape scot free into the bosom of society, he consoles himself with

the remark that the law must be observed to the letter, at whatever cost. These false notions, however,
are not universally adopted. There are wise men who
think differently, and their view must ultimately prevail."

He never dreamed that these eccentricities of the
English might possibly have some connection with
their liberties. He accounted for them on scientific
principles. "In countries where a damp climate and
a want of elasticity in the air gives a gloomy cast to
the character of the people, serious subjects are sure to
be popular. Hence it is that the English are naturally inclined to busy themselves about their government,
while the French are not."

Government having assumed the place of Providence, people naturally invoked its aid for their private
wants. Heaps of petitions were received from persons
who wanted their petty private ends served, always for
the public good.[b] The chests which contained them
were, perhaps, the only spot where all classes of society under the old regime freely intermingled. Sad reading, this: farmers begging to be reimbursed the value
of lost cattle or horses; men in easy circumstances
begging a loan to enable them to work their land to
more advantage; manufacturers begging for monopolies to crush out competition; business men confiding
their pecuniary embarrassments to the intendant, and
begging for assistance or a loan. It would appear that
the public funds were liable to be used in this way.

Men of rank were not unfrequent applicants for favors. They might be recognized by the lofty tone in
which they begged. They came to solicit from the in-

tendant delays in which to pay their share of the land-tax, which was their chief burden; or they asked that it be remitted altogether. I have read a great number of petitions of this kind from noblemen, some of very high degree; the ground alleged is usually the inadequacy of the petitioner's income, or his pecuniary straits. Men of rank always addressed intendants simply "Sir;" on these occasions they addressed him "*Monseigneur,*" as every body else did.

Pride and poverty are often amusingly combined in these petitions. One reads as follows: "Your warm heart can never surely insist on the payment of a strict twentieth by a man of my rank, as you might with men of the common sort."

In times of scarcity, which recurred frequently during the eighteenth century, the people of each province flew to the intendant, and seemed to expect food from him as a matter of course.[c] The act was redeemed by wholesale denunciations of the government. All the sufferings of the people were laid to its charge; it was loudly blamed for the severity of the weather.

Let no one again express surprise at the wonderful ease with which centralization was re-established in France at the beginning of this century. It had been overthrown by the men of 1789; but its foundations were deep in the minds of its very destroyers, and upon these it was rebuilt anew stronger than ever.

CHAPTER VII.

HOW THE CAPITAL OF FRANCE HAD ACQUIRED MORE PREPONDER-
ANCE OVER THE PROVINCES, AND USURPED MORE CONTROL OVER
THE NATION, THAN ANY OTHER CAPITAL IN EUROPE.

IT is not situation, or size, or wealth which makes some capital cities rule the countries in which they stand; that phenomenon is caused by the prevailing form of government.

London, which is as populous as many a kingdom, has, up to this time, exercised no sovereign control over Great Britain.

No citizen of the United States ever supposes that New York could decide the fate of the American Union, nor does any citizen of the State of New York fancy that that city could even direct state affairs at will; yet New York contains as many inhabitants to-day as Paris did when the Revolution broke out.

Moreover, Paris bore to the rest of the kingdom the same proportion, so far as population was concerned, during the religious wars as it did in 1789; yet it was powerless at the former period. At the time of the Fronde, Paris was nothing more than the largest French city; in 1789 it was France.

In 1740 Montesquieu wrote to a friend, "France is nothing but Paris and a few distant provinces which Paris has not yet had time to swallow up." In 1750 the Marquis de Mirabeau, a man of chimerical views, but occasionally profound in his way, said of Paris without naming it, "Capitals are necessities, but if the head grow too large, the body becomes apoplectic and wastes away. What will the consequence be if, by drawing all the talent of the kingdom to this metropolis, and leaving to the provincials no chance of reward or motive for ambition, the latter are placed in a sort of quasi dependence, and converted into an inferior class of citizens?" He adds that this process is effecting a silent revolution by depopulating the provinces of their notables, leading men, and men of ability.

The foregoing chapters have explained pretty fully the causes of this phenomenon; the reader's patience may be spared their repetition here.

The Revolution did not escape the notice of government, but it only viewed the fact in its bearing on the capital, whose rapid increase seemed to presage increased difficulties of administration. Numerous royal ordinances, especially in the seventeenth and eighteenth centuries, endeavored to check its growth. The monarchy steadily concentrated in Paris all the national life of France, and yet desired to see Paris remain small. People were forbidden to build new houses, or were bound to build them in the most costly manner, in the worst localities. But each successive ordinance admitted that, notwithstanding its predecessors, Paris had increased steadily. Six times did Louis XIV. exert his omnipotent will to check the expansion of the city, but each effort was a failure; the capital expanded in spite of decrees. Its power swelled even more rapidly than its volume, which was due less to its own exertions than to events beyond its walls.

For, simultaneously with its extension, the local

franchises of the rural districts were fading away, all symptoms of independent vigor were vanishing, provincial characteristics were being effaced, the last flicker of the old national life was dying out. Not that the nation was growing sluggish ; on the contrary, it never knew a more active time ; but the only mainspring of movement was at Paris. One illustration, chosen out of a thousand, may make this plainer. I find reports to the minister on the book business, in which it is stated that, during the sixteenth and at the beginning of the seventeenth century, there were large printing-offices in many provincial cities, but that now there are no printers to be found, and no work to be done. Yet it is not to be questioned but there were far more books printed at the close of the eighteenth century than during the sixteenth. The secret is, simply, that mind had ceased to radiate from any point but the centre ; Paris had swallowed up the provinces.

This preliminary revolution was fully accomplished before the French Revolution broke out.

The famous traveler, Arthur Young, left Paris a few days after the assembling of the States-General, and before the capture of the Bastille ; he was struck with the contrast between city and country. In Paris, all was activity and noise ; political pamphlets appeared in such quantities that ninety-two were counted in one week. "I never saw such a fever of publishing," said he, "even at London." Outside of Paris he could find nothing but inertia and silence ; no pamphlets, and but few journals. The provinces were roused and ready to move, but not to take the initiative ; when the people met, it was to hear the news from Paris. Young ask-

ed the people of each city what they purposed doing.
"Their answer was always the same, 'We are but a
provincial city; you must go and see what they are
going to do at Paris.' These people," he adds, "dare
not hold an opinion till they know how it is received
at Paris."

Surprise has been expressed at the remarkable ease
with which the *Constituante* assembly destroyed at a
blow provinces in some cases older than the monarchy,
and parceled out the kingdom into eighty-three distinct sections, as if it had been virgin soil in the New
World. Europe was not prepared for any such act,
and viewed it with surprise and horror. "This is the
first time," said Burke, "that men have so barbarous-
ly torn their country to pieces." It did look as though
they had torn living bodies, but in reality they had only
dismembered corpses.

At the very time that Paris was becoming all-powerful, another noteworthy change was taking place within its borders. It had long been a city of trade, business, and pleasure; it now became an industrial and
manufacturing city. This change gave it a new and
formidable character.

It had long been inevitable. Even in the Middle
Ages Paris had been the most industrious, as it was
the largest city of the kingdom; latterly, the distance
between it and its rivals had increased. Arts and industrial energy followed the government. As Paris
became more and more the arbiter of taste, the only
centre of power and of art, the focus of national activity, the manufacturing life of the country gradually
concentrated itself there.

Though I place, in general, but little reliance on the statistical tables of the old regime, I believe it may be safely asserted that during the sixty years which preceded the French Revolution, the number of workmen at Paris was more than doubled, though the whole population of the city during the same period only increased one third.

Independently of these general causes, peculiar motives attracted mechanics from all parts of France to Paris; and when they came, they lived mostly together, and ultimately monopolized whole wards. The burdens laid on mechanics by the fiscal policy of the government were lighter at Paris than in the provinces; nor was it so easy any where as there to obtain the freedom of a trade-company. Residents of the suburbs of Saint Antoine and of the Temple enjoyed peculiar privileges in this respect. Louis XVI. enlarged still further the prerogatives of the Saint Antoine suburb, in the design of collecting an immense number of operatives there, or, as that unfortunate monarch phrased it, "being desirous of showing a new mark of our favor to the workmen of the Saint Antoine suburb, and relieving them from burdens which are alike injurious to their interests and to the freedom of trade."

Toward the period of the Revolution the number of factories, manufactures, and blast-furnaces had become so great at Paris as to alarm the government. Industrial progress had aroused strange fears in the mind of officials. A decree of council in 1782 declares that "the king, fearing lest the rapid increase of factories should lead to so large a consumption of firewood as to deprive the city of its proper supply, prohibits the establishment of new works of this kind within fifteen leagues of the capital." No one suspected the real danger to be apprehended from the agglomeration of workmen.

It was thus that Paris became the mistress of France, and thus that the army that was to master Paris was mustered.

It is generally admitted nowadays, I believe, that administrative centralization and the omnipotence of Paris have had much to do with the fall of the various governments we have had during the last forty years. I shall have but little difficulty in proving that the ruin of the old monarchy was in a great measure due to the same causes, and that they exercised no small influence in bringing about that revolution which was the parent of all the others.

CHAPTER VIII.

THAT FRENCHMEN HAD GROWN MORE LIKE EACH OTHER THAN ANY OTHER PEOPLE.

THE careful student of the old regime in France soon meets with two apparently contradictory facts.

It appears that every body in the upper and middle classes of society, the only classes which are heard of, is exactly like his neighbor.

At the same time, this homogeneous mass is split into an immense multitude of small bodies, and each body contains an exclusive set, which takes no concern for any interests but its own.

When I think of these infinite subdivisions, and the want of union and sympathy they must have produced, I begin to understand how a great revolution could overthrow such a society, from top to bottom, in a moment. The shock must have leveled, at a blow, all party walls, and left behind it the most compact and homogeneous social body ever seen in the world.

I have already described how provincial peculiarities had gradually worn off. That change tended powerfully to assimilate the French people. National unity loomed through the surviving distinctions of rank. The laws were uniform. As the eighteenth century advanced, the number of edicts, declarations, and Orders in Council, which applied the same rules with equal force to all parts of the kingdom, became larger

and larger.   Subjects as well as rulers entertained
ideas of a general uniform system of legislation that
should bear equally on all : this was a prominent feature in all the schemes of reform which saw the light
during the thirty years preceding the Revolution.   Two
centuries before, the basis for such schemes may be said
to have been wanting.

Not only had all the provinces grown like each other, but the men also.   A marked resemblance began
to exist between men of all ranks and stations ; or, at
all events, among those who were not comprised in the
class known as " the people."

This is clearly shown in the *cahiers* of the various
classes presented in 1789.   Their authors had evidently different interests to serve, but in all other respects
they were alike.

At former meetings of the States-General, on the contrary, the interests of the middle classes were common
to the nobility, their aims were the same, their intercourse free from antagonism ; but they seemed to be
two distinct races.

Time had maintained and occasionally aggravated
the privileges which kept them apart, but in all other
respects it had singularly labored to produce a resemblance between them.

The impoverishment of the nobility had gone on
steadily for several centuries.   A man of rank observed sadly in 1755, " Notwithstanding their privileges, the nobility are falling daily deeper into difficulties and destruction, while the Third Estate inherits
their fortunes."   No change had been made in the
laws which protected the property of the aristocracy,

or in their economical condition. Yet they grew poorer every where as they lost their power.

One is almost inclined to fancy that human institutions, like the human body, contain, besides the particular organs appointed to perform specific functions, a central hidden force which is the vital principle. When this force is subdued, though the organs seem to act as usual, the whole machine languishes and dies. The French nobility still retained the use of entails (which, according to Burke, were more frequent and more binding in France than in England), laws of primogeniture, irredeemable ground-rents, and, generally, the beneficial rights they derived from feudal customs; they had been released from military service, but paid fewer taxes than ever, thus getting rid of the burden while they retained the privilege. They enjoyed, moreover, many other pecuniary advantages which their fathers had never had, and yet they grew poorer gradually as they mixed less in the theory and practice of government. It was their poverty which mainly led to the extensive subdivision of landed property that has already been noted.[d] Men of rank sold their land piecemeal to the peasantry, reserving nothing but seigniorial rents, which furnished a nominal, not a substantial competency. Several French provinces, such as Limousin, which Turgot describes, were full of petty impoverished noblemen, who had no land left, and who lived on the produce of seigniorial rights and ground-rents.

"In this province," said an intendant, "at the beginning of the century, there were several thousand noble families, but not fifteen out of the whole number had an income of twenty thousand livres." I find a memorandum addressed by the intendant of Franche-Comté to his successor in 1750, in which it is said that "the nobility of this section of country are of high rank, but very poor, and as proud as they are poor. The contrast between their former and their present condition is humiliating. It is a very good plan to keep them poor, in order that they shall need our aid and serve our purposes. They have formed," he adds, "a society into which no one can obtain admission unless he can prove four quarterings. It is not incorporated by letters patent; but it is tolerated, as it meets but once a year, and in the presence of the intendant. These noblemen hear mass and dine together, after which they return home, some on their Rosinantes, some on foot. You will enjoy this comical assembly."

All over the Continent, in the countries where the feudal system was being displaced and no new aristocracy founded, as was the case in France, the nobility were relapsing into poverty. Their decline was peculiarly marked among the German nations bordering on the Rhine. England alone presented a contrast. There the old noble families had not only kept, but largely increased their fortunes, and were the chiefs of the nation in wealth as well as in power. The new families which had grown up by their side competed with them, but could not surpass them in magnificence.

In France, the commoners (*roturiers*) inherited all the property lost by the nobility; they seemed to fatten on their substance. The laws did not hinder commoners from ruining themselves, or help them to acquire wealth; yet they did acquire it constantly, and became as rich or richer than men of rank. They often invested their means in the same kind of property as the nobles held; though usually residents of the city, they often owned country estates, and occasionally even seigniories.

Both classes were educated alike, and led similar lives, hence more points of resemblance. The commoner was as well informed as the nobleman, and had obtained his information from the same source. Both were equally and similarly enlightened; both had received the same theoretical and literary education. Paris had become the sole preceptor of France, and shaped all minds in the same form and mould.

There was, no doubt, at the close of the eighteenth century, a difference between the manners of the noble and the commoner, for nothing resists the leveling process so long as that superficial varnish called manners. But at bottom all the classes which ranked above the people were alike. Their ideas were the same; so were their habits, tastes, pleasures, books, and language. They differed in point of rights alone.

I doubt whether the same fact existed to the same extent in any other country. Common interests had closely knit together the various social classes in England, but they differed widely in habits and ideas; for political liberty, so long enjoyed by that admirable power, though it unites men by close relations and mutual dependence, does not always assimilate them one to another; it is despotism which, in the long run, inevitably renders them mere duplicates one of the other, and types of selfishness.

CHAPTER IX.

L ET us now glance at the reverse of the picture, and see how these same Frenchmen, who had so many features in common, were, notwithstanding, split into more isolated groups than any other people or their own ancestry.

There is reason to believe that, at the time the feudal system was established in Europe, the class since known as the nobility did not form a *caste*, but was composed originally of the chief men of the nation, thus forming a real aristocracy. That is a question which I do not purpose to discuss in this place. I merely observe that in the Middle Ages the nobility had become a caste; that is to say, its distinguishing mark was birth.

It resembled an aristocracy inasmuch as it was the governing body; but birth alone decided who should stand at the head of that body. All who were not of noble birth were excluded from its ranks, and filled a station in the state which might vary in dignity, but was always subordinate.

Wherever the feudal system took root in Europe, it led to the establishment of castes; in England alone it gave birth to an aristocracy.

I have always been surprised that a fact so strikingly peculiar to England, and which is the only true key to the peculiarities of her laws, her spirit, and her history, should have obtained so little notice among philosophers and statesmen. Custom seems to have blinded the English to its importance. It has often been half noticed and half described, but never, I think, fully and clearly realized. Montesquieu, who visited Great Britain in 1739, certainly did write, "I am in a country which does not resemble the west of Europe;" but he went no farther.

The contrast between England and the rest of Europe arose, indeed, less from her Parliament, her liberty, her freedom of the press, and her jury system, than from another and more important peculiarity. England was the only country where castes had been not altered, but thoroughly abolished: noblemen and people engaged in the same avocations, entered the same professions, and, what is more significant, intermarried with each other. The daughter of the greatest nobleman in the land might marry, without dishonor, a man of no hereditary rank.

If you want to ascertain whether castes, and the ideas, habits, and barriers to which they give rise, are really abolished in any nation, look at the marriages which take place there. There you will find the decisive test. Sixty years of democracy have not wholly effaced privileges of caste in France; old families, mixed and confounded with new ones in every thing else, still scorn connection with them by marriage.

It has often been said that the English nobility were more prudent, more skillful, more open than the nobility of any other country. The truth is, that there had not been, for a long period of time, any nobility at all in England, in the old circumscribed meaning of the word.

The revolution which destroyed it is lost in the night of time, but the English tongue is a surviving witness of the change. Many centuries since, the meaning of the word "gentleman" changed in England, and the word "roturier" ceased to exist. When Molière wrote Tartuffe in 1664, it would have been impossible to give a literal English version of the line,

"Et tel que l'on le voit, il est bon gentilhomme."

Language can be made to throw farther light on the science of history. Follow, for instance, the meanings of the word gentleman throughout its career. Our word "gentilhomme" was its father. As distinctions of classes became less marked in England, its signification widened. Century after century, it was applied to lower and lower classes in the social scale. The English at last bore it with them to America, where it was indiscriminately applied to all classes. Its history is, in fact, that of democracy.

In France, the word "gentilhomme" never acquired more latitude than it possessed at first. Since the Revolution it has become disused, but not modified. The word which described members of the caste was preserved unaltered, because the caste itself was retained as widely distinct as ever from other classes of society.

I will go farther. I maintain that the caste had grown more distinct and exclusive than ever; that the movement of French society had been exactly opposite to that which took place in England.

While the citizen and the noble had grown more like each other, the distance between them had increased; their mutual resemblance had rather alienated than united them.

During the Middle Ages, when the feudal system was in full vigor, the holders of seigniorial lands (who were technically styled vassals), whether nobles or not, were constantly associated with the seignior in the government of the seigniory. That was, in fact, the principal condition of their tenure. They were bound by their titles not only to follow their seignior in arms, but to assist him, for a given time each year, in rendering justice in his court, and administering the government of the seigniory. Seigniorial courts were the mainspring of feudal government; they figure in all the old laws of Europe, and I have found marked traces of them in many parts of Germany even in our own time. A learned feudist, Edme de Fréminville, who thought proper, thirty years before the Revolution, to write a voluminous work on feudal rights and the renewal of court rolls, informs us that he has seen "many seigniorial titles by which the vassals bound themselves to attend, every fortnight, at the seignior's court, there to sit, jointly with him or his judge in ordinary, in judgment upon disputes and lawsuits between the people of the seigniory." He adds, that he has "found as many as eighty, a hundred and fifty, and even two hundred vassals, a great proportion of whom were *roturiers*, pledged to this service in a seigniory." This I quote, not as a proof of the custom— such evidence abounds—but as an instance of the early and long-continued association of the peasantry with men of rank. They were constantly engaged together in the transaction of the same business. What the seigniorial courts did for small rural landholders, the Provincial States, and, at a later period, the States-General, effected for the middle class in cities.

It is impossible to read the extant records of the States-General and Provincial States of the fourteenth century without being amazed at the weight and power exercised by the Third Estate in these assemblies.

As individuals, the burghers of the fourteenth century were, no doubt, very inferior to those of the eighteenth; collectively, they occupied a higher and more solidly established rank. Their right to take part in the government was uncontroverted; their share in political assemblies was always large, often paramount. The other classes were daily reminded of the necessity of making terms with them.

It is quite striking to notice how easily the nobility and the Third Estate then combined for purposes of action or defense—no easy matter to contrive at a later day. Many of the States-General of the fourteenth century derived an irregular and revolutionary character from the disasters of the time; but the Provincial States of the same period, on which there is no reason to suppose any abnormal influence was operating, contain singular evidence of this harmony. In Auvergne the Three Estates combined to carry out most important measures, and appointed commissioners, chosen equally from each, to superintend their execution. Champagne witnessed a similar spectacle at the same time. Nor is it necessary to do more than hint at the famous league between the nobles and citizens of several cities, by which the leaguers bound themselves, at the beginning of the same century, to defend their national franchises and provincial privileges against the encroachments of the royal power.[e] [f] Our history, at that age, is full of similar episodes, which seem to have been borrowed from the history of England. They disappear entirely in later times.

With the disorganization of the seigniorial governments, the increasing infrequency or total cessation of meetings of the States-General, and the ruin of national and local liberties together, the middle classes ceased to associate in public life with men of rank. There was no longer any necessity for their meeting and coming to a mutual understanding. They became daily more independent of each other, and more complete strangers. By the eighteenth century the change was accomplished; the two classes only met accidentally in private life. They were not only rivals, but enemies.

A feature which appears peculiar to France was the seeming aggrandizement of individual noblemen at the cost of the order. While the nobility, as an order, was losing its political power, men of rank were acquiring new privileges and augmenting their old ones. The former had lost its corporate authority, but still the new master chose his chief servants more exclusively than ever from among its members. It was easier for a commoner (*roturier*) to become an officer under Louis XIV. than Louis XVI. Commoners often obtained office in Prussia at a time when the fact was unexampled in France. All the new privileges were hereditary and inseparable from blood. The more the nobility ceased to be an aristocracy the more it became a caste.

Let us take the most odious of these privileges, the exemption from taxes : it is easily seen that from the fifteenth century to the French Revolution it was constantly on the increase.   It became more valuable as the taxes swelled.   When the *taille* was but 1,200,000 livres under Charles VII., the privilege of not being bound to contribute was not worth much; but it was considerable when the tax yielded 80,000,000, under Louis XVI.   When the taille was the only tax from which the nobility were exempt, their privileges might pass unnoticed; but when similar taxes had been created in a thousand different shapes and with a thousand different names, when four other imposts had been placed on the same footing as the taille, and new impositions, such as royal *corvées* on all public works, military duty, &c., had been laid on every class save the nobles only, their privileges appeared immense.[g] True, the inequality, great as it was, seemed still greater, for the nobleman's farmer had often to pay the very taxes which his master flattered himself he escaped ; but, in these matters, the semblance of injustice is more mischievous than the reality.

Louis XIV., when laboring under the financial difficulties which at last overwhelmed him, toward the close of his reign, created two taxes, a capitation-tax and a land-tax of a twentieth, which were to be paid by all his subjects indiscriminately.   But, as though the privilege of the nobility was so intrinsically respectable that it deserved consideration even in cases where it did not apply, care was taken to preserve a distinction in the manner of levying it.[h][i][k] It was exacted of the people harshly and with marks of degradation; the nobles were respectfully and gently requested to pay.[l]

The taxes had been unequal all over Europe, but the inequality was more plainly seen and severely felt in France than abroad. The bulk of the taxes in Germany were indirect, and the exemption from direct taxes, enjoyed by the nobility, was only partial—they paid less than other people. They were taxed specially, too, in lieu of the military service they had once been bound to render.

Now, of all the methods that have been devised for the division of nations into classes, unequal taxes are the most pernicious and effective. They tend to isolate each class irremediably; for when the tax is unequal, the line is drawn afresh every year between the taxables and the exempts; the distinction is never allowed to fade. Every member of the privileged class feels a pressing and immediate interest in keeping it up, and maintaining his isolation from the taxable community.

All, or nearly all public measures begin or end with a tax. Hence, when two classes of citizens do not feel the taxes alike, they cease to have common interests and feelings in common; they do not require to meet for consultation; they have no opportunity and no desire to act in concert.

Burke draws a flattering picture of the old constitution of France, and makes a point in favor of the institution of nobility, that commoners might obtain rank by procuring office; he evidently infers an analogy between this feature of our institutions and the open aris-

tocracy of England. Nor can it be denied that Louis
XI. bestowed titles freely in order to reduce the power
of the nobility, and that his successors did the same
thing to get money. Necker states that in his time as
many as four thousand offices carried with them noble
rank. No similar feature existed elsewhere in Europe.
Yet the analogy which Burke seeks to establish between France and England was none the less false.

The real secret of the stanch attachment of the
middle classes of England to their aristocracy did not
lie in the fact that it was an open body; it flowed rather from the undefined extent and unknown limits of
that body. Englishmen bore with their aristocracy less
because they could obtain admission within its pale,
than because they never knew when they were within,
and could always consider themselves part and parcel
of it, could share its authority, and derive *éclat* or profit from its power.

In France, on the contrary, the barrier which separated the nobility from the other classes, though easily
surmounted, was always conspicuous, and known by
outward and odious marks. The parvenu who overstepped it was separated from his former associates by
privileges which were onerous and humiliating for them.

The plan of raising commoners to the nobility, therefore, far from weakening their hatred of the superior
class, increased it beyond measure. New nobles were
viewed by their old equals with most bitter envy.
Hence it was that the Third Estate evinced far more
dislike of the new than of the old nobility, and demanded constantly that the entrance to the ranks of the nobility should be, not enlarged, but narrowed.

At no time in our history was it so easy to become a noble as in 1789, and at no time had the nobility and the commonalty been so distinct and separate. Not only did the nobles exclude from their electoral colleges every one who was the least tainted with plebeian blood, but the commoners exhibited equal anxiety to keep out of their ranks all who looked like men of rank. In certain provinces, new nobles were rejected by one party because they were not deemed noble enough, by the others because they were too noble. This happened, it is said, to the celebrated Lavoisier.

The burghers presented a very similar spectacle. They were as widely distinct from the people as the nobles from them.

Nearly the whole middle class under the old regime lived in the cities. Two causes had produced this result: the privileges of men of rank and the *taille*. Seigniors residing on their estates could afford to be good-natured and patronizing to the peasantry, but they were insolent to a degree to their neighbors of a higher rank. And the more political power they lost, the more proud and overbearing they became. Nor could it be otherwise; for when they were stripped of their authority, they no longer needed to conciliate partners in the business of government, while, on the other hand, they tried to console themselves for the sacrifice of substantial authority by an immoderate abuse of its outward semblance. Their absence from their estates was rather an increased inconvenience than a relief to their neighbors; absenteeism had not even that advantage, and privileges exercised by attorney were only the more intolerable.

I question, however, whether the taille and the other taxes which had been placed on the same footing were not still more effective causes than these.

It would be easy to explain, and that in a few words, why the taille was a more oppressive tax in the country than in the cities; but the reader may not consider such an explanation requisite. It will suffice, therefore, to say that the middle classes domiciled in cities were enabled, in many various ways, to evade the tax, wholly or partially, which they could not have done had they been living on their property in the country. Above all, a city residence saved them from the risk of being chosen to levy the taille. This they dreaded more than the tax itself, and very justly, for there was not, in the whole range of society under the old regime, or even in any society, I believe, a position worse than that of parochial collector of the taille. I shall have occasion to demonstrate this hereafter. Yet, with the single exception of men of rank, no resident of a village could escape the office. Rather than submit to the burden, rich commoners leased their estates and went to live in the nearest city. Turgot is consistent with the secret documents which I have had occasion to consult when he declares that "the collection of the taille converts the landholding commoners of the country into city burghers." This, it may be observed by the way, was one of the reasons why France was more plentifully sprinkled with towns, and especially small towns, than any other country of Europe.

Inclosed within city walls, the rich commoner lost his rural tastes and feelings. He ceased to take an interest in the toils and concerns of the class he had deserted. His life had henceforth but one object: he aspired to become a public functionary in his adopted city.

It is a grave error to suppose that the rage for office-seeking, which stamps the French of our day, the middle classes especially, sprung up since the Revolution: it dates from a much more ancient period, though constant encouragement has steadily developed and intensified it.

The offices of the old regime were not always like ours, but I think they were more numerous; there was no end to the small ones. Between 1693 and 1709 alone, it has been calculated that forty thousand were created, all within reach of the most slender commoner. I have myself counted, in a provincial town of no great size, in the year 1750, the names of one hundred and nine persons engaged in administering justice, and a hundred and twenty-six more busied in executing their orders. The middle classes really coveted government places with unexampled ardor. The moment a man acquired a little capital, instead of investing it in trade, he bought an office directly. Not even the close companies or the taille have proved as injurious to the commercial and agricultural interests of France as this mania for places. When no offices were vacant, the place-hunters set their imagination to work and soon invented new ones. I find a published memorial of a Sieur Lemberville, in which he proves that inspectors of this or that branch of industry are absolutely needed, and winds up by offering himself for the future office. Who has not known a Lemberville? A man possessed of some education and means did not think

it decorous to die without having been a public functionary. "Each in his way," said a contemporary,
"wants to be something by his majesty's favor."

The only substantial difference between the custom
of those days and our own resides in the price paid
for office. Then they were sold by government, now
they are bestowed; it is no longer necessary to pay
money; the object can be attained by selling one's
soul.

Interest, to a still greater extent than locality or
habits of life, drew a line between the middle classes
and the peasantry. Complaint is made about the privileges of the nobles, and very justly; but what must
be said of those of the middle classes? Thousands
of offices carried with them exemptions from this or
that impost. One exempted its holder from serving
in the militia, another from performing *corvées*, a third
from paying the taille. "Where is the parish," said
a writer of the time, "that does not contain, besides
nobles and clergy, a number of inhabitants who have
procured some exemption from taxes by obtaining office under government?" The number was so great,
in fact, as to produce at times a sensible falling off in
the product of the *taille;* and, now and then, this inconvenience led to the abolition of several useless offices. I have no doubt that exemptions were as frequent among the middle classes as among the nobility,
and even more so.

These wretched privileges excited the envy of those
who did not enjoy them, and filled their possessors
with selfish pride. Nothing more common, during the
whole of the eighteenth century, than hostility and

jealousy between cities and the surrounding country. Turgot declares that " the towns are monopolized by selfishness, and are always ready to sacrifice the village and country parts in their district." On another occasion, he reminds his sub-delegates how "often" they have been " obliged to repress the tendency of cities to usurp the rights and encroach upon the privileges of the villages and country parts in their district."

The middle classes contrived to make strangers and enemies of the lower classes in the cities also. Most of the local taxes were devised so as to fall mainly upon the latter. Turgot remarks somewhere that the middle classes usually contrived to escape the payment of town dues; and this I have found to be correct.

But the most striking characteristic of the middle classes was their fear of being confounded with the people, and their violent desire to escape in some way from popular control.

"If it be the king's pleasure," said the burghers of a city in a memorial to the comptroller-general, "that the office of mayor become elective, it would be fitting that the choice of the electors should be restricted to the principal notables, and even to the presidial."

We have had occasion to notice how steadily the kings pursued the policy of stripping the cities of their political rights. This is the leading feature of their tactics from Louis XI. to Louis XV. The burghers often aided in the accomplishment of these schemes, and sometimes suggested them.

At the time of the municipal reform of 1764, an intendant consulted the municipal officers of a small town on the subject of retaining an elective magistracy, chosen partly by the lower classes. They replied that, to tell the truth, "the people had never abused the franchise, and it would no doubt be agreeable to confirm them in the right of choosing their masters; still it was better, for the sake of order and the public tranquillity, that the matter should be left to the decision of the notables." The sub-delegate of the same town reported that he had invited to a secret conference "the six leading citizens of the place," who were unanimously of opinion that the best thing to do was to have the magistrates elected, not by the assembly of notables, as the municipal officers proposed, but by a small committee selected from the various bodies which composed the assembly. The sub-delegate, who was more favorable to popular freedom than these citizens, reported their opinion, but added that "it was hard for mechanics to be deprived of control over moneys exacted from them in virtue of taxes imposed by those among their fellow-citizens who, by reason of the exemption from taxes they enjoyed, were often disinterested in the matter."

To complete the picture, let us glance at the middle classes independently of their relations to the people, as we examined the nobility independently of its bearing on the middle classes.

The first striking feature in this small part of the nation is infinite subdivision. The French people really seem to resemble those pretended elementary substances which science is unceasingly resolving into new elements the closer it examines them. I have studied a small town in which I found the names of thirty-six different bodies of citizens. These various bodies, small as they were, were constantly hard at work reducing their size; they were ever throwing off some foreign particle or other, and trying to reduce their condition to that of simple elements. This operation had cut down some of them to not more than three or four members. They were none the less quarrelsome and consequential on that account. Peculiar privileges, among which the least decorous were still marks of honor, distinguished each class from the others, and endless was the struggle for precedence among them. Intendant and courts were stunned with the clamor of their quarrels. " It has just been decided that the holy water must be given to the presidial before the city corporation. The Parliament hesitated, but the king evoked the case, and decided it in Council. It was high time; the whole city was in a ferment on the subject." If one body is granted precedence over another at the assembly of notables, the injured corporation withdraws; it will abandon its public duties rather than see, as it says, its dignity insulted. The corporation of barbers in the city of La Flêche decided " to express in this manner the natural grief which it felt at the precedence awarded to the bakers." A portion of the notables of a city refused to perform their functions, " because," said the intendant, " some mechanics had obtained admission to the assembly, and with these the leading citizens could not humble themselves by associating." Another intendant observed, " If the rank of alderman be given to a notary, that will disgust the other notables,

for the notaries are men of low birth, not sons of notables, and have been clerks in their youth." The six
leading citizens, whom I have mentioned above, who
were so ready to strip the people of their political
rights, were greatly perplexed when called upon to des-
ignate who should be notables, and what should be the
order of precedence among them. On this point they
expressed their views rather by doubts and hints than
straightforward suggestions: "They were afraid," they
said, " of hurting the feelings of their fellow-citizens."

The friction between these small bodies sharpened
the peculiar vanity of the French, but extinguished the
proper pride of the citizen. Most of these corporations existed in the sixteenth century, but then, after
having transacted the business of their exclusive association, they mingled with the other citizens for the
transaction of the general concerns of the city. In the
eighteenth century no such intermixture took place,
for symptoms of municipal life had become rare, and
city business was managed by hired agents. Each of
these small societies lived for itself alone, thought of
nothing but its own affairs, had no interest in any concerns but those which were exclusively its own.

Our ancestors had no such word as "individuality," which we have coined for our use. They did not
need it, because in their time there were no individuals wholly isolated and unconnected with some group
or other; but each of the small groups of which French
society was composed was intensely selfish, whence
arose a sort of collective individuality, so to speak,
which prepared men's minds for the true individuality
of the present day.

The strangest feature of the old society was the similarity which existed among all these individuals thus grouped in different sets ; they were so alike that when they changed their surroundings it was impossible to recognize them ; moreover, in their hearts they regarded the petty barriers which split them into rival cliques as equally contrary to public interest and common sense.   In theory they were all for unity. Each held to his set because others did the like ; but they were all ready to fuse together into one mass, provided no one obtained peculiar advantages, or rose above the common level.

CHAPTER X.

HOW THE DESTRUCTION OF POLITICAL LIBERTY AND CLASS DIVIS-
IONS WERE THE CAUSES OF ALL THE DISEASES OF WHICH THE
OLD REGIME DIED.

OF all the fatal diseases which assailed the constitution of the old regime, the most deadly was
the one I have just described.   Let us return to the
source of this strange and terrible malady, and see how
many other troubles had the same origin.

Had the English wholly lost their political liberties
and all the local franchises dependent thereon during
the crisis of the Middle Ages, it is reasonable to suppose that the classes which comprise their aristocracy
would have held themselves quite aloof from the people, as the corresponding classes did in France.   It
was the spirit of liberty which compelled them to remain within reach of the people, in order to come to
an understanding with them when required.

It is curious to note how ambition prompted the
English nobility to mix familiarly with their inferiors,
and to treat them as equals when necessity seemed to
require it.   Arthur Young, from whom I have quoted
already, and whose work is one of the most instructive that can be consulted on Old France, relates how,
while he was staying at the country-house of the Duke
of Liancourt, he expressed a wish to converse with
some of the most skillful and intelligent farmers of the
neighborhood.   The duke sent his intendant for them,

upon which the Englishman remarks: "An English nobleman, in the like case, would have asked three or four farmers to dinner with his family, and would have had them sit by the side of the noblest ladies. I have seen that a hundred times over in our island, but you may travel from Calais to Bayonne without seeing any thing of the kind here."

Beyond a doubt, the British aristocracy was naturally more haughty and more averse to familiarity with its inferiors than the same class in France, but the necessities of its position imposed restraints. It was willing to sacrifice any thing for power. For centuries the only alterations in the taxes were made in favor of the poorer classes. Notice, I beg, how widely neighbors may be made to differ by different political principles!m In the eighteenth century, in England, the only exemptions from taxes were enjoyed by the poor, in France by the rich. There the aristocracy had assumed all the burdens in order to enjoy the power of governing; here they steadily refused to pay taxes, as their only consolation for the loss of political power.

During the fourteenth century, the maxim *N'im-pose qui ne veut* (no taxation without the consent of the taxables), appears to have been as solidly established in France as in England. It was frequently quoted; deviations from it were regarded as acts of tyranny, absolute conformity with it constitutional. At this period our institutions were analogous, in many respects, to those of the English. But thenceforth the destinies of the two nations began to deviate, and became more unlike from century to century. They might be compared to two lines, which, starting from adjacent points in slightly different directions, separate more widely the more they are prolonged.

I venture to assert that when the nation, wearied out by the long disorders which had accompanied the captivity of King John and the insanity of Charles VI., allowed the kings to impose a tax without its consent, the nobles basely concurring on condition that they should be exempt, they sowed the seed of all the abuses and mischiefs which troubled the old regime during its existence, and led to its violent death; and I admire the singular sagacity of Commines when he says, " When Charles VII. gained the right of imposing the taille at will without the consent of the States, he greatly changed his spirit (*son âme*) and that of his successors, and dealt his kingdom a wound that will bleed for a long time to come."

See how the wound has been enlarged by time; trace the consequences of this one act.

Forbonnais remarks with truth, in his learned " Researches on French Finances," that, during the Middle Ages, monarchs usually lived on the produce of their domains; "and as extraordinary necessities," he adds, " were met by extraordinary taxes, they bore equally on the clergy, the nobility, and the people."

Most of the general taxes, voted by the three orders during the fourteenth century, were of this character. Nearly all the taxes established at this time were indirect, that is to say, they bore on all consumers indiscriminately. When the tax was direct, it bore, not on property, but on incomes. For instance, nobles, clergy, and commoners were required to abandon to the king a tithe of their income. And the rule with regard to taxes laid by the States-General applied with equal force to those which were laid by the Provincial States within their territories.

It is true that even then the direct tax, called *taille*, did not bear on men of rank, who were exempt in consideration of serving gratuitously as soldiers in time of war. But the *taille*, as a general tax, was restricted in its operation; it applied to seigniories more than to the kingdom.

When the king first undertook to impose a tax of his own will and mere motion, he was well aware that policy indicated the selection of one which did not bear upon the nobility, and which they—who were the most powerful class in the kingdom, and the only rivals of the sovereign—would not be provoked to resist; and, accordingly, he chose the *taille*.

Inequalities enough existed already between the various classes of Frenchmen; this new distinction was more sweeping than all, and aggravated while it confirmed the others. Thenceforth, in proportion to the increased necessities which were produced by the enlarged ambition of the central power, the *taille* increased and multiplied, till the original amount levied was decupled, and every new tax was a *taille*.[n] Year by year the tax-gathering divided society anew, and re-erected the barrier between the taxables and the exempts. The first condition of the tax being its imposition, not on those who could afford to pay it, but on those who could not afford to resist it, government was driven into the monstrous anomaly of sparing the rich and burdening the poor. It is said that Mazarin once intended to supply a pressing exigency by a tax on the principal houses in Paris; but, meeting with more resistance than he had anticipated, he simply added the five millions he wanted to the *taille* levy. His design had been to tax the most wealthy citizens; in fact, he taxed the poorest; but the treasury got the money.

Taxes so unequal yielded a limited revenue; but there was no limit to the necessities of the throne. Still, king after king refused to convoke the States in order to obtain subsidies, and refrained from taxing the nobility lest the annoyance should provoke them to insist on a return to constitutional usage. Hence those prodigious and mischievous financial *tours de force*, which marked the history of the French treasury during the last three centuries of the monarchy.

A careful study of the financial and administrative history of the old regime shows to what straits and dishonest shifts the want of money will reduce a government, however mild it may be, so long as it is unchecked, and fears neither publicity on the one hand, nor revolution—that safeguard of popular liberty—on the other.

That history teems with instances of royal properties sold, then resumed as inalienable; of violated contracts; vested rights trampled; public creditors sacrificed at every crisis; the public faith constantly broken.°

Privileges, granted as perpetual, were constantly revoked. If it were possible to sympathize with the sufferings of martyrs to vanity, one would pity those unfortunate new-made noblemen who, during the seventeenth and eighteenth centuries, were so often called upon to pay for honors and unjust privileges, whose price they had fully paid at the time of the original purchase. Louis XIV., for instance, annulled all the titles of nobility that had been granted during the ninety-two years previous, though most of them had been granted by himself. Their possessors could only retain them on paying more money, " all these titles having been granted by surprise," says the edict. An example which Louis XV. took care to imitate eighty years afterward.

It was pronounced illegal for militia-men to serve by substitute, as the practice would tend to enhance the value of recruits.

Cities, corporations, hospitals, were forced to repudiate their engagements in order to lend their money to the king. Parishes were hindered from undertaking useful works for fear that the *taille* might be less regularly paid if their resources were divided.

It is related that M. Orry and M. Trudaine, who were respectively comptroller-general and director-general of the department of Bridges and Roads, formed a plan for the commutation of seigniorial *corvées* on highways into an annual payment in money, to be applied to repairing the roads of each canton. There is much instruction in the reason which deterred these able officials from executing their design; they were afraid, it is said, that it would be impossible to prevent the treasury from embezzling the money, and obliging the people both to labor on the roads and to pay for their repairs besides. I do not hesitate to say that no private individual could escape ruin if he conducted his affairs as the great monarch in all his glory managed the public business.

All the old mediæval institutions, whose faults were aggravated as every thing around them improved, may be traced to a financial origin ; the same is true of the pernicious innovations of a later date. To pay the debts of a day, powers were created which lasted centuries.

A particular tax, called the freehold duty (*droit de franc fief*), had been laid at a very remote period on commoners who possessed estates noble. This duty created the same division among lands as existed among men ; and each helped the other. The freehold duty hindered the fusion of the nobility and the people on the neutral ground of real estate ; and I dare say it was more effective than any thing else in keeping them apart. It opened a gulf between the nobleman and his neighbor. In England, nothing so powerfully aided the fusion of the two classes as the abolition, in the seventeenth century, of all the distinguishing marks which served to separate feudal lands from freeholds.

During the fourteenth century the feudal freehold duty was light, and only exacted at long intervals. During the eighteenth, when the feudal system was nearly abolished, it was rigorously levied every twenty years, and amounted to a twelvemonth's income of the land. Sons paid it on succeeding to their father. The agricultural society of Tours stated, in 1761, that "this duty was infinitely injurious to the progress of agricultural science. No tax levied by the king's government is so vexatious or so onerous in the country parts as this one." Another contemporary observed that "this imposition, which was originally paid but once in a lifetime, has become a very cruel exaction." The nobility wished to see it abolished, for it operated to hinder commoners from buying their estates;[p] but the necessities of government involved its maintenance, and even its extension.

The Middle Ages have been unjustly blamed for much of the mischief produced by the trade-corporations. There is every reason to believe that, in the origin, trade-companies and trade-unions were formed merely for the purpose of uniting the members of each craft together, and establishing a sort of free government for each branch of industry, in order to assist and control the operatives. It does not appear that Saint Louis contemplated any thing beyond this.

It was not till the beginning of the sixteenth century, when the revival of civil and religious liberty was in full progress, that the idea of placing labor on the footing of a privilege to be purchased of government was first broached. It was not till then that each craft became a small, close aristocracy, and a start was given to those monopolies which were so injurious to the progress of the arts and so odious to our ancestors. From the time of Henry III., who generalized, if he did not actually create the evil, to that of Louis XVI., who extirpated it, it may be said that the system of trade-companies acquired fresh strength and extension every year; and this, while the progress of society as steadily aggravated their inconvenience, and common sense revealed their absurdity. Year after year the close corporation system was adopted by new trades, while the privileges of the old companies were constantly on the increase. The evil reached its climax at the period which is usually termed the glorious portion of the reign of Louis XIV.; for that was the time when the government stood in most urgent need of money, and was most firmly resolved not to appeal to the country.

Letronne remarked very justly in 1775, " Government established trade-corporations solely for the purpose of obtaining money from them, either by the sale of patents, or by the creation of offices which the corporations were bound to buy up. The edict of 1673 carried out thoroughly the principles of Henry III. by obliging all corporations to purchase charters from government; the next step was compelling all trades not incorporated to form companies. This wretched business yielded three hundred thousand livres."

We have already seen how the constitutions of cities were overthrown, not from political motives, but in order to supply the public coffers with resources.

The same pecuniary necessities, coupled with a fixed aversion to appeal to the States, led to the sale of offices—a feature in the old regime which gradually assumed such proportions that history may be searched in vain for a parallel. It owed its origin to fiscal ingenuity. But it was so well contrived that for three centuries it fed the vanity of the middle classes, and directed the whole of their energies toward the acquisition of place; it stamped on the national heart that rage for offices, which became the source alike of our revolutions and our servitude.

As the finances became more embarrassed, new offices were created, with exemptions from taxation or privileges by way of salary; and, as they were created to supply the wants of the treasury, and not the re-

quirements of the public service, an immense number
of them were useless or positively mischievous.[q]   As
early as 1664, when Colbert instituted an inquiry into
the subject, it was discovered that the capital invested in this miserable business nearly amounted to five
hundred millions of livres.   It is said that Richelieu
abolished a hundred thousand offices.   They rose
anew under fresh names.   For a trifle of money, people trafficked away the right of directing and controlling their own servants.   The net result of this system was a government machine, so vast, so complicated, so cumbrous, and so inefficient, that it was actually found necessary to let it stand idle, while a new
instrument, constructed with more simplicity and better adapted for use, performed the work which these
countless functionaries were supposed to do.[r]

It may be affirmed that none of these detestable institutions could have lasted twenty years if it had
been lawful to discuss their merits.   None would have
been established or extended if the States had been
consulted, or if their complaints had been noticed when
they were convened.   On the rare occasions when the
States met during the later ages of the monarchy, they
were uniformly presented as a grievance.   These assemblies frequently traced all the abuses of which they
complained to the king's usurpation of the right of
levying taxes arbitrarily, or, to use the energetic expressions of the fifteenth century, "of his enriching
himself out of the substance of the people without the
advice and consent of the three Estates."   They did not
confine their remonstrances to their own wrongs; they
strenuously demanded, and often succeeded in enforc-

ing respect for the rights of the provinces and cities. Some members protested at every session against the inequality of the public burdens. They repeatedly demanded the abolition of trade-corporations. They assailed the sale of offices century after century with increasing warmth. "To sell offices," they said, "is to sell justice, which is infamous." When the system of venal offices was firmly established, they complained of its abuse as persistently as ever. They exclaimed against the creation of useless and dangerous privileges; but all was in vain. These institutions were barricades against the people. They were devised in order to obviate the necessity of convening the States, and to conceal from the public eye taxes which the government dared not exhibit in an honest light.

Nor were the good kings any better in this respect than the bad ones. It was Louis XII. who systematized the sale of offices, and Henry IV. who first sold hereditary ones. So weak was personal virtue against the vice of the system!

It was the desire to avoid meeting the States which led to the original grant of political power to the Parliaments, whence the judiciary became mixed with government in a manner that could not but be prejudicial to business. Policy dictated the establishment of new guarantees in the room of those that were taken away; for the French, who are patient enough under moderate despotisms, do not like the sight of them; and it is always wise to surround absolute power in France with a fence which, though it may not impede its movements, may conceal them from the public eye.

In fine, it was through fear lest the nation, whose money the kings wanted, should insist upon the restoration of its liberties, that class divisions were kept up; for by this means organized resistance or a common understanding was rendered impossible, and the government was certain of having to deal with each small clique separately. In the long course of French history, there reigned many distinguished sovereigns, several who were men of wit, some who were men of talent, while nearly all were men of courage; but there was not a single one who tried to efface class distinctions, or to promote union otherwise than as a condition of dependence. I am wrong; there was one who did desire to see the people united, and tried with all his heart to unite them, and that one—wonderful mystery of God's judgments!—was Louis XVI.!

The great crime of the old kings was the division of the people into classes. Their subsequent policy followed as a matter of course; for when the wealthy and enlightened portion of a people are debarred from combination for public purposes, self-government becomes impossible, and tyranny becomes a necessity.

Turgot, in a secret report to the king, observes sadly, "The nation is composed of several disunited classes and a divided people; hence no one takes thought for any thing but his own private interest. Public spirit is a thing unknown. Villages and cities have no mutual relations with each other, nor have the counties (*arrondissements*) in which they are situate. They are even unable to come to an understanding for the repair of the common roads. An incessant warfare is carried on between rival claims and pretensions; the decision is invariably referred to your majesty or your servants. An order from you is required before people will pay taxes, or respect the rights of their neighbors, or even exercise their own."

It was no slight task to reunite people who had been strangers to each other, or foes for so many centuries. It was very difficult to teach them to come to an understanding for the transaction of their common business. Division was a comparatively easy achievement. We have furnished the world with a memorable illustration of the difficulty of the reverse process. When, sixty years ago, the various classes into which French society was divided were suddenly brought together, after a separation of several centuries, their only points of contact were their old sores; they only met to tear each other in pieces. Their rival jealousies and hatreds survive to this day.

CHAPTER XI.

OF THE KIND OF LIBERTY ENJOYED UNDER THE OLD REGIME, AND
OF ITS INFLUENCE UPON THE REVOLUTION.

IT is impossible to form an accurate conception of
the government of the old regime, and of the society which produced the Revolution, without pursuing
somewhat farther the perusal of this book.

The spectacle of a people so divided and narrowed
into cliques, with a royal authority so extensive and
powerful, might lead to the impression that the spirit
of independence had disappeared with public liberty,
and that all Frenchmen were equally bowed in subjection. Nothing of the kind was the case. The government was sole and absolute manager of the public business, but it was not master of individual citizens.

Liberty survived in the midst of institutions already
prepared for despotism; but it was a curious kind of
liberty, not easily understood to-day. A very close inspection can alone discern the precise proportions of
good and evil which it contained.

While the central government was displacing all the
local authorities, and absorbing the whole power of the
kingdom, its action was often impeded by institutions
which it had either created or refrained from destroying,
by old usages and customs, by rooted abuses. These
nurtured a spirit of resistance in the minds of individuals, and preserved the characters of a good many from
losing all their temper and outline.

The central government had the same character, used
the same means, sought the same ends that it does to-
day, but its power was less.   Bent on making money
out of every thing, it had sold most of the public offices, and made away with the privilege of disposing
of its patronage at will.[s]   One of its passions had been
the detriment of the other; its avarice had counteract-
ed its ambition.   It could not carry out its measures
without employing agents whom it had not trained to
the work, and whom it could not discharge for inefficiency.   Its positive commands were thus often neu-
tralized by the loose manner in which they were carried
out.   This strange radical vice of the system operated
as a sort of check against the omnipotence of government—a breakwater, irregular in form and badly built,
but still serving to break the shock and weaken the
force of authority.

Again, the government had not as many favors to
dispose of, in the shape of charitable assistance, honors, and money, as it has to-day ; its power of seduc-
tion, like its power of control, was less.

It was not itself aware of the exact limits of its
powers.   None of them were solidly established or regularly recognized.   Its sphere was immense, but it traversed it with uncertain step, groping its way through
obscure and unknown paths.   And that obscurity, which
veiled the limits of its powers, and shrouded all its
rights, favorable as it was to the encroachments of
royalty, was likewise favorable to the defense of popular freedom.

With the consciousness of its recent rise and slender
origin, the administration was invariably timid in the

face of obstacles. It is a striking sight to see, in the correspondence of the ministers and intendants of the eighteenth century, how quickly this government, which was so overbearing and despotic when all was submission, lost its presence of mind at the first show of resistance, was alarmed by the mildest criticism, and terrified at the least noise. On these occasions it stopped short, hesitated, tried to compromise matters, and often withdrew from the contest at the sacrifice of a portion of its legitimate authority. Such was the course best suited to the weak selfishness of Louis XV. and the benevolence of his successor. These sovereigns, besides, never supposed for a moment that any one thought of dethroning them. They were strangers to the harshness and distrust which fear has since often planted in the hearts of rulers. They never perceived that they were trampling people under foot.

Many of the prejudices, and privileges, and false notions which stood in the way of the foundation of wholesome liberty, encouraged in many minds a spirit of independence and even insubordination.

The nobility held the government proper in supreme contempt, though they had occasional relations with its agents. Even after their power was gone, the nobles preserved some relic of the pride of their ancestors, who rebelled alike against servitude and against law. They took no thought for the liberty of the masses, and willingly allowed the government to lay its hand heavily on them; but they had no notion of submitting to it themselves, whatever resistance might cost. At the outbreak of the Revolution, the language and tone of the nobility toward the king and his agents

were infinitely more haughty than those of the Third
Estate, though the latter was on the point of overturn-
ing the throne, by whose side the former were to fall.
The nobility claim the invention of nearly all the guarantees of the rights of the subject that were enjoyed
during our thirty-seven years of representative government. Their old *cahiers*, in spite of their errors and
prejudices, breathe the spirit of a great aristocracy.[t]
It will always be a subject of regret that the French
nobility was destroyed and uprooted instead of being
subjected to the control of the laws. The error deprived the nation of a portion of its substance, and
dealt liberty a wound that will never heal. The nobility had been the first class in the kingdom, and had
enjoyed undisputed greatness for so many centuries,
that it had acquired a high-mindedness, a self-reliance,
a sense of responsibility, which rendered it the most
solid portion of the social frame. Virile itself, it imparted virility to the other classes of society. Its ex-
tirpation weakened its very assailants. It can never
be wholly restored—can never revive of itself ; it may
regain the titles and estates of its ancestors, but their
spirit, never.

The clergy, who have since been abjectly servile in
civil matters to any and every temporal authority, and
the most audacious flatterers of any monarch who con-
descended to appear to favor the Church, were then
the most independent body in the nation, the only one
whose peculiar liberties were safe from assault.

When the provinces had lost their franchises, and
the city charters were a mere name, when ten nobles
could not meet to discuss business without the ex-

press permission of the king, the French Church held its periodical assemblies just as usual. Nor were the several ecclesiastical authorities without fixed limits.[u] Substantial guarantees shielded the lower clergy from the oppression of their superiors. No arbitrary power in the hands of the bishop schooled them to passive obedience to the king. I have no intention of discussing the old constitution of the Church ; I only observe that it did not teach the priests political servility.

Many ecclesiastics, moreover, were men of rank, and carried with them into the Church the pride and intractability of their class. All held a high rank in the state, and enjoyed privileges. The very feudal rights which militated so gravely against the moral power of the Church, imparted to its individual members a feeling of independence toward the civil authority.

Above all, the possession of real estate endowed the clergy with the feelings, and necessities, and opinions, and even the passions of citizens. I have had the patience to read most of the reports and debates of the old provincial assemblies, especially those of Languedoc, where the clergy took an unusual share in the details of government, and the reports of the provincial assemblies which were held in 1779 and 1787; and, bringing to bear on these documents our modern ideas, I have been amazed to find bishops and *abbés*, many of whom were as eminent in holiness as in learning, report ably on the opening of a road or the construction of a canal, argue with knowledge and science on the best means of increasing the agricultural yield of lands, of improving the condition or developing the industry of the people, and prove themselves always the equals, and often the superiors of the laymen with whom they were associated.[v]

I venture to think, in opposition to the generally received opinion, that systems which debar the Catholic clergy from the possession of landed property, and provide for their remuneration in money, serve no interests but those of the Papacy and the temporal power, and deprive the people of a very important element of liberty.

For a man whose best qualities are under foreign control, and who can have no family in the land he inhabits, there can be but one substantial motive for patriotism—the ownership of real estate. Remove that motive, and he ceases to belong to any one place rather than another. A stranger to civil society, he lives where chance has planted him, without sharing any of the interests which surround him. His conscience is in the hands of the Pope, his livelihood in those of the sovereign. He has no country but the Church. In political troubles, he thinks of nothing but its dangers and its advancement. If it be free and prosperous, what matters the rest? His normal political state is indifference. An excellent member of the Christian city, he is but a poor citizen of any other. Feelings and ideas such as his, in a body intrusted with the education of youth and the censorship of morals, can not but enervate the national spirit for all the concerns of public life.

To form a correct idea of the changes that can be wrought in men's minds by changes in their condition, one must read once more the *cahiers* presented by the clerical order in 1789.

Though frequently intolerant, and sometimes obstinately wedded to their ancient privileges, the clergy gave proof on that occasion that they were as resolute foes to despotism and as stanch friends of civil and political liberty as the nobility or the Third Estate.[w] They demanded that individual liberty should be secured, not by promises, but by a proceeding analogous in character to the writ of *habeas corpus*. They called for the destruction of state prisons, the abolition of unconstitutional courts and evocations, public debates, an irremovable judiciary; the distribution of offices among all classes of citizens, and the adoption of merit as the sole test of eligibility; a less oppressive and less ignominious recruiting system, to admit of no exemptions; the commutation of all feudal rights, which, they said, being part of the feudal system, were inimical to liberty; free labor; the abolition of inland custom-houses; an increase in the number of private schools, until there was one, and that a free school, in each parish; lay charitable institutions, such as workhouses, in the rural districts; all sorts of encouragements to agriculture.

So far as politics proper were concerned, they proclaimed loudly that to the nation alone belonged the indefeasible and inalienable right of making laws and imposing taxes. No Frenchman, they said, can be compelled to pay a tax which he did not vote either in person or by representative. They demanded free elections and annual meetings of the States-General, declared that it was their office to discuss all great public measures in presence of the nation, to make general laws which no special customs or privileges could defeat, to vote supplies, and control even the king's household. They insisted on the inviolability of the persons of deputies and the responsibility of ministers. They also demanded the establishment of provincial assemblies in every province and municipalities in every city. Of divine right not one word said they.

I doubt whether, on the whole, even taking into account the startling vices of some of its members, the world ever saw a more remarkable body than the Catholic clergy at the time the Revolution broke out. They were enlightened; they were national; their private virtues were not more striking than their public qualities; and yet they were largely endowed with faith, sufficient to bear them up against persecution. I began to study the old regime full of prejudice against the clergy; I have ended my task, and feel nothing but respect for them. They had no faults, in truth, but those which are inseparable from all corporations, whether political or religious, when they are solidly built and closely knit together, namely, a tendency to extension, an intolerant spirit, and an instinctive, and occasionally a blind devotion to the special interests of the corporate body.

Nor were the middle classes of the old regime less superior to their modern successors in point of independence and spirit. Many of the very vices of their organization led to this result. It has already been mentioned that they were even more given to place-hunting, and that there were more places within their reach than there are now; but mark the difference between the two. Government could neither give nor take away these places. They increased the dignity of their incumbents, without in any way rendering them slaves to the ruling power. Thus the very cause of the servility of so many men to-day was formerly the most powerful motive for independence and self-respect.

The immunities which, unhappily, divided the middle and lower classes, converted the former into a species of sham aristocracy, and armed it occasionally with pride and a spirit of resistance worthy of the genuine. The public good was often forgotten in the little private cliques which they formed; but the clique interests never.[x] There were common privileges, there was a corporate dignity to be defended, and there was no chance of concealment for the complaisant coward. People were, so to speak, actors on a very small but uncommonly conspicuous stage, with the same audience always before them, and always ready to applaud or hiss.

The art of stifling the sound of resistance was not brought to such perfection as it has been since. France was not so well deafened as it is in our day. It was, on the contrary, well adapted for the transmission of sound, and, though no political liberty could be seen, one had only to speak loud to be heard at a great distance.

The oppressed were secured a hearing in the courts of justice. The political and administrative institutions of the country were those of a despotism, but we were still a free people in our courts of law. The administration of justice under the old regime was cumbrous, complicated, slow, and costly—grave faults, no doubt; but it was never servile to the supreme power;

and this is the very worst form of venality. That capital vice, which not only corrupts the judge, but soon infects the whole body of the people, was unknown in the old courts. Judges were not only irremovable, but looked for no promotion; both conditions are essential to independence, for the power of punishing may be dispensed with if that of rewarding be retained.

True, the royal authority had stripped the common courts of their jurisdiction over cases in which the government was interested, but it had not stripped them of their terrors. They might be prevented from judging cases, but they could not be hindered from receiving complaints and expressing their opinions. And as the judicial idiom had preserved the plain simplicity of the old French tongue, which called things by their right names, it was not uncommon for judges to qualify the measures of the government with such epithets as arbitrary and despotic.ʸ The irregular interference of the courts in the administration of government, which often proved a hindrance to the transaction of business, occasionally served as a safeguard of liberty; the greater evil was limited by the lesser.

In the heart of the magistracy and around it, the new ideas of the day had not wholly crushed out the vigorous habits of thought of olden time. No doubt the Parliaments thought more of themselves than of the public good; but still, when it was necessary to defend their independence and their honor, they were always intrepid, and gave heart to all who surrounded them.

When the Parliament of Paris was dissolved in 1770, every one of the magistrates who composed it submitted to the loss of rank and power rather than yield to the king. More than this: courts of another kind, such as the Court of Aids (*cour des aides*), which were neither assailed nor menaced, voluntarily exposed themselves to the same fate when that fate had become a matter of certainty. Nor was even this all. The leading advocates who had practiced before the Parliament spontaneously shared its fate. They resigned glory and profit, and preferred silence to pleading before a dishonored magistracy. I know of nothing grander than this in the history of any free people; and yet this took place in the eighteenth century, close to Louis the Fifteenth's court.

The nation had borrowed many habits from the courts. It was from the courts that we learned the only portion of the education of a free people which we owe to the old regime, that is to say, the principle that all decisions should be preceded by discussion, and subject to appeal; the use of publicity, and the love of forms. The government itself had borrowed largely from the language and usages of the courts. The king felt bound to assign reasons for his edicts; the Council's Orders were preceded by long preambles, intendants notified the public of their ordinances by the ministry of bailiffs. All the old administrative bodies, such as the Treasury Board, and the select-men, transacted business publicly, and heard rival petitioners or applicants by counsel. All their habits and forms were so many barriers against the arbitrary power of the sovereign. But the people proper, especially in the rural districts, had no means of resisting oppression except by violence.

Most of the means of defense I have just pointed

out were beyond their reach; no one could avail himself of them unless his position in society was such that he could make himself seen and heard. But outside the ranks of the people, any one in France who had the courage might, if he chose, yield a conditioned obedience, and resist even while he yielded.

The king addressed the nation in the language of a chief, not a master. At the commencement of the reign of Louis XVI., the monarch declared in the preamble of an edict, "We glory in commanding a free and generous nation." One of his ancestors had expressed the same idea in older style, when, on thanking the States-General for the boldness of their remonstrances, he exclaimed, "We had rather speak to freemen than to slaves."

The men of the eighteenth century were strangers to that passionate love for ease which is the mother of servitude; which, equally tame and tenacious, combines with several of the private virtues, such as family affection, regular habits, respect for religion, lukewarm but assiduous devotional habits; which tolerates honesty, and justifies heroism, and is remarkably successful in producing respectable men and cowardly citizens. They were better and worse.

The French of those days loved merriment and adored pleasure; their habits were perhaps more irregular, their passions and ideas more disorderly than those of their descendants, but they were strangers to the modern and decent sensuality of our day. Persons in the higher classes sought ornament rather than comfort, honor rather than money. Comfort did not even absorb the attention of the middle classes; more delicate and higher enjoyments were constantly sought in preference. Money was never the great end of life. "I know my countrymen," proudly wrote a contemporary; "skilled in melting and scattering the metals, they are not calculated to worship them, and are quite prepared to return to their old idols, valor, glory, and, I will add, magnanimity."

Care must be taken not to measure the baseness of men by their degree of submission to the sovereign power: that gauge would be a false one. Submissive as the men of the old regime were to the will of the king, they were strangers to submission of another kind; they had not learned to bow the knee to illegitimate or disputed authority, which inspires not honor, but contempt, and secures submission through the fear of injury or the hope of reward. That degrading form of servitude was unknown in olden time. The king inspired feelings such as no absolute monarch of later times has ever been able to awaken, and which the Revolution so thoroughly uprooted that we can hardly understand them. They loved him like a father, and respected him as they respected their God. When they submitted to his arbitrary commands, it was less from compulsion than from love, and their soul often remained their own, even in a state of complete subjection. For them, the greatest evil of obedience was constraint; it is the least in our time. The greatest evil now is the servility which prompts obedience. Let us beware how we despise our ancestors; we have no right to do so. Would to God that we could recover, even with their faults and their prejudices, a little of their greatness.

It would then be an error to consider the old regime as a period of servility and dependence. There was much more liberty then than there is now,[z] [a] but it was an irregular and intermittent kind of liberty, bound up with the class system and notions of privileges and exemptions—a sort of liberty which encouraged rebellion against law as well as against oppression, and always left a portion of the people destitute of the most natural and obvious safeguards. Yet, stunted and deformed as it was, it was fertile. It was to that liberty that so many individuals owed the preservation of their natural character, with its color and outline, when centralization was laboring to reduce the character of the whole nation to a dead level and one uniform line. It was that which kept self-respect alive, and often raised the love of glory above all other passions. It was that which formed those vigorous souls, those proud and bold geniuses, whose appearance on the scene we are soon to witness, and who made the French Revolution alike the admiration and the terror of subsequent generations. It would be strange indeed if such masculine virtues as theirs had been brought to light in a land where liberty was unknown.

But if this disorderly and unwholesome sort of liberty prepared the French to overthrow despotism, it unfitted them, to an unexampled degree, perhaps, for replacing it by the peaceful and free government of law.

CHAPTER XII.

HOW THE CONDITION OF THE FRENCH PEASANTRY WAS WORSE IN
SOME RESPECTS IN THE EIGHTEENTH CENTURY THAN IT HAD BEEN
IN THE THIRTEENTH, NOTWITHSTANDING THE PROGRESS OF CIV-
ILIZATION.

IN the eighteenth century, the French peasantry
were no longer a prey to small feudal despots.
They rarely suffered violence at the hands of government. They enjoyed civil liberty and possessed land;
but they were shunned by all the other classes of society and led a life of unexampled isolation. The consequences of this new and singular form of oppression
deserve to be examined separately and with some attention.

At the very beginning of the seventeenth century,
Henry IV. complained, says Peréfix, that the nobility
were deserting the rural districts. The desertion had
become general by the middle of the eighteenth: all the
documents of the time—treatises on political economy,
intendants' correspondence, reports of agricultural societies—concur in deploring the fact. It is, moreover,
indisputably proved by the capitation registers. The
capitation-tax was levied at the actual place of residence of the taxable: all the great and a portion of the
lesser nobility paid it at Paris.

No men of rank remained in the country districts
but those whose means did not allow them to move.
A man of this class was strangely situate among the

peasantry. He was no longer their ruler, and had no reasons for conciliating, or aiding, or guiding them, while, on the other hand, he did not share their burdens, and consequently felt no sympathy for sufferings which did not afflict him, or for wrongs to which he was a stranger. Though they had ceased to be his subjects, he had not become their fellow-citizen. The position is without parallel in history.

There resulted from it a sort of absenteeism of heart, if I may use the expression, which was even more effective than absenteeism of body. The man of rank who resided on his estate often thought and acted as his steward would have done in his absence. He viewed his tenants merely in the light of debtors, and rigorously exacted from them his full due according to law, thus rendering the remains of the feudal system harder to bear than its entirety had formerly been.[b] [c]

He was often in involved and needy circumstances, and lived meanly in his chateau, his main thought being how he could save money for the winter at Paris. With their peculiar directness of mind, the people gave him the name of the least of all birds of prey; they called him the hobby.

There were individual exceptions, of course; but history regards classes only. No one denies that there were at this time many rich landowners who concerned themselves for the welfare of the peasantry, without being compelled to do so by duty or interest; but these were rebels against the law of their condition, which, in spite of themselves, enjoined indifference on the one side and hatred on the other.

It has been common to ascribe the general desertion

of the country parts by the nobility to the policy of particular kings or ministers: some have traced it to Richelieu, others to Louis XIV. During the last three centuries of the monarchy it certainly was the aim of the monarchs to keep the nobility apart from the people, and to attract the former to the court. That aim was pursued with especial vigor in the seventeenth century, when the nobility were still feared by the kings. One of the questions addressed to intendants was, "Do the noblemen of your province prefer remaining there, or leaving their homes?" The answer of one intendant regretted that in his province men of rank preferred the company of mere peasants to the society of the court and their duty to the king. The province of which this was said was Anjou, which afterward became La Vendée. These noblemen, who were said to be slow to perform their duty to the king, were the only ones who defended the French monarchy in the field, and died for it; they owed this glorious distinction solely to their influence over the peasantry, among whom they were censured for preferring to reside.

Care must be taken, however, not to ascribe the migration of the nobility into the capital to the direct influence of this or that king. The true and principal cause of the phenomenon lay not in the policy of individuals, but in the slow, unceasing operation of institutions; this is proved by the utter incapacity of the government to arrest the mischief, when in the eighteenth century it was so minded. When the nobility lost, irretrievably, their political rights, and the local franchises were taken away, the migration became universal. No stimulus was required to wean the nobles from the country ; they had no wish to stay there : rural life had no charms for them.

What I have said of the nobility applies equally to rich landowners in general. Centralization stripped the rural districts of their rich and enlightened inhabitants. I might explain how, moreover, it prevented agriculture from arriving at perfection ; for, as Montesquieu profoundly observes, " The yield of land depends less on its fertility than on the freedom of its occupants." But I do not wish to digress.

We have seen already how the middle classes deserted the country parts and took refuge in cities. Nothing is better established by the documents of the old regime. One rarely sees, say they, more than one generation of rich peasants. The moment a farmer acquires a little property, he takes his son from the plow, sends him into the city, and buys him some small office. Hence arose the strange dislike which farmers even still seem to feel for the calling which has enriched them. The effect has outlived the cause.

In fact, the only well-bred man, or, as the English would say, the only gentleman who lived permanently among the peasantry, and associated with them, was the parish curate ; and the curate would have become the master of the rural classes, in spite of Voltaire, had he not been so notoriously connected with the political hierarchy, whose odium he shared together with its privileges. [d]

The peasant, then, was widely separated from the upper classes of society. He was kept aloof from all who could help or guide him. The higher his fellows rose in influence and station, the more they avoided him. He seemed to have been picked out of the whole nation, and set aside.

No such state of things existed in any other great nation of civilized Europe, nor had it been of long duration in France. The peasant of the fourteenth century was liable to more oppression, but he had better claims to assistance. If the aristocracy tyrannized over him occasionally, they never abandoned him.

Villages in the eighteenth century were assemblages of poor, ignorant, and coarse persons; with unskilled magistrates, universally despised; with a syndic who could not read; with a collector who could not add up the accounts on which his neighbors' and his own fortune depended. Their old seigniors, despoiled of their authority, had come to consider it degrading to be concerned in their government. They viewed the distribution of the taille, the militia levy, the regulation of *corvées*, as servile duties only fit for a syndic. No one but the central power paid any attention to village affairs; and, as it was distant, and had nothing to fear from the villagers, it noticed them no further than was necessary to get money from them.

See, now, what became of this forsaken class, over which no one tried to tyrannize, but which no one tried to aid or enlighten.

The weightiest of the feudal burdens had certainly been lightened or removed, but they had been succeeded by others perhaps even more oppressive. Peasants were relieved from many grievances which had afflicted their ancestors, but they endured sufferings which the latter had never known.

It is notorious that the increase of the taille—tenfold in two centuries—fell wholly on the agricultural classes. A word must be said here of the manner in which it was levied in the country, in order to show what barbarous laws may be established or maintained in a civilized age, when the leading minds of the nation have no personal interest in changing them.

I find a sketch of the taille, in a confidential circular of the comptroller-general to the intendants, dated 1772. It is a masterpiece of accuracy and brevity. "In the greater part of the kingdom," says the minister, "the taille is arbitrarily distributed and levied, under a joint and several responsibility, on the persons of taxables and not on property; it varies constantly in consequence of the fluctuations in the means of those who pay it." That is the whole story; impossible to sketch with more art the lucrative evil.

The sum to be paid by each parish was fixed yearly. As the minister observed, it varied incessantly, so that the farmer could never tell how much he would have to pay from year to year. In each parish a peasant was chosen at haphazard every year, and appointed collector; it was his business to distribute the tax among his fellow-parishioners.

I promised to describe the office of collector. Listen to the Provincial Assembly of Guienne: it is an impartial witness, being wholly composed of persons who are exempt in virtue of royal appointments. It declared in 1779: "As no one is willing to take the office of collector, it must be held alternately by every one. Hence the tax is levied every year by a new collector, about whose capacity and honesty no inquiry is made.

The tax levy is what might be expected: it bears the mark of the collector's fears, his weaknesses, or his vices. How could it be otherwise? He is wholly in the dark. Who can tell the exact income of his neighbor, or the proportion it bears to that of others? Yet the collector is bound to decide the exact amount of each; and for the proceeds of the tax his property and his person are liable. He usually loses half his time, for two years, in running after the tax-payers. Those who can not read are obliged to find a neighbor to take their place."

A short while before, Turgot had said of another province, "The post of collector often drives its incumbent to despair, and nearly always ruins him. In each village, all the families in easy circumstances are thus successively reduced to poverty."

The unfortunate individual was, however, armed with prodigious power—a tyrant as well as a martyr. While he was ruining himself, he held the fortune of every one else in his hands. In the language of the provincial assembly, "Family affection, personal friendships and spites, a desire for vengeance, a wish to conciliate, fears of displeasing a rich man who has work to give—all these render it almost impossible that he can discharge his duties justly." Fear often made the collector pitiless. In some parishes he did not show his face without a band of bailiffs and followers at his back. "Unless he is backed by bailiffs," writes an intendant in 1764, "the taxables will not pay." "At Villefranche alone," says the provincial assembly quoted above, "six hundred bailiffs and followers are always kept on foot."[e]

To escape this violent and arbitrary taxation, the French peasant of the eighteenth century imitated the Jew of the Middle Ages. . He assumed the garb of poverty if he was accidentally in easy circumstances; the idea of a competency terrified him. I find this proved by a document which does not date from Guienne, but from a hundred leagues from thence. The Agricultural Society of Maine announced in its report of 1761 that it had intended to distribute cattle as prizes, but had " abandoned the design from apprehensions that the distribution of such prizes might awaken jealousies which the arbitrary mode of distributing the taxes might enable defeated competitors to gratify in future years."

This system of taxation trained every one, in fact, to spy out his neighbors, and denounce to the collector their progress toward affluence: all were educated to be informers and natural enemies. What more would one expect to hear of the dominions of a rajah of Hindostan?

There were parts of France, however, where the taxes were uniform and mild; these were some of the *pays d'états.*[f] It is true that these provinces had reserved the right of taxing themselves. In Languedoc, for instance, the taille bore wholly on landed property, and did not vary with the owner's means. Every thirty years the whole province was divided into three classes of lands, according to fertility, and the proportion to be borne by each estate was carefully fixed and recorded in a register. Every one knew beforehand precisely how much he had to pay. If he failed to pay, he, or rather his land, was alone responsible. If he felt aggrieved by the levy, he had the right of demanding a comparison of his quota with that of any other resident of the parish he chose to select, by the process we now call an "appeal for proportionate equality."

It will be seen that this system is precisely the one which we pursue to-day; it has been extended to the whole country without alteration. It is worthy of remark, that while we have borrowed from the old regime the form of our public administration, we have abstained from imitating it in other respects. Our administrative methods are copied from those of the old provinces. We have taken the machine, but rejected its product.

The habitual poverty of the country people had given rise to maxims well calculated to keep them poor. Richelieu, in his Political Testament, says, "If the people were well off, it would be difficult to restrain them within legal bounds." Rulers in the eighteenth century did not go quite so far, but they believed the peasant would not work without the spur of need; misery appeared to them the only safeguard against idleness. I have heard the very same theory advanced in reference to the negroes in our colonies. So general has this belief been, that most political economists have felt it necessary to refute it at length.

It is well known that the primitive object of the taille was to enable the king to hire soldiers in lieu of the nobles and vassals who were bound to service; yet in the seventeenth century the military service was again exacted, as has been mentioned, under the name of militia, and this time the burden fell wholly upon the people, and almost exclusively on the peasantry.

That militia duty was often strenuously refused or evaded is well established by the immense number of police reports referring to the apprehension of refractory militia-men or deserters that are to be found in every intendant's office. It was, it seems, the most odious of all the burdens that were laid on the peasantry. They fled into the woods to avoid serving, or resisted the levies with force of arms. This appears surprising in view of the ease with which a system of compulsory conscription is enforced to-day.

The intense aversion which the old regime peasantry felt for the militia system was due less to the principle of the law than to the manner in which it was executed; to the length of time during which the risk hung over men's heads (a man was liable till he was forty, unless he married); to the arbitrary revision of the lots, which often made a good number as fatal as a bad one; to the legal impossibility of procuring a substitute; to the disgust inspired by a hard, dangerous vocation, in which it was wholly impossible to rise; but, above all, to the reflection that this great burden bore on them alone, and on the most wretched individuals among them. The ignominious distinction established between them and other classes imbittered their actual wrongs.

I have examined the reports of several drawings for militia-men, in various parishes, in the year 1769. The exempts are enumerated: one is the servant of a gentleman; another, watchman at an abbey; a third is only valet of a burgher, it is true, but his master "lives nobly." No one, as a rule, was exempt but persons in easy circumstances. When a farmer, for instance, paid heavy taxes for several years, his sons were exempt: this was called encouraging agriculture. Political economists, much as they admired equality in other matters, made no objection to this privilege; they only desired to extend it to other cases, or, in other words, to increase the burden of the poorest and most unprotected peasantry. One of them observes that "soldiers are so badly paid, so poorly lodged, dressed, and fed, and kept in such strict dependence, that it would be too cruel to choose them out of any class but the very lowest."

Up to the close of the reign of Louis XIV. the highroads were not repaired at all, or were kept in repair at the cost of the state and of the road-side landowners: it was at that period that the plan of keeping them in repair at the expense of the peasantry, by *corvées*, was first commenced. It seemed so excellent a mode of securing good roads without paying for them, that in 1737 a circular of Comptroller-general Orry applied it to the whole of France. Intendants were authorized to imprison refractory peasants, or to send bailiffs for them.[g]

Thenceforth, measurably with the extension of trade and the desire for good roads, *corvées* were extended and increased.[h] A report made in 1779 to the Provincial Assembly of Berry states that the annual value of labor performed by the peasantry in *corvées* in that poor province was 700,000 *livres*. A similar estimate was made for lower Normandy in 1787. No better indication of the sad condition of the country-people could be found. Social progress enriched all other classes of society, but impoverished the peasantry. Civilization was a blessing to all but them.

It is stated in the correspondence of the intendants about the same period, that the peasantry must not be allowed to perform their regular *corvées* on private roads, for they are all required on the highways, or, as the phrase was, on the king's highway.[i] The strange notion that the cost of keeping the roads in repair ought to be borne by the poorest persons in the community, and those who travel the least—new as it was—took such root in the minds of those who were gainers by it, that they soon came to believe that no other system was feasible. An attempt was made in 1776 to commute *corvées* for a tax payable in money: the new tax was as unequally distributed as the old imposition.

Corvées, on ceasing to be seigniorial and becoming royal, were gradually applied to all public works. In 1719 they were exacted for the construction of barracks. "*The parishes must send their best workmen,*" said the ordinance, "*and give up all other work for this.*" *Corvées* were exacted for the conveyance of convicts to the galleys,[k] and of beggars to charitable institutions; for the removal of military baggage from place to place, when troops were moved.[l] This was no slight task at a time when every regiment was encumbered with heavy baggage: it was requisite to gather from the neighborhood for many miles around an immense number of carts and oxen. This kind of compulsory labor, which was hardly felt at first, became a very heavy burden when the standing armies became large. I have seen pressing demands from contractors, insisting on the employment of *corvées* for the conveyance of timber from the forests to ship-yards.[m] Labor of this description was usually remunerated, but the price was low and unalterable. This ill-advised imposition sometimes became so burdensome as to frighten the receivers of the taille. In 1751 a receiver was apprehensive lest "the expense to which the peasantry were put for the repairs of the roads would incapacitate them from paying the taille."

Could these oppressive measures have been carried into effect if beside the peasantry there had stood rich and enlightened men, with the will and the power, if not to protect them, at least to intercede on their behalf with the master, who held the fortune of rich and poor alike in his hand?

I have read a letter, written in 1774 by a wealthy landholder to the provincial intendant on the subject of opening a road. The road, says he, would insure the prosperity of the village, and he explains why; then he recommends the establishment of a fair, which could not fail to double the price of produce; and, lastly, this excellent citizen advises the foundation of a school, with some small help from government, as the best method of procuring industrious subjects for the king. None of these ideas had occurred to him until he had been confined a couple of years by a *lettre de cachet* in his chateau. "It is my exile on my estate," he adds ingenuously, "which has convinced me of the extreme utility of all these projects."

It was especially in time of scarcity that observers noticed the rupture of the old bonds of patronage and dependence which had formerly linked the great landowners and the peasantry together. At these critical periods the central government was terrified by a consciousness of its weakness.   It tried to recall to life the individual influences or the political associations it had destroyed, but they gave no sign, and it saw with surprise that the people it had killed were really dead.

When the suffering was very great, especially in the poorer provinces, some intendants, like Turgot, issued illegal ordinances, compelling the rich landowners to feed their peasantry till the harvest came round. I have seen letters from several curates, dated 1770, advocating the taxation of the richest landowners of their parishes, laymen and ecclesiastics alike—" men who own large estates, on which they never· reside, and which only serve to give them an income which they spend elsewhere."

Villages were always infested with beggars, for, as Letronne remarks, the poor are relieved in the cities, but in the country, especially in winter, there is no one to help them, and they have no choice but to beg.

These unfortunate people were sometimes furiously persecuted.   The Duke of Choiseul undertook in 1767 to put down mendicity throughout France.   The intendant's correspondence bears witness to the rigor with which he proceeded.   Orders were given to the police to arrest simultaneously all the beggars in the kingdom: it is said they seized fifty thousand.   All able-bodied vagabonds were sent to the galleys; for the others, some forty poor-houses were opened in various parts of the kingdom.   It would have answered better to have opened the hearts of the rich.

The government of the old regime, which was so mild and so timid, so fond of formalities and delays in dealing with the upper classes, was often rough and always prompt in dealing with the lower, especially with the peasantry. I have never been able to discover, in all the documents I have examined, a single instance where a burgher was arrested by order of an intendant, but peasants were arrested daily for *corvées*, militia duty, mendicity, and a thousand other matters. One class was entitled to be judged by an independent tribunâl, after a long and public hearing; the other was dragged before the police magistrate (*prévôt*), who decided summarily and without appeal.[n]

" The immense distance which separates the people from other classes of society," says Necker in 1785, "tends to divert attention from the manner in which power may be used against individuals. Were it not for the gentleness and humanity of the French character, and the spirit of the age, the subject would be an endless source of sorrow to those who can sympathize with sufferings which they do not share."

But the oppressive character of the system was more conspicuous in the improvement it prevented than in the injury it caused. Free, and landholders as they were, the peasantry were almost as ignorant as, and often more wretched than the serfs their ancestors. In the midst of a prodigious development of art and science, they made no industrial progress; they remained dark and uncivilized in a world that glittered with intelligence. They had never learned to use the quickness and keenness of their race; they could not even succeed in their own calling—agriculture. A celebrated English agricultural writer described what he saw as being "farms dating from the tenth century." They excelled in nothing but warfare; for, as soldiers, they could not help mingling with other social classes.

Such was the depth of wretchedness and solitude in which the French peasantry were hermetically sealed. I was surprised and almost alarmed by discovering that, less than twenty years before the Catholic faith was abolished without resistance and the churches profaned, the government often adopted the following method of ascertaining the population of a canton: the curates reported the number of communicants at Easter; to this an approximate figure was added for children under age and sick persons; and the total was assumed to be the exact population. Yet the ideas of the time, strangely altered and disguised, were making their way into the peasant's mind by devious and crooked channels, though nothing of them appeared on the surface. Manners, customs, belief— all were unchanged: the peasant was not only resigned, he was in good spirits.

Care must be taken not to misunderstand the gayety which the French have often exhibited in the greatest affliction. It is a mere attempt to divert the mind from the contemplation of misfortune which seems inevitable; it by no means indicates insensibility. Throw open a door by which these men may escape from the misery which they appear to bear so lightly, and they will rush through it with such force as to pass over any obstacle that stands in the way, without even noticing it.

We see these things very plainly from our point of view, but they were hidden from contemporaneous observers. The upper classes never easily read the mind of their inferiors, and least of all of the peasantry. Their education and their social habits endow the latter with habits of judging which are peculiar to themselves, and which other classes do not acquire; and when rich and poor have no interests, or grievances, or business in common, the obscurity which wraps their respective minds becomes impenetrable; they may live side by side for centuries without understanding each other. It is curious to note the astonishing feeling of security which pervaded the upper and middle classes of society at the time the Revolution began, to hear their ingenious lucubrations on the virtues of the people, on their gentleness, their affectionate disposition, their innocent pleasures, when '93 is close at hand. A ridiculous, but a terrible spectacle!

Let us stop here, before proceeding further, and observe, through all the small facts I have noticed, one of the greatest of God's laws for the government of society.

The French nobility will not mix with the other classes. Men of rank succeed in throwing off all their public burdens. They fancy that by doing so they may preserve their rank without its troublesome appendages, and at first sight it really seems they can; but before long an internal disease assails them, and reduces them gradually. They grow poorer as their privileges multiply. The middle classes, from which they had taken such care to keep aloof, grow rich and enlightened beside them, without them, in spite of them. The very men they had refused to accept as associates or fellow-citizens are about to become their rivals, their enemies, and, ere long, their masters.

Though they have been relieved from the responsibility of guiding, protecting, assisting their vassals, they estimate that they have lost nothing, because their titles and their pecuniary privileges still remain intact.   As they are still the first men in the country in rank, they persuade themselves that they still hold rule ; and, in fact, they are still surrounded by those whom in notarial acts they style " their subjects," while others are their vassals, their tenants, their farmers.   But, in reality, they govern no one.   They stand quite alone, and from the blow that threatens to overwhelm them, their only resource will be in flight.

Though the career of the nobility and that of the middle classes had differed widely, there was one point of resemblance between them : both had kept themselves aloof from the people.   Instead of uniting with the peasantry, the middle classes had shrunk from the contact of their miseries ; instead of joining them to combat the principle of inequality of ranks, they had only sought to aggravate the injustice of their position: they had been as eager for exceptional rights as the nobility for privileges.   Themselves sprung from the ranks of the peasantry, they had so lost all recollection and knowledge of their former character, that it was not till they had armed the peasants that they perceived they had roused passions which they could neither gauge, guide, nor restrain, and of which they were destined to be the victims as well as the authors.

The ruin of the great house of France, which once promised to spread over the whole Continent, will always be a subject of wonder, but no careful student of its history can fail to comprehend its fall.   With few exceptions, all the vices, all the errors, all the fatal prejudices which I have sketched, owed either their origin, or their continuance, or their development to the exertions made by most of our kings to create distinctions of classes in order to govern more absolutely.

But when the work was complete—when the nobility were isolated from the middle classes, and both from the peasantry—when each class contained a variety of small private associations, each as distinct from the others as the classes themselves, the whole nation, though homogeneous, was composed of parts that did not hold together. There was no organization that could resist the government, but there was none that could assist it. So it was that, the moment the groundwork moved, the whole edifice of the French monarchy gave way and fell with a crash.

Nor did the people, in taking advantage of the faults of their masters, and throwing off their yoke, wholly succeed in eradicating the false notions, the vicious habits, the bad propensities these masters had either imparted or allowed them to acquire. They have at times used liberty like slaves, and shown themselves to be as incapable of self-government as they were void of pity for their old teachers.

I shall now pursue my subject, and, losing sight of the ancient and general predisposing causes of the great revolution, pass to some specific facts of more recent date, which determined finally its locality, its origin, and its character.

CHAPTER XIII.

HOW, TOWARD THE MIDDLE OF THE EIGHTEENTH CENTURY, LITER-
ARY MEN BECAME THE LEADING POLITICIANS OF THE COUNTRY,
AND OF THE EFFECTS THEREOF.

FRANCE had long been the most literary nation
of Europe, but her men of letters had never exhibited the mental peculiarities, or occupied the rank
which distinguished them in the eighteenth century.
Nothing of the kind had ever been witnessed either
here or abroad.

They took no part in public business, as English
authors did ; on the contrary, they had never lived so
much out of the world.   They held no public office,
and, though society teemed with functionaries, they had
no public functions to discharge.

But they were not strangers to politics, or wholly
absorbed in abstract philosophy and belles-lettres, as
most of the German literary men were.   They paid
sedulous, and, indeed, special attention to the subject
of government.   They were to be heard day after day
discoursing of the origin and primitive form of society,
of the primordial rights of the governed and governing
power, of the natural and artificial relations of men one
to the other, of the soundness or the errors of the prevailing customs, of the principles of the laws.   They
made thorough inquiries into the Constitution, and
criticised its structure and general plan.   They did
not invariably devote particular or profound studies to

these great problems. Many merely glanced at them in passing, often playfully, but none omitted them altogether. Abstract and literary views on political subjects are scattered throughout the works of that day; from the ponderous treatise to the popular song, none are wholly devoid of this feature.

The political systems of these writers were so varied that it would be wholly impossible to reconcile them together, and mould them all into a theory of government.

Still, setting details aside, and looking only to main principles, it is readily discerned that all these authors concurred in one central point, from whence their particular notions diverged. They all started with the principle that it was necessary to substitute simple and elementary rules, based on reason and natural law, for the complicated and traditional customs which regulated society in their time.

It will be ascertained, on close inquiry, that the whole of the political philosophy of the eighteenth century is really comprised in that single notion.

It was not new. For three thousand years it had been floating backward and forward through the minds of men without finding a resting-place. How was it that it contrived to engross the attention of all the authors of the day just at this time? How did it happen that, instead of lying buried in the brain of philosophers, as it had done so often, it became so absorbing a passion among the masses, that idlers were daily heard discussing abstract theories on the nature of human society, and the imaginations of women and peasants were fired by notions of new systems? How came it that literary men, without rank, or honors, or riches, or responsibility, or power, monopolized political authority, and found themselves, though strangers to the government, the only leading politicians of the day? I desire to answer these queries briefly, and to show how facts which seem to belong to the history of our literature alone exercised an influence over our revolution that was both extraordinary and terrible, and is still felt in our time.

It was not chance which led the philosophers of the eighteenth century to advocate principles so opposed to those on which society rested in their day. They were naturally suggested by the spectacle they had before them. They had constantly in view a host of absurd and ridiculous privileges, whose burden increased daily, while their origin was growing more and more indistinct; hence they were driven toward notions of natural equality. They beheld as many irregular and strange old institutions, all hopelessly jarring together and unsuited to the time, but clinging to life long after their virtue had departed; and they naturally felt disgusted with all that was ancient and traditional, and—each taking his own reason for his guide—they sought to rebuild society on some wholly new plan.°

These writers were naturally tempted to indulge unreservedly in abstract and general theories of government. They had no practical acquaintance with the subject; their ardors were undamped by actual experience; they knew of no existing facts which stood in the way of desirable reforms; they were ignorant of the dangers inseparable from the most necessary revolutions, and dreamed of none. There being no approach toward political liberty, the business of government was not only ill understood, it was not understood at all. Having no share in it themselves, and seeing nothing that was done by those who had, these writers lacked the superficial education which the habit of political freedom imparts even to those who take no part in politics. They were hence bolder in their projects of innovation, fonder of theory and system, more prone to despise the teaching of antiquity and to rely on individual reason than is usually the case with speculative writers on politics.

Ignorance of the same kind insured their success among the masses. If the French people had still participated in the government by means of States-General, if they had still taken part in the administration of the public business in Provincial Assemblies, it is certain that they would have received the lucubrations of these authors with more coolness; their business habits would have set them on their guard against pure theory.

Had they seen a possibility of changing the spirit without wholly destroying the form of their old institutions, as the English did, they might have been reluctant to adventure upon absolute novelties; but there was not a man whose fortune, or whose comfort, or whose person, or whose pride was not daily interfered with by some old law, or old institution, or old decayed authority, and each particular grievance seemed altogether incurable short of the total destruction of the constitution of the country.

We had, however, saved one right from the general

wreck—that was the right of philosophizing freely on the origin of society, on the natural principles of government, and the primitive rights of man.

A rage for this political literature seized all who were inconvenienced by the legislation of the day, including many who were naturally but little prone to indulge in abstract speculations. Tax-payers, wronged by the unjust distribution of the taille, warmed over the principle of the natural equality of man. Farmers, whose harvests were spoiled by rabbits kept by their noble neighbors, rejoiced to hear that reason repudiated all privileges without exception. Popular passions thus disguised themselves in a philosophic garb; political aspirations were forcibly driven into a literary channel, and men of letters, taking the direction of public opinion, temporarily occupied the position which in free countries belongs to party leaders.

Nor could their claim to that place be disputed. A vigorous aristocracy will not only conduct public business, but will make public opinion, and give the keynote to authors, and authority to principles; but these prerogatives had passed away from the French nobility long before the eighteenth century; they had lost credit and power together. The place they had occupied in the public mind was vacant, and no one could gainsay the authors for seizing upon it.

The aristocracy rather favored than impeded their usurpation. Forgetting that established theories, sooner or later, inevitably become political passions, and find expression in acts, they made no objection to the discussion of doctrines that were wholly subversive of their private rights, and even of their existence. They considered them ingenious exercises for the mind, amused themselves by taking part in them, and peacefully enjoyed their immunities and privileges, while they serenely discoursed on the absurdity of all existing customs.

Astonishment is expressed at the blindness with which the upper classes of the old regime helped to ruin themselves; but where could they have learned better? Ruling classes can no more acquire a knowledge of the dangers they have to avoid without free institutions, than their inferiors can discern the rights they ought to preserve in the same circumstances. More than a century had elapsed since the last trace of public life had disappeared in France. During the interval, no noise or shock warned conservatives of the impending fall of the ancient edifice. Appearances remaining unchanged, they suspected no internal revolution. Their minds had stood still at the point where their ancestors had left off. The nobility were as jealous of the royal prerogative in 1789 as they had been in the fifteenth century, as the reports of the States-General prove. On the other hand, on the very eve of his wreck in the democratic storm, the unhappy Louis XVI., as Burke very truly observes, could see no rival to the throne outside the ranks of the aristocracy; he was as suspicious of the nobles as if he had been living in the time of the Fronde. He felt as certain as any of his ancestors that the middle and lower classes were the surest supports of the throne.

But of all the strange phenomena of these times, the strangest to us, who have seen so many revolutions, is the absence of any thought of revolution from the mind of our ancestors. No such thing was discussed, because no such thing had been conceived. In free communities, constant vibrations keep men's minds alive to the possibility of a general earthquake, and hold governments in check; but in the old French society that was so soon to topple over, there was not the least symptom of unsteadiness.

I have read attentively the cahiers of the Three Estates presented to the States-General in 1789; I say the Three Estates—nobility and clergy as well as Third Estate. I observe that here a law and there a custom is sought to be changed, and I note it. Pursuing the immense task to the end, and adding together all the separate demands, I discover with terror that nothing less is demanded than the simultaneous and systematic repeal of all the laws, and abolition of all the customs prevailing in the country; and I perceive at once that one of the greatest revolutions the world ever saw is impending. Those who are to be its victims to-morrow suspect nothing; they delude themselves with the notion that this elaborate old society can be transformed without a shock, and with the help of reason alone. Unhappy creatures! how had they forgotten the quaint old maxim of their fathers four hundred years ago, "He that is too desiring of liberty and franchess must needs fall into serfage."

That the nobles and middle classes, shut out as they had been for so long from public life, should exhibit this singular inexperience, was not surprising; but it was singular that the members of the government, ministers, magistrates, and intendants, should be equally blind. Of these, many were able men at their trade;

they were thoroughly versed in the administrative science of the period; but of the great science of government in the abstract, of the art of watching social movements and foreseeing their results, they were as ignorant as the people themselves; for this branch of the business of public men can only be taught by the practical working of free institutions.

This is finely illustrated in the memorial which Turgot presented to the king in 1775, in which he advised the creation of a representative assembly. It was to be freely elected by the people, to meet for six weeks every year, but to exercise no effective authority. It might devote attention to administrative details, but without meddling with the government; express opinions rather than wishes; discuss laws without making them. "Such an assembly," said he, "would enlighten the king without fettering him, and afford a safe outlet for public opinion. It would not be authorized to impede necessary measures of government, and could be easily restrained within these limits by his majesty in case it tried to overstep them." It would have been difficult to misapprehend more grossly the tendency of a measure or the spirit of the age. Toward the close of revolutions, it has certainly often happened that Turgot's idea has been successfully realized, and the forms of liberty established without its substance. Augustus performed the experiment with success. When a nation has been wearied by long strife, it will submit to be duped for peace sake; and in these cases history apprises us that it will suffice to collect from various parts of the country obscure dependents of government, and make them play the part of a political assembly at a fixed rate of wages. This performance has been repeatedly witnessed. But at the outset of revolutions such enterprises have always failed, for they excite, without satisfying, men's minds. Every citizen of a free state is aware of this truth; Turgot, with all his administrative science, knew nothing of it.

Now when it is borne in mind that this French nation, which had so little experience of business, and so little to do with its own government, was, at the same time, the most literary of all the nations of the world, it may be easily understood how writers became a power in the state, and ended by ruling it.

In England, political writers and political actors were mixed, one set working to adapt new ideas to practice, the other circumscribing theory by existing facts; whereas in France, the political world was divided into two separate provinces without intercourse with each other. One administered the government, the other enunciated the principles on which government ought to rest. The former adopted measures according to precedent and routine, the latter evolved general laws, without ever thinking how they could be applied. The one conducted business, the other directed minds.

There were thus two social bodies: society proper, resting on a framework of tradition, confused and irregular in its organization, with a host of contradictory laws, well-defined distinctions of rank and station, and unequal rights; and above this, an imaginary society, in which every thing was simple, harmonious, equitable, uniform, and reasonable.

The minds of the people gradually withdrew from

the former to take refuge in the latter. Men became indifferent to the real by dint of dwelling on the ideal, and established a mental domicile in the imaginary city which the authors had built.

Our revolution has often been traced to American example. The American Revolution, no doubt, exercised considerable influence over ours, but that influence was less a consequence of the deeds done in America than an inference from the prevailing ideas in France. In other European countries the American Revolution was nothing more than a strange and new fact ; in France it seemed a striking confirmation of principles known before. It surprised them, it convinced us. The Americans seemed merely to have carried out what our writers had conceived ; they had realized what we were musing. It was as if Fénélon had been suddenly transported into the midst of the Sallentines.

It was something entirely new for men of letters to direct the political education of a great nation : this, more perhaps than any thing else, contributed to form the peculiar character and results of our revolution.

The people imbibed the temper and disposition of the authors with their principles. They were so long sole tutors of the nation, and their lessons were so wholly unchecked and untried by practical experience, that the whole nation acquired, by dint of reading them, their instincts, their mental complexion, their tastes, and even their natural defects. When the time for action came, men dealt with political questions on literary principles.

The student of our revolution soon discovers that

it was led and managed by the same spirit which gave
birth to so many abstract treatises on government.
In both he finds the same love for general theories,
sweeping legislative systems, and symmetrical laws;
the same confidence in theory; the same desire for
new and original institutions; the same wish to reconstruct the whole Constitution according to the rules
of logic, and in conformity with a set plan, instead of
attempting partial amendments.   A terrible sight!
For what is a merit in an author is often a defect in
a statesman, and characteristics which improve a book
may be fatal to a revolution.

The political style of the day was somewhat indebt-
ed to the prevailing literature; it bristled with vague
expressions, abstract terms, ambitious words, and literary phrases.   The political passions of the day gave
it currency among all classes, even the lowest.   Long
before the Revolution, the edicts of Louis XVI. often
spoke of natural laws and the rights of man.   Peasants, in petitions, styled their neighbors "fellow-citizens;" the intendant, "a respectable magistrate;" the
parish curate, the "minister of the altar;" and God, the
"Supreme Being."   They might have become sorry
authors had they but known orthography.

These peculiarities have taken such root in the
French mind that they have been mistaken for its natural characteristics, whereas they are, in fact, only the
result of a strange system of education.   I have heard
it stated that the taste, or, rather, the rage we have
shown during the last sixty years for general principles, systems, and grand verbiage in political matters,
proceeded from an idiosyncracy of our race—a pecul-

iarity of the French mind; as though a feature of this kind would be likely to remain hidden for ages, and only to see the light at the close of last century.

It is singular that we should have retained the habits which literature created, though we have almost entirely lost our old love for letters.   I was often surprised, during the course of my public life, to see men who hardly ever read the works of the eighteenth century, or, indeed, any others, and who despised literary men, exhibit a singular fidelity to leading defects to which the old literary spirit gave birth.

CHAPTER XIV.

HOW IRRELIGION BECAME A GENERAL RULING PASSION AMONG
FRENCHMEN IN THE EIGHTEENTH CENTURY, AND OF THE INFLU-
ENCE IT EXERCISED OVER THE CHARACTER OF THE REVOLUTION.

EVER since the great revolution of the sixteenth century, when the spirit of free inquiry was evoked to decide which of the various Christian traditions were true and which false, there had constantly appeared, from time to time, inquisitive or daring minds which disputed or denied them all. The train of thought which in the time of Luther had expelled from the Catholic fold several millions of Catholics drove a few Christians every year out of the pale of Christianity. Heresy had been followed by unbelief.

It may be said generally that in the eighteenth century Christianity had lost a large portion of its power all over Europe; but in most countries it had been reluctantly abandoned rather than violently rejected. Irreligion had spread among sovereigns and wits, but it had made no progress among the middle classes and the people; it was a fashionable caprice, not a popular opinion. "A vulgar error prevails in Germany," says Mirabeau in 1787, "to the effect that the Prussian provinces are full of atheists. The truth is, that, if there are a few freethinkers here and there, the people are as religious as any nation in the world, and among them fanatics are quite common." He adds that it is a pity Frederick II. does not authorize the marriage of

Catholic priests, and allow married ecclesiastics to retain their rank and functions: "This measure, I venture to say, would be worthy of so great a man." In France irreligion had become a passion, general, ardent, intolerant, oppressive; but nowhere else.

The scenes that took place in France were without precedent. Established religions had often been violently attacked, but the fury which assailed them was always inspired by zeal for some new religion. Even the false and detestable religions of antiquity met with no violent or general opposition until Christianity arose to supplant them. Previous to that event they had died of old age, quietly, in the midst of doubt and indifference. In France the Christian faith was furiously assailed, but no attempt was made to raise up another religion on its ruins. Ardent efforts were made to eradicate from men's souls the faith that was in them, and leave them empty. A multitude of men engaged warmly in this ungrateful work. Absolute infidelity, than which nothing is more repugnant to man's natural instincts, or produces more discomfort of soul, appeared attractive to the masses. It had formerly given rise to a sickly languor: it now engendered fanaticism and propagandism.

The accidental coincidence of several leading writers, impressed with a sense of unbelief in Christianity, is not sufficient to account for this extraordinary event; for why should all these writers, without exception, turn their attention to this quarter in preference to others? How did it happen that not one out of all of them took the opposite side? Why was it that, unlike their predecessors, they found a ready ear and a predisposition in their favor among the people? The answers to these queries must be sought in peculiarities of time and place; in the same direction, too, we must look for the secret of the success of these writers. Voltaire's spirit had long existed in the world, but Voltaire's reign never could have been realized except in France during the eighteenth century.

Let us first acknowledge that the church in France was not more open to attack than elsewhere. Fewer vices and abuses had in fact crept into the French Church than were seen in many foreign churches; the French clergy were more tolerant than their predecessors or their neighbors. The real causes of the phenomenon are to be found rather in the state of society than in that of the Church.

In searching for them, we must carefully keep in view the proposition established in the last chapter, namely, that the opposition aroused by the faults of government, being excluded from the political world, took refuge in literature, whereby men of letters became the real chiefs of the party that was to overthrow all the social and political institutions of the country.

That point established, the question presents itself in another form. It is not, What were the faults of the Church of that day as a religious institution? but, Wherein was it an obstacle to the progress of the Revolution, and an inconvenience to the writers who were its chief leaders?

The fundamental principles of the Church were at war with those which they desired to see prevail in the civil government of the country. The Church was founded on traditions ; they professed the greatest contempt for all institutions claiming respect in virtue of their antiquity. It recognized a higher authority than individual reason ; they allowed of no appeal from reason. It clung to the notion of a hierarchy; they insisted on leveling all ranks. The two could never come to an understanding, unless both admitted that political and religious societies, being essentially different, can not be governed by like principles; and as they were far from any admission of this kind, it seemed to the reformers absolutely necessary to destroy the religious institutions of the time in order to reach the civil institutions, which were constructed on their basis and model.

The Church was, moreover, the first of all political bodies, and the most odious, though not the most oppressive. It had become a political body in defiance of its vocation and its nature; it shielded vice in high places, while it censured it among the people; it threw its sacred mantle over existing institutions, and seemed to demand for them the immortality it expected for itself. Attacks upon such a body were sure of public sympathy.

Besides these general reasons, the writers of the day had particular, and, so to speak, personal motives for directing their first attack against the Church. The clergy represented that portion of the government which was nearest and most diametrically opposed to them. Other authorities made themselves felt from time to time; but the Church, specially intrusted with the superintendence of ideas and the censorship of let-

ters, was a daily thorn in their side. It opposed them
when they stood forth on behalf of the general liberties
of mankind, and consequently they were driven, in
self-defense, to attack it as the outwork of the place
they were assaulting.

The Church, moreover, appeared the weakest and
most defenseless of all the outworks which lay before
them. Its power had declined as that of the sovereign
had gained strength. Once his superior, then his
equal, it was now merely his subordinate. The pair
had exchanged gifts; the Church had been glad to give
its moral influence in return for the use of the phys-
ical power of the sovereign. He enforced submission
to the Church, it taught respect for the crown. It was
a dangerous bargain, so near revolutionary times, and
sure to be disadvantageous to the power which relied
on faith, not force.

Though the kings still styled themselves eldest sons
of the Church, they were not particularly dutiful. They
took far better care of their own authority than of that
of the Church. They did not allow it to be openly
molested, but neither did they prevent insidious and
covert attacks upon it.

The species of constraint laid upon the enemies of
the Church increased instead of diminishing their power. Oppression sometimes checks intellectual movement, but as often it accelerates it; it invariably happens that such a censorship of the press as then existed multiplies its power a hundred fold.

Authors were persecuted sufficiently to warrant complaint, but not to justify terror. They labored under
inconveniences, which goaded them on to the struggle

without overwhelming them.   Prosecutions against
them were almost always noisy, slow, and fruitless;
they were better calculated to encourage than to repress
free speech.   A thoroughly free press would have been
safer for the Church.

"You think our intolerance," Diderot wrote to Hume
in 1768, "more favorable to intellectual progress than
your unrestricted liberty: D'Holback, Helvetius, More-
let, and Suard, are not of your opinion."   The Scotch-
man was, however, in the right; he had the experience
of a freeman.   Diderot judged like a man of letters,
Hume like a statesman.

If I ask the first American I meet, either at home
or abroad, whether he considers religion to be of service
to law and social order, he will answer unhesitatingly
that civilized society, especially if it be free, can not
exist without religion.   Respect for religion is in his
eyes the best safeguard for political stability and private security.   Those who know least about government know this much.   There is no country in the
world where the boldest political doctrines of the eighteenth century philosophers have received so general a
practical application as in America.   But, notwithstanding the unlimited freedom of the press, their infidel doctrines have never made any progress there.

As much may be said of the English.   Our irreligious philosophy was preached to them before our philosophers were born; it was Bolingbroke who completed Voltaire's education.   Throughout the eighteenth
century infidelity had famous champions in England.[p]
Able writers, profound thinkers, embraced its cause.
But they won no victories with it, because all who had

any thing to lose by revolutions hastened to the support of the established faith.   Even men who mixed
in French society, and did not reject the doctrines of
our philosophers, considered them dangerous.   Great
political parties, such as exist in every free country,
found it to be their interest to espouse the cause of the
Church; Bolingbroke was seen to join hands with the
bishops.   Animated by this example, and encouraged
by a consciousness of support, the clergy fought with
energy in their own defense.   Notwithstanding the vice
of its constitution, and the abuses of all sorts which
teemed within its organization, the Church of England
stood the shock unmoved; writers and speakers sprang
forth from its ranks, and defended Christianity with
ardor.   Infidel theories were discussed, refuted, and rejected by society, without the least interference on the
part of government.

But why need we seek illustrations abroad?   Where
is the Frenchman who would write such books as these
of Diderot or Helvetius at the present day?   Who
would read them?   I might almost say, Who knows
their titles?   We have had experience enough of public life, incomplete as it has been, during the last sixty
years, to lose all taste for this dangerous style of literature.   See how each class in turn has learned, at the
rough school of revolutions, the necessity of respecting
religion.   The old nobility were the most irreligious
class of society before 1789, and the most pious after
1793; the first attacked, they were the first to recover.   When the middle classes were struck down in the
midst of their victory, they in their turn drew toward
religion.   Respect for religion gradually made its way

into the breast of every one who had any thing to lose by popular disorders, and infidelity disappeared or lay hidden in the general dread of revolution.

Very different was the state of society toward the close of the old regime. Politicians were out of practice, and were so ignorant of the part which religion plays in the government of empires, that infidelity found proselytes among those who were the most vitally interested in the maintenance of order and the subordination of the people. Nor yet proselytes alone, but propagandists, who made an idle pastime of disseminating impiety.

The Church of France, which had up to that time been prolific in great orators, sank under the desertion of those whom a common interest should have rallied to its side, and made no sign. At one moment it seemed as though it would have compromised for the retention of its wealth and rank by the sacrifice of its faith.

The assailants of Christianity being as noisy as its adherents were mute, the latter began to fear that they were singular in their opinions, and, dreading singularity more than error, they joined the crowd without sharing its creed. Thus the whole nation was credited with the sentiments of a faction, and the new opinions seemed irresistible even to those whose conduct was the main secret of their imposing appearance. The phenomenon has been often witnessed since in France, in connection not only with religion, but with very different matters.

No doubt an extensive influence was exercised over our Revolution by the general discredit into which religious creeds had fallen at the close of the eighteenth

century.   Its character was moulded, and a terrible
aspect imparted to its physiognomy by this peculiar
circumstance.

I have endeavored to trace the effects produced by
irreligion in France, and I am satisfied that it was by
unsettling men's minds, rather than by degrading their
hearts or corrupting their morals, that it led them into
such strange excesses.

When religion fled from men's souls, they were not
left void and debilitated, as is usually the case ; its
place was temporarily occupied by ideas and feelings
which engrossed the mind and did not allow it to col-
lapse.

If the men of the Revolution were more irreligious
than we are, they were imbued with one admirable
faith which we lack : they believed in themselves.
They had a robust faith in man's perfectibility and
power; they were eager for his glory, trustful in his
virtue.   They had a proud reliance in their own
strength ; and though this often leads to errors, a people without it is not fit for freedom.   They had no
doubt but that they were appointed to transform society and regenerate the human race.   These sentiments
and passions had become a sort of new religion, which,
like many religions which we have seen, stifled selfishness, stimulated heroism and disinterestedness, and
rendered men insensible to many petty considerations
which have weight with us.

I have studied history extensively, and I venture to
affirm that I know of no other revolution at whose
outset so many men were imbued with a patriotism
as sincere, as disinterested, as truly great.   The na-

tion exhibited the characteristic fault, but likewise the characteristic virtue of youth, or, rather, the virtue which used to be characteristic of youth; it was inexperienced, but it was generous.

For all this, infidelity produced immense evil.

Throughout most of the political revolutions that the world had experienced, the assailants of civil laws had respected religious creeds. In like manner, the leaders of religious revolutions had rarely undertaken to alter the form and character of civil institutions, and to abolish the whole framework of government. In the greatest social convulsions there had thus always remained one solid spot.

When the French Revolution overthrew civil and religious laws together, the human mind lost its balance. Men knew not where to stop or what measure to observe. There arose a new order of revolutionists, whose boldness was madness, who shrank from no novelty, knew no scruples, listened to no argument or objection. And it must not be imagined that this new species of beings was the spontaneous and ephemeral offspring of circumstances, destined to perish when they passed away; it has given birth to a race which has spread and propagated throughout the civilized world, preserving a uniform physiognomy, uniform passions, a uniform character. We found it in existence at our birth; it is still before us.

CHAPTER XV.

HOW THE FRENCH SOUGHT REFORMS BEFORE LIBERTIES.

IT is noteworthy that of all the ideas and feelings which prepared the Revolution, the idea of political liberty, properly so called, was the last to make its appearance, as the desire for it was the first to vanish.

The old edifice of government had long been insecure; it shook, though no man struck it. Voltaire was hardly thinking of it. Three years' residence in England had enabled him to understand that country without falling in love with it. He was delighted with the skeptical philosophy that was freely taught among the English, but he was not struck with their political laws, which he rather criticised than praised. His letters on England, which are one of his master-pieces, hardly contain any allusion to Parliament: he envies the English their literary liberty, but cares little for their political liberty, as though the one could exist for any length of time without the other.

About the middle of the century, a class of writers devoted their attention to administrative questions; they had many points in common, and were hence distinguished by the general name of economists or physiocrats. They are less conspicuous in history than the philosophers; they exercised a less direct influence in causing the Revolution, but still I think its true nature can best be studied in their writings. The philosophers confined themselves, for the most part, to abstract and general theories on the subject of government; the economists dealt in theories, but also deigned to notice facts. The former furnished ideal, the latter practical schemes of reform. They assailed alternately all the institutions which the Revolution abolished; not one of them found favor in their eyes. All those, on the other hand, which are credited especially to the Revolution, were announced beforehand and warmly lauded by them: it is not easy to mention one whose substantial features are not to be found in some of their writings.

Their books, moreover, breathe that democratic and revolutionary spirit with which we are so familiar. They hate, not certain specific privileges, but all distinctions of classes; they would insist upon equality of rights in the midst of slavery. Obstacles they regard as only fit to be trampled on. They respect neither contracts nor private rights; indeed, they hardly recognize individual rights at all in their absorbing devotion to the public good. Yet they were quiet, peaceable men, of respectable character, honest magistrates, able administrators; they were carried away by the peculiar spirit of their task.

Their contempt for the past was unbounded. "The nation," said Letronne, "is governed on wrong principles; every thing seems to have been left to chance." Starting from this idea, they set to work to demand the demolition of every institution, however old and time-honored, which seemed to mar the symmetry of their plans. Forty years before the Constituent Assembly divided France into departments, one of the economists suggested the alteration of all existing territorial divisions and of the names of all the provinces.

They conceived all the social and administrative reforms effected by the Revolution before the idea of free institutions had once flashed upon their mind. They were in favor of the removal of all restrictions upon the sale and conveyance of produce and merchandise. But of political liberty they took no thought; and when it first occurred to them they rejected the idea. Most of them were strongly opposed to deliberative assemblies, to local and subordinate authorities, and to the various checks which have been established from time to time in free countries to counterbalance the supreme government. "The system of counterpoises," said Quesnay, "is a fatal feature in governments." A friend of his was satisfied that "the system of counterpoises was the fruit of chimerical speculations."

The only safeguard against despotism which they proposed was public education; for, as Quesnay said, "Despotism is impossible in an enlightened nation." "Mankind," says one of his disciples, "have invented a host of fruitless contrivances to obviate the evils arising from abuses of power by governments, but they have generally neglected the only one that could really be of service, namely, a general permanent system of public education in the essence of justice and natural order." Such was the literary nonsense they wanted to substitute in the place of political guarantees.

Letronne bitterly deplores the government's neglect of the rural districts, and describes them as having no roads, no industry, no intellectual progress; but he never seems to have imagined that they would have been better regulated if their affairs had been intrusted to the people themselves.

Even Turgot, with all his peculiar breadth of view and rare genius, was but little fonder than they of political liberty. He had no taste for it till late in life, when public opinion pointed in that direction. Like the economists, he conceived that the best of all political guarantees was public education afforded by the state; but he desired it to be conducted in a particular spirit, and according to a particular plan. His confidence in this intellectual course of medicine—or, as a contemporary styled it, this "educational mechanism on fixed principles"—was unbounded. "I will venture to answer," said he to the king, in a memorial on the subject, "that in ten years the nation will be so thoroughly altered that you shall not recognize it; and that, in point of enlightenment, morality, loyalty, and patriotism, it will surpass every other nation in the world. Children now ten years old will then be men, trained in ideas of love for their country, submissive to authority from conviction, not from fear, charitable to their fellow-countrymen, habituated to obey and to respect the voice of justice."

It was so long since political liberty had flourished in France that its conditions and effects had been well-nigh forgotten. More than this, its shapeless relics, and the institutions which seemed to have been framed to take its place, rather aroused prejudice against it. Most of the surviving state assemblies exhibited the spirit as well as the forms of the Middle

Ages, and hindered instead of assisting social progress. The Parliaments, which were the only substitutes for political bodies, could not arrest the mischief done by government, and often impeded it when it desired to do good.

The economists did not think it possible to use these old institutions as instruments for the accomplishment of the Revolution, nor did they approve the idea of intrusting the business to the nation as sovereign; they doubted the feasibility of effecting so elaborate and intricate a reform by the aid of a popular movement. Their designs, they thought, could be best and most easily accomplished by the crown itself.

The royal power had not taken its rise in the Middle Ages, and bore no mediæval stamp. They discovered in it good as well as bad points. It shared their proclivity for leveling all ranks, and making all laws uniform. It detested as heartily as they did the old institutions which had grown out of the feudal system, or which favored oligarchy. It was the best organized, the greatest and strongest government machine in Europe. Its existence seemed to them a very fortunate accident; they would have called it providential had it been the fashion then as now to allude to Providence on all possible occasions. Letronne observes that "France is much more happily situated than England; for here reforms that will change the whole state of the country can be accomplished in a moment, whereas in England similar measures are always exposed to be defeated by party strife."

Their idea, then, was not to destroy, but to convert

the absolute monarchy. " The state must govern according to the laws of natural order (*règles de l'ordre essentiel*)," says Mercier de la Rivière; " on these conditions it should be absolute." " Let the state," said another, "understand its duty thoroughly; this secured, it should be untrammeled." All of them, from Quesnay to Abbé Bodeau, were of the same mind.

They were not satisfied with using the royal power to effect social reforms; they partly borrowed from it the idea of the future government they proposed to establish. The one was to be, in some measure, a copy of the other.

The state, said the economists, must not only govern, it must shape the nation. It must form the mind of citizens conformably to a preconceived model. It is its duty to fill their minds with such opinions and their hearts with such feelings as it may judge necessary. In fact, there are no limits either to its rights or its powers. It must transform as well as reform its subjects; perhaps even create new subjects, if it thinks fit. " The state," says Bodeau, "moulds men into whatever shape it pleases." That sentence expresses the gist of the whole system.

The immense social power conceived by the economists differed from the power they had before them in point of origin and character as well as magnitude. It was not of divine origin; it owed nothing to tradition; it was impersonal: it was called the state, not the king; it was not the heirloom of a family, it was the collective product and representative of the whole nation. Individual rights gave way to it as the sum of the rights of all.

They were quite familiar with the form of tyranny which we call democratic despotism, and which had not been conceived in the Middle Ages. No more social hierarchies, no distinctions of class or rank; a people consisting of individuals entirely equal, and as nearly alike as possible; this body acknowledged as the only legitimate sovereign, but carefully deprived of the means of directing or even superintending the government; over it a single agent, commissioned to perform all acts without consulting his principals: to control him, a public sense of right and wrong, destitute of organs for its expression; to check him, revolutions, not laws; the agent being *de jure* a subordinate agent, in fact a master: such was the plan.

Finding nothing in their neighborhood conformable to this ideal of theirs, they went to the heart of Asia in search of a model. I do not exaggerate when I affirm that every one of them wrote in some place or other an emphatic eulogium on China. One is sure to find at least that in their books; and as China is very imperfectly known even in our day, their statements on its subject are generally pure nonsense. They wanted all the nations of the world to set up exact copies of that barbarous and imbecile government, which a handful of Europeans master whenever they please. China was for them what England, and afterward America, became for all Frenchmen. They were filled with emotion and delight at the contemplation of a government wielded by an absolute but unprejudiced sovereign, who honored the useful arts by plowing once a year with his own hands; of a nation whose only religion was philosophy, whose only aristocracy were men of letters, whose public offices were awarded to the victors at literary tournaments.

It is generally believed that the destructive theories known by the name of socialism are of modern origin. This is an error. · These theories are coeval with the earliest economists. While some of them wanted to use the absolute power they desired to establish to change the forms of society, others proposed to employ it in ruining its fundamental basis.

Read the *Code de la Nature* by Morelly; you will find there, together with the economist doctrines regarding the omnipotence and the boundless rights of the state, several of those political theories which have terrified France of late years, and whose origin we fancy we have seen—community of property, rights of labor, absolute equality, universal uniformity, mechanical regularity of individual movements, tyrannical regulations on all subjects, and the total absorption of the individual in the body politic.

" Nothing," says the first article of this code, " belongs wholly to any one. Property is detestable, and any one who attempts to re-establish it shall be imprisoned for life, as a dangerous madman and an enemy of humanity." The second article declares that "every citizen shall be kept, and maintained, and supplied with work at the public expense. All produce shall be gathered into public garners, to be distributed to citizens for their subsistence. All cities shall be built on the same plan; all private residences shall be alike. All children shall be taken from their families at five years of age, and educated together on a uniform plan." This book reads as if it had been written yesterday.

It is a hundred years old: it appeared in 1755, simultaneously with the foundation of Quesnay's school. So true it is that centralization and socialism are natives of the same soil: one is the wild herb, the other the garden-plant.

Of all the men of their age, the economists would seem the least out of place at the present day; their passion for equality is so violent, their love of liberty so variable, that they wear a false air of contemporaries of our own. When I read the speeches and writings of the men who made the Revolution, I feel that I am in the company of strangers; but when I glance at the writings of the economists, I begin to fancy that I have lived with them, and just heard them talk.

About 1750 the nation at large cared no more for political liberty than the economists themselves; when it fell into disuse, the taste for it, and even the idea of it, were soon lost. People sought reforms, not rights. Had the throne then been occupied by a monarch of the calibre and character of Frederick the Great, I have no doubt he would have accomplished many of the reforms which were brought about by the Revolution; and that not only without endangering his throne, but with a large gain of power. It is said that M. de Machault, one of the ablest ministers of Louis XV., conceived this idea, and communicated it to his master; but such enterprises are not executed at second-hand; a man capable of accomplishing them could not fail to conceive them himself.

Twenty years changed the face of things. France had a glimpse of political liberty, and liked it. Many indications prove this. The provinces began to desire once more to administer their own government. Men's minds became imbued with the notion that the people at large were entitled to a share in their own government. Recollections of the old States-General were revived. National history contained but this single item which the people loved to recall. The economists were carried away by the current, and compelled to clog their absolute scheme with some free institutions.

When the Parliaments were destroyed in 1771, the public, which had suffered severely from their evils, was profoundly affected by their fall. It seemed as if the last barrier against the royal prerogative had been destroyed.

Voltaire was indignant at the symptom. He wrote to his friends, "Nearly all the kingdom is in a state of effervescence and consternation; the provinces ferment as violently as the capital. Yet the edict seems to me to be pregnant with useful reforms. To abolish all venal offices; to establish courts that will administer justice gratuitously; to prevent litigants from coming to Paris from all parts of the kingdom to ruin themselves; to burden the crown with the expense of the seigniorial courts—are not these great services rendered to the nation? Have not these Parliaments been barbarous and intolerant? Really I admire the 'Welches' for taking the side of these insolent and indocile burghers. For my part, I think the king is right; if one must serve, I hold it better to serve a well-bred lion, who is naturally stronger than I am, than two hundred rats of my own breed." And he adds, by way of excuse, "Think how infinitely I ought to appreciate the kindness of the king in relieving seigniors of the cost of their courts."

Voltaire had been absent from Paris for many years, and fancied that the public mind was just as he had known it. This was not the case. The French were not satisfied now with desiring to see their affairs well managed; they wanted to manage them themselves. It was already visible that the great revolution which was in preparation would be effected, not only with the consent of the people, but by their hands.

I think that from this moment the radical revolution, which was to ruin simultaneously the worst features of the old regime and its redeeming traits, became inevitable. A people so badly trained for action could not undertake reforms without destroying every thing. An absolute sovereign would have been a less dangerous reformer. And, for my part, when I remember that this revolution, which destroyed so many institutions, and ideas, and habits that were inimical to liberty, also destroyed others without which liberty can hardly exist, I am inclined to think that, had it been accomplished by a despot, it would have left us perhaps fitter to become a free nation than it did, though it was done in the name of and by the sovereign people.

The preceding remarks must be carefully borne in mind by all who desire to understand the history of our Revolution.

At the time the French conceived a desire for political liberty, they were imbued with a number of notions on the subject of government which were not only difficult to reconcile with liberty, but were almost hostile to it.

In their ideal society there was no aristocracy but that of public functionaries, no authority but the government, sole and all-powerful, director of the state, tutor of individuals. They did not wish to depart from this system in the search for liberty; they tried to conciliate the two.

They attempted to combine an unlimited executive with a preponderating legislative body—a bureaucracy to administer, a democracy to govern. Collectively, the nation was sovereign—individually, citizens were confined in the closest dependence; yet from the former were expected the virtues and the experience of a free people, from the latter the qualities of a submissive servant.

It is to this desire of adjusting political liberty to institutions or ideas which are either foreign or hostile to it, but to which we were wedded by habit or attracted by taste, that we owe the many vain experiments of government that have been made during the last sixty years. Hence the fatal revolutions we have undergone. Hence it is that so many Frenchmen, worn out by fruitless efforts and sterile toil, have abandoned their second object and fallen back on their first, declaring that there is, after all, a certain pleasure in enjoying equality under a master. Hence we resemble the economists of 1750 more closely than our fathers of 1789.

I have often asked myself what was the source of that passion for political liberty which has inspired the greatest deeds of which mankind can boast. In what feelings does it take root? From whence does it derive nourishment?

I see clearly enough that when a people is badly governed it desires self-government; but this kind of love for independence grows out of certain particular temporary mischiefs wrought by despotism, and is never durable; it passes away with the accident which gave it birth. What seemed to be love for liberty turns out to be mere hatred of a despot. Nations born to freedom hate the intrinsic evil of dependence.

Nor do I believe that a true love for liberty can ever be inspired by the sight of the material advantages it procures, for they are not always clearly visible. It is very true that, in the long run, liberty always yields to those who know how to preserve it comfort, independence, and often wealth; but there are times when it disturbs these blessings for a while, and there are times when their immediate enjoyment can only be secured by a despotism. Those who only value liberty for their sake have never preserved it long.

It is the intrinsic attractions of freedom, its own peculiar charm—quite independently of its incidental benefits—which have seized so strong a hold on the great champions of liberty throughout history; they loved it because they loved the pleasure of being able to speak, to act, to breathe unrestrained, under the sole government of God and the laws. He who seeks freedom for any thing but freedom's self is made to be a slave.

Some nations pursue liberty obstinately through all kinds of dangers and sufferings, not for its material benefits; they deem it so precious and essential a boon that nothing could console them for its loss, while its enjoyment would compensate them for all possible afflictions. Others, on the contrary, grow tired of it in the midst of prosperity; they allow it to be torn from them without resistance rather than compromise the comfort it has bestowed on them by making an effort. What do they need in order to remain free? A taste for freedom. Do not ask me to analyze that sublime taste; it can only be felt. It has a place in every great heart which God has prepared to receive it: it fills and inflames it. To try to explain it to those inferior minds who have never felt it is to waste time.

CHAPTER XVI.

THAT THE REIGN OF LOUIS XVI. WAS THE MOST PROSPEROUS ERA
OF THE OLD MONARCHY, AND HOW THAT PROSPERITY REALLY
HASTENED THE REVOLUTION.

IT can not be questioned but the exhaustion of
France under Louis XIV. commenced long before the reverses of that monarch. Symptoms of weakness may be detected in the most glorious years of
his reign. France was ruined before she had ceased
to conquer. Who has not read the terrible essay on
Statistics of Administration which Vauban has left
us ? In memorials addressed to the Duke of Burgundy at the close of the seventeenth century, before
the outbreak of the disastrous war of Succession, all
the intendants allude to the growing decay of the nation, and do not speak as though it were of recent
origin. One observes that population has greatly
fallen off within his province of late years ; another
says that such a town, formerly rich and flourishing,
now affords no demand for labor. One reports that
there used to be manufactures in the province, but
they have been abandoned ; another, that the soil was
more productive, and agriculture more flourishing twenty years ago than it is now. An intendant of Orleans
was positive that population and production had fallen
off twenty per cent. within thirty years. Partisans of
despotism and warlike sovereigns should be recom-
mended to read these documents.

As these evils grew out of the faults of the Constitution, neither the death of Louis XIV. nor even the advent of peace restored public prosperity. Writers on government and social economy, in the first half of the eighteenth century, invariably held to the opinion that the provinces were not recovering—that their decline was steadily progressive. They asserted that Paris alone was increasing in size and wealth. Intendants, ministers, men of business, agreed with men of letters on this point.

I confess that, for my part, I disbelieve this steady decline of France during the first half of the eighteenth century; but the universality of the belief in it, even among those who were best fitted to judge, shows that no sensible progress was being made. All the public documents of the time which I have seen, in fact, indicate a sort of social lethargy. The government revolved in the old routine circle, creating nothing new; cities made hardly any effort to render the condition of their inhabitants more comfortable and more wholesome; no private enterprise of any magnitude was undertaken.

About thirty or forty years before the Revolution broke out, the scene changed. Every portion of the social body seemed to quiver with internal motion. The phenomenon was unprecedented, and casual observers did not notice it; but it gradually became more characteristic and more distinct. Year after year it became more general and more violent, till the whole nation was aroused. Beware of supposing that its old life is going to be restored! 'Tis the awakening of a new spirit, which gives life only in order to destroy.

Every one is dissatisfied with his condition, and seeks to change it. Reform is the cry on every side. But it is sought impatiently and angrily; men curse the past, and dream of a state of things opposite in every particular to that which they see before them. The spirit soon penetrates the government itself; transforms it inwardly without changing its outward form; leaves the laws as they were, but alters their administration.

I have said elsewhere that the comptroller-general and the intendants of 1740 were very different personages from the comptroller-general and the intendants of 1780. This is shown in detail in the official correspondence of the time. At both periods intendants were invested with the same authority, employed the same agents, used the same arbitrary means; but their objects were different. In 1740 intendants were engrossed with the business of keeping their province in order, levying militia, and collecting the taille; in 1780 their heads were full of schemes for enriching the public. Roads, canals, manufactures, commerce, and agriculture above all, absorbed their attention. Sully was then the fashionable model of an administrator.

It was at this period that the agricultural societies I have mentioned began to be established; that fairs began to be common, and prizes to be distributed. I have seen circulars from the comptroller-general which read more like agricultural treatises than public state papers.

The change that had come over the spirit of the governing class was best seen in the collection of the taxes. Though the laws were as unequal, as arbitrary, as harsh as ever, their faults were materially alleviated in practice.

M. Mollien, in his Memoirs, observes that, when he "began to study the fiscal laws, he was terrified by what he discovered: exceptional courts allowed to sentence men to fine, imprisonment, corporal punishment for mere omissions; tax-farmers exercising plenary authority over persons and property on the sole responsibility of their own oath, &c. Fortunately, he did not confine his studies to the letter of the law, and he soon discovered that there was as much difference between the text of the law and its application, as there was between the style of living of the old and modern school of financiers. The courts were always inclined to extenuate offenses and mitigate penalties."

The Provincial Assembly of Lower Normandy said, in like manner, in 1787, "The tax levy may lead to abuses and vexations innumerable; we are, however, bound to admit that in practice the law has been carried out with moderation and discretion of late years."

Official documents abundantly justify this assertion. They prove conclusively that life and liberty were respected; they indicate, moreover, a general concern for the ills of the poor: a new sentiment. The state rarely employed violence with the poor, but often remitted their taxes or granted them alms. The king subscribed to all the country work-houses or poor-houses, and occasionally founded new ones. I find that more than 80,000 *livres* were distributed by the state in charity, in Haute-Guienne alone, in the year 1779; 40,000 in Touraine in 1784; 48,000 in Normandy in 1787. Louis XVI. would not always leave this branch of public business to his ministers; he often took charge of it himself. When a decree was drawn to fix the indemnity due to the peasantry for the damage done to their fields by the royal game in the neighborhood of the captainries, the king drafted the preamble himself, and indicated the method which the peasants were to pursue in order to obtain speedy justice. Turgot describes this good and unfortunate sovereign bringing him the draft in his own handwriting, and saying, "You perceive that I work, too, on my side." If the old regime were described as it really was during the last years of its existence, the portrait would be flattering and very unfaithful.

Simultaneously with these changes in the mind of governed and governors, public prosperity began to develop with unexampled strides. This is shown by all sorts of evidence. Population increased rapidly; wealth more rapidly still. The American war did not check the movement: it completed the embarrassment of the state, but did not impede private enterprise; individuals grew more industrious, more inventive, richer than ever.

An official of the time states that in 1774 "industrial progress had been so rapid that the amount of taxable articles had largely increased." On comparing the various contracts made between the state and the companies to which the taxes were farmed out, at different periods during the reign of Louis XVI., one perceives that the yield was increasing with astonishing rapidity. The lease of 1786 yielded fourteen millions more than that of 1780. Necker, in his report of 1781, estimated that " the produce of taxes on articles of consumption increased at the rate of two millions a year."

Arthur Young states that in 1788 the commerce of Bordeaux was greater than that of Liverpool, and adds that "of late years maritime trade has made more progress in France than in England; the whole trade of France has doubled in the last twenty years."

Due allowance made for the difference of the times, it may be asserted that at no period since the Revolution has public prosperity made such progress as it did during the twenty years prior to the Revolution.[q] In this respect, the thirty-seven years of constitutional monarchy, which were periods of peace and rapid progress for us, can alone compare with the reign of Louis XVI.

Considering the vices of the government and the burdens which weighed upon industry, the spectacle of this great and increasing prosperity is astonishing; so astonishing, indeed, that some political writers, finding themselves incapable of explaining the fact, have denied it altogether, on the same principle that Molière's doctor refused to believe that a patient could be cured contrary to rule. How was it possible that France could prosper and grow rich with unequal taxes, diversified customs, town dues, feudal rights, trade guilds, venal offices, etc.? For all these, France did begin to grow rich and develop its resources on all sides; and for the simple reason that, independently of these misshapen and inharmonious machines, which seemed better calculated to retard than to accelerate social progress, society was held together and driven toward public prosperity by two very simple but very powerful agents: the one a government, strong without being despotic, which maintained order every where; the other a nation whose upper classes were the most enlightened and the freest people on the Continent, and in which individuals were at liberty to make money if they could, and to keep it when made.

Though the king used the language of a master, he was, in reality, the slave of public opinion. From public opinion he derived all his inspirations; he consulted it, feared it, flattered it. Absolute in theory, he was limited in practice. As early as 1784, Necker said in a public document, "Foreigners rarely realize the authority wielded by public opinion in France; they can not readily understand the nature of that invisible power which rules even over the royal palace. It does so, however." He mentions the fact as a matter beyond dispute.

It is a superficial error to ascribe the greatness and power of a nation to the mechanism of its legislation; for in this matter the product is due less to the perfection of the instrument than to the strength of the power used. Look at England; how much more complicated, and varied, and irregular do her laws seem than ours!r Yet where is the European nation whose public credit stands higher, or in which private property is more extensive, more varied, and safer, or society sounder or more opulent? The fact does not spring from the excellence of this or that law, but from the spirit which pervades the whole body of English legislation. The imperfection of special organs is immaterial, the vital spirit is so strong.

Measurably with the increase of prosperity in

France, men's minds grow more restless and uneasy; public discontent is imbittered; the hatred of the old institutions increases. The nation visibly tends toward revolution.

More than this, those districts where progress makes the greatest strides are precisely those which are to be the chief theatre of the Revolution. The extant archives of the old district of Ile de France prove that the old regime was soonest and most thoroughly reformed in the neighborhood of Paris. In no other *pays d'élection* were the liberty and property of the peasant so well secured. *Corvées* had disappeared long before 1789. The taille was more moderate, more regular, more evenly distributed there than in any other part of France. A perusal of the law which reformed it in 1772 is absolutely essential to those who would understand how powerful an intendant could be, whether for good or for evil. In this law the tax appears in a new light. Government commissioners visit each parish once a year and convene the whole community; the relative value of estates is settled publicly; the means of each citizen ascertained by fair discussion; the taille is distributed with the concurrence of all who are to pay it. The arbitrary power of the syndic, the old useless recourse to violence, are done away with. The taille retains its inherent vices, no doubt, under the best system of collection; it is levied on one class of taxables only, and weighs upon their industry as well as upon their property, but in all other respects it is a very different affair from the tax of the same name in the neighboring districts.[s]

On the other hand, the old regime was nowhere in so high a state of preservation as on the borders of the Loire, especially near its mouth, in the swamps of Poitou and the moors of Brittany. That is the very place where the civil war broke out, and the Revolution was resisted with most obstinacy and violence. So that it would appear that the French found their condition the more insupportable in proportion to its improvement.

One is surprised at such an anomaly, but similar phenomena abound in history.

Revolutions are not always brought about by a gradual decline from bad to worse. Nations that have endured patiently and almost unconsciously the most overwhelming oppression, often burst into rebellion against the yoke the moment it begins to grow lighter. The regime which is destroyed by a revolution is almost always an improvement on its immediate predecessor, and experience teaches that the most critical moment for bad governments is the one which witnesses their first steps toward reform. A sovereign who seeks to relieve his subjects after a long period of oppression is lost, unless he be a man of great genius. Evils which are patiently endured when they seem inevitable, become intolerable when once the idea of escape from them is suggested. The very redress of grievances throws new light on those which are left untouched, and adds fresh poignancy to their smart: if the pain be less, the patient's sensibility is greater.[t] Never had the feudal system seemed so hateful to the French as at the moment of its proximate destruction. The arbitrary measures of Louis XVI.—insignificant as they were—seemed harder to bear than all the despotism of Louis XIV.   The short imprisonment of Beaumarchais aroused more emotion in Paris than the Dragonnades.

No one in 1780 had any idea that France was on the decline; on the contrary, there seemed to be no bounds to its progress.   It was then that the theory of the continual and indefinite perfectibility of man took its rise.   Twenty years before, nothing was hoped from the future; in 1780 nothing was feared. Imagination anticipated a coming era of unheard-of felicity, diverted attention from present blessings, and concentrated it upon novelties.

Besides these general reasons for the phenomenon, there were others of a particular nature and equally potent.   Though the administration of the finances had been improved with the other departments, it was still marked by the faults which are inseparable from absolute governments.   It was secret and irresponsible, and hence many of the mischievous practices of Louis XIV. and XV. were still in use.   The very efforts which the government made to develop public prosperity, the assistance it occasionally lavished upon the needy, the public works it undertook, increased its expenses without proportionally increasing its revenue; hence the king's embarrassments were even greater than those of his predecessors.   Like them, he often made his creditors suffer; like them, he borrowed on all sides privately, and without calling for tenders. His creditors were never sure of their interest; indeed, their only guarantee for their capital was the personal faith of the sovereign.

An observer who is reliable, for he was an eye-witness, and better placed for observation than most people, says on this subject, "The French ran great risks in dealing with their own government. If they invested money in its securities, they were never sure of the time when the interest would be paid. If they built ships, mended roads, clothed soldiers for the government, they had no security for repayment of their advances, no certainty when the debt would be considered due; in fact, they were forced to calculate the chances of losing on a contract with ministers just as they would do on a bottomry bond." He adds, very sensibly, "At this time, especially when the development of industry created an unusual thirst for the acquisition of property, and a new liking for ease and comfort, those who had lent money to the state felt more keenly than they would have done at another time the bad faith of the creditor who, of all others, ought to have been the last to forget the sanctity of a contract."

The abuses with which the French government was charged were not new, but the light in which they were viewed was. More crying faults had existed in the financial department at an earlier period, but since then changes had taken place, both in government and in society, which made them more keenly felt than before.

Within the last twenty years the government had acquired an unwonted activity, and had taken part in all kinds of new enterprises. It had thus become the largest consumer of industrial products, and the greatest contractor in the kingdom. A prodigious increase had taken place in the number of those who had money relations with it, who were interested in its loans, speculated in its bargains, or were its salaried servants. At no former period were private fortunes so deeply involved with the state finances. Bad financial management had formerly been a public evil, now it became disastrous to a thousand private families. In 1789 the state owed nearly 600 millions to creditors who were themselves in debt, and whose grievances were aggravated by the personal injury inflicted on them by the remissness of the state. And be it remarked that the irritation of this class of malcontents increased in proportion to their number; for a speculative mania, a thirst for riches, a taste for comfort spreading as business became extended, troubles of this kind appeared intolerable to those who, thirty years before, might have borne them without complaint.

Hence it happened that capitalists, merchants, manufacturers, and other business men or financiers—who are usually the most conservative class of the community, and the stanchest supporters of government, and who will submit patiently to laws which they despise or detest—were now more impatient and more resolutely bent on reform than any other section of the people. They were especially determined on a revolution in the financial department, never dreaming that a radical change in that branch of the government must involve the ruin of the whole.

How could a catastrophe have been avoided? On one side, a nation in which the desire for wealth increased daily; on the other, a government unceasingly engaged in exciting and disturbing men's minds, now inflaming their avarice, now driving them to despair—rushing to its ruin by both roads.

CHAPTER XVII.

A S the people had not appeared for a single instant
on the public stage for a hundred and forty years,
the possibility of their ever appearing there was forgotten, and their insensibility was regarded as a proof of
deafness.   Hence, when some interest began to be tak-
en in their lot, they were discussed publicly as though
they had not been present.   It appeared as though it
was supposed that the discussion would only be heard
by the upper classes, and that the only danger was lest
these might not be made to understand the case.

The very classes which had most to fear from popular fury declaimed loudly and publicly against the
cruel injustice which the people had so long suffered.
They took pleasure in pointing out to each other the
monstrous vices of the institutions which weighed upon
the people.   They employed rhetoric to paint their
sufferings and the inadequate rewards for their labor.
Thus, in their endeavor to relieve the lower classes,
they roused them to fury.   I am not speaking of writers—I allude to the government, to its chief agents,
themselves members of the privileged classes.

When the king endeavored to abolish *corvées* thir-
teen years before the Revolution, he stated in the preamble of the ordinance, "With the exception of a few
provinces (*pays d'états*), nearly all the roads of the
kingdom have been made gratuitously by the poorest

portion of our subjects. The whole burden has fallen
upon those who have no property but their labor, and
whose interest in the roads is very slender; the landowners, who are really interested in the matter—for
their property increases in value in proportion to the
improvement in the roads—are privileged exempts.
By compelling the poor to keep the roads in repair, to
give their time and their labor for nothing, we have
deprived them of their only safeguard against poverty
and hunger, in order to make them toil for the benefit
of the rich."

When an effort was made, at the same time, to remove the restraints which the system of industrial corporations imposed on workmen, it was proclaimed in
the king's name "that the right to labor is the most
sacred of all properties; that any law which infringes
that right is essentially null and void, as being inconsistent with natural right; that the existing corporations are, moreover, abnormal and tyrannical institutions, the product of selfishness, cupidity, and violence." Such expressions were perilous indeed; but
it was more dangerous still to utter them in vain. A
few months later, corporations and *corvées* were re-established.

It was Turgot, it is said, who put these words in
the king's mouth. Most of his successors followed
the example. When the king announced, in 1780,
that from that time forth the augmentations of the
taille would be made public by registry, he took pains
to add as a commentary, "The persons liable to pay
the taille have been not only tormented by the vexatious manner in which it is collected, but have been

exposed besides to unexpected augmentations in the amount levied, and that to such an extent that the taxes paid by the poorest portion of our subjects have increased much more rapidly than those levied on the richer classes." Again, when the king, not daring to equalize all the taxes, endeavored to establish the principle of equality in the collection of those which were already paid by all classes in common, he said, "His majesty hopes that the rich will not complain of being placed on the same level as the poor in the performance of a duty which they ought long ago to have shared more equally."

In times of scarcity, especially, greater efforts seem to have been made to inflame the passions of the people than to supply their necessities. An intendant, desirous of stimulating the charity of the rich, would speak of "the injustice and the harshness of those landowners who owe all they have to the labor of the poor, and who leave the unfortunate laborers, broken down in their service, to perish of hunger." On a similar occasion, the king declared that it was "his majesty's intention to protect the poor against schemes which compelled them to work for the rich at a rate of wages fixed by the latter, and thus exposed them to lack the very necessaries of life. The king will not permit one portion of mankind to be surrendered to the cupidity of another."

To the close of the monarchical era, the struggle between the various administrative branches of government gave rise to all sorts of manifestations of this kind; each disputant accused his rival of being the cause of the people's misery. This is seen distinctly in the quarrel which took place between the king and the Parliament of Toulouse on the subject of the movement of breadstuffs. The Parliament declared that "the false policy of the government endangered the subsistence of the poor;" and the king replied that it was "the ambition of the Parliament and the greed of the rich which caused the public distress." Thus on both sides efforts were made to convince the people that their sufferings were the work of their superiors.

These matters were not stated in private letters; they are to be found in public documents, which the government and the Parliament took care to print by thousands. In the course of his explanations, the king told some harsh truths both of his predecessors and of himself. "The state treasury," said he once, "has been embarrassed by the profusion of several reigns. Several of our inalienable domains have been sold far below their value." "Industrial corporations," he is made to say on another occasion, with more truth than prudence, "are the especial product of the fiscal greed of kings." Farther on he says, "If money has often been thrown away in useless expenses, and the taille has increased beyond measure, the fact must be charged upon the administrators of the finances, who, finding an increase of the taille the easiest, because the most secret method of meeting their difficulties, have had recourse to that plan, though almost any other would have been less burdensome to our subjects."[a]

All this was addressed to the educated classes, in order to prove the merit of measures which certain private interests opposed. As for the people, it was taken for granted that they heard all, but understood nothing.

It must be admitted that the very benevolence which prompted the relief of these poor people concealed a large share of contempt for them. One is reminded of Madame de Duchatelet, who, according to Voltaire's secretary, had no objection to undress before her servants, as she was not convinced that valets were men.

Nor was the dangerous language quoted above confined to Louis XVI. or his ministers. The very privileged classes who were the most immediate objects of popular hatred never spoke otherwise. It must be acknowledged that the upper classes in France concerned themselves about the condition of the poor long before they learned to fear them : their interest in popular sufferings was prior to the first suspicion that those sufferings might eventuate in their ruin. This is especially visible in the ten years which preceded 1789. The peasantry were the theme of constant conversations, of abiding sympathy. Remedies for their evils were suggested incessantly. Light was thrown on their chief grievances, and the fiscal laws which pressed heavily on them were loudly censured. But their new friends were as thoughtless in their sympathy as they had formerly been in their insensibility.

Read the reports of the Provincial Assemblies which were convened in some parts of France in 1779, and, at a later period, throughout the kingdom ; study the public documents which they have left us, and you will be touched with the humanity and amazed at the singular imprudence of their language.

The Provincial Assembly of Normandy declared, in

1787, that " the money appropriated by the king to the roads has often been so used as to be convenient to the rich, but useless to the poor. It has often been employed to render the approach to a chateau more agreeable, while the entry of a bourg or village has been neglected." At the same assembly, the two orders of the nobility and the clergy, after having described the vices of the system of *corvées*, offered spontaneously to devote 50,000 *livres* to the improvement of the roads, " so that," as they say, " the internal communications of the province may be made practicable without costing the people any thing." It would have been less onerous to the privileged classes to have substituted a general tax for the *corvées*, and to have paid their share ; but even in abandoning the benefit of unequal taxation, they liked to preserve the name of being exempt. They sacrificed the useful portion of their rights, but they preserved what was odious.

Other assemblies, wholly composed of persons who were, and intended to remain, exempt from the taille, painted, in equally sombre colors, the evils which that tax inflicted on the poor. They drew a frightful sketch of its abuses, and scattered copies broadcast. And, singular to state, with these striking marks of interest in the people's welfare, they intermingled, from time to time, public expressions of contempt. The people had inspired sympathy without ceasing to inspire disdain.

The Provincial Assembly of Upper Guienne, pleading with warmth the cause of the peasantry, alluded to them as " *ignorant and gross beings, turbulent spirits, and rude and indocile characters.*" Turgot,

who did so much for the people, used language very
similar.[v]

Expressions as harsh were commonly used in documents destined to a wide publicity, and intended to be
seen by the peasantry.   It was as if the writers had
been living in one of those European countries like
Gallicia, where the upper classes speak a different
tongue from the lower, and can not be understood by
them.   Feudal lawyers of the eighteenth century, who
often evince an unusual spirit of justice, moderation,
and tenderness for copyholders and other feudal debtors, still occasionally speak of *low peasants*.   These
insults appear to have been technical (*de style*), as the
notaries say.

Toward 1789, the sympathy for the people grew
warmer and more imprudent.   I have had in my hands
circulars, addressed by several Provincial Assemblies,
in the early part of 1788, to the people of several parishes, inquiring for the details of their grievances.   One
of these was signed by an *abbé*, a nobleman of high degree, three men of rank, and a burgher, all members
of the assembly and acting in its name.   This commission directed the syndic of each parish to convene
the peasantry, and inquire of them what complaints
they had to make of the manner in which the taxes
were levied upon them.   " We are aware," it said,
" that most of the taxes, and especially the gavel and
the taille, are disastrous in their effects upon farmers ;
but we desire to ascertain the particulars of each abuse."
Nor does the curiosity of the Assembly rest there.
They want to know the number of persons who are
exempt from taxation in the parish ; whether they are

noblemen, ecclesiastics, or commoners; what is the nature of their privileges; what is the value of their property; whether they reside on their estates; whether
the parish contains much Church property, or, as the
phrase then was, much land in mortmain, not mer-
chantable; and what its value may be. Even these
inquiries fall short of their requirements. They desire
to know what sum of money would represent the share
which each privileged person would have to bear in
taxes, taille and its accessories, capitation-tax, *corvées*,
if taxation weighed equally on all.

This was simply inflaming the passions of each individual by the recital of his wrongs, pointing out
their authors to him, encouraging him by indicating
the smallness of their number, stealing into his inmost
heart to light up his cupidity, his envy, his hatred.
It seemed as though the Jacquerie, the Maillotins, the
Sixteen, had been wholly forgotten; and as if no one
knew that the French, who are naturally the gentlest
and even the kindest people in the world so long as
they are in repose, become the most barbarous race
alive when violent passions pervert their natural disposition.

I have, unhappily, been unable to procure all the answers which the peasants made to these murderous inquiries, but I have found a few of them, and they suffice to indicate the spirit of the whole.

They give with care the name of every privileged
person, whether belonging to the nobility or the middle classes. Occasionally they describe, and invariably criticise his mode of life. They enter into curious
calculations with regard to the value of his property;

they enlarge upon the number and nature of his privileges, and especially upon the injury which they inflict upon the neighborhood.   They enumerate the
bushels of wheat which he receives by way of dues;
they estimate enviously his revenue, which they say
is advantageous to no one.   The curate's fees—his
salary, as they have already begun to say—are excessive; they remark bitterly that the Church exacts money for every thing, and that a poor man can not even
be buried gratuitously.   As for the taxes, they are all
ill-distributed and oppressive; not one obtains favor
at their hands, and all are spoken of in violent language breathing absolute fury.

"The indirect taxes are odious," they say; "not
a household but the tax-gatherer invades; nothing is
sacred either from his eyes or his hands.   The registry duties are crushing.   The receiver of the taille is
a tyrant whose cupidity shrinks from no measure of
annoyance for honest people.   The bailiffs are no better; no honest farmer is safe from their ferocity.   The
collectors are obliged to ruin their neighbors in order
to save themselves from the voracity of these despots."

The inquiry is no mere preliminary of the Revolution; it is part of it, speaks its language, wears its
features.

One among the many points of difference between
the religious revolution of the sixteenth century and
the French Revolution is especially striking.   In the
sixteenth century, most of the nobility took the side of
the new religion from ambitious or interested motives;
while the people, on the contrary, embraced it from
conviction, and without expecting any profit from the

change. In the eighteenth century this was not the case. It was disinterested principle and generous sympathy which roused the upper classes to revolution, while the people were agitated by the bitter feeling of their grievances, and a rage to change their condition. The enthusiasm of the former fanned the flame of popular wrath and covetousness, and ended by arming the people.

CHAPTER XVIII.

OF CERTAIN PRACTICES BY MEANS OF WHICH THE GOVERNMENT
COMPLETED THE REVOLUTIONARY EDUCATION OF THE PEOPLE.

THE government had long labored to plant and fasten in the popular mind several of those ideas which are now called revolutionary—principles of hostility to individual and private rights, and arguments in favor of appeals to violence.

The king set the example of treating the oldest and most solidly established institutions with contempt. Louis XV. shook the monarchy, and hastened the Revolution as much by his innovations as by his vices, by his energy as by his dissipation. When the people saw the Parliament—an institution coeval with, and apparently as strong as the monarchy—fall and disappear, they inferred, in a vague manner, that a period of violence was at hand, when age would prove no guarantee of respectability, and novelty no indication of risk.

During the whole course of his reign, Louis XVI. talked of nothing but reform. The Revolution overthrew very few institutions whose overthrow he did not foreshadow. He issued ordinances abolishing some of the worst, but he restored them soon afterward, as though he intended only to uproot them, leaving to others the task of pulling them down.

Some of the reforms which he effected changed vio-

lently and unexpectedly old and respected customs;
others did violence to acquired rights. They paved
the way for the Revolution less by striking down obstacles which stood in its way than by showing the
people how it might be brought about. The mischief
was aggravated by the pure and disinterested motives
of the king and his advisers; for no example is so dangerous as that of violence employed by well-meaning
people for beneficial objects.

Long before, Louis XIV. had publicly promulgated
in his edicts the theory that all the lands in the kingdom had been in the origin conditionally granted by
the state, which was therefore the only real landowner
—the actual holders having mere possessory rights,
and an imperfect and questionable title. This doctrine
sprang out of the feudal system, but it was never openly professed in France till that system was on the point
of death; courts of justice never admitted it. It was
the mother of modern socialism, which thus, strange
to say, seems to have been the offspring of royal des-
potism.ʷ

During the subsequent reigns, the government took
pains to teach the people, in practical lessons which
they could easily understand, that private property
was to be regarded with contempt. During the second half of the eighteenth century the government was
seized with a mania for public works; it took possession without scruple of all the lands it required for its
enterprises, and threw down the houses which stood in
its way. The Department of Bridges and Roads was,
then as now, smitten with admiration for the geomet-
rical charm of the straight line. It would have noth-

ing to do with roads in which there was the slightest curve; to avoid a bend, it would cut through a thousand estates. Properties thus injured or destroyed were always arbitrarily and tardily paid for; sometimes they were not paid for at all.[x]

When the Provincial Assembly of Lower Normandy took the administration of the province out of the hands of the intendant, it was ascertained that the price of all the lands taken by public authority during the twenty years previous was yet unpaid. The debt which the state thus owed to this little corner of France amounted to 250,000 *livres*. But few large landholders were injured; the burden fell chiefly on the smaller proprietors, for lands were very generally parceled out into small lots. Here were a large number of persons whose own experience taught them that private rights were not for a moment to be balanced against the public interest: a doctrine they were not likely to forget when the time came for its application to their own benefit.

In many parishes persons had bequeathed sums of money to be employed in supporting charitable institutions for the benefit of the parishioners in certain specific cases. Most of these institutions were either destroyed or transformed during the later period of the monarchy, by mere Orders in Council, that is to say, by the arbitrary will of government. The fund was usually taken away from the village, and bestowed on neighboring hospitals. Carrying out the principle still farther, the government simultaneously diverted the property of the hospitals from its original destination, and applied it to purposes of which the founder of the

charity would doubtless have disapproved. Much of
this property had been left to the hospitals, to be held
by them inalienably : the government authorized them
to sell it, and to pay over the price to the public treasury, which was to pay interest thereon. This, the administrators said, was making a better use of the be-
quest than the testator himself had done. They forgot
that the very best way to teach men to violate the individual rights of the living is to disregard the wishes
of the dead. No subsequent government has displayed such marked contempt for testamentary injunctions
as the old monarchy. Never, on any occasion, did it
evince any of those fastidious scruples which in England rally the whole weight of the social body to the
support of the citizen's last will, and secure for his
memory a respect that is never paid to his person.

Requisitions, compulsory sales of produce, the *maximum*, were all in use under the government of the old
regime. I find that in times of scarcity the public officials would fix the price at which farm produce must
be sold, and punish farmers who refused to send their
grain to market by the imposition of a fine.

But the most pernicious of all lessons was that inculcated by judicial proceedings in criminal cases in
which the people were concerned. Poor men were far
better protected against the rich and the powerful than
is generally supposed. But when they had to deal
with the state, they were judged, as I said before, by
abnormal tribunals composed of partial judges : the
proceedings were speedy and delusive ; the decision,
which was final, might be anticipated by preliminary
execution. " His majesty appoints the provost of po-

lice (*prévôt de la maréchaussée*) and his lieutenant to
take cognizance of all movements and assemblages to
which the scarcity of provisions may give rise; ordains that cases shall be heard and decided by them
summarily and without appeal; and forbids all courts
of justice to take cognizance of any such." This Order in Council was the law throughout the eighteenth
century. Police reports of the time show that, in cases
of this character, suspected villages were surrounded
at night; houses were entered before daybreak; peasants designated for arrest were seized without other
warrant or authority. They were often detained for
a length of time in prison before they could speak to a
judge, though edicts declared that every person accused should be examined within twenty-four hours
after his arrest. That provision of the law was neither less formal nor more respected than it is in our
own day.

It was thus that a benign and solidly-established
government taught the people, day by day, the system
of criminal procedure best adapted to the requirements
of revolution and the desires of tyranny. It kept open
school, and to the last gave to the lower classes this
perilous education. Even Turgot faithfully copied his
predecessors in this respect. When his legislation of
1775 on the subject of breadstuffs gave rise to resistance in the Parliament and riots in the country parts,
he obtained from the king an ordinance which removed
the cases of the rioters from the jurisdiction of the ordinary courts, and gave them exclusively to the cognizance of the provost. "The police jurisdiction," the
ordinance said, "is principally designed to repress pop-

ular disturbances when it is desirable that speedy examples be made." Under this ordinance, peasants traveling out of their parish without a certificate signed by the curate and the syndic were liable to prosecution before the provost, arrest, and punishment as vagabonds.

It is true that, under terrible forms, the monarchy of the eighteenth century concealed moderate penalties. Its principle was rather to terrify than to injure; or, rather, it was arbitrary and violent from habit and indifference, but, at the same time, instinctively gentle. But summary judicial proceedings were none the less popular with government. The lighter the penalty, the easier the vice of its infliction was forgotten. The mildness of the sentence cloaked the harshness of the trial.

I venture to state—for I hold the proofs in my hand —that precedents and examples for very many of the proceedings of the revolutionary government were found in the records of the measures employed against the lower classes during the two last centuries of the monarchy. The old regime furnished the Revolution with many of its forms; the latter merely added the atrocity of its genius.

CHAPTER XIX.

HOW GREAT ADMINISTRATIVE CHANGES HAD PRECEDED THE POLIT-
ICAL REVOLUTION, AND OF THE CONSEQUENCES THEREOF.

BEFORE the form of the government was altered, most of the laws regulating the condition of persons and the administration of public business had been repealed or modified.[y]

The destruction of trade-companies and their partial and incomplete restoration afterward had wholly changed the relation formerly existing between master and workman. That relation was now uncertain—constrained. Neither was the old dominical authority in a state of preservation, nor the guardianship of the state fully developed; so that, between the two, the mechanic, cramped and embarassed, knew not to which side he ought to look for protection or control. This state of uncertainty and anomaly, in which all the lower classes of the large cities had been suddenly placed, led to very grave consequences when the people appeared on the political stage.

A year before the Revolution a royal edict overturned the whole judicial system. New jurisdictions were created, old ones abolished, all the old rules governing the competency of judges changed. Now I have already had occasion to remark that the number of persons who were employed in France, either in hearing cases or executing judgments, was immense. In fact, nearly all the middle class had something to do with the courts. Hence the effect of the law was to disturb the condition and means of several thousand families, whose situation was rendered uncertain and precarious. Nor was it less prejudicial to litigants, who, in the judicial confusion, had some trouble in finding out the law which was applicable to their case, and the court that was to hear it.

But it was especially the radical reform effected in the government proper, in 1787, which threw public business into disorder, and brought trouble into the home of every private family.

I stated that in the *pays d'élection*, that is to say, in three fourths of France, the whole government of each district (*généralité*) was placed in the hands of a single man, the intendant, who was not only uncontrolled, but without advisers.

In 1787 provincial assemblies were created, which became the real governors of the country. In every village an elective municipal body took the place of the old parochial assemblies, and, generally speaking, of the syndic also.

Thus a system diametrically opposed to the past, and completely subversive, not only of the old methods of transacting business, but of the relative positions of men, had to be applied to every part of the country by one uniform plan, quite independently of old usages and of the particular situation of the several provinces. So profoundly was the old government imbued with the unitarian spirit of the Revolution by whose hands it was to perish.

It was then plainly seen how large an influence habit exercises over the working of political institutions, and how much more easily men manage their affairs with obscure and complicated laws to which they are used than with a far simpler system which is new to them.

There were in France, under the old regime, all kinds of authorities, infinitely diversified according to locality, with powers of unknown and unlimited scope, so that the field of action of each was always common to several others; yet business was transacted in an orderly and tolerably easy manner.   The new authorities, on the contrary, which were few in number, carefully limited in their sphere, and harmoniously adjusted, were no sooner put in force, than they encroached upon one another, and clashed, throwing every thing into confusion and paralyzing each other.

The new system, moreover, had a great fault, which alone would have rendered its execution difficult, at the outset especially; all the authorities it created were corporate.

Under the old monarchy, but two methods of governing were known.   Where the government was in the hands of a single individual, he acted without the concurrence of any assembly.   Where, on the other hand, assemblies were used, as was the case in *pays d'états* and in cities, the executive power was confided to no one in particular: the assembly not only governed and controlled the administration, it executed the laws, either directly or through the medium of temporary committees which it appointed.

These being the only two plans known, when one was abandoned the other was adopted.   It is not a little singular that, in so enlightened a society, and one in which government had so long played a leading part, no one should have thought of combining the two systems, and drawing a distinction between the executive branch and that which was supervisory or directory, without disuniting them. This idea, simple as it is, never struck any one; it is a discovery which dates from this century, and almost the only discovery in administrative science that we can fairly claim. We shall perceive the effects of the contrary system when we see the old administrative methods applied to politics, the traditions of the detested old regime followed, and the plan of the Provincial States and small municipalities adopted by the National Convention. Causes which had formerly led to nothing but embarassment in the transaction of public business then gave rise to the Reign of Terror.

The Provincial Assemblies of 1787 were authorized to administer their own government, and to supersede the intendant in almost all matters. They were intrusted with the distribution and levy of the taille, under the authority of the central government, and with the selection and general direction of all public works. All the agents of the Bridges and Roads, from the inspector to the overseer of works, were under their immediate orders. The assemblies decided according to their own discretion what was to be done, reported to the ministers, suggested the names of persons deserving reward. They were the guardians of the *communes*, heard most of the lawsuits which had formerly been brought before the intendant, &c., and discharged a variety of functions that were ill suited to a corporate and irresponsible body, especially when composed of persons who were entirely new to such duties.

The confusion was completed by an error; the intendant was stripped of his power, but the office was retained.   After being deprived of their absolute authority, the intendants were expected to aid the assembly and supervise its acts—as though a fallen functionary could ever help to execute and enter into the spirit of laws which dispossess him.

A similar course was adopted with regard to the office of sub-delegate.   District assemblies were appointed to discharge its functions under the direction of the Provincial Assembly, and on similar principles.

From all that we can learn of the proceedings of the Provincial Assemblies of 1787, including their own reports, it would appear that from the first they found themselves at war, sometimes open, sometimes secret, with the intendants, who employed all their superior business experience in defeating the aims of their successors.[z]   One assembly complains that it can hardly succeed in wresting from the hands of the intendant the most necessary papers.   Another is accused by the intendant of seeking to usurp powers which the edicts reserve to him.   He appeals to the minister, who makes no answer, or answers doubtfully, being as new to the business as the others.   Sometimes the assembly decides that the intendant has been guilty of maladministration, that the roads he has made are in the wrong direction or in bad repair; he is accused of ruining the communities whose guardian he was.   In their inexperience, every thing is obscure to the assemblymen, and they often hesitate, send to distant assemblies for advice, keep couriers constantly on the road from one to another.   The intendant of Auch pretends that he

is entitled to oppose the assembly, which had authorized a *commune* to tax itself; the assembly replies
that in this matter the intendant may offer advice, but
nothing more, and sends to the assembly of Ile de
France to ask what that body thinks on the point.

These recriminations and interchange of opinions
often delay, and sometimes stop altogether, the transaction of public business. National life seems suspended. The Provincial Assembly of Lorraine—a mere
echo of others—declares that " the stagnation of public business is complete, and all good citizens are afflicted thereat."

Others of these new administrations go wrong by
excessive activity and self-reliance; they are full of a
restless and disturbing zeal, which prompts them to
want to change all the old methods with a stroke of
the pen, and to correct the most deeply-rooted abuses
in a day. Under the pretext that they are henceforth
the guardians of cities, they assume the management
of municipal affairs; in a word, their efforts to improve
matters succeed in throwing every thing into confusion.

Now consider the immense influence which the government had long exercised in France, the multitude
of interests which it affected, the vast number of affairs
which depended on it for support or aid; bear in mind
that private individuals relied more on it than on themselves to secure the success of their own business, to
develop their industry, to insure their means of subsistence, to make and mend their roads, to preserve
the peace among them, and to guarantee their well-
being; and then calculate how many individuals must
have been personal sufferers by its disorder.

The vices of the new organization were more conspicuous in the villages than any where else; for there it not only disturbed the old divisions of authority, but changed suddenly the relative position of individuals, and drove the several orders into mutual hostility.

When Turgot, in 1775, proposed to the king to reform the administration of the rural districts, the greatest difficulty he met with, as he states himself, arose from the unequal distribution of taxes. For the chief parochial business was the distribution, levy, and appropriation of the taxes, and how was it possible to make people, on whom they pressed unequally, and some of whom were wholly exempt from them, deliberate and act in concert on their subject? Every parish contained some men of rank, or churchmen, who paid no taille, peasants who were partially or wholly exempt, others who paid an integral share. These formed three distinct parishes, each of which would have required a separate administration. The problem was insoluble.

Nowhere was the inequality of taxation so conspicuous as in the country; nowhere were people so divided into distinct and mutually hostile classes. Before attempting a collective administration and a free government in villages, the taxes should have been equalized, and distinctions of class and rank modified.

This was not the plan pursued when reform was attempted in 1787. Within the parish, the old distinctions of rank were maintained with the unequal taxation which marked them; yet the whole government was intrusted to elective bodies. This led directly to most singular results.

The curate and the seignior had no business to appear in the assembly which elected municipal officers; for they were respectively members of the orders of the clergy and the nobility, while the officials elected were the special representatives of the Third Estate.

But when the Municipal Council was chosen, the curate and the seignior were members *ex officio*, for it would not have been seemly to exclude from the government of the parish its two leading inhabitants. It was the seignior who presided over the municipal councilors, though he had not contributed to elect them, and could not take part in the bulk of their acts. Neither seignior nor curate, for instance, could vote on the distribution or levy of the taille, in consequence of their exemption. In return, the Council could not interfere with their capitation-tax, which continued to be regulated according to particular forms by the intendant.

Lest this president—so carefully isolated from the body which he was said to direct—should still exercise an indirect influence in opposition to the interest of the order to which he did not belong, it was proposed to disfranchise his tenants; and the Provincial Assemblies, to which the point was referred, considered the proposal proper, and in conformity with correct principle. Other men of rank, resident in the parish, were excluded from this municipal body, unless they were elected by the peasants; and then, as the regulation is careful to observe, they were representatives of the Third Estate alone.

The seignior then only appeared there to exhibit his subjection to his old subjects, who were now his mas-

ters, while he was more like their prisoner than their
chief.   Indeed, the principal object of the assemblage
appeared to be less to bring the different ranks together than to show them how widely they differed,
and how adverse their interests were.

Was the office of syndic still so discredited that it
was never willingly accepted, or had it risen in importance side by side with the community whose chief
agency it was?   No one knew precisely.[a]   I have seen
a letter from a village bailiff of 1788, complaining in-
dignantly that he has been elected syndic, " which is
in violation of the privileges of his office."   The comptroller-general replied that the ideas of this personage
required to be rectified ; " that he must be made to
understand that it was an honor to be elected by his
fellow-citizens ; and that, moreover, the new syndics
would not resemble the functionaries hitherto known
by the title, and might expect more consideration at
the hands of government."

On the other hand, the moment the peasantry became a power in the state, the leading citizens of the
parishes and men of rank were suddenly attracted to
their side.   A seignior and high justiciary of a village
near Paris complained that the edict prevented his
taking part, even as a simple inhabitant of the parish,
in the proceedings of the parochial assembly.   Others
" consent," they said, " to devote themselves for the
public good, and accept the office of syndic."

It came too late.   In proportion to the advances of
the wealthy classes, the people of the rural districts
shrank back ; when they tried to mingle with them,
the people sheltered themselves in the isolation into

which they had been driven. Some municipal assemblies declined to admit their seignior as a member; others made all sorts of objections to the reception of commoners who were rich. The Provincial Assembly of Lower Normandy states, "We are informed that several municipal assemblies have refused to admit absentee landholders, who, as commoners, have an indisputable right to seats there. Other assemblies have declined to admit farmers who owned no land within their jurisdiction."

Thus all was novelty, obscurity, conflict between the secondary laws, even before the chief laws which regulated the government of the state had been touched. Those which were still in force were shaken, and there was not a law or a regulation which the government had not announced its intention to abolish or modify.

Our Revolution, then, was preceded by a sudden and thorough remodeling of all administrative rules and habits. The event is barely remembered now, yet it was one of the greatest perturbations that ever marked the history of a great people. It was a first revolution, which exercised a prodigious influence over the second, and rendered it a very different affair from all former or subsequent revolutions.

The first English revolution, though it overthrew the political constitution of the country, and for a time abolished royalty itself, barely touched the secondary class of laws, and made no change in the prevailing customs and usages. Justice and government were administered in the old forms and in the beaten track. At the height of the civil war, it is said that the twelve judges of England continued their semi-annual circuits throughout the country to hold the assizes. The agitation was not universal. The effects of the revolution were circumscribed, and English society, though shaken at the top, was unmoved at the base.

We have ourselves seen in France, since 1789, several revolutions which have altered the whole edifice of government. Most of them have been very sudden, and have been achieved by violence, in open violation of existing laws. Yet none have given rise to long continued or general disorder; they have been scarcely felt, in some cases hardly noticed by the majority of the nation.

The reason is that, since 1789, the administrative system has always remained untouched in the midst of political convulsions. The person of the sovereign or the form of the central power has been altered, but the daily transaction of business has neither been disturbed nor interrupted. Each citizen has remained subject to the laws and usages which he understood, in the small matters which concerned him personally. He had to deal with secondary authorities, with which he had done business before, and which were rarely changed. For if each revolution struck off the head of the government, it left its body untouched and alive, so that the same functionaries continued to perform their functions, in the same spirit, and according to the same routine, under every different political system. They administered justice or managed public affairs in the name of the king, then in that of the republic, lastly in that of the emperor. Fortune's wheel turning on and on, the same individuals began again to administer and manage in the same way for the king, for the republic, for the emperor; what mattered the name of the master? It was their business to be good administrators and managers—not citizens. Thus, the first shock over, it seemed as though nothing had changed in the country.

At the outbreak of the Revolution, those branches of the government which, though subordinate, are most felt by individuals, and exercise the largest and most steady influence on their welfare, had just been overturned; the government had suddenly changed all its agents and all its principles. At first the state did not seem to have felt a severe shock from this sweeping reform; but every Frenchman had experienced a slight commotion. Not a man but was affected either in his rank, or in his habits, or in his business. Though great state affairs continued to be transacted in a sort of regular order, in those smaller transactions which constitute the routine of every-day life, no one knew whom to obey, where to apply, how to act.

Every part of the nation being thus thrown off the level, one final blow was enough to set the whole in motion, and produce the greatest convulsion and the most terrible disorders that were ever witnessed.

CHAPTER XX.

HOW THE REVOLUTION SPRANG SPONTANEOUSLY OUT OF THE PRE-
CEDING FACTS.

I DESIRE, in conclusion, to put together some of the features which I have separately sketched, and, having drawn the portrait of the old regime, to watch the Revolution spring from it by its own unaided effort.

Let it be borne in mind that France was the only country in which the feudal system had preserved its injurious and irritating characteristics, while it had lost all those which were beneficial or useful; and it will seem less surprising that the Revolution which was to abolish the old constitution of Europe should have broken out there rather than elsewhere.

Let it also be borne in mind that France was the only feudal country in which the nobility had lost its old political rights, lost the right of administering government and leading the people, but had nevertheless retained and even largely increased its pecuniary indemnities and the individual privileges of its members; had, in its subordinate position, remained a close body, growing less and less of an aristocracy and more and more of a caste; and it will at once be understood why its privileges seemed so inexplicable and detestable to the French, and why their hearts were inflamed with a democratic envy that is not yet extinguished.

Let it be borne in mind, finally, that the nobility was separated from the middle classes, which it had eschewed, and from the people, whose affections it had lost; that it stood alone in the midst of the nation, seemingly the staff of an army, really a group of soldierless officers; and it will be easy to conceive how, after an existence of a thousand years, it was overthrown in a single night.

I have shown how the royal government abolished the provincial liberties, usurped the place of the local authorities in three fourths of the kingdom, and monopolized public business, great and small; and I have also shown how Paris consequently became of necessity the master of the country instead of the capital, or rather, became itself the whole country. These two facts, which were peculiar to France, would alone suffice to show how a revolt could achieve the overthrow of a monarchy which had endured so violent shocks during so many centuries, and which, on the eve of its destruction, seemed immovable to its very assailants.

Political life had been so long and so thoroughly extinguished in France—individuals had so entirely lost the habit of mixing in public affairs, of judging for themselves, of studying popular movements, and even understanding the people at all, that the French quite naturally drifted into a terrible revolution without seeing it—the very parties who had most to fear from it taking the lead, and undertaking to smooth and widen the way for its approach.

In the absence of free institutions, and, consequently, of political classes, active political bodies, or organized parties, the duty of leading public opinion, when it revived, naturally fell to the lot of philosophers. Hence it might be expected that the Revolution would be conducted less in view of specific facts than in conformity with abstract principles and general theories. It might be conjectured that, instead of assailing specific laws, it would attack all laws together, and would assume to substitute for the old Constitution of France a new system of government which these writers had conceived.

The Church was mixed with all the old institutions that were to be destroyed. Hence it was plain that the Revolution would shake the religious while it overthrew the civil power; and this done, and men's minds set free from all the restraints which religion, custom, and law impose on reformers, it was impossible to say to what unheard-of lengths of boldness it might not go. Every careful student of the state of the country could perceive that there were no lengths of boldness that were too distant, no pitch of violence too frantic to be attempted.

"What!" cried Burke, in one of his eloquent pamphlets, " one can not find a man that can answer for the smallest district; not a man who can answer for his neighbor. People are arrested in their houses for royalism, for moderation, or any thing else, and no one ever resists." Burke had no idea of the state in which the monarchy he so deeply regretted had left us. The old government had deprived the French of the power and the desire to help each other. When the Revolution broke out, there were not ten men in the greater part of France who were in the habit of acting in concert, in a regular manner, and providing for their own defense; every thing was left to the central power. And so, when that power made way for an irresponsible sovereign assembly, and exchanged its former mildness for ferocity, there was nothing to check or delay it for an instant. The same cause which had overthrown the monarchy had rendered every thing possible after its fall.

At no former period had religious toleration, gentleness in the exercise of authority, humanity, and benevolence, been so generally advocated or so thoroughly accepted as sound doctrine as during the eighteenth century: the very spirit of war—last refuge of the spirit of violence—had been limited, and its rigors softened. Out of the bosom of this refined society how inhuman a revolution was about to spring! And yet the refinement was no mere pretense, for no sooner had the first fury of the Revolution been deadened than the spirit of the laws and political customs was softened and assuaged.

To comprehend the contrast between the benign theories and the violent acts of the Revolution, one must remember that it was prepared by the most civilized classes of the nation, and executed by the roughest and most unpolished. The former having no bond of mutual union, no common understanding among themselves, no hold on the people, the latter assumed the whole direction of affairs when the old authorities were abolished. Even where they did not govern they inspired the government; and a glance at the way they had lived under the old regime left no room for doubt as to what they would prove.

The very peculiarities of their condition endowed them with some rare virtues. They had long been free and landholders; they were temperate and proud in their independent isolation. They were hardened to toil, careless of the refinements of life, resigned to misfortune however great, firm in the face of danger. A simple, manly race, hereafter to constitute armies under which Europe shall bow the neck; but hence, also, a dangerous master. Crushed for centuries under the weight of abuses which no one shared with them, living alone, and brooding silently over their prejudices, their jealousies, and their hatreds, they were hardened by their hard experience, and were as ready to inflict as to bear suffering.

Such was the French people when it laid hands on the government, and undertook to complete the work of the Revolution. It found in books a theory which it assumed to put in practice, shaping the ideas of the writers to suit its passions.

The careful student of France during the eighteenth century must have noticed in the preceding pages the birth and development of two leading passions, which were not coeval, and not always similar in their tendencies.

One—the deepest and most solidly rooted—was a violent, unquenchable hatred of inequality. It took its rise and grew in the face of marked inequalities; drove the French with steady, irresistible force to seek to destroy utterly all the remains of the mediæval institutions; and prompted the erection on their ruins of a society in which all men should be alike, and as equal in rank as humanity dictates.

The other—of more recent date, and less solidly rooted—prompted men to seek to be free as well as equal.

Toward the close of the old regime these two passions were equally sincere, and apparently equally active ; they met at the opening of the Revolution, and, blending together into one, they took fire from contact, and inflamed the whole heart of France. No doubt 1789 was a period of inexperience, but it was also a period of generosity, of enthusiasm, of manliness, of greatness—a period of immortal memory, upon which men will look back with admiration and respect when all who witnessed it, and we who follow them, shall have long since passed away. The French were then proud enough of their cause and of themselves to believe that they could enjoy freedom and equality together. They planted, therefore, free institutions in the midst of democratic institutions. Not content with pulverizing the superannuated laws which divided men into classes, castes, corporations, and endowed them with rights more unequal even than their ranks, they likewise annulled at a blow those other laws which were a later creation of the royal power, and which had stripped the nation of all control over itself, and set over every Frenchman a government to be his preceptor, his tutor, and, in case of need, his oppressor. Centralization fell with absolute monarchy.

But when the vigorous generation which began the Revolution perished or became enervated, as all generations must which undertake such enterprises ; when, in the natural course of events of this character, the love of liberty had been discouraged and grown languid in the midst of anarchy and popular despotism, and the bewildered nation began to grope around for a master, immense facilities were offered for the restoration of absolute government; and it was easy for the genius of him who was destined both to continue and to destroy the Revolution to discover them.

The old regime contained, in fact, a large body of institutions of modern type which, not being hostile to equality, were susceptible of being used in the new order of things, and yet offered remarkable facilities for the establishment of despotism. They were sought for and found in the midst of the ruins. They had formerly given birth to habits, passions, and ideas which tended to keep men divided and obedient; they were restored and turned to account. Centralization was raised from its tomb and restored to its place; whence it happened that, all the checks which had formerly served to limit its power being destroyed, and not revived, there sprang out of the bosom of a nation which had just overthrown royalty a power more extensive, more detailed, more absolute than any of our monarchs had ever wielded. The enterprise seemed incredibly bold and unprecedentedly successful, because people only thought of what they saw before them, and forgot the past. The despot fell; but the most substantial portion of his work remained: his administrative system survived his government. And ever since, whenever an attempt has been made to overthrow an absolute government, the head of Liberty has been simply planted on the shoulders of a servile body.

During the period that has elapsed since the Revolution, the passion for liberty has frequently been extinguished again, and again revived. This will long be the case, for it is still inexperienced, ill regulated, easily discouraged, easily frightened away, easily overcome, superficial, and evanescent. Meanwhile, the passion for equality has retained its place at the bottom of the hearts it originally penetrated, and linked with their dearest sentiments. While the one is incessantly changing, now increasing, now diminishing, now gaining strength, now losing it, according to events, the other has remained uniformly the same, striving for its object with obstinate and often blind ardor, willing to sacrifice every thing to gain it, and ready to repay its grant from government by cultivating such habits, ideas, and laws as a despotism may require.

The Revolution will ever remain in darkness to those who do not look beyond it; it can only be comprehended by the light of the ages which preceded it. Without a clear view of society in the olden time, of its laws, its faults, its prejudices, its suffering, its greatness, it is impossible to understand the conduct of the French during the sixty years which have followed its fall; and even that view will not suffice without some acquaintance with the natural history of our nation.

When I examine that nation in itself, I can not help thinking it is more extraordinary than any of the events of its history. Did there ever appear on the earth another nation so fertile in contrasts, so extreme in its acts—more under the dominion of feeling, less ruled by principle; always better or worse than was anticipated—now below the level of humanity, now far above; a people so unchangeable in its leading features that it may be recognized by portraits drawn two or three thousand years ago, and yet so fickle in its daily opinions and tastes that it becomes at last a mystery to itself, and is as much astonished as strangers at the sight of what it has done; naturally fond of home and routine, yet, once driven forth and forced to adopt new customs, ready to carry principles to any lengths and to dare any thing; indocile by disposition, but better pleased with the arbitrary and even violent rule of a sovereign than with a free and regular government under its chief citizens; now fixed in hostility to subjection of any kind, now so passionately wedded to servitude that nations made to serve can not vie with it; led by a thread so long as no word of resistance is spoken, wholly ungovernable when the standard of revolt has been raised—thus always deceiving its masters, who fear it too much or too little; never so free that it can not be subjugated, nor so kept down that it can not break the yoke; qualified for every pursuit, but excelling in nothing but war; more prone to worship chance, force, success, eclat, noise, than real glory; endowed with more heroism than virtue, more genius than common sense; better adapted for the conception of grand designs than the accomplishment of great enterprises; the most brilliant and the most dangerous nation of Europe, and the one that is surest to inspire admiration, hatred, terror, or pity, but never indifference?

No nation but such a one as this could give birth to a revolution so sudden, so radical, so impetuous in its course, and yet so full of missteps, contradictory facts, and conflicting examples. The French could not have done it but for the reasons I have alleged; but, it must be admitted, even these reasons would not suffice to explain such a revolution in any country but France.

I have now reached the threshold of that memorable Revolution. I shall not cross it now. Soon, perhaps, I may be enabled to do so. I shall then pass over its causes to examine it in itself, and to judge the society to which it gave birth.

APPENDIX.

OF THE *PAYS D'ETATS*, AND LANGUEDOC IN PARTICULAR.

IT is not my intention to examine in detail, in this place, the condition of affairs in each of the *pays d'états*, as they stood before the Revolution.

I merely design to state how many there were; which of them were distinguished by local activity; on what footing they stood as regards the royal government; wherein they departed from the rules I have mentioned, and in what particulars they were governed by these rules; and, lastly, to show, by the example of one of them, what they all might have become.

States had existed in most of the French provinces —that is to say, their government had been administered by members of the Three Estates (*gens des trois états*), as it was then the fashion to say; in other words, by an assembly composed of representatives of the clergy, the nobility, and the burghers. This provincial institution, like most of the political institutions of the Middle Ages, had flourished in a similar form throughout almost all civilized Europe, or, at all events, in every country into which German customs and ideas had made their way. In many German provinces States existed up to the French Revolution; in the others they did not disappear till the seventeenth or eighteenth century. For two centuries sovereigns had uniformly and steadily waged war against them, sometimes openly, sometimes secretly. No attempt had been any where made to adapt them to the improved condition of the times; but monarchs had never let slip an opportunity of destroying them, or deforming them when this was the worst they could do.

In France there were but five provinces of any extent, and a few small, insignificant districts, in which States still existed in 1789. Provincial liberty, properly speaking, subsisted in two only, Bretagne and Languedoc; every where else the substantial features of the institution had been taken away, leaving only the semblance behind.

I shall examine Languedoc separately, and at some length.

It was the largest and most populous of the *pays d'états*. It contained more than two thousand *communes*, or, as they were then called, communities, and nearly two millions of inhabitants. It was, moreover, the best ordered and prosperous, as well as the largest of these provinces. We may therefore learn, from an inquiry into its condition, what provincial liberty was under the old regime, and to what extent, in those sections of country where it was most vigorous, it had been subordinated to the royal power.

In Languedoc the Estates could not meet without an express order from the king. Each member must have received individually a letter addressed to him inviting him to be present at each session. Hence a malcontent of the time remarked: "Of the three bodies which compose our Estates, one, the clergy, is appointed by the king, as all livings and bishoprics are in his gift; and the two others are assumed to be in the same position, for the king can prevent any member from being present by simply withholding the invitation, though the member excluded has not been exiled or even put on his trial."

The period when the session of the Estates must end was likewise fixed by the king. An Order in Council limited their ordinary sessions to forty days. The king was represented in the assembly by commissioners who had seats whenever they chose to demand them, and were the organ of the government. The authority of the Estates was strictly limited. They could come to no important decision, pass no appropriation bill, without an Order in Council approving the measure: they could neither impose a tax, nor effect a loan, nor institute an action at law without the express permission of the king. All their rules, including those which regulated their own sittings, were invalid till the king had sanctioned them. Their receipts and expenditures, their budget, as we should say at present, was subject to the same control.

The government exercised the same political rights in Languedoc as elsewhere. Whatever laws it chose to promulgate, whatever general rules it laid down, whatever measures it took, applied to Languedoc as well as the *pays d'élection*. It performed the natural functions of government, maintained the same police, employed the same agents there as elsewhere, and created, from time to time, a host of new functionaries, whose offices the province was obliged to buy up at very high rates.

Languedoc, like the other provinces, was governed

by an intendant. In every district this intendant had sub-delegates, who were in relation with the heads of the communities, and directed them. The intendant was public guardian, precisely as in the *pays d'élection*. The smallest village, buried in the gorges of the Cevennes, could not make the least outlay without being authorized by an Order in Council from Paris. That branch of legal business which is now called the Department of Private Claims (*contentieux administratif*) was even more extensive there than elsewhere. The intendant had original jurisdiction over all questions of highways and roads, and generally over all disputes in which the government was, or chose to consider itself, interested. Nor were government agents less carefully protected there than elsewhere against prosecutions by citizens who were aggrieved by them.

Wherein, then, did Languedoc differ from the other provinces? How came it to be so envied by its neighbors? It differed from the rest of France in three respects:

1st. It possessed an assembly composed of substantial men, enjoying the confidence of the people and the respect of the general government. No government functionary, or, as they were called, king's officer, could be a member. The assembly discussed freely and seriously the affairs of the province every year. The proximity of this centre of intelligence obliged the government to exercise its privileges very cautiously and moderately: though its agents and its tendencies were the same there as elsewhere, they produced very different results.

2dly. Many public works were carried on in Languedoc at the cost of the king and directed by his agents ; others were partly defrayed and substantially directed by the crown ; but a still larger number were executed at the cost of the province. When the king had once approved the design and authorized the outlay necessary for the latter, they were prosecuted by officials chosen by the States, under the inspection of commissioners selected from the assembly.

3dly. The province was entitled to levy, in the way it liked best, a portion of the royal taxes, and all the taxes that were required for its own necessities.

We shall now see the use which Languedoc made of these privileges. It is a matter which deserves close attention.

A most striking feature in the *pays d'élection* was the rarity of local taxes. The general taxes were often burdensome, but the province spent little or nothing on itself. In Languedoc, on the contrary, enormous sums were spent by the province for public works ; in 1780 the annual appropriation exceeded 7,000,000 *livres*.

The central government was occasionally shocked at such extravagance. It began to fear that such appropriations would exhaust the province, and incapacitate it from paying the royal taxes. It reproached the States with a want of moderation. I have read a memorial in which the assembly replied to these criticisms. A few extracts from that document will depict the spirit which animated that little government better than any thing I could say.

The memorial admits that the province has certainly undertaken and is prosecuting immense works ; but, instead of apologizing therefor, it declares that, if the king has no objection, this policy will be still farther carried out.   The province has already improved and facilitated the navigation of the chief rivers which cross its territory, and is now engaged in prolonging the Burgundy Canal—which was constructed under Louis XIV., and is now inadequate—through Lower Langue-doc, by Cette and Agde to the Rhone.   It has adapted the port of Cette to commercial purposes, and keeps it in repair at great expense.   These outlays, it is ob-served, are for national rather than provincial objects, but the province has made them, as it will be the chief gainer by the works.   It is further engaged in drain-ing and reclaiming the marsh of Aigues-Mortes.   But its chief outlays have been for roads.   It has either opened or repaired all the high roads which traverse its surface and lead into neighboring provinces.   It has mended all the roads between the different cities and bourgs of Languedoc.   All these roads are ex-cellent even in winter, and compare very favorably with the hard, rough, ill-kept roads which are met with in most of the neighboring provinces, such as Dau-phiné, Quercy, and Bordeaux (which, it is observed, are *pays d'élection*).   On this head the memorial refers to the judgment of travelers and merchants; nor with-out reason, for Arthur Young, who traveled through the country a year afterward, notes, "Languedoc, *pays d'état*—good roads, made without *corvées*."

If the king will grant permission, continues the memorial, the Estates will do more yet; they will undertake to improve the parish roads, which affect as many interests as the others.   "For if produce," continued the memorial, "can not find its way from the producer's barn to the market, it is of very little use to provide for its exportation to a distance." "The principle of the States with regard to public works," the memorial adds, "has always been to look at their usefulness, not at their cost." Rivers, canals, roads, give value to all products of the soil and of industry, by facilitating their conveyance at all seasons and at small expense to a market, and spreading commercial activity throughout the province; they are always worth more than they cost. Moreover, works of this character, if undertaken moderately, and spread uniformly over the territory of the province, sustain the value of labor, and give employment to the poor. "The king," adds the memorial, proudly, "need be at no expense for the establishment of work-houses in Languedoc, as he has been obliged to do in the rest of France. We seek no favors of the kind: the works of public utility which we undertake ourselves stand us in the stead of work-houses, and furnish a remunerative demand for all our labor."

The more I study the regulations which the king permitted the States of Languedoc to establish in those branches of administration which were left under their control, the more I admire the wisdom, the equity, the mildness which characterize them, and the more satisfied am I of the superiority of the policy of the local government over that which obtained in the provinces administered by the king.

The province was divided into communities, towns, or villages—into administrative districts, which were called dioceses; and, lastly, into three great departments, called *sénéchaussées*. Each of these divisions was separately represented in the Assembly; each had its own separate government, which acted under the direction of the States or the king. Public works for the benefit of any particular division were only undertaken when that division expressed a desire for them. If the work demanded by the community would be beneficial to the diocese, the latter was bound to bear a proportionate share of the expense. If the sénéchaussée was interested, it paid a share. But diocese, sénéchaussée, and province were all bound to contribute to works which the interests of a community required, if they were necessary, and beyond the means of the body directly concerned; for, as the States frequently observed, "The fundamental principle of our constitution is that all the divisions of the province are jointly and severally liable to each other, and bound to contribute to each other's progress."

Works undertaken by the province were required to have been planned deliberately; and to have received the assent of all the secondary bodies concerned. All labor consumed was paid for in cash; *corvées* were unknown. I have stated that in *pays d'élection* land taken for objects of public utility was always tardily and inadequately paid for, and that occasionally the owner was not paid at all. This was one of the leading grievances of the Provincial Assemblies when they met in 1787. Some even complained that it was impossible to estimate the debts that had been thus incurred, as the property taken had been destroyed or transformed before it had been valued. In Languedoc, every foot of land taken from its owner was carefully valued before it was touched, and *the value paid before the expiration of a year from the time the works were begun.*

This system of the States of Languedoc with regard to public works appeared so excellent to the central government, that, without imitating, it admired it. The Royal Council, after having authorized its establishment, had it printed at the royal printing-office, and sent it to the intendants as a useful document to consult.

All that I have said with regard to public works is applicable, even in a greater degree, to that other and equally important branch of the provincial administration, the collection of the taxes. When one examines this department, first in the kingdom, then in the province, it seems impossible to believe that both are parts of the same empire.

I had occasion some time since to mention that the system used in Languedoc for the distribution and collection of the taille was substantially the same as the one now employed for the collection of our modern imposts. I shall not again revert to the subject, but will add simply that the province was so well convinced of the superiority of its method that, whenever the king established new taxes, the States paid heavily for the right of levying them in their own way, and by the hands of their own agents.

Notwithstanding all the outlays I have enumerated, the financial condition of Languedoc was so prosperous, and her credit so well established, that the central government often applied to it for endorsements, and borrowed in the name of the province at lower rates than would have been charged to the crown. I find that Languedoc borrowed in its own name, but for the use of the king, in the later years of the monarchy, 73,200,000 *livres.*

Yet the government watched these provincial liberties with a very jealous eye. Richelieu first mutilated, then abolished them. The weak and slothful Louis XIII., who loved nothing, detested them: he had such a dislike for provincial privileges, according to Boulainvilliers, that he would fly into a rage at the mere mention of the subject. Weak minds always find energy enough to hate things which oblige them to exert themselves; their whole vigor is concentrated upon that one point, and, weak as they are every where else, they contrive to hate with some force. Good fortune happily restored the Constitution of Languedoc during the infancy of Louis XIV.; and that monarch, regarding it as his work, respected it. Louis XV. suspended it for a couple of years, but suffered its restoration afterward.

The creation of municipal offices involved great indirect dangers for the province. This detestable institution tended not only to destroy the constitution of cities, but to disfigure that of provinces. I am not aware whether the deputies of the Third Estate in the Provincial Assemblies had ever been chosen in view of the business they had to perform; certain it is that for a long period of time they had not been so elected. The only legitimate representatives of the middle classes and the people were the municipal officers of cities.

So long as the cities chose their magistrates freely by universal suffrage, and generally for a short period of time, but little inconvenience was occasioned by the fact that these deputies had not been specially appointed to represent the people, and defend their interest at that particular moment. Perhaps the mayor, council, or syndic was as faithful an exponent of the popular will as if he had been expressly chosen to represent the people in the assembly. But it will at once be understood that this ceased to be the case when the official had acquired his office for money. In this case he represented no one but himself, or, at best, only the small interests and petty passions of his coterie. Yet the powers of the magistrate by purchase were the same as those of the elected magistrate had been. Hence a total change in the character of the institution. Instead of a firm body of popular representatives, the nobility and the clergy had to contend in the Provincial Assembly with no one but a few isolated, timid, and powerless burghers; the Third Estate became more and more insignificant in the government as it grew more and more powerful in society. This was not the case in Languedoc, as the province always took care to buy up the offices which the king established from time to time. For this object a loan of more than four millions of livres was effected in the year 1773 alone.

Other causes, more potent still, had operated to imbue these old institutions with a modern spirit, and imparted to the States of Languedoc an indisputable superiority over all others.

In that province, as in a large portion of the South, the taille was a tax on the realty, not on the person. It was regulated by the value of the property, not the

fortune of the owner. True, certain lands enjoyed a
privilege of exemption. These lands had formerly all
belonged to the nobility; but, in the course of events
and the progress of industry, part of them had fallen
into the hands of commoners, while, on the other hand,
noblemen had in many cases become proprietors of
lands subject to the taille. The absurdity of privileges was enhanced, no doubt, by their transfer from
persons to property; but their burden was diminished,
because, inconvenient as they were, they involved no
humiliation. They were no longer inseparably bound
up with class ideas; they created no class interests
hostile to those of the public; they threw no obstacle
in the way of a general administration of the public
business by all classes. Nor was there, in fact, any
part of France in which all classes mixed so freely, or
on so decided a footing of equality as in Languedoc.

In Bretagne, all men of rank were entitled to be
present in person at the States; hence these latter bore
some resemblance to Polish Diets. In Languedoc, the
nobility was represented in the States by twenty-three
deputies; the clergy was represented by twenty-three
bishops. It is worthy of remark, that the cities had
as many members as the other two orders combined.

There was but one assembly, and votes were taken
by heads, not by orders; hence the Third Estate naturally became the preponderating body, and gradually imbued the whole assembly with its peculiar spirit.
The three magistrates, known as syndics-general, who
were intrusted with the general management of business before the States, were always lawyers, that is to
say, commoners. The nobility was strong enough to

maintain its rank, but not to rule. The clergy, on the other hand, though counting many men of rank among its members, always maintained a good understanding with the Third Estate. It took an ardent interest in many of the schemes proposed by the burghers, labored in concert with them to augment the material property of citizens, and extend commerce and industry, and often placed at their service its extensive knowledge of men, and its peculiar skill in the management of affairs. It was almost always an ecclesiastic who was sent to Versailles to discuss with ministers questions that were in dispute between the States and the crown. It may be said that during the whole of the last century the government of Languedoc was administered by burghers, under the control of noblemen, and with the aid of bishops.

Thanks to the peculiar constitution of the province, the spirit of the new era penetrated Languedoc easily, and made many modifications in its old system without destroying any thing.

This might have been the case every where. A portion of the perseverance and energy that were employed by the kings in abolishing or crippling the Provincial States would have sufficed for their improvement and adaptation to the necessities of modern civilization, had those monarchs ever sought any thing beyond extending and maintaining their own power.

N O T E S.

Note a, *page* 29.

INFLUENCE OF THE ROMAN LAW IN GERMANY.—HOW IT HAD REPLACED THE GERMANIC LAW.

AT the close of the Middle Ages the Roman law became the chief and almost the only study of the German lawyers, most of whom, at this time, were educated abroad at the Italian universities. These lawyers exercised no political power, but it devolved on them to expound and apply the laws. They were unable to abolish the Germanic law, but they did their best to distort it so as to fit the Roman mould. To every German institution that seemed to bear the most distant analogy to Justinian's legislation they applied Roman law. Hence a new spirit and new customs gradually invaded the national legislation, until its original shape was lost, and by the seventeenth century it was almost forgotten. Its place had been usurped by a medley that was Germanic in name, but Roman in fact.

I have reason to believe that this innovation of the lawyers had a tendency to aggravate the condition of more than one class of Germans, the peasantry especially. Persons who had up to that time succeeded in preserving the whole or a part of their liberty or their property, were ingeniously assimilated to the slaves or emphyteutic tenants of the Roman law, and lost rights and possessions together.

This gradual transformation of the national law, and the efforts which were made to prevent its accomplishment, were plainly seen in the history of Wurtemberg.

From the rise of the county of this name in 1250 to the creation of the duchy in 1495, the whole legislation of Wurtemberg was indigenous in character. It consisted of customs, local city laws, ordinances of seigniorial courts, or statutes of the States. Ecclesiastical affairs alone were regulated by foreign, that is to say, by canon law.

But from the year 1495 a change took place. Roman law began to penetrate the legislation of the duchy. The *doctors,* as they were called—that is to say, the individuals who had studied at foreign schools—connected themselves with the government, and took the management of the high courts. From the commencement to the middle of the fifteenth century, a struggle between them and the politicians of the day was carried on, similar in character, though different in result from the struggle that took place in England at the very same time. At the Diet of Tubingen in 1514 and the following Diets, the lawyers were attacked violently by the representatives of feudal institutions and the city deputies; they were loudly charged with invading all the courts of justice, and altering the spirit or the letter of all the laws and customs. At first, victory seemed to rest with the assailants. They obtained of government a promise that honorable and enlightened persons, chosen from the nobility and the States of the duchy—not doctors—should be set over the higher courts, and that a commission, consisting of government agents and representatives of the States, should be appointed to draft a bill for a Code to have force throughout the country. Useless effort! The Roman law soon expelled the national law from a large section of the legislative sphere, and even planted its roots in the section where the latter was allowed to subsist.

German historians ascribe this triumph of foreign over domestic law to two causes: 1st. The attraction exercised over the public mind by ancient literature, which necessarily led to a contempt for the intellectual products of the national genius; and, 2dly. The idea—with which the Germans of the Middle Ages, and even their laws, were imbued—that the Holy Empire was a continuation of the Roman Empire, and hence that the legislation of the latter was an heirloom of the former.

These causes do not suffice to explain the simultaneous introduction of Roman law into every Continental country. I think that the singular availability of the Roman law—which was a slave-law—for the purposes of monarchs, who were just then establishing their absolute power upon the ruins of the old liberties of Europe, was the true cause of the phenomenon.

The Roman law carried civil society to perfection, but it invariably degraded political society, because it was the work of a highly civilized and thoroughly enslaved people. Kings naturally embraced it with enthusiasm, and established it wherever they could throughout Europe; its interpreters became their ministers or their chief agents. Lawyers furnished them at need with legal warrant for violating the law. They have often done so since. Monarchs who have trampled the laws have almost always found a lawyer ready to prove the lawfulness of their acts—to establish learnedly that violence was just, and that the oppressed were in the wrong.

Note b, page 3.

TRANSITION FROM FEUDAL TO DEMOCRATIC MONARCHY.

As all European monarchies became absolute about the same time, it is not probable that the constitutional change was due to accidental circumstances which occurred simultaneously in every country. The natural supposition is that the general change was the fruit of a general cause operating on every country at the same moment.

That general cause was the transition from one social state to another, from feudal inequality to democratic equality. The nobility was prostrate; the people had not yet risen up; the one was too low, the other not high enough to embarrass the movements of the supreme power. For a period of a hundred and fifty years kings enjoyed a golden age. They were all-powerful, and their thrones were stable, advantages usually inconsistent with each other. They were as sacred as the hereditary chiefs of a feudal monarchy, and as absolute as the masters of a democracy.

Note c, page 32.

DECLINE OF FREE GERMAN CITIES.—IMPERIAL CITIES (*Reichstadten*).

According to the German historians, these cities reached their highest point of prosperity during the fourteenth and fifteenth centuries. They were then the refuge of the wealth, of the arts, of the learning of Europe, the mistress of commerce, and the centre of civilization. They ended, especially in northern and southern Germany, by forming, with the surrounding nobility, independent confederations, as the Swiss cities had done with the peasantry.

They were still prosperous in the sixteenth century; but their decline had begun. The Thirty Years' War hastened their downfall; they were nearly all destroyed or ruined during that period.

The Treaty of Westphalia, however, made special mention of them, and maintained their condition as "immediate states," that is to say, communities independent of all control but the emperor. But neighboring monarchs on one side, and on the other the emperor himself, whose power, after the Thirty Years' War, was nearly confined in its exercise to these small vassals of the empire, constantly encroached on their sovereignty. They still numbered fifty-one in the eighteenth century. They occupied two benches at the Diet, and had a separate vote. But, practically, their influence over the direction of public affairs was gone.

At home they were overloaded with debts, chiefly arising from the fact that they were still taxed in proportion to their past splendor, and also, in some degree, from their defective administration. It is not a little remarkable that this maladministration appeared to flow from some secret disease that was common to all of them, whatever their constitution happened to be. Aristocratic and democratic forms of government provoked equal discontent. Aristocracies were said to be mere family coteries, in which favor and private interest controlled the government. Democracies were said to be under the sway of intrigue and corruption. Both forms of government were accused of dishonesty and profligacy. The Emperor was constantly obliged to interfere in their affairs to restore order. Their population was falling off, their wealth vanishing. They were no longer the centres of German civilization; the arts had fled from them to take refuge in new cities created by kings, and representing the modern era. Trade had deserted them. Their former energy, their patriotic vigor, had disappeared. Hamburg alone continued to be a great centre of wealth and learning; but this flowed from causes peculiar to itself.

Note d, *page* 38.

DATE OF THE ABOLITION OF SERFDOM IN GERMANY.

It will be seen from the following table that serfdom has only been very recently abolished in the greater part of Germany. Serfdom was abolished,

1. In Baden not till 1783.
2. In Hohenzollern in 1789.
3. Schleswig and Holstein in 1804.
4. Nassau in 1808.
5. Prussia. Frederick William I. abolished serfdom in his domains in 1717. The code of Frederick the Great, as has been observed, pretended to abolish it throughout the kingdom, but in reality it only abolished its hardest form, *leibeigenschaft*; it preserved the milder form, called *erbuntertahnigkeit*. It did not cease entirely till 1809.

6. In Bavaria serfdom disappeared in 1808.

7. A decree of Napoleon's, dated Madrid, 1808, abolished it in the Grand-duchy of Berg, and in several small territories, such as Erfurth, Baireuth, &c.

8. In the kingdom of Westphalia its destruction dates from 1808 and 1809.

9. In the principality of Lippe-Detmold from 1809.

10. In Schomberg-Lippe from 1810.

11. In Swedish Pomerania from 1810.

12. In Hesse-Darmstadt from 1809 and 1811.

13. In Wurtemberg from 1817.

14. In Mecklenburg from 1820.

15. In Oldenburg from 1814.

16. In Saxony for Lusatia from 1832.

17. In Hohenzollern-Sigmaringen from 1833 only.

18. In Austria from 1811. In 1782, Joseph II. had abolished the *leibeigenschaft;* but serfdom in its mild form—*erbuntertah-nigkeit*—lasted till 1811.

Note e, *page* 38.

A portion of Germany, such as Brandenburg, old Prussia, and Silesia, was originally peopled by the Slavic race, and was conquered and partly occupied by Germans. In those countries serfdom was always much harsher than in the rest of Germany, and left much plainer traces at the close of the eighteenth century.

Note f, *page* 39.

CODE OF FREDERICK THE GREAT.

Of all the works of Frederick the Great, the least known, even in his own country, and the least striking, is the Code drawn up by his orders, and promulgated by his successor. Yet I doubt whether any of his other works throws as much light on the mind of the man or on the times in which he lived, or shows as plainly the influence which they exercised one upon the other.

This Code was a real constitution in the ordinary sense of the word. It regulated not only the mutual relations of citizens, but also their relations to the state. It was a civil code, a criminal code, and a charter all in one.

It rests, or appears to rest, on a certain number of general principles, expressed in a highly philosophical and abstract form, and which bear a strong resemblance in many respects to those which are embodied in the Declaration of the Rights of Man in the Constitution of 1791.

It proclaims that the welfare of the commonwealth and of its inhabitants is the aim of society and the limit of law; that laws can not restrain the freedom and the rights of the citizen save for public utility; that every member of the commonwealth ought to labor for the public good in proportion to his position and his means; that the rights of individuals ought to give way to those of the public.

It makes no allusion to any hereditary rights of the sovereign, nor to his family, nor even to any particular right as distinguished from that of the state. The royal power was already designated by no other name than that of the state.

On the other hand, it alludes to the rights of man, which are founded on the natural right of every one to pursue his own happiness without treading on the rights of others. All acts not forbidden by natural law, or a positive state law, are allowable. Every citizen is entitled to claim the protection of the state for himself and his property, and may defend himself by using force if the state does not come to his defense.

These great principles established, the legislator, instead of evolving from them, as the constitution of 1791 did, the doctrine of popular sovereignty, and the organization of a democratic government in a free society, turns sharp round and arrives at another conclusion, democratic enough, but not liberal. He considers the sovereign the sole representative of the state, and invests him with all the rights which he has stated belong to society. The sovereign does not figure in the Code as the representative of God; he is the representative, the agent, the servant of society, as Frederick stated at full length in his works; but he is its sole representative, he wields its whole authority alone. The head of the state, on whom the duty of securing the public welfare—which is the sole object of society—devolves, is authorized to direct and regulate all the actions of individuals in this view.

Among the chief duties of this all-powerful agent of society, I find such as these mentioned: maintaining order and public safety at home, so that every citizen shall be guaranteed against violence; making peace and war; establishing all laws and police regulations; granting pardons; annulling criminal prosecutions.

Every association in the country, and every public establishment, is subject to his inspection and superintendence in the interest of the general peace and security. In order that the head of the state may be able to perform his duties, he must have certain revenues and lucrative rights ; hence he is allowed to tax private fortunes, persons, professions, commerce, industry, articles of consumption. Public functionaries acting in his name must be obeyed as he is in all matters within the scope of their duties.

Under this very modern head we shall now see a thoroughly Gothic body placed. Frederick has taken away nothing but what might impede the action of his own power, and the whole will form a monstrous being, which looks like a compromise between two creations. In this strange production Frederick evinces as much contempt for logic as care for his own power, and anxiety not to create useless difficulties in attacking what was still capable of defense.

With the exception of a few districts and certain localities, the inhabitants of the rural districts are placed in a state of hereditary serfdom ; not only is the land clogged with *corvées* and inherent services, but, as has been seen already, similar burdens attach to the persons of the peasants.

Most of the privileges of landholders are recognized anew by the Code—or, it might be said, in contradiction to the Code ; for it is expressly stated that, wherever the new legislation clashes with local customs, the latter must prevail. It is formally declared that the state can not abolish any of these privileges except by purchase, according to the legal forms.

True, the Code states that serfdom, properly so called (*leibeigenschaft*), is abolished in so far as it interferes with personal liberty ; but the hereditary subjection which takes its place (*erbuntertahnigkeit*) is, after all, a species of serfdom, as the text shows.

According to the Code, the burgher remains wholly distinct from the peasant. Between the noble and the burgher, an intermediate class, consisting of high functionaries who are not noble, ecclesiastics, professors of learned schools, gymnasia, and universities, is placed.

Superior to the burghers, these personages were not to be confounded with the nobility, to whom they were clearly understood to be inferior. They could not purchase equestrian estates, or fill the highest posts in the civil service. Nor were they *hoffähig* ; that is to say, they could but rarely appear at court, and never with their families. As was the case in France, these distinctions became more insulting in proportion to the increasing knowledge and influence of this class, which, though excluded from the most brilliant posts, filled all those where business of importance was transacted.   The privileges of the nobility necessarily gave birth to irritation, which mainly contributed to cause the revolution here, and make it popular in Germany.   The principal author of the Code was a burgher, but no doubt he merely obeyed the instructions of his master.

The old constitution of Europe is not in such ruin in this part of Germany that Frederick thinks it safe to allow his contempt for it to lead him to destroy its relics.   Generally speaking, he deprives the nobility of the right of assemblage and corporate action ; leaving to each nobleman his privileges, he limits and regulates their use.   Hence it happens that this Code, drawn up by the orders of a disciple of one of our philosophers, and put in force after the outbreak of the French Revolution, is the most authentic and latest legislative document which gives a legal warrant for the feudal inequalities which the Revolution was about to abolish throughout Europe.

The nobility is declared to be the first body in the state.   Men of rank, it states, are to be preferred to all others for posts of honor, if they are capable of filling them.   None but they are to possess noble estates, create substitutions, enjoy rights of chase, justiciary rights inherent to noble estates, and rights of presentation to clerical livings ; none but they can assume the name of their estates.   Burghers, specially authorized to acquire noble estates, can only enjoy the rights and honors attached to such possessions within these limits.   A burgher owning a noble estate can not leave it to an heir burgher unless he be heir in the first degree. When there are no such heirs and no heirs noble, the property must be sold at auction.

One of the most characteristic portions of the Code of Frederick the Great is its criminal provision for political offenses.

Frederick's successor, Frederick William II., who, notwithstanding the feudal and absolutist provisions above noted, fancied he detected revolutionary tendencies in this work of his uncle's, and refrained from promulgating it till 1794, was only reconciled to it by the excellent penal provisions which served to counteract its bad principles.   Nor has there ever been any thing since devised more complete of the kind.   Not only are revolts and conspiracies punished with the greatest rigor, but disrespectful criticisms of government are repressed with equal severity.   It is forbidden to purchase or to distribute dangerous writings ; printer, publisher, and vender are all responsible for the act of the author.

Public balls and masquerades are declared to be public meetings, which can not take place without the authority of the police. Similar rules govern dinners in public places. Liberty of the press and of speech are under close and arbitrary supervision. It is forbidden to carry fire-arms.

By the side of this work, which was more than half borrowed from the Middle Ages, are provisions whose spirit borders on socialism. Thus it is declared that it devolves on the state to provide food, work, and wages for all who can not support themselves, and have no claim for support on the seignior or the *commune;* they must be provided with work suited to their strength and capacity. The state is bound to provide establishments for relieving the poor. It is authorized to abolish establishments which tend to encourage idleness, and to distribute personally to the poor the money by which these establishments were supported.

Boldness and novelty in point of theory, and timidity in practice characterize every portion of this work of Frederick the Great. On the one side, that great principle of modern society—that all are equally subject to taxes—is loudly proclaimed; on another, provincial laws containing exemptions to this rule are allowed to subsist. It is affirmed that all lawsuits between the sovereign and the state must be tried in the same forms and according to the same rules as all other cases; but, in fact, this rule was never carried into effect when the interests or passions of the king were opposed to it. The mill of Saint Souci was ostentatiously shown to the people, and justice was quietly made subject to royal convenience in other cases.

What proves that this Code, which assumed to be such a novelty, really made but few changes, and is therefore a curious study of German society in this section of country at the close of the eighteenth century, is that the Prussian nation hardly noticed its publication. Lawyers were the only persons who studied it; and even in our time there are many enlightened men who have never read it.

Note g, *page* 41.

PROPERTY OF THE GERMAN PEASANTS.

Many families among the peasantry were not only free and landholders, their property constituted a species of perpetual *majorat*. Their estate was indivisible, and passed by descent to one of the sons—usually the youngest—as was the case in some English customs. He was expected to endow his brothers and sisters.

The *erbgütter* of the peasantry were spread more 'or less over the whole of Germany, for the land was nowhere absorbed by the feudal tenures. Even in Silesia, where the nobility owned immense estates comprising most of the villages, other villages were possessed by the inhabitants, and were wholly free. In certain parts of Germany, such as the Tyrol and Frise, the rule was that the peasantry owned the land by *erbgütter.*

But in the greater part of the German countries this kind of property was an exception sometimes rarely met with. In the villages where it occurred, landholders of this kind constituted a sort of aristocracy among the peasantry.

Note h, *page* 41.

POSITION OF THE NOBILITY AND DIVISION OF LAND ALONG THE RHINE.

From information obtained on the spot, and from persons who lived under the old regime, it appears that in the Electorate of Cologne, for instance, there were a great number of villages without seigniors, and governed by agents of the king; that in the places where the nobility lived, their administrative powers were very limited; that their position (individually at all events) was rather brilliant than powerful; that they possessed honors and offices, but no direct control over the people. I also ascertained that in the same electorate property was much divided, and that many of the peasants owned the land they occupied. The fact was ascribed to the poverty that had long oppressed many of the noble families, and obliged them to sell their estates to the peasants for an annual rent or a sum of money. I have had in my hands a schedule of the population and estates within the Bishopric of Cologne at the beginning of the eighteenth century : it indicated that, at that time, one third of the soil belonged to the peasantry. From this fact arose sentiments and ideas which predisposed these people to a far greater extent than the inhabitants of other parts of Germany to welcome a revolution.

Note i, *page* 42.

HOW THE USURY LAWS FAVORED SUBDIVISION OF LAND.

At the close of the eighteenth century it was still illegal to lend money on interest, whatever was the rate charged. Turgot says that this law was observed in many places as late as 1769. These laws are still in force, says he, but they are often violated. Consular judges allow interest on loans, while the ordinary courts condemn the practice. Dishonest debtors still prosecute their creditors criminally for having lent money without alienating the capital.

Independently of the effects which such laws as these must have had on commerce, industry, and the morals of business men, they affected the division and tenure of lands to a very great extent. They caused an immense increase of perpetual rents, as well ground-rents (*foncières*) as others. They compelled the old land-owners, instead of borrowing in times of need, to sell small portions of their domains, partly for a given sum, partly for a rent; hence leading, first, to the infinite subdivision of estates, and, secondly, to the creation of a multitude of perpetual rents on their little properties.

Note k, *page* 46.

EXAMPLE OF THE IRRITATION CAUSED BY TITHES TEN YEARS BEFORE THE REVOLUTION.

In 1779, a petty lawyer of Lucé complains in a bitter and revolutionary tone that curates and other large titheholders are selling at exorbitant prices to farmers the straw which has been paid them by way of tithes, and which the farmers absolutely need for manure.

Note l, *page* 46.

EXAMPLE OF THE MANNER IN WHICH THE PRIVILEGES OF THE CLERGY ALIENATED THE AFFECTION OF THE PEOPLE FROM THEM.

In 1780, the prior and canons of the Priory of Laval complain of being made to pay duty on articles of consumption, and on the materials required for the repair of their buildings. They argue that the duty is an accessory of the taille, and that, being exempt from the one, they ought not to be liable for the other. The minister tells them to apply to the *election*, with recourse to the Court of Aides.

Note m, *page* 46.

FEUDAL RIGHTS EXERCISED BY PRIESTS.—ONE EXAMPLE OUT OF A THOUSAND.

The Abbey of Cherbourg, in 1753, possessed seigniorial rents, payable in money or produce, in almost all the villages in the neighborhood of Cherbourg : one village alone paid 306 bushels of wheat. It owned the barony of Sainte Geneviève, the barony and seigniorial mill of Bas du Roule, and the barony of Neuville au Plein, at least ten leagues distant. It received, moreover, tithes from twelve parishes on the peninsula, some of which were at a great distance from the abbey.

Note n, *page* 49.

IRRITATION AMONG THE PEASANTRY PROCEEDING FROM THE FEUDAL RIGHTS, ESPECIALLY THOSE OF THE CHURCH.

Letter written shortly before the Revolution by a peasant to the intendant. It is no authority for the facts it states, but it indicates admirably the state of feeling in the class to which the writer belonged :

" Though we have but few nobles in this part of the country," it says, " it must not be supposed that real estate is free from rents ; on the contrary, nearly all the fiefs belong to the Cathedral, or the archbishopric, or the collegiate church of Saint Martin, or the Benedictines of Noirmontiers, of Saint Julien, or some other ecclesiastics, against whom no prescription runs, and who are constantly bringing to light old musty parchments whose date God only knows !

" The whole country is infected with rents. Most of the farm-lands pay every year a seventh of a bushel of wheat per acre, others wine ; one pays the seignior a fourth of all fruits, another a fifth, another a twelfth, another a thirteenth—the tithes being always paid on the gross. These rights are so singular that they vary from a fourth part of the produce to a fortieth.

" What must be thought of these rents in kind—in vegetables, money, poultry, labor, wood, fruit, candles ? I am acquainted with rents which are paid in bread, in wax, in eggs, in headless pigs, in rose shoulder-knots, in bouquets of violets, in golden spurs, &c. ; and there are a host of seigniorial dues besides these. Why has France not been freed from all these extravagant rents ? Men's eyes are at last being opened ; one may hope every thing from the wisdom of the present government. It will stretch a kindly hand to the poor victims of the exactions of the old fiscal system, called seigniorial rights, which could not be alienated or sold.

" What must be thought of this tyranny of mutation fines ? A purchaser exhausts his means in acquiring a property, and is obliged to pay besides in expenses to secure his title, contracts, actual entry, *procès-verbaux*, stamp, registry, *centième denier*, eight *sous* per *livre;* after which he must exhibit his title to his seignior, who will exact the mutation fine on the gross price of his purchase, now a twelfth, and now a tenth. Some claim a fifth, others a fifth and a twenty-fifth besides. All rates are demanded; I know some who charge a third of the price paid. No, the most ferocious and the most barbarous nations of the known world have never invented such or so many exactions as our tyrants heaped on the heads of our forefathers." (This literary and philosophical tirade is sadly defective in orthography.)

"What! the late king permitted the commutation of ground-rents on city property, but excluded those on farms! He should have begun with the latter. Why not permit poor farmers to break their chains, to pay off and get rid of the hosts of seigniorial dues and ground-rents, which are such an injury to the vassal and so small a gain to the seignior? No distinction should have been made between city and country, seigniors and private individuals.

" The stewards of the owners of ecclesiastical estates rob and plunder the farmers at every mutation. We have seen a recent example of the practice. The steward of our new archbishop gave notice to quit to all the farmers holding under leases from M. de Fleury, his predecessor, declared all their leases null and void, and turned out every man who refused to submit to his rent being doubled, and to pay a large bonus besides, though they had already paid a bonus to M. de Fleury's steward. They have thus been deprived of seven or eight years' holding, though their leases were executed in due form, and have been driven out upon the world on Christmas eve, the most critical period of the year, owing to the difficulty of feeding cattle. The King of Prussia could have done nothing worse."

It appears, in fact, that, with regard to Church property, leases granted by one titulary did not bind his successor. The writer of the letter states what is true when he says that feudal rents were redeemable in cities, but not in the country; a new proof of the neglect in which the peasantry lived, and of the manner in which all who were placed above them contrived to provide for their own interest.

Note o, page 49.

Every institution that has long been dominant, after establishing itself in its natural sphere, extends itself, and ends by exercising a large influence over those branches of legislation which it does not govern. The feudal system, though essentially political, had transformed the civil law, and greatly modified the condition of persons and property in all the relations of private life. It had operated upon successions by creating unequal divisions of property—a principle carried out in certain provinces even among the middle classes (as witness Normandy). It had affected all real estate, for there were but few tracts of land that were wholly freed from its effects, or whose possessors felt none of the consequences of its laws. It affected the property of *communes* as well as that of individuals. It affected labor by the impositions it laid upon it. It affected incomes by the inequality of taxation, and, in general, the pecuniary interest of every man in every business : landowners, by dues, rents, *corvées ;* farmers in a thousand ways, among others by rights of banality, ground-rents, mutation-fines, &c. ; traders, by market-dues ; merchants, by tolls, &c. In striking it down, the Revolution made itself perceived and felt at the same time at all points by every private interest.

Note p, *page* 59.

PUBLIC CHARITIES GRANTED BY THE STATE.—FAVORITISM.

In 1748—a year of great famine and misery, such as often occurred in the eighteenth century—the king granted 20,000 pounds of rice. The Archbishop of Tours claimed that he alone had obtained the gift, and that it ought to be distributed by him alone, and in his diocese. The intendant argued that the gift was made to the whole province, and should be distributed by him to all the parishes. After a long contest, the king, to settle the quarrel, doubled the quantity of rice given to the province, so that the archbishop and the intendant might each distribute half. Both agreed that it ought to be distributed by the curates. No one thought of the seigniors or the syndics. It appears from the correspondence between the intendant and the comptroller-general that the former accused the archbishop of wishing to give the rice to his favorites, and especially to the parishes which belonged to the Duchess of Rochechouart. The collection also contains letters from noblemen which demand aid for their parishes in particular, and letters from the comptroller-general which make reference to the parishes of certain individuals.

Public charities are always liable to abuses under every system ; but when distributed from a distance, without publicity, by the central government, they are actually futile.

Note q, *page* 59.

EXAMPLE OF THE MANNER IN WHICH THESE PUBLIC CHARITIES
WERE DISTRIBUTED.

A report, made in 1780 to the Provincial Assembly of Upper Guienne, states, " Out of the sum of 385,000 livres which his majesty has granted to this province from the year 1773, when workhouses were established, to the year 1779 inclusive, the *election* of Montauban, capital and place of residence of the intendant, has alone had more than 240,000 livres, most of which has been spent in the *commune* of Montauban."

Note r, *page* 60.

POWERS OF THE INTENDANT FOR THE REGULATION OF MANUFAC-
TURES.

The archives of the intendants' offices are full of papers which refer to the regulation of industrial enterprises by the intendants.

Not only is labor subject to the inconvenience of trade-companies, guilds, &c., it is liable to be affected by every whim of government, that is to say, of the Council in great matters, of the intendants in small ones. The latter are constantly giving directions about the length of woofs, the kind of thread to use, the pattern to prefer, errors to avoid. Independently of the sub-delegates, they have local inspectors of manufactures under their orders. In this particular centralization had gone farther than it now does ; it was more capricious, more arbitrary ; it created a swarm of public functionaries, and gave rise to general habits of submission and dependence.

Note also that these habits were imparted to the middle classes, merchants, and traders, which were about to triumph, to a far greater extent than to the classes that were on the point of defeat. Hence, instead of destroying, the Revolution tended to confirm and spread them.

The preceding remarks have been suggested by the perusal of a quantity of correspondence and documents taken from the intendant's office of the Ile de France, and indorsed, " Manufactures and Fabrics," " Drapery," " Drugs." I have found in the same place reports from the inspectors to the intendant giving full and detailed accounts of their visits of inspection to factories ; moreover, various Orders in Council, passed on reports of the intendant, prohibiting or permitting manufactures of certain stuffs, or in certain places, or in certain methods.

The dominant idea in the intercourse of these inspectors with the manufacturer—who, by the way, is treated very cavalierly—seems to be that their duty and the rights of the state compel them to see that the manufacturer not only acts fairly toward the public, but looks after his own interest. They consequently feel bound to make him adopt the best methods, and admonish him on the most trifling details of his business, larding the whole with a profusion of penalties and heavy fines.

Note s, *page* 61.

SPIRIT OF THE GOVERNMENT OF LOUIS XI.

Nothing indicates more clearly the spirit of the government of Louis XI. than the constitutions he gave to cities. I have had occasion to study very closely those which he gave to most of the cities of Anjou, Maine, and Touraine.

All these constitutions are framed on the same plan, and all reveal the same designs. Louis XI. appears in a new light in these charters. He is generally regarded as the enemy of the nobility, but the sincere though somewhat brutal friend of the people. They reveal him as a hater alike of the political rights of the people and of those of the nobility. He uses the middle classes to lower the nobility and keep down the people : he is both anti-aristocratic and anti-democratic—the model of the burgher king. He loads city notables with privileges in the view of increasing their importance, grants them titles of nobility in order to cheapen rank, and thus destroys the popular and democratic city governments, and places the whole authority in the hands of a few families, attached to his policy, and pledged to his support by every tie of gratitude.

Note t, *p.* 62.

A CITY GOVERNMENT IN THE EIGHTEENTH CENTURY.

I select from the Inquiry into City Governments, made in 1764, the papers which relate to Angers; they contain an analysis, attacks upon, and defenses of the constitution of this city, emanating from the presidial, the city corporation, the sub-delegate, and the intendant. As the same facts occurred in many other places, the picture must not be regarded as a solitary example.

MEMORIAL OF THE PRESIDIAL ON THE PRESENT STATE OF THE MUNICIPAL CONSTITUTION OF ANGERS, AND ON THE REFORMS THAT IT NEEDS.

" The Corporation of Angers never consults the people at large even on the most important occasions, unless it is compelled to do so; hence its policy is unknown to every one but its own members. Even the movable aldermen have only a superficial acquaintance with its mode of proceeding."

(The tendency of all these little burgher oligarchies was, in truth, to consult the people at large as little as possible.)

The corporation is composed of twenty-one officers, in virtue of a decree of 29th March, 1681, to wit:

A mayor, who becomes noble *ex officio*, and whose term is four years;

Four movable aldermen, who hold office for two years;

Twelve consulting aldermen, who are elected and hold office for life;

Two city counsel;

One counsel holding the reversion of the office;

A clerk.

They enjoy many privileges: among others, their capitation-tax is fixed at a moderate sum; they are exempt from lodging soldiers, arms, or baggage; they are exempt from dues *de cloison double et triple*, from the old and new excise, from the accessory dues on articles of consumption, even from benevolences, " from which latter they have asserted their own freedom," says the presidial. They enjoy, moreover, allowances in the shape of lights, and in some cases salaries and lodgings.

We see from this that a post of perpetual alderman at Angers was not to be despised in those days. Note here, as every where else, the contrivances to secure exemptions from taxes for the rich. The memorial goes on to say that " these offices are eagerly sought by the richest citizens, who desire them in order to reduce their capitation-tax, and increase that of their fellow-citizens in proportion. There are at this moment several municipal officers who pay 30 livres of capitation, and ought to pay 250 to 300 livres; one, among others, ought, in proportion to his fortune, to pay 1000 livres at least." In another part of the memorial it is said that among the richest inhabitants of the place are more than forty officers, or widows of officers (office-holders), whose rank exempts them from the heavy capitation-tax paid by the city. The tax consequently falls upon an infinite number of poor mechanics, who, believing themselves overtaxed, constantly complain of the amount of their tax—unjustly so, for there are no inequalities in the division of the burden laid upon the city.

The General Assembly is composed of seventy-six persons:
The mayor;
Two deputies of the chapter;
A syndic of the clerks;
Two deputies of the presidial;
A deputy of the university;
A lieutenant-general of police;
Four aldermen;
Twelve consulting aldermen;
A king's attorney near the presidial;
A city counsel;
Two deputies of the woods and forests;
Two of the *election;*
Two of the salt warehouse;
Two of the *traites;*
Two of the mint;
Two of the advocates and attorneys;
Two of the consular judges;
Two of the notaries;
Two of the shop-keepers;
And, lastly, two deputies from each of the sixteen parishes.

These latter are understood to be the special representatives of the people; they are, in fact, the representatives of industrial corporations, and the council is so arranged, as the reader has seen, that they are sure to be in a minority.

When posts in the corporation become vacant, the General Assembly chooses three candidates for each vacancy.

Most of the posts in the city government are free to persons of all professions; the Assembly is not—as others which I have noticed—obliged to choose a magistrate or a lawyer to fill a vacancy. To this the presidial objects strongly.

According to the same presidial, which seems terribly jealous of the city corporation, and whose main objection to the constitution was, I suspect, that it did not confer privileges enough on the presidial, " the General Assembly is too numerous, and composed of persons too devoid of intelligence to be consulted on any matters but sales of the city property, the negotiation of loans, the establishment of town dues, and the election of municipal officers.

All other business should be transacted by a smaller body, wholly composed of *notables*. No one should be a member of this assembly but the lieutenant-general of the *sénéchaussée*, the king's attorney, and twelve other notables chosen out of the six bodies, the clergy, the magistracy, the nobility, the university, the merchants, and the burghers, and others who do not belong to any of these six classes. The first choice of notables should be made by the Assembly, and future elections by the assembly of notables or the body from which each notable is chosen."

A resemblance existed between these public functionaries, who thus become members of municipal bodies as office-holders or notables, and the functionaries of the same title and character in our day. But their position was very different from that of modern office-holders—a fact which can not be safely overlooked; for nearly all these old functionaries were city notables before they obtained office, or only sought office in order to become notables. They had no notion of either resigning their rank or being promoted; this alone creates a vast difference between them and their successors in office.

MEMORIAL OF THE MUNICIPAL OFFICERS.

This document shows that the city corporation was created in 1474 by Louis XI. upon the ruins of the old democratic constitution of the city, and that its principle was of the nature explained above; that is to say, nearly all political power was vested in the middle classes; the people were kept at a distance, or weakened; a vast number of municipal officers were created in order to muster partisans for the scheme; hereditary titles of nobility were granted in profusion, and all sorts of privileges were secured to the burgher administrators.

The same paper also contains letters patent from successors of Louis XI., which recognize this new constitution and curtail still further the power of the people. It mentions that in 1485 the letters patent granted with this view by Charles VIII. were assailed by the people of Angers before the Parliament, just as, in England, disputes relative to the charter of a city would have been carried before the courts. In 1601 a decree of Parliament again fixed the political rights which were authorized by the royal charter. From thenceforth, no other controlling authority appears but the Royal Council.

It appears from the same memorial that mayors, like all other city officers, were selected by the king out of a list of three names presented by the General Assembly; this was in virtue of an Order in Council of 22d June, 1708. It also appears that, in virtue of Orders in Council of 1733 and 1741, the small traders were entitled to one alderman (perpetual) or councilor. Finally, the memorial shows that at that time the corporation was intrusted with the distribution of the tax levied for the capitation, equipment, lodgings, provisions of the poor, of the troops, of the revenue service, of foundlings.

Then follows an enumeration of the great labors which devolve upon municipal officers. They fully justify, in the opinion of the memorialists, the privileges and the permanent rank which they enjoy, and which, it is plain, they are much afraid of losing. Many of the reasons which they assign for the severity of their office-labors are curious, such as the following : " Their financial duties have been much increased by the extensions which are constantly being made to the aid dues, the gabel, the stamp and registry dues, and the unlawful exactions of registry dues and freehold duties. They have been involved, on the city's behalf, in perpetual lawsuits with the financial companies in reference to these taxes ; they have had to go from court to court, from the Parliament to the Council, in order to resist the oppression under which they are groaning. An experience and a public service of thirty years enable them to state that the life of man is hardly long enough to defend one's self against the stratagems and the traps which the agents of the revenue-farmers are constantly laying for the citizen, in order to preserve their commissions."

Curiously enough, it is to the comptroller-general that these things are said, and said with the view of winning his support for the privileges of the class that expresses these views. So deeply rooted was the habit of viewing the companies which farmed the taxes as an adversary that might be abused on all sides without objection from any one. This habit steadily spread and gained strength ; men learned to view the treasury as an odious tyrant, hateful to all : the common enemy instead of the common agent.

"All offices were first united with the corporation," adds the same memorial, " by an Order in Council of the 4th September, 1694, in consideration of a sum of 22,000 livres ;" that is to say, the offices were redeemed that year for that sum. By an order of 26th April, 1723, the offices created by the edict of 24th May, 1722, were also united to the corporation, or, in other words, the city was permitted to redeem them. By another order of 24th May, 1723, the city was authorized to borrow 120,000 livres for the acquisition of the said offices. Another, of 26th July, 1728, authorized it to borrow 50,000 livres to redeem the office of clerk-secretary of the City Hall. "The city," says the memorial, "has paid its money to preserve the freedom of its elections, and to secure to the officers it elects for one or two years, or for life, the various prerogatives attached to their offices." Some of the municipal offices were re-established by the edict of November, 1733; an order was subsequently obtained at the instance of the mayor and aldermen, allowing the city to purchase an extension of its rights, for a term of fifteen years, for a sum of 170,000 livres.

This is a fair criterion of the policy of the government of the old regime, as regards cities. It compelled them to contract debts, then authorized them to establish extraordinary taxes to liquidate them. And to this it must be added that afterward many of these taxes, which were naturally temporary, were made perpetual, and then the government got its share.

The memorial continues: "The municipal officers were never deprived of their judicial functions till the establishment of royal courts. Until 1669, they had sole cognizance of disputes between masters and servants. The accounts of the town dues are rendered before the intendant, in obedience to the decrees establishing or continuing the said dues."

The memorial makes it plain that the representatives of the sixteen parishes, who, as above mentioned, had seats in the General Assembly, were chosen by companies, corporate bodies, or communities, and were the mere organs of these bodies. They were bound by their instructions on all points.

In fine, this memorial shows that, at Angers as elsewhere, no expenses could be incurred by the city without the concurrence of the intendant and the Council. And it must be acknowledged that, when the government of a city is intrusted to certain men to be used as their private property, and when these men receive no salary, but enjoy in lieu thereof privileges which exonerate them from all responsibility to their fellow-citizens for maladministration, the guardianship of the state may seem a necessity.

The whole of this memorial, which is clumsily drawn up, indicates a state of great alarm on the part of these officials lest the existing state of things should be changed. All kinds of reasons, good and bad, are accumulated together, and pressed into the service of the *statu quo*.

MEMORIAL OF THE SUB-DELEGATE.

The intendant, having received these two contradictory memorials, asks for the opinion of his sub-delegate. He gives it:

"The memorial of the municipal councilors," says he, "does not deserve attention; its only aim is to subserve their own privileges. That of the presidial may be beneficially consulted, but there is no reason for granting them all the prerogatives they desire."

He admits that the constitution of the civic body has long needed reform. Besides the immunities already mentioned, which were enjoyed by all the municipal officers of Angers, he states that the mayor, during his term of service, was lodged at a cost of at least 600 francs; that he received 50 francs salary, and 100 francs for expenses of his office, besides the *jetons*. The attorney-syndic was also lodged, and so was the clerk. In order to escape aid and town dues, the municipal officers had fixed upon a presumed amount of consumption by each of them; and by accounting for this, they could introduce into the city as many casks of wine or other merchandise as they pleased.

The sub-delegate does not propose to deprive the councilors of their exemption from taxes; but he thinks their capitation-tax, which is now fixed at a very low figure, should be settled every year by the intendant. He also advises that these officials should be made to contribute with every one else to the *don gratuit*, their exemption from which is without authority or precedent.

The municipal officers, says the memorial, are intrusted with the preparation of the capitation-rolls for the people. They perform this duty carelessly and arbitrarily, whence the intendant is regularly overwhelmed every year with petitions and reclamations. It would be desirable that this tax should be distributed hereafter, in the interest of each community or company, by its members, in a general and stable manner; and that municipal officers should in future fix the capitation of burghers only, and of persons belonging to no public body, such as certain workmen and the servants of privileged persons.

The memorial of the sub-delegate confirms what the municipal officers have already stated in regard to the redemption, in 1735, of the municipal offices, for the sum of 170,000 livres.

LETTER FROM THE INTENDANT TO THE COMPTROLLER-GENERAL.

Armed with these various documents, the intendant writes to the minister: "The public interest and that of the citizens," he says, "require a reduction in the number of municipal officers, whose privileges have become a heavy burden on the public."

"I am struck," he adds, "with the enormous amount of money that has been repeatedly paid for the redemption of municipal offices at Angers. A similar sum, employed usefully, would have done the city much good ; as it is, it has only made people feel the weight of the authority and of the privileges of these officials.

"The internal abuses of this government fully deserve the attention of the Council. Independently of *jetons* and candle, which consume the annual appropriation of 2127 livres (this was the sum set apart for this class of expenditures in the normal budget, which was occasionally imposed on cities by the king), the public money is squandered and employed for clandestine purposes by these officers. The king's attorney, who has held his office for thirty or forty years, has obtained such a mastery over the administration, of which he alone understands the details, that the citizens have been unable to obtain the least information with regard to the employment of their money." In consequence, the intendant proposes to the minister to reduce the corporation to a mayor serving for four years, six aldermen serving for six years, one king's attorney serving for eight, and a perpetual clerk and receiver.

In other respects the Constitution which he proposes for Angers is precisely the same as the one he elsewhere proposed for Tours. In his opinion,

1st. The government should preserve the General Assembly, but merely as an electoral body for the election of municipal officers.

2d. It should create an extraordinary Council of Notables, whose functions should be those with which the edict of 1764 appeared to invest the General Assembly. This council to be composed of twelve persons, holding office for six years, and elected, not by the General Assembly, but by the twelve bodies esteemed notable, each body electing one. He designates as notable bodies,

The presidial,
The university,
The *election*,
The office of woods and forests,
The salt warehouse,
The office of the *traites*,
The mint,
The advocates and attorneys,
The consular judges,
The notaries,

The traders (*marchands*),
The burghers (*bourgeois*).

As will be remarked, nearly all these notables were public functionaries, and all the public functionaries were notables. From this, as from a thousand other papers in these collections, it may be inferred that the middle classes were then as great place-hunters and as destitute of independent ambition as they are now. The only difference is, as I remarked in the text, that formerly the petty importance afforded by these places was bought, whereas now candidates beg the government to grant them the charity of a place for nothing.

It is here seen that the whole real power in the municipality is vested in the extraordinary council, and the administration of the city is thus further confined to a small circle of burghers.   The only assembly in which the people continue to exercise the least interference is now confined to the electing of municipal officers whom it can not instruct.   It is to be remarked, also, that the intendant is more unbending and antipopular in his principles than the king, who seemed in his edict to have transferred most of the public authority to the General Assembly, and again, that the intendant is far more liberal and democratic than the burghers.   This last inference is at all events a fair one from the memorial I have quoted in the text, from which it appears that the notables of another city were desirous of excluding the people from the election of municipal officers in opposition to the views of the intendant and the king.

It may be noticed that the intendant recognizes two distinct classes of notables under the names of *bourgeois* and *marchands*. It may not be useless to give an exact definition of these words, in order to show into how many small fragments the *bourgeoisie* was divided, and by how many petty vanities it was actuated.

The word *bourgeois* had a general and also a particular meaning; it meant the members of the middle classes at large, and it also meant a certain number of men within those classes.   "*Bourgeois,*" says a memorial filed at the inquiry of 1764, " are individuals whose birth and fortune enable them to live without engaging in lucrative pursuits."   Other portions of the memorial show that the word *bourgeois* does not apply to persons who belong to companies or industrial corporations ; it is not so easy to say to whom it does apply.   " For," as the same memorial says, " many persons assume the title of *bourgeois* whose only claim to it is their idleness, who have no fortune, and lead a rude, obscure life. *Bourgeois* should, on the contrary, always be distinguished by their fortune, their birth, their talents, manners, and mode of life. Mechanics composing trade-companies have never been classed in the rank of notables."*

Traders (*marchands*) were another class of individuals who, like the *bourgeois*, belonged to no company or corporation: but where were the limits of this little class? " Must we," says the same memorial, " confound small, low-born dealers with wholesale merchants ?" To overcome the difficulty, the memorial proposes to have the aldermen draw up every year a table of notable traders (*marchands*), to be handed to their chief or syndic, who shall invite to the deliberations at the city hall none but those who are thereon inscribed. Care will be taken to inscribe on this table no traders who may have been domestics, porters, wagoners, or followers of other low trades.

Note u, *page* 66.

One of the most striking features of the administration of cities in the eighteenth century is, not the absence of all representation and intervention of the public in city business, but the extreme variability of the rules governing such administration. Civic rights were constantly bestowed, taken away, restored, increased, diminished, modified in a thousand ways, and unceasingly. No better indication of the contempt into which all local liberties had fallen can be found than these eternal changes of laws which no one seemed to notice. This mobility would alone have sufficed to destroy all initiative or recuperative energy, and all local patriotism in the institution which is best adapted to it. It helped to prepare the great work of destruction which was to be effected by the Revolution.

Note v, *page* 67.

A VILLAGE GOVERNMENT IN THE EIGHTEENTH CENTURY (TAKEN FROM THE PAPERS OF THE INTENDANT'S OFFICE IN THE ILE DE FRANCE).

The affair which I am about to relate is one instance out of a thousand which illustrates the forms and the dilatory methods used by parochial governments, and shows what a general parochial assembly really was in the eighteenth century.

---

* In the text the words *bourgeois* and *bourgeoisie* are translated " burghers" or " the middle classes," according to the context. The exact meaning of the French word is often doubtful, and the search for an exact English equivalent almost always hopeless.—TRANS.

The parsonage-house and steeple of a rural parish—that of Ivry, Ile de France—required repair. To whom was application to be made to make the repairs? Who was to pay for them? How was the money to be procured?

1st. Petition from the curate to the intendant, setting forth that the parsonage-house and steeple need immediate repairs; that his predecessor had caused useless buildings to be erected adjoining the parsonage-house, and had thus altered and deformed the character of the spot; and that the inhabitants, having permitted him to do this, ought to bear the expense of all needful repairs, having their recourse on the late curate's heirs for the expense.

. 2d. Ordinance of monseigneur the intendant (29th August, 1747), ordering the syndic diligently to convene an assembly to deliberate on the necessity of the repairs.

3d. Deliberation of the inhabitants, by which they declare that they do not object to the parsonage-house being repaired, but as for the steeple, they hold that, as it is built on the choir, which the curate, as a large tithe-holder, is bound to repair, he must pay for any repairs it may need. [An Order in Council of April, 1695, had, in fact, imposed the duty of keeping the choir in repair upon the tithe-holder, leaving the tithe-payers to look after the nave.]

4th. New ordinance of the intendant, which, in view of the conflict of statements, orders an architect, the *Sieur* Cordier, to visit and examine the parsonage-house and steeple, hear evidence, and make estimates of the works.

5th. Authentic report of all these proceedings, testifying that a certain number of landholders of Ivry, apparently men of rank, burghers, and peasants, appeared before the intendant's commissioner, and gave evidence for or against the pretensions of the curate.

6th. New ordinance of the intendant, directing that the estimates prepared by his architect be laid before the landholders and inhabitants in a general assembly convoked with due diligence by the syndic for the purpose.

7th. New parochial assembly in pursuance of the ordinance, in which the people declare that they adhere to their expressed opinions.

8th. Ordinance of the intendant, directing, first, that in presence of his sub-delegate at Corbeil, the curate, syndic, and principal inhabitants of the parish being also present, the contracts for the work according to the estimates shall be given out; and, secondly, that, whereas the want of repairs involves absolute danger, the whole cost shall be levied upon the inhabitants, without prejudice to the legal rights of those who conceive that the cost of repairing the steeple should be borne by the curate as tithe-holder.

9th. Notice to all parties to be present at the office of the sub-delegate at Corbeil, where the contracts are to be given out.

10th. Petition of the curate and several inhabitants, praying that the costs of the preliminary proceedings be not charged, as usual, against the contractor, lest they should deter bidders from coming forward.

11th. Ordinance of the intendant, directing that all expenses incurred in order to bring the affair to issue be settled by the sub-delegate, added to the contract, and included in the imposition.

12th. Authority from several notables of the parish to the Sieur X. to be present on their behalf at the execution of the contract, and confirm it according to the architect's estimates.

13th. Certificate of the syndic, stating that the usual notices and advertisements have been made.

14th. Official report of the contract:

Expenses of repairs .... 487*l.*
Legal expenses pertaining thereto .... 237*l.* 18*s.* 6*d.*
724   18   6

15th. Lastly, Order in Council (23d July, 1748), authorizing an impost to raise this sum.

It may have been noticed that frequent allusions are here made to the parochial assembly. The following report of one of these assemblies will show how matters were usually managed on these occasions.

NOTARIAL ACT.—" This day, at the close of the parochial mass, at the usual and customary place, was present at the assembly held by the inhabitants of the said parish before X., notary at Corbeil undersigned, and the witnesses hereinafter mentioned, the Sieur Michaud, vine-dresser, syndic of the said parish, who presented the ordinance of the intendant authorizing the assembly, read the same, and applied for an official certificate of his due diligence in the premises:

" And then and there appeared an inhabitant of the said parish, who stated that the steeple was upon the choir, and, consequently, that its repairs should be charged to the curate; did furthermore appear —— (here follow the names of various parishioners, who, on the contrary, consent to the request of the curate); and thereafter appeared fifteen peasants, mechanics, masons, and vine-dressers, who declare themselves of the same mind as the preceding persons. Did also appear the Sieur Raimbaud, vine-dresser, who declared that he would agree to whatever monseigneur the intendant decided in the premises. Did also appear the Sieur X., doctor of the Sorbonne, curate, who persists in the allegations and conclusions of his request.

"Whereof the said parties have required of us official certificate.

"Done and passed at the said place of Ivry, in front of the burial-ground of the said parish, before the undersigned; and the meeting aforesaid lasted from eleven o'clock in the morning till two."

It will be noticed that this parish assembly was a mere administrative inquiry, in the same form and as costly as judicial inquiries; that it never led to a vote or other clear expression of the will of the parish; that it was merely an expression of individual opinions, and constituted no check upon government. Many other documents indicate that the only object of parish assemblies was to afford information to the intendant, and not to influence his decision even in cases where no other interest but that of the parish was concerned.

It may be remarked, also, that this affair gives rise to three separate inquiries; one before the notary, another before the architect, and a third before two notaries, to ascertain whether the people have not changed their minds.

The impost of 724 *liv*. 18 *s*., authorized by the Order of 23d July, 1748, bears upon all landholders, whether privileged or not. This was generally the case in affairs of this kind; but the share of the various rate-payers was not fixed on uniform principles. Persons who paid the taille were taxed in proportion to their taille. Privileged individuals, on the other hand, were taxed in proportion to their assumed fortunes, which gave them a great advantage over the former class.

It appears, finally, that in this matter the distribution of the impost was made by two collectors, inhabitants of the village; not elected, nor serving in their turn, as was usually the custom, but chosen and appointed by the intendant's sub-delegate.

Note w, *page* 67.

The pretext which Louis XIV. put forward for destroying the municipal liberty of towns was the maladministration of their finances; yet the evil, according to Turgot, continued to exist, and even assumed larger proportions after the reform of this monarch.

He adds that most cities are heavily in debt at the present time, partly for moneys lent to government, and partly for expenses or decorations which municipal officers—who dispose of other people's money, who render no account, and receive no instructions —are constantly incurring, in order to increase the splendor or the profit of their position.

Note x, *page* 72.

THE STATE WAS GUARDIAN OF CONVENTS AS WELL AS COMMUNES; INSTANCE THEREOF.

The comptroller-general, authorizing the intendant to pay over 15,000 livres to the Convent of Carmelites, to which certain indemnities were due, desires the intendant to satisfy himself that the money, which represents a capital, is properly invested. Similar instances abound.

Note y, *page* 79.

HOW THE ADMINISTRATIVE CENTRALIZATION OF THE OLD REGIME CAN BE BEST JUDGED IN CANADA.

The physiognomy of governments can be best detected in their colonies, for there their features are magnified, and rendered more conspicuous. When I want to discover the spirit and vices of the government of Louis XIV., I must go to Canada. Its deformities are seen there as through a microscope.

A number of obstacles, created by previous occurrences or old social forms, which hindered the development of the true tendencies of government at home, did not exist in Canada. There was no nobility, or, at least, none had taken deep root. The Church was not dominant. Feudal traditions were lost or obscured. The power of the judiciary was not interwoven with old institutions or popular customs. There was, therefore, no hindrance to the free play of the central power. It could shape all laws according to its views. And in Canada, therefore, there was not a shadow of municipal or provincial institutions; and no collective or individual action was tolerated. An intendant far more powerful than his colleagues in France; a government managing far more matters than it did at home, and desiring to manage every thing from Paris, notwithstanding the intervening 1800 leagues; never adopting the great principles which can render a colony populous and prosperous, but, instead, employing all sorts of petty, artificial methods, and small devices of tyranny to increase and spread population; forced cultivation of lands; all lawsuits growing out of the concession of land removed from the jurisdiction of the courts and referred to the local administration; compulsory regulations respecting farming and the selection of land—such was the system devised for Canada under Louis XIV. : it was Colbert who signed the edicts. One might fancy one's self in the midst of modern centralization and in Algeria. Canada is, in fact, the true model of what has always been seen there. In both places the government numbers as many heads as the people; it preponderates, acts, regulates, controls, undertakes every thing, provides for every thing, knows far more about the subject's business than he does himself—is, in short, incessantly active and sterile.

In the United States, on the contrary, the English anti-centralization system was carried to an extreme. Parishes became independent municipalities, almost democratic republics. The republican element, which forms, so to say, the foundation of the English constitution and English habits, shows itself and develops without hindrance. Government proper does little in England, and individuals do a great deal; in America, government never interferes, so to speak, and individuals do every thing. The absence of an upper class, which renders the Canadian more defenseless against the government than his equals were in France, renders the citizen of the English colonies still more independent of the home power.

In both colonies society ultimately resolved itself into a democratic form. But in Canada, so long as it was a French possession at least, equality was an accessory of absolutism; in the British colonies it was the companion of liberty. And, so far as the material consequences of the two colonial systems are concerned, it is well known that in 1763, at the conquest, the population of Canada was 60,000 souls, that of the English provinces 3,000,000.

Note z, page 80.

AN EXAMPLE, CHOSEN AT HAPHAZARD, OF THE GENERAL REGULA-
TIONS WHICH THE COUNCIL OF STATE WAS IN THE HABIT OF
MAKING FOR THE WHOLE OF FRANCE, AND BY WHICH IT CREATED
SPECIAL MISDEMEANORS OF WHICH THE GOVERNMENT COURTS
HAD SOLE COGNIZANCE.

I take the first which I happen to find. Order in Council of 29th April, 1779, which enacts that thereafter throughout the kingdom all sheep-growers and sheep-dealers shall mark their sheep in a peculiar manner, under penalty of 300 *livres* fine. "His majesty orders the intendant to see this order obeyed," it says, whence it follows that it devolved upon the intendant to pronounce penalties incurred. Another instance: An Order in Council of 21st December, 1778, forbids express companies and wagoners to warehouse the goods they have in charge, under pain of 300 *livres* fine. "His majesty enjoins upon his lieutenant general of police and his intendants to see to it."

Note a, page 92.

The Provincial Assembly of Guienne cries aloud for new brigades of horse-police, just as in our day the council-general of the department of Aveyron or Lot no doubt demands new brigades of *gendarmerie*. Always the same idea — *gendarmerie* constitute order, and order can not be had with the gendarme except through government. The report adds: "Complaint is daily made that there is no police in the country." (How could there be? Noblemen take no concern for any thing, burghers live in town; and the community is represented by a rude peasant, and has no power at all.) "It must be admitted that, except in some *cantons* in which benevolent and just seigniors use their influence over their vassals to prevent those appeals to violence to which the country people are prone, in consequence of the rudeness of their manners and the roughness of their character, there exists hardly any where any means of controlling these ignorant, rough, and hot-headed men."

Such was the manner in which the nobles of the Provincial Assembly allowed themselves to be spoken of, and in which the Third Estate, comprising half the assembly, spoke of the people in public documents.

Note b, page 93.

Tobacco licenses were as eagerly sought after under the old regime as at present. The most distinguished people begged them for their dependents. Some, I find, were granted at the request of noble ladies, some to please archbishops.

Note c, page 94.

Local life was more thoroughly extinguished than almost seems credible. One of the roads leading from Maine into Normandy had become impassable. Who calls for its repair? The district of Touraine, which it crosses? The province of Normandy, or that of Maine, both vitally interested in the cattle-trade of which it is the outlet? Some canton particularly injured by the bad condition of the road? Neither district, nor province, nor canton utter a word. The duty of attracting the attention of government to the road is left to the traders who use it, and whose wagons stick in the mud. They write to Paris to the comptroller-general, and beg him to come to their rescue.

Note d, *page* 103.

VARYING VALUE OF SEIGNIORIAL RENTS AND DUES ACCORDING TO PROVINCES.

Turgot says in his works: "I must remark that the importance of these dues is very different in most of the rich provinces, such as Normandy, Picardy, and the vicinity of Paris. In the latter, riches usually consist in the produce of land; the farms are large, close together, and bring high rents. The seigniorial rents of large farms form a very small portion of the income from them, and are regarded rather as honorary than lucrative. In poorer and worse-farmed provinces, seigniors and men of rank possess but little land of their own; farms, which are much subdivided, are burdened with heavy rents in produce, and all the co-tenants are jointly responsible for their payment. These rents eat up the clearest portion of the income of the land, and constitute the bulk of the seignior's revenue."

Note e, *page* 111.

DISCUSSION OF PUBLIC AFFAIRS ANTAGONISTIC TO THE ESTABLISHMENT OF CASTES.

The unimportant labors of the agricultural societies of the eighteenth century show how the general discussion of public affairs militated against castes. Though these assemblages took place thirty years prior to the Revolution, in the midst of the old regime, the mere fact that they discussed questions in which all classes were interested, and that all classes mingled in the discussion, drew men together and effected a sort of fusion. Ideas of reasonable reform suggested themselves to the minds even of the privileged classes, and yet they were mere conversations about agriculture.

I am satisfied that no government but one which relied wholly on its own strength, and invariably dealt with individuals singly, as that of the old regime did, could have maintained the ridiculous and insane inequality which existed at the time of the Revolution. The least touch of self-government would have soon altered or destroyed it.

Note f, *page* 111.

Provincial liberties may survive national liberty for a time, when they are of old standing, and interwoven with manners, customs, and recollections, and the despotism is new. But it is unreasonable to suppose that local liberties can be created at will, or maintained for any length of time, when general liberty is extinct.

Note g, *page* 112.

Turgot gives a statement of the extent of the privileges of the nobility, in the matter of taxation, in a memorial to the king. It appears to me to be quite correct.

1st. Privileged persons may claim exemption from taxes for a farm which consumes the labor of four plows. Such a farm in the neighborhood of Paris would usually pay 2000 francs of taxes.

2dly. The same privileged persons pay nothing for woods, meadows, rivers, ponds, or inclosed lands near their chateau, whatever be their extent. Some cantons are almost wholly laid out in meadow or vineyard; in these, seigniors who have their lands managed by a steward pay no impost whatever. All the taxes fall on the taille-payers. The advantage of this is immense.

Note h, *page* 113.

INDIRECT PRIVILEGE IN RESPECT OF TAXES.—DIFFERENCE IN THE MANNER OF COLLECTION WHEN THE TAX IS LEVIED ON ALL ALIKE.

Turgot draws a picture of this, which I have reason to believe is correct.

" The indirect advantages of the privileged classes with regard to the capitation-tax are very great. The capitation-tax is naturally an arbitrary impost; it is impossible to divide it among the citizens at large otherwise than blindly. It was found convenient to take the taille rolls, which were already made, as a basis. A special roll was made for the privileged classes; but, as the latter made objections, and the taille-payers had no one to speak for them, it came about that the capitation of the privileged classes was gradually reduced in the provinces to a very small sum, while the taille-payers paid as much for capitation as the principal of the taille."

Note i, page 112.

ANOTHER EXAMPLE OF INEQUALITY IN THE COLLECTION OF A
UNIFORM TAX.

It is known that local imposts were levied on all classes equally;
"which sums," say the Orders in Council authorizing these expenditures, "shall be levied on all persons without distinction, whether
privileged or not, jointly with the capitation-tax, or in proportion
thereto."

Note that, as the capitation-tax of taille-payers, which was assimilated to the taille, was always heavier than the capitation of
privileged persons, the very plan which seemed to favor uniformity kept up the inequality between the two.

Note k, page 112.

SAME SUBJECT.

I find in a bill of 1764, which designed to render the taxes uniform, all sorts of provisions that were intended to preserve a distinction in favor of the privileged classes in respect to the tax levy.
For instance, no property of theirs could be appraised for taxation
except in their presence or in the presence of their attorney.

Note l, page 112.

HOW THE GOVERNMENT ADMITTED THAT, EVEN IN THE CASE OF
TAXES WEIGHING ALIKE ON ALL CLASSES, THE TAX OUGHT TO
BE COLLECTED DIFFERENTLY FROM THE PRIVILEGED AND UN-
PRIVILEGED CLASSES.

"I see," said the minister in 1766, "that the most difficult taxes
to collect are those which are due by nobles and privileged persons, in consequence of the consideration which the tax-collectors
feel bound to pay to these persons. It has resulted from this that
they are heavily in arrears on their capitation-tax and twentieths
(the taxes which they paid in common with the people)."

Note m, page 125.

Arthur Young, in his Journey in 1789, draws a picture in which
the condition of the two societies is so agreeably sketched and so
skillfully set that I can not resist giving it here.

In traveling through France during the emotion caused by the
capture of the Bastille, Young was arrested in a village by a mob,

who, seeing no *cocarde* on his hat, were about to drag him to jail. To get out of the scrape, Young improvises the following little speech:

"'Gentlemen, it has just been said that the taxes are to be paid just as before. The taxes must be paid, certainly, but not as before. They must be paid as they are in England. We have many more taxes than you; but the Third Estate, the people, pays none of them; they fall upon the rich. In my country, windows pay a tax; but a man who has only six in his house pays nothing. A seignior pays his twentieths and the taille, but the owner of a small garden escapes scot free. Rich men pay for their horses, their carriages, their servants, for the right of shooting their own partridges; but small landholders know nothing of these taxes. More than this: we have, in England, a tax that is levied on the rich for the maintenance of the poor. If, then, taxes are still to be paid, they must be paid on a new plan. The English plan is the best.'

"As my bad French," adds Young, "suited their patois well enough, they understood what I said. They applauded every word of this speech, and concluded that I might be a good fellow—an impression which I confirmed by crying *Vive le Tiers!* They then let me pass with a hurrah."

Note n, *page* 127.

The church of X., election of Chollet, was falling into ruin. Measures were being taken to repair it, according to the plan indicated by the Order of 16th December, 1684, that is to say, by a tax on all the citizens. When the collectors proceed to levy the tax, the Marquis of X., seignior of the parish, declares that, as he undertakes to repair the choir without assistance, he can not be expected to contribute to the tax. The other inhabitants reply very reasonably that, as seignior and large tithe-holder (he possessed, no doubt, the tithes enfeoffed), he was bound to repair the choir, and that he was by no means, on that account, relieved from his obligation to contribute to the other repairs. On reference to the intendant, he decides against the marquis and in favor of the collectors. The records of the affair contain more than ten letters of the marquis, each more pressing than the last, begging that the other people of the parish be made to pay in his stead, and condescending to call the intendant "monseigneur," and even to "supplicate him."

Note o, *page* 128.

EXAMPLE OF THE MANNER IN WHICH THE GOVERNMENT OF THE
OLD REGIME RESPECTED ACQUIRED RIGHTS, FORMAL CONTRACTS,
AND CITY OR ASSOCIATE LIBERTIES.

Royal declaration " suspending, in time of war, repayment of all
loans made to the crown by cities, bourgs, colleges, communities,
hospitals, poor-houses, corporations of artisans and tradesmen, and
others, for the payment of which town or other dues were pledged;
interest to accrue on the same."

This was not only suspending payment at the time fixed, but
laying hands on the security pledged for the payment of the loan.
Similar measures were common under the government of the old
regime ; they could never have occurred in a country where a
free press or free assemblies existed. Compare these proceedings
with those which have taken place in England and America in
the like circumstances. Here the contempt for right was not
less flagrant than the contempt for local liberties.

Note p, *page* 131.

The case cited in the text is not the only one in which the privileged classes perceived that they were affected by the feudal dues
which weighed upon the peasantry. An agricultural society, composed wholly of privileged persons, said, thirty years before the
Revolution,

" Irredeemable rents, whether ground-rents or feudal rents at-
taching upon land, become so onerous to the debtor when they are
considerable, that they ruin him and the land too. He is forced
to neglect his farm, for he can not effect loans on a property so
burdened, nor can he find a purchaser for it. If the rent were
redeemable, he would soon find a lender to advance money to pay
it off, or a purchaser to extinguish it. One is always glad to improve a property of which one believes one's self peaceable owner.
It would be of infinite service to agriculture if a means could be
found of rendering these rents redeemable. Many feudal seigniors
are convinced of this, and would gladly concur in any arrange-
ment for the purpose. It would therefore be desirable to indicate
a plan for redeeming all these ground-rents."

Note q, *page* 133.

All public functionaries, including the agent of the tax-farmers,
enjoyed exemptions from taxes. The privilege was granted them

by the ordinance of 1681. An intendant says, in a letter address-ed to the minister in 1782, " The most numerous class of privi-leged persons consists of clerks of the gabel, of *traites*, of the do-main, of the post, of aids, and other excise of all kinds. One or more of these are to be found in every parish."

The object was to prevent the ministers from proposing to the Council a measure to extend the exemption from taxes to the clerks and servants of these privileged agents. The farmers-gen-eral, says the intendant, are always asking for extensions of the privilege, in order to obtain clerks without paying them a salary.

Note r, *page* 133.

Venal offices were not wholly unknown abroad. In Germany some small sovereigns had introduced the system; but they had applied it to but few offices, and these subordinate ones. The sys-tem was carried out on a grand scale in France only.

Note s, *page* 138.

One must not be surprised—though it certainly seems surpris-ing—to see functionaries of the old government, closely connected with the administration, go to law before the Parliament about the limits of their respective powers. The fact is easily explained : the questions at issue were questions of public administration, but they were also questions of private property. What here appears to be an encroachment of the judiciary was, in fact, nothing but a consequence of the fault which the government committed in selling offices. All places being bought, and their incumbents be-ing paid by fees, it was impossible to alter the functions of an office without injuring individual rights which had been purchased for a valuable consideration. One example out of a thousand : the lieutenant general of police of Mans institutes an action against the financial department of that city to claim the right of paving the streets, and obtaining fees thereon, that being, he says, part of the police of the streets, which devolves upon him. The de-partment replies that the very title of its commission intrusts it with the paving of the streets. This time it is not the king's council which decides between them ; as the point involved is chiefly the interest of the capital invested by the lieutenant in the purchase of his office, the case goes before the Parliament. In-stead of being a government question, it is a civil suit.

Note t, *page* 140.

ANALYSIS OF THE CAHIERS OF THE NOBILITY IN 1789.

The French Revolution is the only one, I believe, at the beginning of which the different classes of society were enabled to present an authentic account of the ideas they had conceived, and express the feelings which animated them, before the Revolution had distorted or modified those ideas and feelings. This authentic account was recorded, as is known, in the *cahiers* which the three orders drew up in 1789. These *cahiers* or *memoires* were drawn up in perfect freedom, in the midst of the widest publicity, by each of the three orders; they were the fruit of long discussion by the parties in interest, and ripe deliberation by their authors; for in those days, when the government spoke to the nation, it did not undertake to answer its own questions. At the time the cahiers were composed, the principal parts of them were collected and published in three volumes, which are to be found in all libraries. The originals are deposited in the national archives, and with them the reports of the assemblies which drew them up, and a portion of the correspondence between M. Necker and his agents in reference to the subject. This collection forms a long series of folio volumes, and is the most precious document we have on the subject of ancient France. All who desire to become acquainted with the spirit of our forefathers at the time of the Revolution should consult it without delay.

I had imagined that perhaps the printed extract, in three volumes, which I have mentioned above, was a one-sided performance, and an unfaithful reflection of this immense collection; but I find, on comparing the two, that the smaller work is a correct miniature of the greater.

The following extract from the cahiers of the nobility shows the spirit which animated the majority of that body. It shows which of their old privileges the nobility desired at all hazards to keep, which they were half inclined to abandon, and which they proposed of their own accord to sacrifice. It discloses especially the views which pervaded the whole body on the subject of political liberty. Curious and melancholy spectacle!

INDIVIDUAL RIGHTS.—The nobility demand, in the first place, that an explicit declaration of the rights of man be made, and that that declaration bear witness to the liberty and secure the safety of all men.

PERSONAL LIBERTY.—They desire that the serfdom of the

glebe be abolished wherever it may still exist, and that means be sought for the extinction of the slave-trade and negro slavery; that all be free to travel whithersoever they will, and to reside where they please, within or without the kingdom, without being liable to arbitrary arrest; that the police regulations be amended, and that the police be under control of the magistracy, even in case of riot; that no one be arrested and judged except by his natural judges; that, in consequence, state prisons and other illegal places of detention be suppressed. Some demand the destruction of the Bastille. The nobility of Paris insist warmly on this point.

All letters of *cachet* should be prohibited. If the danger of the state requires the arrest of a citizen who can not be handed over directly to the ordinary courts of justice, measures must be taken to prevent injustice, either by notifying the Council of State, or in some other way.

The nobility desire that all special commissions, irregular courts, privileges of *committimus*, reprieves, be abolished; that the most severe penalties be laid upon all who execute or order the execution of an arbitrary command; that the ordinary courts—which alone should be preserved—take all necessary measures to secure individual liberty, especially in criminal matters; that justice be administered gratuitously, and useless jurisdictions abolished. One cahier says, " Magistrates were made for the people, not the people for magistrates." They demand that an honorary counsel and advocates for the poor be established in every bailiwick; that all examinations be public, and prisoners be allowed to defend themselves; that in criminal matters the prisoner be provided with a counsel, and the judge assisted by a number of citizens of the same order as the prisoner, who shall decide upon the fact of the crime or misdemeanor charged (reference is here made to the constitution of England); that penalties be proportioned to offenses, and uniform; that capital punishment be employed more rarely, and all corporal punishments, torture, &c., be abolished; that the condition of prisoners be improved, especially those who are confined before their trial.

The cahiers demand that an effort be made to respect individual liberty in the recruiting service both of soldiers and sailors. It should be allowable to avoid military service by paying a sum of money. No lots should be drawn save in the presence of deputies of the three orders. Finally, an attempt should be made to reconcile military discipline and subordination with the rights of the citizen and the freeman. Blows with the flat of the sword should be forbidden.

LIBERTY AND INVIOLABILITY OF PROPERTY.—Property should be inviolable, and should never be molested save for the necessities of the public weal. In such cases the government should pay a high price, and that promptly. Confiscations should be abolished.

LIBERTY OF TRADE, LABOR, AND INDUSTRY.—Freedom of labor and trade should be secured. In consequence, all monopolies should be taken from trade-companies, as well as other privileges of the kind. No custom-houses should exist except on the frontier.

LIBERTY OF RELIGION.—The Catholic faith shall be the only dominant religion in France, but all other religions shall be tolerated, and persons who are not Catholics shall be reinstated in their properties and civil rights.

LIBERTY OF THE PRESS, INVIOLABILITY OF LETTERS IN THE POST-OFFICE.—The liberty of the press shall be secured, and a law shall fix beforehand the restrictions that may be established in the interest of the public. No works but such as treat of religious doctrine shall be liable to ecclesiastical censorship; in the case of all others, it shall be sufficient that the names of the author and printer are known. Many demand that charges against the press be tried before jury.

All the cahiers insist energetically on the inviolability of secrets confided to the post, so that private letters may never be brought in accusation against individuals. The opening of letters, say they, bluntly, is the most odious form of espionage, as it violates the public faith.

EDUCATION.—The cahiers of the nobility confine themselves to recommending that all proper means be taken to spread education, both in cities and in the country, and that each boy be taught with a view to his future vocation. They insist on the necessity of teaching children the political rights and duties of the citizen, and suggest that a catechism on the principal points of the Constitution be used in schools. They do not, however, point out any means to be used to facilitate and spread education. They merely demand educational establishments for the children of the poor nobility.

CARE TO BE TAKEN OF THE PEOPLE.—Many of the cahiers demand that the people be treated with more consideration. They exclaim against the police regulations, in virtue of which they say hosts of mechanics and useful citizens are daily thrust into prisons and jails without any regular commitment, and often on mere suspicions, a manifest violation of natural liberty. All the cahiers demand that *corvées* be definitely abolished. A majority of bailiwicks desire that rights of banality and toll be made redeemable. Many demand that the collection of various feudal dues be rendered less oppressive, and that the freehold duty be abolished. One cahier observes that the government is interested in facilitating the purchase and sale of lands. This is precisely the reason that will soon be urged for abolishing at a blow all seigniorial rights, and throwing all mainmortable lands into the market. Many cahiers ask that the right of pigeon-houses be rendered less prejudicial to agriculture. As for the establishments for the preservation of the king's game, known by the name of captainries, they demand their immediate abolition, as being subversive of the rights of property. They desire to see, in lieu of the present taxes, new ones established which shall be less onerous to the people.

The nobility demand that an effort be made to disseminate plenty and comfort throughout the rural districts; that looms and factories of coarse stuffs be established in the villages, so as to occupy the country-people during the idle season; that in each bailiwick public store-houses be founded, under the inspection of the provincial governments, to provide for seasons of famine, and sustain the regularity of prices; that attempts be made to improve agriculture and better the condition of the country parts; that more public works be undertaken, and especially that marshes be drained, and means taken to guard against inundations, &c.; finally, that special encouragements be offered to agriculture and trade in all the provinces.

The cahiers suggest that, instead of the present hospitals, small establishments of the kind be founded in every district; that the poor-houses be abolished, and replaced by work-houses; that a charitable fund be placed at the disposal of the Provincial States; that surgeons, physicians, and midwives be appointed for every county to tend the poor gratuitously, and paid by the province; that the Courts of Justice should always be open to the poor, free of charge; that thought be taken for the establishment of blind, deaf and dumb asylums, foundling-hospitals, &c.

In all these matters the nobility express their general views as to what reforms are needed; they do not enter into details. It is easy to see that they have been less frequently brought into contact with the poor than the lower order of clergy, and that, having seen less of their sufferings, they have reflected less on the subject of a remedy.

OF ELIGIBILITY TO OFFICE, OF THE HIERARCHY OF RANKS, AND OF THE HONORARY PRIVILEGES OF THE NOBILITY. — It is chiefly, or, rather, it is only when they come to deal with distinctions of rank and class divisions that the nobles turn their backs on the prevailing spirit of reform. They make important concessions, but, on the whole, they adhere to the spirit of the old regime. They feel that they are fighting for life. Their cahiers thus demand energetically that the nobility and the clergy be maintained as distinct orders. They even desire that a method be devised for preserving the purity of the order of the nobility ; that, for instance, the practice of selling titles or coupling them with certain offices be prohibited, and that rank be the reward of long and meritorious services rendered to the state. They wish that all the false nobles could be found out and prosecuted. All the cahiers, in short, demand that the nobility be maintained in all its honors. Some think it would be well for men of rank to wear a distinctive badge.

Nothing could be more characteristic than such a demand ; nothing could indicate more plainly the similarity between the noble and the commoner. Generally speaking, the nobility, while abandoning many of their beneficial rights, cling with anxiety and warmth to those which are purely honorary. They want not only to preserve those which they possess, but also to invent new ones. So conscious were they that they were being dragged into the vortex of democracy : so terribly did they dread perishing there. Singular fact ! Their instinct warned them of the danger, but they never perceived it.

As to the distribution of office, the nobility demand that posts in the magistracy be no longer sold, but that any citizen of suitable age and capacity be eligible as a candidate to be presented by the nation to the king. In respect to military rank, a majority of the cahiers are against excluding the Third Estate, and conceive that a man who has deserved well of his country ought to be able to attain the highest rank. Several cahiers say, " The order of the nobility disapproves all laws which close the door of military preferment to the order of the Third Estate." Some few, however, suggest that noblemen alone should have the right of entering the army as officers without passing through the inferior grades. Nearly all the cahiers demand that uniform rules be established with regard to promotion, that advancement be not wholly obtained by favor, and that, with the exception of the highest posts, promotion proceed by seniority.

As for clerical functions, they demand that elections be re-established for the distribution of livings, or, at all events, that the king appoint a committee to guide him in distributing ecclesiastical preferment.

They say that henceforth pensions must be granted with more discrimination, and not accumulated in certain families; that no citizen must receive two pensions, or draw pay for two offices at once; that survivorships must be abolished.

CHURCH AND CLERGY.—When they have done with their own rights and peculiar constitution, and turn to the privileges and constitution of the Church, the nobility are not so timid; they have a very sharp eye for abuses.

They demand that the clergy be deprived of all exemptions from taxes; that they pay their debts, and do not call upon the nation to pay them; that the monastic orders be thoroughly reformed. Most of the cahiers declare that these institutions have departed from the spirit of their founders.

Most of the bailiwicks desire that tithes be rendered less injurious to agriculture; several demand their entire abolition. One cahier says that "tithes are for the most part exacted by those curates who give themselves the least trouble to supply their flocks with spiritual food." The first Order, as is seen, handled the second unceremoniously. Nor was it more respectful in dealing with the Church itself. Many bailiwicks formally assert the right of the States-General to suppress certain religious orders, and apply their property to other uses. Seventeen bailiwicks declare that the States-General may regulate ecclesiastical discipline. Many say that there are too many fête-days; that they injure agriculture, and favor drunkenness; that, in consequence, a great number of them must be suppressed, and Sundays kept instead.

POLITICAL RIGHTS.—As to these, the cahiers recognize the right of all Frenchmen to take part directly or indirectly in the government, that is to say, to be electors and eligible. But this right is restricted by the distinction of ranks; that is to say, no one can be elected but by and for his Order. This principle laid out, representation should be so devised as to secure to each Order an active share in the public affairs.

Opinions are divided as to the way of taking votes in the assembly of the States-General: a majority advocate voting by Order, others think this rule ought not to apply to questions of taxation, and others, again, object to it altogether. These latter say, "Each member shall have a vote, and all questions shall be decided by a majority of votes. This is the only rational plan, and the only one that can extinguish that *esprit de corps* which has been the only source of our misfortunes, draw men together, and lead them to the result which the nation is entitled to expect of an assembly in which patriotism and the virtues are enlightened by learning." Still, as this innovation might be fraught with danger if hastily introduced in the present state of the public mind, many are for postponing its adoption to subsequent assemblies of the States-General. In any event, the nobility demand that each order preserve the dignity that is meet in Frenchmen; that, consequently, the old humiliating forms which were imposed on the Third Estate—such as bending the knee—be abolished. One cahier says that the "sight of one man on his knees before another is offensive to the dignity of man, and indicates an unnatural inequality among men whose essential rights are the same."

OF THE FORM OF GOVERNMENT AND ITS CONSTITUTIONAL PRINCIPLES.—As to the form of government, the nobility demand the maintenance of royalty, the preservation of legislative, judicial, and executive powers in the hands of the king, but, at the same time, the establishment of fundamental laws for the purpose of guarding the rights of the nation against the exercise of arbitrary power.

Consequently, all the cahiers proclaim that the nation is entitled to be represented in the States-General, which body must be numerous enough to secure its independence. They desire that these States meet at periodical intervals, and at every change of monarch without special summons. Many bailiwicks express a wish to see this assembly permanent. If the States-General are not convened at the time appointed, it ought to be lawful to refuse to pay taxes. Some cahiers propose that during the interval between the sessions of the States a small committee be intrusted with the duty of watching the administration; but the bulk oppose this scheme flatly, on the ground that such a committee would be unconstitutional. The reason they allege is curious. They say there would be reason to fear that so small a body could easily be seduced by government.

The nobility deny to ministers the right of dissolving the assembly, and propose that they be prosecuted before the courts when they disturb it with their intrigues; they desire that no official, or person in any way dependent on government, shall be a deputy; that the persons of deputies shall be inviolable, and that they shall not be liable to account for opinions expressed in debate; finally, that all sittings of the assembly shall be public, and that the nation be made a spectator by printing the debates.

The nobility unanimously demand that the principles which must govern the state administration be applied to the administration of every portion of the national territory; hence, that in every province, district, and parish, assemblies be established composed of members freely elected for a limited period.

Many cahiers think that the offices of intendant and receiver-general should be abolished; all are of opinion that thenceforth the business of distributing taxes, and managing provincial business, should be left to the provincial assemblies. They advise that a similar plan be adopted with regard to county and parochial assemblies, which henceforth should be under the control of the Provincial States.

DIVISION OF POWERS: LEGISLATIVE POWER.—In dividing power between the assembled nation and the king, the nobility ask that no law shall take effect until it has been sanctioned by the States-General and the king, and recorded in the registers of the courts appointed to enforce it; that the business of establishing and fixing the quotas of taxes shall belong exclusively to the States-General; that subsidies voted shall only be considered as having been appropriated for the interval between one session of the States and another; that all taxes, established or levied without the consent of the States, shall be deemed illegal, and that all ministers and collectors who shall have ordered or levied such taxes shall be prosecuted for extortion; that, on the same principle, no loan shall be contracted without the consent of the States-General, but that a limited credit shall be opened by the States, to be used by government in case of war or sudden calamity, until a new session of the States can be called; that all the national treasuries shall be under the supervision of the States; that the expenses of each department shall be fixed by them, and that the most careful precautions shall be taken to prevent any appropriation being exceeded.

Most of the cahiers demand the suppression of those vexatious imposts known by the names of insinuation dues, *centième denier*, ratification dues, and comprised under the title of *régie* of the king's domains (one cahier says: "The word *régie* would alone suffice to condemn them, since it implies that property which actually belongs to citizens is owned by the king"); that all the public domains which are not sold shall be placed under the government of the Provincial States, and that no ordinance or edict for raising extraordinary taxes shall be issued, except with the consent of the three orders of the nation.

The idea of the nobility obviously was to transfer the whole administration of the finances, including loans, taxes, and this class of imposts, to the nation as represented by the general and provincial assemblies.

JUDICIAL POWER.—In the same way, the organization of the judiciary tends to make the power of the judges largely dependent upon the assembled nation.   Thus several cahiers declare :

"That magistrates shall be responsible for their acts to the assembled nation ;" that they shall only be dismissed with the consent of the States-General ; that no court shall, on any pretext whatever, be disturbed in the exercise of its functions without the consent of these States ; that delinquencies of the Court of Cassation and of the Parliaments shall be judged by these States.   Most of the cahiers recommend that no judges but such as the people present for office be appointed by the king.

EXECUTIVE POWER.—This is wholly reserved to the king, but it is limited in order to prevent abuses.

Thus, as to the administration, the cahiers demand that the accounts of the various departments be printed and made public, and that the ministers be responsible to the nation assembled ; and in like manner, that the king be bound to communicate his intentions to the States-General before he can employ the troops on foreign service.   At home, the troops shall not be used against the people without a requisition from the States-General.   The standing army shall be limited ; and in ordinary seasons, two thirds only shall be kept in effective service.   As to the foreign troops which the king may have in his service, they must be kept away from the heart of the kingdom, and stationed on the frontier.

The most striking feature of the cahiers of the nobility—a feature which no extract can reproduce — is the perfect harmony which exists between these noblemen and their age.   They are imbued with its spirit and speak its language.   They speak of "the inalienable rights of man," "principles inherent to the social compact."   In treating of individuals, they speak of their rights ; in alluding to society, they talk of its duties.   Political principles seem to them "as absolute as moral truths, both the one and the other having reason for their basis."   When they want to abolish the remains of serfdom, they say they must "efface the last traces of human degradation."   They sometimes call Louis XVI. a "citizen king," and constantly allude to the crime of "high-treason against the nation," with which they are so soon themselves to be charged. In their eyes, as in those of every one else, public education seems the grand panacea, and its director must be the state. One cahier says that "the States-General will give their attention to forming the national character by modifying the education of children." Like their contemporaries, they are fond of uniformity in legislative measures, always excepting every thing that concerns the existence of the Orders. They seek a uniform administration, uniform laws, &c., as ardently as the Third Estate. They call for all kinds of reforms, and those radical enough. They are for abolishing or transforming all the taxes without exception, and the whole judicial system, with the exception of the seigniorial courts, which only need improvement. Like all other Frenchmen, they regard France as a trial-field—a sort of political model-farm —in which every thing should be tried, every thing turned upside down, except the little spot in which their particular privileges grow. To their honor, it may even be said that they did not wholly spare that spot. In a word, it is seen from these cahiers that the only thing the nobles lacked to effect the Revolution was the rank of commoners.

Note u, *page* 141.

EXAMPLE OF THE RELIGIOUS GOVERNMENT OF AN ECCLESIASTICAL PROVINCE IN THE MIDDLE OF THE EIGHTEENTH CENTURY.

1. The archbishop.
2. Seven vicars general.
3. Two ecclesiastical courts called officialities : the one, known as the "metropolitan officiality," having cognizance of all sentences of the suffragans; the other, known as the "diocesan officiality," having cognizance, first, of all personal affairs among the clergy, and, secondly, of all disputes regarding the validity of marriages, in reference to the sacrament. This last tribunal is composed of two judges : there are attorneys and notaries attached to it.
4. Two fiscal courts : one, styled the diocesan office, has original jurisdiction over all disputes which may arise respecting the taxes of the clergy in the diocese (the clergy, as is known, imposed their own taxes). This tribunal consisted of the archbishop, presiding, and six other priests. The other court hears appeals from the other diocesan offices of the ecclesiastical province. All these courts admit lawyers, and hear cases pleaded in due form.

Note v, page 142.

SPIRIT OF THE CLERGY IN THE PROVINCIAL STATES AND ASSEM-
BLIES.

What I say in the text of the States of Languedoc applies
equally to the Provincial States which assembled in 1779 and 1787,
especially those of Haute Guienne.   The members of the clergy
are distinguished in this assembly for their learning, their activity,
their liberality.   The proposition to make the reports of the assembly public comes from the Bishop of Rodez.

Note w, page 143.

This liberal tendency of the clergy in political matters, which
was evidenced in 1789, was not the fruit of the excitement of the
moment; it was of old standing.   It was witnessed in Berri in
1779, when the clergy offered 68,000 *livres* as a free gift if the
provincial administration were allowed to subsist.

Note x, page 145.

Note that political society was disjointed, but that civil society
still held together.   In the heart of the different classes individuals were linked together; there even subsisted some trace of the
old bond of union between seigniors and people.   These peculiarities of civil society had their influence on politics; men thus
united formed irregular and ill-organized masses, but bodies that
were certain to be found refractory by government.   The Revolution burst these ties, and substituted no political bonds in their
stead; it thus paved the way for both equality and servitude.

Note y, page 146.

EXAMPLE OF THE TONE IN WHICH THE COURTS SPOKE OF CERTAIN
ARBITRARY MEASURES.

It appears from a memorial laid before the comptroller-general
by the intendant of the district of Paris, that it was the custom
of that district that each parish should have two syndics, one
elected by the people in an assembly over which the sub-delegate
presided, the other appointed by the intendant, and directed to
superintend his colleague.   A quarrel took place between the two
syndics of the parish of Rueil, the one who was elected refusing
to obey his colleague.   The intendant induced M. de Breteuil to
imprison the refractory syndic for a fortnight in the prison of La

Force ; on his liberation he was discharged, and a new syndic appointed in his stead. Thereupon the syndic appealed to the Parliament. I have not been able to find the conclusion of the proceedings, but the Parliament took occasion to declare that the imprisonment of the syndic and the nullification of his election could not but be considered " arbitrary and despotic acts." The courts were sometimes badly muzzled in those days.

Note z, page 150.

The educated and wealthy classes, the burghers included, were far from being oppressed or enslaved under the old regime. On the contrary, they had generally too much freedom ; for the crown could not prevent them from securing their own position at the sacrifice of the people's, and, indeed, almost always felt bound to purchase their good-will or soothe their animosity by abandoning the people to their mercy. It may be said that a Frenchman belonging to this class in the eighteenth century was better able to resist government and protect himself than an Englishman of the same period would have been in the like case. The crown felt bound to use more tenderness and deal more gently with him than the English government would have done to a man of the same standing. So wrong it is to confound independence with liberty. No one is less independent than a citizen of a free state.

Note a, page 150.

A REASON WHICH OFTEN COMPELLED THE GOVERNMENT OF THE OLD REGIME TO USE MODERATION.

In ordinary times, the most perilous acts for governments are the augmentation of old or the creation of new taxes. In olden times, when a king had expensive tastes, when he rushed into wild political schemes, when he let his finances fall into disorder, or when he needed large sums of money to sustain himself by gaining over his opponents, by paying heavy salaries that were not earned, by keeping numerous armies on foot, by undertaking extensive works, &c., he was obliged to have recourse to taxation, and this at once aroused all classes, especially that one which achieves violent revolutions—the people. Nowadays, in the same circumstances, loans are effected, which are not immediately felt, and whose burden falls on the next generation.

Note b, *page* 152.

One of the many examples of this is to be found in the *election* of Mayence. The chief domains of that *election* were farmed out to farmers-general, who hired as sub-farmers small wretched peasants, who had nothing in the world, and to whom the most necessary farm-tools had to be furnished. It is easy to understand how creditors of this stamp would deal harshly with the farmers or debtors of the feudal seignior whom they represented, and would render the feudal tenure more oppressive than it had been in the Middle Ages.

Note c, *page* 152.

ANOTHER EXAMPLE.

The inhabitants of Montbazon had entered on the taille-roll the stewards of a duchy owned by the Prince of Rohan, in whose name it was worked. The prince, who was no doubt very rich, not only has "this abuse," as he calls it, corrected, but recovers a sum of 5344 *livres* 15 *sous*, which he had been wrongfully made to pay, and has the same charged to the inhabitants.

Note d, *page* 154.

EXAMPLE OF THE EFFECT OF THE PECUNIARY RIGHTS OF THE CLERGY IN ALIENATING THE AFFECTIONS OF THOSE WHOSE ISOLATION SHOULD HAVE MADE THEM FRIENDS OF THE CHURCH.

The curate of Noisai declares that the people are bound to repair his barn and wine-press, and proposes that a local tax be imposed for the purpose. The intendant replies that the people are only bound to repair the parson's house; the curate, who seems more attentive to his farm than to his flock, must himself repair his barn and wine-press. (1767.)

Note e, *page* 157.

The following passage is taken from a clear and moderate memorial presented in 1788 by the peasantry to a provincial assembly: "To the other grievances incident to the collection of the taille must be added that of the bailiff's followers. They usually appear five times during the levy. They are, in general, invalid soldiers or Swiss. At each visit they remain four or five days in the parish, and for each of them 36 sous a day are added to the tax-levy. As for the distribution of the tax, we will not expose the well-known abuses of authority, or the bad effects of a distribution made by persons who are often incapable, and almost invariably partial and vindictive. These causes have, however, been a source of trouble and strife. They have led to lawsuits which have been very costly to litigants, and very advantageous to the places where the courts sit."

Note f, page 158.

SUPERIORITY OF THE METHODS USED IN THE PAYS D'ÉTATS ADMITTED BY OFFICIALS OF THE CENTRAL GOVRENMENT ITSELF.

In a confidential letter dated 3d June, 1772, and addressed by the Director of Taxes to the intendant, it is stated, "In the *pays d'états* the imposition is a fixed percentage, which is exacted and really paid by the taxable. This percentage is raised in the levy in proportion to the increase in the total required by the king (a million, for instance, instead of 900,000 *livres*). This is a very simple matter. In our districts, on the contrary, the tax is personal, and, to a certain degree, arbitrary. Some pay what they owe, others only half, others a third, others a quarter, and some nothing at all. How is it possible to increase such a tax one ninth, for instance?"

Note g, page 161.

ARBITRARY IMPRISONMENT FOR CORVÉES.

Example.—It is stated in a letter of the high provost in 1768, " I ordered three men to be arrested yesterday on the requisition of M. C., the assistant engineer, for not having performed their *corvée*. The affair made quite a stir among the women of the village, who cried, 'Nobody thinks of the poor people when the *corvée* is in question; nobody cares how they live—do you see?'"

Note h, page 161.

OF THE MANNER IN WHICH THE PRIVILEGED CLASSES ORIGINALLY UNDERSTOOD THE PROGRESS OF CIVILIZATION IN REFERENCE TO ROADS.

The Count of K., in a letter to the intendant, complains of the want of zeal with which a road that is to pass near his place is prosecuted. He says it is the fault of the sub-delegate, who is not energetic enough, and does not force the peasantry to perform their *corvées*.

Note i, *page* 162.

There were two means of making roads. One was by *corvées* for all heavy work requiring mere manual labor; the other—and the least valuable resource—was by imposing a general tax, whose proceeds were placed at the disposal of the Department of Bridges and Roads for the construction of scientific works. The privileged classes, that is to say, the principal landholders, who were of course the parties most interested in the roads, had nothing to do with *corvées;* and as the general tax in favor of the Bridge and Road Department was always joined with the *taille*, and levied on those who paid it, they escaped that too.

Note k, *page* 162.

INSTANCE OF CORVÉES FOR THE REMOVAL OF CONVICTS.

A letter dated 1761, and addressed to the intendant by the commissioner of the chain-service, states that the peasants were forced to transport the convicts in carts; that they did so very reluctantly; that they were often maltreated by the keepers of the convicts, "who," says the letter, "are coarse, brutal men, while the peasants, who dislike this duty, are often insolent."

Note l, *page* 162.

Turgot's sketches of the inconveniences and annoyances of *corvées* for the transportation of military baggage do not seem to me exaggerated now that I have read the documents bearing on the subject. He says, among other things, that the first inconvenience of the system is the extreme inequality with which this heavy burden is borne. It falls wholly on a small number of parishes, who are exposed to it by the misfortune of their position. The distance to be traversed is often five, six, and sometimes ten or fifteen leagues; three days are consumed in the journey and the return. The sum allowed is not one fifth the value of the labor. These *corvées* are almost invariably required in summer during harvest-time. The oxen are almost always overdriven, and often come home sick, so that many farmers prefer paying 15 or 20 *livres* to furnishing a cart and four oxen. The work is done in a most disorderly manner; the peasantry are constantly in prey to the violence of the soldiery. Officers almost always exact more than the law allows: they sometimes compel the farmers to yoke saddle-horses to carts, whereby the animals are often lamed. Soldiers will insist on riding on carts that are already heavily laden ; in their impatience at the slow gait of the oxen, they will prick them with their swords, and if the farmer objects he is very roughly handled.

Note m, *page* 162.

EXAMPLE OF THE APPLICATION OF CORVÉES TO EVERY THING.

The marine intendant of Rochefort complains that the peasants are indisposed to perform their *corvées* by carting the timber that has been purchased by the naval purveyors in the various provinces. (This correspondence shows that the peasants were, in fact, still—1775—bound to *corvées* of this kind, for which the intendant fixed their remuneration.) The Minister of Marine sends the letter to the intendant of Tours, and says that the carts required must be supplied. The intendant, M. Ducluzel, refuses to sanction *corvées* of this nature. The Minister of Marine writes him a threatening letter, in which he notifies him that he will apprize the king of his resistance. The intendant replies directly (11th December, 1775), and states firmly, that during the whole ten years of his service as intendant at Tours, he has always refused to authorize these *corvées,* in consequence of the abuses they involve—abuses which the rates of wages do not compensate ; " for," says he, " the cattle are often lamed by drawing heavy logs over roads as bad as the weather in which this service is usually required of them." The secret of this intendant's firmness seems to have been a letter of M. Turgot's, filed with the correspondence, and dated 30th July, 1774, when Turgot entered the ministry ; the letter states that Turgot never sanctioned these *corvées* at Limoges, and approves M. Ducluzel for refusing to sanction them at Tours.

Other portions of this correspondence show that purveyors of timber frequently exacted these *corvées* without being authorized to do so by a bargain with the state. They saved at least a third in freight. A sub-delegate gives the following instance of this profit : " Distance to draw the logs from the place where they are cut to the river, over roads almost impassable, six leagues ; time consumed, two days. The *corvéables* are paid at the rate of six *liards* a league per cubic foot ; they will thus receive 13 *fs.* 10 *s.* for the journey, which will barely cover the expenses of the farmer, his assistant, and the cattle yoked to his cart. He loses his own time, his trouble, and the labor of his cattle."

On 17th May, 1776, a positive order of the king to insist on this *corvée* is intimated to the intendant by the minister. M. Ducluzel having died, his successor, M. L'Escalopier, hastens to obey, and to promulgate an ordinance stating that " the sub-delegate is empowered to distribute the duty among the parishes; and all persons liable to *corvées* in the said parishes are hereby ordered to be present, at the hour directed by the syndics, at the place where the timber lies, and to cart it at the rate that shall be fixed by the sub-delegate."

Note n, *page* 165.

INSTANCE OF THE MANNER IN WHICH THE PEASANTRY WERE OFTEN TREATED.

1768. The king remits 2000 francs of the taille to the parish of Chapelle Blanche, near Saumur. The curate claims a portion of this sum to build a steeple, and so rid himself of the noise of the bells which incommodes him in his parsonage. The inhabitants object and resist. The sub-delegate takes the side of the curate, and has three of the principal inhabitants arrested at night, and locked up in jail.

Another example : Order of the king to imprison for two days a woman who has insulted two troopers of the horse-police. Another to imprison for a fortnight a stocking-maker who has spoken ill of the horse-police. In this case the intendant replies that he has already had the fellow arrested, for which he is warmly praised by the minister. The police, it seems, had been insulted in consequence of the arrests of beggars, which had shocked people. When the intendant arrested the stocking-maker, he gave out that any person thereafter insulting the police would be still more severely punished.

The correspondence between intendant and sub-delegates (1760 –1770) shows that the former ordered the arrest of mischievous persons, not to bring them to trial, but to get them out of the way. The sub-delegate asks permission to keep two dangerous beggars he has arrested in perpetual confinement. A father protests against the imprisonment of his son, who has been arrested as a vagabond because he traveled without papers. A landowner of X. demands that a neighbor of his, who has lately come to settle in his parish, whom he aided, but who is conducting himself badly toward him and annoying him, be forthwith arrested. The intendant of Paris begs his colleague of Rouen to oblige him thus far, as the petitioner is his friend.

To some one who desired to have some beggars set at liberty, the intendant replied "that poor-houses must not be considered prisons, but mere establishments intended for the detention of beggars and vagabonds by way of *administrative correction*." This idea found its way into the Penal Code. So well preserved have been the notions of the old regime in this matter.

Note o, page 172.

It has been said that the character of the philosophy of the eighteenth century was a sort of adoration of human intellect, an unlimited confidence in its power to transform at will laws, institutions, customs. To be accurate, it must be said that the human intellect which some of these philosophers adored was simply their own. They showed, in fact, an uncommon want of faith in the wisdom of the masses. I could mention several who despised the public almost as heartily as they despised the Deity. Toward the latter they evinced the pride of rivals—the former they treated with the pride of parvenus. They were as far from real and respectful submission to the will of the majority as from submission to the will of God. Nearly all subsequent revolutionaries have borne the same character. Very different from this is the respect shown by Englishmen and Americans for the sentiments of the majority of their fellow-citizens. Their intellect is proud and self-reliant, but never insolent; and it has led to liberty, while ours has done little but invent new forms of servitude.

Note p, page 187.

Frederick the Great says in his Memoirs, "The Fontenelles, the Voltaires, the Hobbeses, the Collinses, the Shaftesburys, the Bolingbrokes—all these great men dealt a deadly blow to religion. Men began to examine what they had stupidly adored. Intellect overthrew superstition. Fables that had long been believed fell into disgust. Deism made many converts. If Epicureanism was fatal to the idolatrous worship of the pagans, Deism was equally fatal to the Judaical visions of our ancestry. The liberty of thought which reigned in England was very favorable to the progress of philosophy."

It may be here seen that Frederick the Great, at the time he wrote these lines, that is to say, in the middle of the eighteenth century, regarded England as the centre of irreligious doctrines. A still more striking fact is the total ignorance displayed by one of the most enlightened and experienced sovereigns of history, of the political utility of religion.   The faults of his masters had injured the natural qualities of his mind.

Note q, *page* 211.

A similar spirit of progress manifested itself at the same time in Germany, and there, as in France, was accompanied by a desire for a change of institutions.   See the picture which a German historian draws of the state of his country at that time:

"During the second half of the eighteenth century," says he, "the new spirit of the age has been introduced even into ecclesiastical territory, on which reforms are commenced.   Industry and tolerance penetrate into every corner of it; it is reached by the enlightened absolutism which has already mastered the greater states.   And it must be acknowledged that at no period during the century has the territory of the Church been ruled by sovereigns as worthy of esteem and respect as those who figured during the ten years which preceded the French Revolution."

Note how this sketch resembles France, where progress and reform took a start at the same moment, and the men who were most worthy of governing appeared just when the Revolution was about to devour them all.

Note, also, how visibly this part of Germany was drawn into the French movement of civilization and politics.

Note r, *page* 212.

HOW THE ORGANIZATION OF THE ENGLISH COURTS PROVES THAT INSTITUTIONS MAY HAVE MADE SECONDARY FAULTS WITHOUT FAILING IN THEIR ORIGINAL OBJECT.

Nations have a faculty of prospering in spite of imperfections in the secondary parts of their institutions, so long as the general principles and spirit of these institutions are imbued with vitality.   This phenomenon is well illustrated by the judicial organization of England during the last century, as we find it in Blackstone.

Two anomalies at once meet the eye: 1st. The laws differ; 2d. They are carried into effect by different tribunals.

1st. As to the laws:

1. One set of laws is in force for England proper, another for Scotland, another for Ireland, another for certain European possessions of Great Britain, such as the Isle of Man and the Channel Islands, others for the colonies.

2. In England alone four systems of law are in use: customary

law, statute law, Roman law, equity. Customary law, again, is subdivided into general customs which apply to the whole kingdom, customs which apply to certain seigniories or towns, and customs which apply to certain classes—such, for instance, as the custom of merchants. Some of these customs differ widely from the others, as, for instance, those which, in opposition to the general spirit of the English laws, direct the equal division of property among children (gavelkind), and those more singular customs still which award a right of primogeniture to the youngest child.

2d. As to the courts:

The law, says Blackstone, has established an infinite variety of courts. Some idea may be formed of their number from the following very brief analysis:

1. One meets first with the courts established out of England proper, such as the courts of Scotland and Ireland, which were not subordinate to the superior courts of England, though they were all, I fancy, subject to appeal to the House of Lords.

2. As to England proper, if my memory serves me, Blackstone counts, 1st. eleven kinds of courts existing at common law, of which four seem, indeed, to have fallen into disuse in his time. 2d. Three kinds of courts exercising jurisdiction over certain cases throughout the country. 3d. Ten kinds of special courts: one of these is local courts, created by special acts of Parliament or existing by custom, either at London or in the towns or boroughs of the provinces. These are so numerous and so varied in their systems and rules that Blackstone abandons the attempt to describe them in detail.

Thus, in England proper, if Blackstone is to be believed, there existed at the time he wrote, that is to say, during the second half of the eighteenth century, twenty-four kinds of courts, of which several were subdivided into various species, each having a particular physiognomy. Setting aside those which seem to have fallen into disuse, there yet remain eighteen or twenty.

Now the least examination of this judicial system brings to light ever so many imperfections.

Notwithstanding the immense number of courts, there are none, it seems, close at hand, which can hear petty cases promptly and at small expense, and hence the administration of justice is embarrassing and costly. Several courts exercise jurisdiction over the same class of cases, whence troublesome doubts are thrown upon the validity of judgments. Nearly all the courts of appeal exercise original jurisdiction of one kind or another, either at common law or as equity courts. There are a variety of courts of appeal. The only point where all business centres is the House of Lords. Suits against the crown are not distinguished from other suits, which would seem a great deformity in the eyes of most of our lawyers. Finally, all these courts judge according to four different systems of laws, one of which consists wholly of precedents, and another—equity—has no settled basis, being designed, for the most part, to contradict the customs or statutes, and to correct the obsolete or over-harsh provisions of these by giving play to the discretion of the judge.

Here are astounding defects. Compare this old-fashioned and monstrous machine with our modern judiciary system, and the contrast between the simplicity, the coherence, and the logical organization of the one will place in still bolder relief the complicated and incoherent plan of the other. Yet there does not exist a country in which, even in Blackstone's time, the great ends of justice were more fully attained than in England; not one where every man, of whatever rank, and whether his suit was against a private individual or the sovereign, was more certain of being heard, and more assured of finding in the court ample guarantees for the defense of his fortune, his liberty, and his life.

This does not indicate that the faults of the judiciary system of England served the ends of justice. It only shows that there may exist in every judiciary system secondary faults which are but a slight impediment to the proper transaction of business, while there are radical faults which, though they coexist with many secondary excellences, may not only interfere with, but absolutely defeat the ends of justice. The former are the easiest to detect; they are instantly noticed by common minds. One can see them at a glance. The others are more difficult to discover, and lawyers are not always the people who perceive or point them out.

Note, also, that the same qualities may be secondary or principal, according to the times and the political organization of society. In aristocratic times, all inequalities, or other contrivances to diminish the privileges of certain individuals before the courts, to guarantee the protection of the weak against the strong, or to give predominance to the action of the government, which naturally views disputes between its subjects with impartiality, are leading and important features. They lose their importance when society and political institutions point toward democracy.

Studying the judiciary system of England by the light of this principle, it will be discovered that, while defects were allowed to exist which rendered the administration of justice among our neighbors obscure, complicated, slow, costly, and inconvenient, infinite pains had been taken to protect the weak against the strong, the subject against the monarch ; and the closer the details of the system are examined, the better will it be seen that every citizen had been amply provided with arms for his defense, and that matters had been so arranged as to give to every one the greatest possible number of guarantees against the partiality and venality of the courts, and, above all, against that form of venality which is both the commonest and the most dangerous in democratic times —subserviency to the supreme power.

In all these points of view, the English system, notwithstanding its secondary faults, appears to me superior to our own. Ours has none of its vices, it is true, but it is not endowed with the same excellences. It is admirable in respect of the guarantees it offers to the citizen in suits against his neighbor, but it fails in the particular that is most essential in a democratic society like ours, namely, the guarantees of the individual against the state.

Note s, *page* 213.

ADVANTAGES ENJOYED BY THE DISTRICT OF PARIS.

This district (*généralité*) enjoyed as large advantages in respect of government charities as of taxes. For example, the comptroller-general writes, on 22d May, 1787, to the intendant of the district of Paris, to say that the king has fixed the sum to be spent in charitable works, in the district of Paris, during the year, at 172,800 livres. Besides this, 100,000 livres are to be spent in cows to be given to farmers. This letter shows that this sum of 172,800 livres was to be distributed by the intendant alone, in conformity with the general rules laid down by the government, and subject to the general approval of the comptroller-general.

Note t, *page* 214.

The administration of the old regime comprised a multitude of different powers, which had been created—rather to help the treasury than the government—at various times, and often intrusted with the same sphere of action. Confusion and conflicts of authority could only be avoided on condition that each power should agree to do little or nothing. The moment they shook off inertia, they clashed and incommoded each other. Hence it happened that complaints of the complications of the administrative system and of the confusion of powers were much more pressing just before the Revolution than they had been thirty or forty years previous. Political institutions had grown better, not worse; but political life was more active.

Note u, *page* 221.

ARBITRARY INCREASE OF THE TAXES.

What the king here says of the taille might have been said with equal truth of the twentieths, as is shown by the following correspondence. In 1772, Comptroller-general Terray had decided upon a considerable increase—100,000 livres—in the twentieths in the district of Tours. M. Ducluzel, an able administrator and a good man, shows all the grief and annoyance he feels at the step in a confidential letter, in which he says, " It is the facility with which the 250,000 livres were obtained by the last increase which has doubtless suggested the cruel step, and the letter of the month of June."

In a very confidential letter from the director of taxes to the intendant, in reference to the same matter, he says, " If you still think the increase as aggravating and revolting, in view of the public distress, as you were good enough to say it was, it would be desirable that you should contrive to spare the province — which has no other defender or protector but yourself—the supplementary rolls, which, being retroactive in their effect, are always odious."

This correspondence likewise shows how sadly some standard rule of action was needed, and how arbitrarily matters were managed even with honest views. Intendant and minister both throw the surplus tax sometimes on agriculture rather than labor, sometimes on one branch of agriculture (vines, for instance) rather than another, according to their own ideas as to which interest requires gentle treatment.

Note v, *page* 224.

STYLE IN WHICH TURGOT SPEAKS OF THE PEOPLE OF THE COUNTRY PARTS IN THE PREAMBLE OF A ROYAL DECLARATION.

" The country communities," says he, " in most parts of the kingdom, are composed of poor, ignorant, and brutal peasants, incapable of self-government."

Note w, *page* 229.

HOW REVOLUTIONARY IDEAS WERE SPONTANEOUSLY GERMINATING
IN MEN'S MINDS UNDER THE OLD REGIME.

In 1779 a lawyer begs the Council to pass an order establishing a maximum price for straw throughout the kingdom.

Note x, *page* 230.

The chief engineer wrote to the intendant, in 1781, on the subject of a demand for increased indemnity : " The applicant forgets that these indemnities are a special favor granted to the district of Tours, and that he is fortunate in obtaining partial repayment for his loss. If all the parties in interest were reimbursed on the scale he proposes, four millions would not suffice."

Note y, *page* 234.

This prosperity did not cause the Revolution ; but the spirit which was to cause it—that active, restless, intelligent, innovating, ambitious, democratic spirit, which imbued the new society, was giving life to every thing, and stirring up and developing every social element before it overthrew the whole.

Note z, *page* 238.

CONFLICT OF THE SEVERAL ADMINISTRATIVE POWERS IN 1787.

Example.—The intermediate commission of the provincial assembly of Ile de France claims the administration of the poorhouse. The intendant insists on retaining control of it, as " it is not kept up out of the provincial funds." During the discussion, the commission applies to the intermediate commissions of other provinces for their opinion. That of Champagne, among others, replies that the same difficulty has been raised there, and that it has, in like manner, resisted the pretensions of the intendant.

Note a, *page* 242.

I find in the reports of the first provincial assembly of Ile de France this assertion, made by the reporter of a committee : " Hitherto the functions of syndic have been more onerous than honorable, and persons who possessed both means and information suitable to their rank were thus deterred from accepting the office."

NOTE REFERRING TO VARIOUS PASSAGES IN THIS VOLUME.

FEUDAL RIGHTS EXISTING AT THE TIME OF THE REVOLUTION, ACCORDING TO THE FEUDAL LAWYERS OF THE DAY.

I do not design to write a treatise on feudal rights, or to inquire into their origin. My object is merely to state which of them were still exercised in the eighteenth century. They have played so important a part in subsequent history, and filled so large a place in the imagination of those who have been freed from them, that I have thought it would be curious to ascertain what they really were at the time the Revolution destroyed them. With this view I have studied, first, the *terriers*, or registers of a large number of seigniories, choosing those which were most recent in date in preference to the older ones. Finding that this plan led to no satisfactory results, as the feudal rights, though regulated by the same general system of laws throughout Europe, varied infinitely in matters of detail in the different provinces and cantons, I resolved to pursue a different method, which was this. The feudal rights gave rise to countless lawsuits. These suits involved such questions as, How were these rights acquired? how were they lost? in what did they consist? which of them required to be based on a royal patent? which on a private contract? which on the local custom or long-established practice? how were they valued in case of sale? what sum of money was each class supposed to represent in proportion to the others? All these had been and still were litigated questions, and a school of lawyers had devoted their whole attention to their study. Of these, several wrote during the second half of the eighteenth century, some shortly before the Revolution. They were not jurisconsults, properly so called; they were legal practitioners, whose sole aim was to furnish the profession with rules of practice for a special and unattractive branch of the law. A careful study of these writers throws light on the intricate and confused details of the subject. I subjoin the most

succinct analysis that I have been able to make of my work.   It
is mainly derived from the work of Edme de Freminville, who
wrote about 1750, and that of Renauldon, written in 1765, and entitled *Traité Historique et Pratique des Droits Seigneuriaux.*

The *cens* (that is to say, the perpetual rent, in money or produce, which the feudal laws impose on certain possessions) still continues, in the eighteenth century, to modify the condition of many
landholders.   It is still indivisible ; that is to say, when the property which owes the *cens* has been divided, it may be exacted from
any one of the owners.   It is not subject to prescription.   Ac-.
cording to some customs, the owner of a property burdened with
cens can not sell it without exposing himself to the *retrait censu-
el ;* that is to say, the creditor of the *cens* may take the property
by paying the same price as the other purchaser.   The custom of
Paris ignores this right.

Lods et ventes (mutation-fine).—The general rule, in those
parts of France where customary law obtains, is that a mutation-
fine is due on every sale of land subject to *cens :* it is a due on the
sale which accrues to the seignior.   These dues differ in different
customs, but they are considerable in all.   They exist also in those
parts of the country where written law obtains ; there they amount
to a sixth of the price, and are called *lods ;* but the seignior, in
these districts, must prove his right.   Throughout the country the
cens creates a privilege for the seignior, in virtue of which he is
preferred to all other creditors.

Terrage or *champart, agrier, tasque.*—These are dues in produce which the debtor of the *cens* pays to the seignior ; the quantity varies according to custom and private agreement.   These
dues were often met with during the eighteenth century.   I believe that, even where customary law obtained, *terrage* required to
be founded on a contract.   It was either seigniorial, or connected
with the land (*foncier*).   It would be superfluous to explain here
the signs by which these two kinds were distinguished ; suffice it
to say that the latter, like ground-rents, was subject to a prescription of thirty years, while the former could never be lost by prescription.   Land subject to *terrage* could not be hypothecated
without the consent of the seignior.

Bordelage.—This was a due which existed only in Nivernais
and Bourbonnais, and consisted in an annual rent payable by all
land subject to *cens*, in the shape of money, grain, and poultry.
This due entailed very rigorous consequences : the non-payment
of it for three years involved the *commise,* or confiscation of the

property to the seignior. The rights of property of debtors of *bordelage* were, moreover, inchoate : in certain cases the seignior was entitled to their inheritance, to the exclusion of the rightful heirs. This was the most rigorous of all the dues of the feudal tenure, and its exercise had gradually been restricted to the rural districts ; for, as the author says, " peasants are mules ready to carry any load."

Marciage was a peculiar right, only exercised in certain places. It consisted in a certain return which was paid by the possessors of property liable to *cens* on the natural death of the seignior.

Enfeoffed tithes.—A large portion of the tithes were still enfeoffed during the eighteenth century. In general, they could only be claimed in virtue of a contract, and did not result from the mere fact of the land being seigniorial.

Parcières were dues levied on the harvest. They bore some resemblance to the *champart* and enfeoffed tithes, and were chiefly in use in Bourbonnais and Auvergne.

Carpot, a due peculiar to Bourbonnais, was to vines what *champart* was to arable land—a right to a portion of the produce. It was one quarter of the vintage.

Serfdom.—Those customs which retain traces of serfdom are called serf customs ; they are few in number. In the provinces where they obtain, no lands, or very few indeed, are wholly free from traces of serfdom. (This was written in 1765.) Serfdom, or, as the author terms it, servitude, was either personal or real.

Personal servitude was inherent in the person, and clung to him wherever he went. Wherever he removed his household, the seignior could pursue and seize him. The authors contain several judgments of the courts based on this right. Among them, one, dated 17th June, 1760, rejects the claim of a seignior of Nivernais upon the succession of one Pierre Truchet. Truchet was the son of a serf under the custom of Nivernais, who had married a free woman of Paris, and died there. The court rejected the seignior's demand on the ground that Paris was a place of refuge from which serfs could not be recovered. The ground of this judgment shows that the seigniors were entitled to claim the property of their serfs when they died in the seigniory.

Real servitude flowed from the possession of certain land, and could not be got rid of except by removing from the land and residing elsewhere.

Corvées were a right by which the seignior employed his vassals or their cattle for so many days for his benefit. *Corvées* at will, that is to say, at the discretion of the seignior, are wholly abolished. They were long since reduced to so many days' work in the year.

Corvées were either personal or real. Personal *corvées* were due by every laborer living on the seigniory, each working at his own trade. Real *corvées* were attached to the possession of certain lands. Noblemen, ecclesiastics, clergymen, officers of justice, advocates, physicians, notaries, bankers, notables, were exempt from *corvées*. The author quotes a judgment of 13th August, 1735, rendered in favor of a notary whose seignior wished to com-. pel him to work for three days in the year in drawing up deeds for the seignior. Also another judgment of 1750, deciding that when the *corvée* is to be paid either in money or in labor, the choice rests with the debtor. *Corvées* must be substantiated by a written document. Seigniorial *corvées* had become very rare in the eighteenth century.

Banality.—There are no banal rights in the provinces of Artois, Flanders, and Hainault. The custom of Paris strictly forbids the exercise of this right when it is not founded on a proper title. All who are domiciled in the seigniory are subject to it—men of rank and ecclesiastics even oftener than others.

Independently of the banality of mills and ovens, there are many others:

1st. *Banality of Factory-mills*, such as cloth-mills, cork-mills, hemp-mills. Several customs, among others those of Anjou, Maine, and Touraine, establish this banality.

2d. *Banality of Wine-presses.*—Very few customs speak of it. That of Lorraine establishes it, as also does that of Maine.

3d. *Banal Bull.*—No custom alludes to it, but it is established by certain deeds. The same is true of banal butcheries.

Generally speaking, this second class of banalities are rarer and less favorably viewed than the others. They can only be established in virtue of a clear provision of the custom, or, in default of this, by special agreement.

Ban of the Vintage.—This was a police authority, which high justiciary seigniors exercised, without special title, throughout the kingdom during the eighteenth century. It was binding on every one. The custom of Burgundy gave to the seignior the right of gathering his crop of grapes one day before any other vine-grower.

Right of Banvin.—This right, which, according to the authors, a host of seigniors exercised either in virtue of the custom or under private contracts, entitled them to sell the wine made on their own estates a certain time—usually a month or forty days—before any other vine-grower could send his wine to market. Of the greater customs, those of Tours, Anjou, Maine, and Marche are the only ones which recognize and regulate this right. A judgment of the Court of Aides, bearing date 28th August, 1751, permits innkeepers to sell wine during the *banvin;* but this was an exceptional case; they were only allowed to sell to strangers, and the wine sold must have come from the seignior's vineyard. The customs which mention and regulate the right of *banvin* usually require that it be founded on written titles.

Right of Blairie.—This is the right in virtue of which high justiciary seigniors grant permission to the inhabitants of the seigniory to pasture their cattle upon the lands within their jurisdiction, or waste lands. This right does not exist in those districts which are governed by written law; but it is well known within the limits of the various customs. It is found under different names in Bourbonnais, Nivernais, Auvergne, and Burgundy. It rests on the assumption that the property of all the land was originally in the seignior, and that, after having distributed the best portions in feuds, copyholds (*censives*), and other concessions, for specific rents, he is still at liberty to grant the temporary use of those lands which are only fit for pasture. *Blairie* is established by several customs; but no one can claim it but a high justiciary, and he must be able to show either a positive title to it, or old acknowledgments of its existence, fortified by long usage.

Tolls.—Originally, say the authors, there existed a vast number of seigniorial tolls on bridges, rivers, and roads. Louis XIV. abolished many of them. In 1724, a commission appointed to inquire into the subject abolished twelve hundred of them; and in 1765 they were still being reduced. The first principle in this matter, says Renauldon, is that a toll, being a tax, must not only be established in virtue of a title, but that title must emanate from the crown. The toll is mentioned as being *de par le roi.* One of the conditions of tolls is that there must be attached to them a tariff of the rates which all merchandise must pay. This tariff must always be approved by an Order in Council. The title, says the author, must be confirmed by uninterrupted possession. Notwithstanding the precautions taken by the legislator, the value of some tolls has largely increased of late years. I know a toll, he adds, which was farmed out for 100 *livres* a century since, and which now brings in 1400; another, farmed out for 39,000 *livres*, now produces 90,000. The chief ordinances and edicts regulating tolls are the 29th title of the ordinance of 1669, and the edicts of 1683, 1693, 1724, and 1775.

The authors whom I quote, though rather prepossessed, in general, in favor of feudal rights, acknowledge that great abuses are practiced in the collection of tolls.

Ferries.—The right of ferry differs sensibly from the right of tolls. The latter is levied on merchandise only; the former on persons, cattle, and vehicles. This right can not be exercised without the king's sanction, and the tariff of rates charged must be included in the Order in Council authorizing or establishing the ferry.

The Right of Leyde (its name varies in different places) is an impost on merchandise sent to fairs or markets. The lawyers I am quoting say that many seigniors erroneously consider this a right appurtenant to high justice, and purely seigniorial; whereas it is a tax which requires the sanction of the king. At any rate, the right can only be exercised by a high justiciary, who receives the fines levied in virtue thereof. And it appears that though theoretically the right of *leyde* could not be exercised except by grant from the king, it was often in part exercised in virtue of a feudal title and long usage.

It is certain that fairs could only be established by authorization of the king.

Seigniors need no specific title or royal grant to regulate the weights and measures that are to be used in the seigniory. It suffices that the right is founded on the custom or long continued usage. The authors say that all the attempts that have been made by the kings to introduce a uniform standard of weights and measures have been failures. No progress has been made in this matter since the customs were drawn up.

Roads.—Rights exercised by the seigniors over the roads.

The highways, which are called the king's roads, belong wholly to the crown. Their establishment, their repairs, crimes committed upon them, are not within the jurisdiction of the seigniors or their judges; but all private roads within the limits of a seigniory belong, without doubt, to the high justiciary. They have entire control over them, and all crimes committed thereon, except cases reserved to the king, are within the jurisdiction of the seigniorial judges. Formerly the seigniors were expected to keep in repair the high roads which traversed their seigniory, and rights of toll, boundary, and *traverse* were granted them by way of indemnity; but the king has since taken the direction of all highways.

Rivers.—All rivers navigable for boats or rafts belong to the king, though they traverse seigniories, any title to the contrary notwithstanding (ordinance of 1669). Any rights which the seigniors may exercise on these rivers—rights of fishing, establishing mills or bridges, or levying tolls—must have been acquired by grant from the king. Some seigniors claim civil or police jurisdiction over these rivers; but any such rights have been usurped or obtained by fraudulent grants.

Small rivers undoubtedly belong to the seigniors whose domain they traverse. They have the same rights of property, jurisdiction, and police, as the king has over navigable rivers. All high justiciaries are universal seigniors of non-navigable rivers flowing through their territory. They need no better title to establish their right of property than the fact of their existence as high justiciaries. Some customs, such as that of Berri, authorize individuals to erect mills on seigniorial rivers flowing through their property without permission from the seignior. The custom of Bretagne granted this right to noblemen. Generally, the law restricts to the high justiciary the right of granting permission to build mills within his jurisdiction. Even traverses can not be made upon a seigniorial river, for the protection of a farm, without permission from the seigniorial judges.

Fountains, Pumps, Retting-tanks, Ponds.—Rain falling upon the highway belongs exclusively to the high justiciary, who alone can make use of it. He can make a pond in any part of his jurisdiction, even on the property of his tenants, by paying them for the land that is submerged. This rule is distinctly laid down by several customs; among others, by those of Troyes and Nivernais. Private individuals can only have ponds on their own land; and even for this, according to several customs, they must obtain leave from the seignior. The customs which require leave to be asked of the seignior forbid his selling permission.

Fishery.—The right of fishery in rivers navigable for boats or rafts belongs to the king. He alone can grant it. His judges have sole cognizance of infractions of the fishery laws. Many seigniors, however, enjoy rights of fishery on these rivers, but they have either usurped them, or hold them by special grant from the king. As for non-navigable rivers, it is forbidden to fish therein, even with line, without the leave of the high justiciary in whose domain they flow. A judgment of 30th April, 1749, condemned a fisherman on this rule. Seigniors themselves must obey the general regulations regarding fisheries in fishing in these rivers. The high justiciary may grant the right of fishing in his river, either as a feud, or for a yearly *cens*.

Hunting.—The right of hunting can not be farmed out like the right of fishery. It is a personal right. It is held to be a royal right, which even men of rank can not exercise within their own jurisdiction, or on their own feud, without the king's permission. This doctrine is laid down in the 30th title of the ordinance of 1669. The seigniorial judges are competent to sit in all cases relative to hunting, except those which refer to the chase of *red* beasts (these are, I imagine, large game, such as stags and deer), which must be left to the royal courts.

The right of hunting is, of all seigniorial rights, the one most carefully withheld from commoners; even the *franc-aleu roturier* does not carry it. The king does not grant it in his pleasures. So strict is the principle, that a seignior can not grant leave to hunt. That is the law. But in practice seigniors constantly grant permission to hunt, not only to men of rank but to commoners. High justiciaries may hunt throughout the limits of their jurisdiction, but they must be alone. Within these limits they are entitled to make all regulations, prohibitions, and ordinances regulating hunting. All feudal seigniors, even without justiciary rights, may hunt within their feud. Men of rank, who have neither feud nor justiciary rights, may hunt upon the lands adjoining their residences. It has been held that a commoner who owns a park within the limits of a high justice must keep it open for the pleasures of the seignior; but the judgment is old; it dates from 1668.

Warrens.—None can now be established without a title. Commoners can establish warrens as well as noblemen, but none but men of rank can have forests.

Pigeon-houses.—Certain customs restrict the right of having pigeon-houses to high justiciaries; others grant it to all owners of feuds. In Dauphiné, Brittany, and Normandy, no commoner can own a pigeon-house; no one but a noble can keep pigeons. Most severe punishments, often corporal, were inflicted on those who killed pigeons.

Such are, according to the authors quoted, the chief feudal rights exacted during the latter half of the eighteenth century. They add that " these rights are generally established. There are a host of others, less known and less extended, which exist only in certain customs or in certain seigniories in virtue of special titles." These rare or restricted rights which the authors enumerate number ninety-nine. Most of them weigh upon agriculture, being dues to the seignior on harvests, or on the sale or transport of produce. The authors say that many of these rights were disused in their time. I fancy, however, that several of them must have been enforced in some places as late as 1789.

Having ascertained from the feudal lawyers of the eighteenth century what feudal rights were still enforced, I wished to ascertain what pecuniary value was set upon them by the men of that day.

One of the authors I have quoted, Renauldon, furnishes the requisite information. He gives a set of rules for legal functionaries to follow in appraising in inventories the various feudal rights which existed in 1765, that is to say, twenty-four years before the Revolution. They are as follows:

Rights of Jurisdiction.—He says, " Some of our customs value the right of jurisdiction, high, low, and middle (*justice haute, basse, et moyenne*), at one tenth the revenue of the land. Seigniorial jurisdictions were then highly important. Edme de Treminville thinks that, in our day, jurisdiction should not be valued higher than a twentieth of the income of the land. I think even this valuation too high."

Honorary Rights.—Though these rights are not easily appreciated in money, our author, who is a practical man, and not easily imposed upon by appearances, advises the appraisers to value them at a very small sum.

Seigniorial Corvées.—The author supplies rules for the valuation of *corvées*, which shows that they were still occasionally enforced. He values the day's work of an ox at 20 *sous*, and that of a man at 5 *sous*, besides his food. This is a fair indication of the wages paid at the time.

Tolls.—With regard to the valuation of tolls, the author says : " No seigniorial rights should be valued at a lower rate than these tolls. They are very fluctuating ; and now that the king and the provinces have taken charge of the roads and bridges which are of most use to trade, many tolls have become useless, and they are being abolished daily."

Right of Fishing and Hunting.—The right of fishery may be farmed out and regularly appraised. The right of hunting can not be farmed out, being a personal right. It is, therefore, an honorary, not a productive right, and can not be estimated in money.

The author then proceeds to speak of the rights of banality, *banvin, leyde, blairie*, and the space he devotes to them shows that they were the most frequently exercised and the most important of the surviving feudal rights. He adds : " There are, besides, a number of other seigniorial rights, which are met with from time to time, but it would be tedious and even impossible to enumerate them here. In the examples we have given, appraisers will find rules to guide them in estimating the rights which we have not specially valued."

Valuation of the Cens.—Most of the customs say that the *cens* must be valued at rather more than $3\frac{3}{10}$ per cent. This high valuation is due to the fact that the *cens* carries with it various casual benefits, such as mutation-fines.

Enfeoffed Tithes, Terrage.—Enfeoffed tithes can not be valued at less than four per cent., as they involve no care, labor, or expense. When the *terrage* or *champart* carries with it mutation-fines to the seignior, this casualty must settle the value at $3\frac{3}{10}$ per cent., otherwise it must be valued like the tithes.

Ground-rents, bearing no mutation-fines or right of redemption —that is to say, which are not seigniorial—must be valued at five per cent.

ESTIMATE OF THE VARIOUS TENURES IN USE IN FRANCE BEFORE THE REVOLUTION.

We only know in France, says the author, three kinds of real estate :

1st. The *franc-aleu*, which is a freehold, exempt from all burdens, and subject to no seigniorial dues or rights, either beneficial or honorary.

Francs-aleux are either noble or common (*roturiers*). Noble *francs-aleux* carry with them a right of jurisdiction, or they have feuds or lands held by *cens* depending on them. They are divided according to feudal law. Common *francs-aleux* have no jurisdiction, or feuds, or lands held by *cens*. They are divided according to the ordinary rules (*roturièrement*). The author considers that the holders of *francs-aleux* are the only landholders who enjoy a complete right of property.

The *franc-aleu* was valued higher than any other kind of tenure. The customs of Auvergne and Burgundy valued it $2\frac{1}{2}$ per cent. The author thinks that $3\frac{1}{3}$ per cent. would be a better valuation.

It must be noticed that common *francs-aleux*, existing within the limits of a seigniorial jurisdiction, were dependent thereon. It was not a sign of subjection to the seignior, but an acknowledgment of the jurisdiction of courts which took the place of the royal tribunals.

2d. Lands held by feudal tenure (*à fief*).

3d. Lands paying *cens*, or, as they are here called in law, *rotures*.

The valuation of lands held by feudal tenure was the lower in proportion to the feudal burdens laid upon them. In some customs, and in that part of the country which was governed by written law, feuds paid nothing but "*la bouche et les mains*," that is to say, feudal homage. In other customs, such as Burgundy, feuds not only owed homage, but were what was called *de danger;* that is to say, they were liable to *commise*, or feudal confiscation, when the owner took possession of them without having rendered "fealty and homage." Other customs, such as that of Paris, for instance, and many more, declared feuds subject not only to fealty and homage, but likewise to re-emption, *quint* and *requint*. Others again, such as that of Poitou and some others, burdened them with a fine on the oath of fealty (*chambellage*), and service on horseback, etc.

The first class of feuds must be valued higher than the others. The custom of Paris set them down at five per cent., which the author thinks very reasonable.

To arrive at a valuation of lands held *en roture* and those subject to *cens*, they must be divided into three classes :

1st. Lands paying the mere *cens*.

2d. Lands liable not only to *cens*, but to other burdens.

3d. Lands mainmortable, subject to real taille, to *bordelage*.

The first two classes of lands *en roture* were common enough in the eighteenth century. The third was rare. The first, says the author, must be valued higher than the second, the second than the third. Indeed, landholders of the third class can hardly be called owners, in the strict sense of the word, as they can not alienate their property without leave from the seignior.

TERRIERS.—The feudal lawyers I have quoted furnish the following rules for drawing up or renewing the seigniorial registers called *terriers*, which I have mentioned in the text. The *terrier*, as is known, was a great register, in which all the deeds establishing rights belonging to the seigniory, whether beneficial or honorary, real, personal, or mixed, were entered at length. It contained all the declarations of the copyholders, the customs of the seigniory, quit-rent leases, etc. In the custom of Paris, the authors say that seigniors may renew their *terriers* every thirty years at the expense of the copyholders. They add, however, that " one is fortunate to find a fresh one every century." The *terrier* could not be renewed (it was a troublesome formality for all those who held under the seignior) without obtaining an authorization which was called *lettres à terrier*. When the seigniory was within the jurisdiction of several Parliaments, this was obtained from the high chancellor; in other cases it was procured from the Parliament. The court named the notary, before whom all vassals, noblemen and commoners, copyholders, emphyteutic lessees, and persons amenable to the seigniorial jurisdiction, were bound to appear. A plan of the seigniory was required to be attached to the *terrier*.

Besides the *terriers*, there were kept in each seigniory other registers called *lièves*, in which the seigniors or their stewards entered the sums they had received from their copyholders, with their names, and the dates of the payments.

THE END.